A Muddy Red River

D. A. Cairns

Published by **Rogue Phoenix Press**

ISBN: **978-1-62420-163-9**

Credits
Cover Artist: Designs by Ms G
Editor: Christie L. Kraemer

Dedication

To Jeanne Haskin

Chapter One

The stage was dark, except for a voyeuristic single spotlight which shone on a nubile dancer. Dressed in nought but satin hot pants and a pink bikini top, she mouthed the words to Blurred Lines as she writhed awkwardly around the microphone stand. Australian holiday maker and hedonist, Rob Archer, took a seat at a small table next to the wall to the left of the stage and gratefully accepted a glass of beer without looking at the waitress. The dancer began to sway gently, apparently abandoning sexy for a vague semblance of cute. Rob compelled his mouth closed and disengaged his eyes in order to survey the room. The temptation to remain riveted to the lame, yet somehow sensual performance of the dancer was mercifully curtailed by the end of the song. He joined the polite applause which mumbled half-hearted appreciation.

To the right of the stage was a circular bar, with a small dais in the centre that was slightly elevated above the level of the bar top. Another two girls were dancing there, similarly dressed in the sleazy attire of good time girls. There were no hot pants for these two though; sparkling G-strings and stilettos adorned their lower halves. An assortment of desperates, mostly foreigners, watched enthusiastically, clapping and cheering whenever either of the girls bent over or thrusted her pelvis. Some simply sat and leered as they nursed drinks and lustful thoughts. These girls seemed more comfortable with the attention, smiling frequently and blowing kisses all over the enchanted men.

Hostesses, or perhaps girlfriends, who could say, decorated the arms and laps of some of the spectators. Rob noticed two groups; one evidently enjoying themselves, the other patently not. He guessed the former were hostesses and the latter, girlfriends. The hostesses maintained intimate and frequent contact with their men. They laughed and smiled, occasionally leaning close to whisper in their partner's ears or to stain their cheeks with lipstick. The girlfriends on the other hand, wore vacant, disinterested looks, wishing they could disappear inside the smoke haze and escape this appalling personal insult.

Rob pulled a cigarette from the packet of *Klong Thips* which lay on the table but before he could light it, a flame appeared, accompanied by a sweet voice.

"You like something else, sir?"

The smoke from the full strength Thai tobacco seared his throat as he inhaled it, igniting the slow burn of the coffin nail. He opened his eyes to find a pair of almond orbs solicitously violating him. He accepted the intrusion.

"Whiskey, please."

"Just whiskey?"

Rob returned her smile then nodded.

"Mekong, okay?"

He nodded again. The waitress winked before walking away and his eyes followed her shapely backside through the dimness, as she headed for the bar. Lipstick was one of the quieter bars in the Nana red light district of Bangkok. Rob had been introduced to the erotic wonders of this part of town by an acquaintance with whom he had shared a few drinks and joints in a number of other sex bars which populated *soi* one and *soi* two on Thailand's world famous Patpong Road. Nana, he said, was way better. Lipstick had a reputation for offering friendly staff, reasonable prices and a wide selection of beautiful ladies, minus the so called lady-boys. So far Rob had found it thus, and he settled into the ambience as the music oozed from every hidden corner of the brooding premises.

The waitress returned, leaning across him and feathering his shoulder with her breasts. "Your drink, sir."

She lingered as he sipped the whiskey, savouring its bite. Her fingers caressed the back of his head, playfully tousling his hair. "Anything else, sir?"

Rob smiled as desire swelled and he surrendered willingly, inviting her to sit with him.

"Just drinks sir. You want friend? I send friend for you."

What a tease! He wrestled his anger into submission and dismissed the waitress with a wave of his hand. She smiled, evidently unoffended, and glided away.

Rob liked being called sir, and he loved the attention. The zing of lust which the waitress's delicate touch had elicited was stunning. Perhaps the atmosphere was pregnant with raunchiness and ribaldry. Perhaps he was desperate and lonely. Whatever the reason for his reaction, Rob felt cheated and frustrated by the waitress. Though he knew the game well, and happily participated whenever given the chance, it could still be incredibly annoying.

He took some more whiskey, appreciating its strength, knowing that subsequent servings would be watered down. The main stage was deserted now, the peephole spotlight swallowed by darkness. Rob turned his attention to the crowd at the bar, which dwindled as the dancing girls finished their routines and stepped down into the arms of the two men who had stuffed their respective bikini tops with the highest amount of five hundred baht notes. He had no idea how they kept track of their earnings when their bodies were engaged in such bawdy acrobatics, another impressive trick of their trade.

One *Klong Thip* chased another, in pursuit of a succession of whiskeys, as Rob sat and watched the next performance, then another. He pressed the side of his watch, raising it closer to eye level as he struggled to read the time. Then he called a waitress over.

"I'd like a friend, please."

"No poplem, sir. You like table friend, short time or long time?"

"What's a table friend?"

The waitress laughed and playfully slapped his arm. "First time you come, huh?"

Inebriation thankfully overrode irritation and embarrassment. "Yeah, first time here."

She moved suddenly, snatching a chair and placing it beside Rob's. With her backside perched on the edge of the chair, she pushed her face close to his. Much to his chagrin, Rob flinched, which made the waitress laugh again; such a cute titter. "I no bite you, silly man."

"Of course not," said Rob, as he closed the distance between them once more. "You surprised me, that's all. I thought you weren't going to sit with me."

Her finger was on his lips before he could utter another syllable. "You want to hear about table friend or you want blah, blah, blah?" Her free hand mimicked a sock puppet.

Rob listened attentively.

"Table friend come sit with you. Talk to you, get your drink, hold your hand and give you head job. Pay first okay, then I send friend. One thousand baht, so cheap, huh?"

Rob's erection was reaching for his wallet, until the image of a woman's head bobbing and banging against the underside of the table as she fellated him caused him to cringe. That was not how he liked to do business.

"How much without the..." he felt awkward saying the word so he gestured instead and cleared his throat.

"No charge. Just *nid noy* extra for drink." Rob was curious as to what exactly she meant by a little bit extra.

She held up two fingers in response to his question.

"Two baht?"

She laughed again, but this time it grated. "Two times."

"Double? Forget it. No thank you."

"Okay," she said calmly, dressing him with her subtle disappointment. "You drink yourself, lonely boy. Bye bye."

Rob reeled in the revelation of the table friend concept. Everywhere else he had been operated under the same rules, only the prices varied. He knew all about short time and long time, and about bar fines. He knew that every man who walked in; accompanied or not, was offered a friend. If there were enough friends to go around, he might be offered a selection. The chosen companion would come and sit with him and make small talk, listen to his problems, massage his ego, get his drinks and maybe even dance with him a little. Then he would be led upstairs to one of the candle lit box sized rooms for some intimate relaxation.

Fear of venereal disease, or the possibility of being robbed at gunpoint while naked had nearly always prevented Rob from going upstairs. He'd heard a story about a guy in a massage parlour in Sydney who had found himself facing the barrel of a sawn off shotgun with nothing but a shrivelling penis and an abnormal heart rate. If the girl had the perfect blend of all things sugar and spice, if she smelled nice and her hair was soft, if she smiled often without forcing it and spoke in liquid whispers, then Rob could have been facing the executioner's chair and he wouldn't have given a damn. On those rare occasions he had succumbed to the feminine charms of a sex bar hostess, it had cost him nothing but a couple of thousand baht, and it had been worth every last satang.

Still, Rob grew restless, each thought laced with regret. If he didn't want some action, then what the hell was he doing here? Some blokes crapped on about curiosity, but that disingenuous line of defence would not have stood up in any barroom banter, let alone in a court of law. Certainly, no mortified wife or girlfriend would have accepted the excuse of inquisitiveness. Rob had neither of those anyway. He was here on a vacation of open ended duration, with the sole intention of seeking and finding pleasure.

The salacious activity inside Lipstick flowed around Rob as though he were a resolute island of morality. He began to wonder if some of his fellow patrons were watching him and wondering why he sat alone; conjecturing about his plans, his intent and his character. Rob mocked himself when the stench of narcissism filled his nostrils. Nobody cared about him. Nobody even knew he was here, apart from the cheeky waitress, who would no doubt forget him as soon as he exited her territory. He was, in truth, a lonely boy.

"Hey, lonely boy."

Rob turned to face the persistent young woman, who had returned accompanied by another young lady. The latter was bereft of the sexy confidence of the waitress and Rob suddenly felt sorry for her; he felt ill at ease himself at the sight of her obvious discomfort. He pulled the adjacent chair out from underneath the table and motioned for her to sit, which she did, albeit stiffly.

"New girl for you. *Feuk yap yap*, no suck."

"You want to practice talking? How much?" The insistence of Thai people that worked in hospitality to blend their broken English with Thai did not assist comprehension.

‘'Just talk. Only half price. I don't like see lonely boy. *Kow jai na?*"

"Yes, I understand." The words thank you did not immediately follow, but by the time Rob had decided the waitress's gesture of goodwill was definitely worth some gratitude, she had gone and it was just Rob and the frightened girl, his table friend.

Awkward situations gained a new cynosure as Rob studied the girl and felt ashamed for doing so. Clearly he had been duped again and the waitress had deceived him with brilliant subterfuge. He was not going to get any value from this table friend, even at half price. These thoughts slapped his conscience, and so, unable to conceive a way to break the deadlock, he determined to leave. He stared at the side of her head as she stared at the table. Rob lit another *Klong Thip*, still wavering, wanting to rescue both himself and the girl. He glanced beyond her to the stage where the spotlight had resumed its prying glare of an even less adept performer than the previous one. The bar stage was occupied with two more pole dancers, or perhaps the same two. Who could tell? Rob looked back at the girl who remained motionless. What the hell was she doing here?

"My name's Rob. What's yours?"

His words shattered the spell of her discomfiture. She looked up and for a fleeting moment their eyes met, before she averted her gaze.

"My name is Jam."

"Sorry, I didn't hear you?"

She turned her head with eyes lowered and spoke in a moderately louder voice. "My name is Jam."

"Sweet," said Rob.

Jam said nothing more.

"You know we eat jam in Australia?" Still nothing. "How is your English, Jam?"

"Okay. I can understand you. I have troubling speaking."

"It sounds pretty good to me."

Rob stubbed out his *Klong Thip* and finished his whiskey.

"Would you like another one?" she asked.

"What in God's name are you doing here, Jam? Surely you don't want to be here. I mean, couldn't you do something else? Don't you want to do something else?"

Jam smiled an infuriatingly enigmatic Thai smile. "I'll get you another drink."

He watched her walk away and his mind changed gears. He no longer wanted Jam as his table friend. That was simply not going to be good enough. Not now that he had broken the ice and sensed a miraculous and unforeseen alignment of the planets occurring high above the blanket of Bangkok's perennial smog. There was something different about this young woman, something special.

A fleeting thought of his older brother back in Australia crossed Rob's mind as he waited for Jam to return. He imagined the disapproval of his life and his pursuit of pleasure for a moment, before swatting it away as he had done so many times before.

Chapter Two

Melisendra simultaneously waltzed into Shane Archer's English language classroom and crashed into his life. A spark of desire ignited a blaze of obsessive infatuation which was so unexpected and so aggressive that Shane had insufficient time to even think of defending the castle of his integrity. His professionalism was pole-axed by the very first smile on her mouth. Unprepared for such a fearsome attack, it was no surprise that Shane was so easily disarmed and defeated. Falling in love with Melisendra was an inevitable outcome of the effortless exertion of her feminine power. The fact that he was married was like a single leaf confronting a cyclone.

He recalled the first day she had graced his presence, seated towards the back of the room where his desk bore a computer and a scrappy collection of papers. Her attention was unwavering, as though every word he uttered was a delicious morsel of food, and she a starving acolyte. Without removing her eyes from him, except for those times when duty required her to attend to the written words before her, she devoured his lesson.

"Teacher," she breathed. "Can you help me, please?"

Words flowed from Melisendra's lips, smoothly attired in a distinct, yet easily comprehensible accent.

"What's up?" said Shane, moving to her side.

She pointed at the page. "What is this word?"

Shane followed her finger to the word in question, taking note of the colour of her fingernails; red, to match the soft cardigan that was draped over her shoulders. He could smell her perfume. His passion stirred.

"Incoherent."

"Incoherent?"

"Yes."

Melisendra looked up at him, frowning in frustrated curiosity. "What does it mean?"

Her tone suggested that knowledge of the meaning of this word might be the single most important piece of information she would ever learn. Her success and her happiness hinged on her comprehension. These thoughts ran through Shane's mind as he searched her eyes, attempting to read her face, such an expressive face. So beautifully expressive; the point of her nose, the fullness of her lips, the way she had applied just enough eyeliner to cause her eyes to shine like the sun.

Suddenly, Shane remembered where he was.

"Incoherent means it doesn't make sense. It doesn't adhere, doesn't stick. It can't be understood."

"Like my speaking?"

Shane lightly touched Melisendra's arm and smiled at her. "Not at all."

He wrestled his focus back to the rest of the class, though none of the other students had noticed his disappearance. He warned himself to be careful. Melisendra was dangerous. If she was playing with him, he needed to know the rules of the game otherwise he would lose and the consequences of such a loss were unthinkable. He wanted her. It was a simple, animalistic impulse; lust. Effort would be required to maintain professionalism and as he could not avoid her, he would have to find some method of dealing with the threat she posed. That was one possible response. The alternative was to play on in ignorance of the rules, and take his chances. Allow Melisendra the advantage for the sake of the thrill. In prospect, the idea was exhilarating. Shane was already losing but perhaps the game was over before it had begun.

During the morning tea break, Melisendra came to speak with Shane as he sat at his desk, sipping tea while staring at the floor.

"Excuse me, teacher."

Her appearance, so close and so intimate, choked Shane, causing him to splutter some tea back into his mug.

"Sorry. Would you like some pine nuts? From my country. They are famous. Very good. I toasted them myself."

Shane accepted a handful of the tiny nuts and asked; "Where are you from?"

"Spain. The nuts are from Castille-Leon. The best in the country, even the world."

"Really?" said Shane, amused by Melisendra's parochialism. "The best in the world?"

Melisendra's finely crafted eyebrows jumped, as though she was both shocked and offended by Shane's challenge against her claims of pine nut supremacy. "Yes," she said earnestly. "Really."

Shane was a patriot too. He was forever trumpeting what a wonderful country Australia was, how good Australians were at sport and how many wonderful inventions came from the minds of great Aussie thinkers. It had a peaceful and stable democracy, clean air, uncluttered streets and natural wonders galore. He actually found it difficult to believe there could be another country on Earth anywhere near as good, despite the fact he had never left the shores of the Great Southland.

"Okay," he said. "I'm sure they're good, but the *best* in the world?"

"Yes," she insisted. They looked into each other's eyes for a very long time without speaking. He felt himself melting under her intense gaze and he was perplexed, both by that fact and his reaction. Paralysed and incarcerated, Shane sat still until Melisendra liberated him.

"Eat them and see," she said.

"Okay. Thanks."

"You're welcome."

Melisendra made a habit thereafter of bringing Shane things to eat in the breaks. She always stayed to chat a little, asking questions, bragging about Spain and Spanish produce. A part of Shane never wanted her to leave, and as she did most of the talking, he was still able to rest his voice which was crucial between teaching sessions. She stood close, her chest at the level of his eyes which compelled him by force of will to look up to her. This he did metaphorically as well. He battled urges to reach out and pull her close, to nestle his face between her breasts. He imagined running his hand up along the inside of her thigh, he fantasized incessantly about her whether she was proximate or absent. While his mind made love to her, his face concentrated on projected platonic wholesomeness. Thoughts of his wife Angela never intruded on these adulterous daydreams.

Clearly, Melisendra did not know her own strength. Or did she? Shane was consumed with thirst for answers to his questions about her intentions. Thus far, he had done nothing to either discourage or encourage her affection. He believed he was being himself, acting normally, at least outwardly. He hoped no one else was aware of the turmoil inside. He hoped Melisendra was unaware of the havoc she was wreaking upon him. Shane needed to know, so he decided to push the envelope, despite the insanity and immorality of such action.

Spontaneous reaction quickly transformed into deliberate and purposeful action. Shane formulated a plan. Each time he worked with Melisendra, he made sure he touched her; her hand, her arm, her shoulder or her back. They were the lightest and seemingly most innocuous of touches. No stroking or caressing. When this initial phase of his plan produced no results, he thought he would try something else. Each time he corrected her written work, he added a little message, just a few words: *Well done - You are very clever - Beautiful work by a beautiful woman - It's lovely to see you today - I like your jumper.* When this failed to stir any reaction, Shane further crossed the line by accessing her student file, retrieving her mobile phone number and sending her a text message. The message read:

If you don't want me to contact you this way, please say so. I would like to talk to you more, but we never have time.

Melisendra did not reply to his text but her behaviour began to change. Upon her arrival in class she stopped greeting him. She did not visit his desk in the breaks, and the food gifts ceased. She also began to criticize him in class, questioning his teaching methods and complaining about the amount of time given to some students at the expense of others. This turn of events greatly disturbed Shane and he understood that he had offended her. He wanted to make amends, and so on the pretext of needing to talk to her about class work he approached her before class began one morning and invited her to step outside to talk.

"Have I done something to upset you?"

Melisendra unloaded a hurt and mystified expression, but Shane was undeterred.

"You've changed. You seem upset with me and I don't like you criticising my teaching in front of the other students."

"No."

Shane stepped closer, reducing the gap between them and lowering his voice, "What do you mean, no?"

There was an edge to her breath and it mingled uncertainly with her perfume as Melisendra held Shane's gaze but said nothing. He saw himself taking her face in his hands and kissing her softly on the lips. He saw her resistance collapsing and her opening her arms and her mouth. He saw her emotional defences fall; the wall torn down by his determination. Silence persisted while such thoughts swirled in Shane's mind, and God only knew what was going on in Melisendra's.

"Are you going to answer me?"

Melisendra began to sway like a dandelion, losing herself as the breeze of Shane's searching gaze blossomed into a wind of interrogation.

"What do you want?"

"I want you to talk to me. Tell me if I have done something to upset you. I thought you were okay with the touching." He reached for her arm and held it briefly to test her resolve. "I thought you were okay with the notes. I thought you liked talking to me and being close to me, because I sure as hell enjoyed it all."

She finally turned away from Shane and glanced back down the hall towards the classroom. "Is it time to go back?"

"I have a theory," said Shane. "Would you like to hear it?"

Silence.

"You were just being yourself. What you call friendliness, many, including myself, call flirtation."

Melisendra frowned.

"Flirtation has a romantic or even sexual element to it. It isn't just being friendly. It suggests something more is going on, that the person or persons doing the flirting are interested in something else, something more than friendship. Something more like..." Shane was struggling for the right words to explain what he meant, and all the while Melisendra was projecting curious innocence.

"Like boys like girls and girls like boys. Does that make sense?"

"No."

Shane suppressed the flick of anger he felt at Melisendra's apparent charade, before suggesting they needed to continue this conversation later.

She shook her head. "I just want to learn English. You're my teacher. And I'm married."

There it was; the giveaway. If only she had omitted those final three words, he might have drowned in perturbed despair. However, with that simple little sentence, Melisendra doused the smouldering ashes of his desire with petrol. Having thought the game had needed to be abandoned, Shane now received a burst of second half adrenalin. It was time to get serious.

He pretended to overlook the remark and gestured for Melisendra to return to class. "Let's talk again later, okay?"

She ignored him.

During class that day, and throughout the week, whenever the opportunity presented itself, or at times even when it didn't and Shane forced the occasion, he continued his pursuit of Melisendra. Deliberately blocking out the fact that what he was doing was unequivocally harassment, he pressed hard, touching her more frequently and for longer, staring at her. He wrote notes which included allusions to her fear and guilt that arose from her strong feelings for him. He tried to tell her as plainly as possible that it was all right to feel the way she did and it would serve her better to accept it rather than fight it. He told her that he liked her and wanted to be with her. He asked her to stay after class and talk to him.

When the day ended, Melisendra quickly packed her belongings and hurried off.

Shane sat at his desk, staring at the wall in bewilderment. Melisendra demonstrated no evidence of being annoyed, but neither did she display any positive reactions to his advances. On top of her charm, intelligence and beauty, this woman was intriguing and enigmatic. If she didn't like what Shane was doing, why didn't she tell him to stop? She wasn't shy, nor was she bereft of the verbal artillery required. Why not simply say; *I am not interested. You have misread my intentions. Stop harassing me.* Why did she wear the same plaid shirt for four consecutive days? Why did Shane think his own behaviour was acceptable? Why was he pursuing her in the first place? Had he been infected by some contagion of lust?

Energetic and confident women who were unselfconsciously attractive had always been magnets for Shane. Passion and intelligence in a beautiful package was irresistible. He had married just such a woman. As he sat and pondered the mysterious Melisendra, he wondered why he was even interested in having an affair. Shane abruptly stiffened on his chair. Was that what he wanted? Or was this a temporary diversion, an amusement? Angela supplied his need. They were having regular sex and it was good too. There was no hesitation, no excuses, no lack of fire and their relationship was good; a two year old marriage which still buzzed with courtship electricity. Why would he want to jeopardize that?

A knock on the door interrupted his musings and he looked up quickly, hoping it was Melisendra.

"Got a moment? I need to talk to you about something," said his manager, Sabeen.

Shane invited her in. She was yet another one of a group of uber-desirable women by whom he was surrounded. They were in his classroom, in the staffroom and in the office. The English as a Second Language industry was, as was the case with its big brother the primary and high school education systems, dominated by female teachers and administrators. Shane smiled at Sabeen, studying her face and trying to decide whether he preferred it with or without spectacles. She hadn't made eye contact with him yet. That was somewhat alarming.

She pulled a seat over beside Shane's desk and sat down heavily, despite her lithe frame.

"What's up?" asked Shane.

'We've had a complaint made against you by one of your students."

A gigantic invisible fist slammed into Shane's chest.

Chapter Three

Dust particles danced like fairies in the thin shafts of sunlight which poked through the half open blinds. Rob recalled a time when, as a child, he believed the dust he could see really was a group of fairies frolicking in the sun. He smiled at the recollection of childish wonder, frivolous fantasy. Dust fairies, the Tooth Fairy, the Easter Bunny and Santa Claus. In some ways it was sad and unfortunate that children had to grow up and suffer the deconstruction of these harmless myths. To have their imaginations tempered and their security blankets rudely snatched away.

Jam stirred beside him. He turned and looked first at the emptiness adjacent to him, then at the floor where she lay. She mumbled something then rolled over on her side, presenting her back to him. She wore cotton pyjamas adorned by jasmine and lotus flowers.

"Wakey wakey," he said. "What time is check-out?"

Jam grumbled a little then she rolled onto her back and exhaled slowly as her eyes fluttered open.

"What is 'check out' time?" she asked.

"When do I have to leave?"

She rubbed her eyes then massaged her temples. "They come to knock on the doors at nine thirty or ten o'clock. I don't think they care very much in the morning."

Jam stood slowly and grabbed a towel from the stand. "Do you want to have a shower?"

'You go first. Can I take you out for breakfast this morning?"

"I don't know."

As she left, Rob felt the room darken and he glanced towards the window. A small electric fan circulated cool air. The sun still shone and the sounds of the city with the traffic and the people bubbled in gently over the quiet of the room. The world was going about its business, unmindful of him, unaware of his absence. Waves of melancholy rode the sounds of external reality. Rob was susceptible to their pernicious attacks. He wasn't even out of bed yet and already the black dog of depression was barking at his door. He remembered fondly the safety and simplicity of childhood, the unadulterated joy of life. Sometimes he wished it were possible to return to that time when all questions had answers, all problems had solutions, and dreams came true on Christmas morning.

Rob became aware of a dull throb in his head and numbness on the left side of his face. His throat was as dry as the Northern Territory's ephemeral Todd River, and hurt as though scorched by the merciless desert sun. He was hung over. God only knew how much whiskey he had put away the previous night. This was his life in Thailand. Every night for two weeks now, hitting the bottle hard and suffering the repercussions every morning. Sometimes this vacation felt more like a kamikaze mission. Hundreds of thousands of baht poured down his throat and sucked into his lungs. At least half a dozen prostitutes used, paid off and dismissed. Meeting Jam had altered the course of Rob's runaway train.

She re-entered the room as his thoughts turned to what exactly had transpired the previous night. He had felt surprisingly sober as he'd followed her up the stairs, along a narrow landing, past several closed doors and into the small room. He recalled feeling nervous, but the details were fuzzy.

"What happened last night, Jam? When we got here?"

"You were very quiet on the way. When we came in, I closed the door and invited you to sit down. You repeated what you said at the table, that you weren't expecting to have sex with me. You just wanted to talk."

Rob detected a note of incredulity in Jam's voice. "You didn't believe me?"

She smiled. "Who comes to Lipstick for conversation?"

He nodded sagely and asked her to continue.

"I had to tell you a second time to sit down and relax. Once you did, I removed your shoes and socks and washed your feet. You were squirming around as though I was torturing you, so I told you to sit still. You mumbled something about stopping the bus and I told you that you weren't on a bus. I began to unbutton your shirt."

"Okay, thanks," interjected Rob. He was becoming aroused by Jam's recount, and as he would no doubt have to get out of the bed soon he did not want to have to conceal the evidence of his excitement.

"I was going to say," continued Jam, "that you asked me not to do, because you knew how to do it yourself. I laughed."

Rob desperately wanted this to stop. There was insufficient alcohol left in his system to deal with the rising embarrassment. "Just cut to the chase."

"What?"

"Tell me if we had sex or not."

"No."

"Could I have a towel please? I'd like to take a shower." Rob felt a sense of pride, an almost tangible righteousness to know he had not had sex with Jam. He felt something different, something unusual and exotic to which he was unaccustomed. It was difficult to reduce the emotion to words, but he was pleased that he had followed through on his decision to not do anything with Jam beyond enjoy her company.

Jam smiled and handed him a fresh white towel. Its softness and her discretion mollified his lingering disquiet. As he climbed out of the bed he realized he was still only wearing his underpants. When Jam turned away, apparently searching for something, Rob wrapped the towel around his waist and asked her the location of the bathroom.

On his way back from the bathroom a man walked towards him wearing a scowl, suggesting his business may have been to evict overstaying guests. Rob smiled half-heartedly at the man who ramped up the look of displeasure on his face and, when close enough, jabbed his index finger into Rob's chest. "You go now!"

The angry little man pressed his finger into Rob's chest one last time for good measure, before glaring at him and heading off down the landing to presumably deliver the same cheery farewell message to the other guests.

Back inside Jam's room Rob found himself alone and, having spied his clothes lain out on the bed, he quickly dressed and then sat to survey the room more closely. Beside the bed there was a small table with a single drawer and on top of it a lamp and a glass ashtray, devoid of butts. A larger table stood against the opposite wall, adjacent to the closet. It housed all Jam's things; women's stuff, make up and perfume, and a framed photograph of a picture perfect young blond woman. On the back of the door hung a couple of skimpy dresses and above the bed was a painting of a tiny boat sailing on a vast calm ocean.

You could sometimes tell a lot about a person by the style and contents of their bedrooms. Rob felt Jam was a clean and simple girl, but other than that there was precious little else to go on. Whatever they had talked about last night had been swallowed by an alcoholic fog and carried far away beyond recollection.

Jam returned. Startled, Rob turned to face her. "Time to go?"

"*Ka*."

"You're going to have to tell me all about yourself over breakfast."

"*Ka*."

Rob hoped Jam would find something to say aside from yes. He followed her out through a back door at the bottom of the stairs. They walked to the end of the *soi*, turned left along Sukhumvit Road and presently entered one of hundreds of *raans*. Before Rob could get comfortable, Jam had ordered breakfast for two.

"You don't waste time, do you?"

After pouring a glass of water for Rob, then one for herself, she settled back in her chair and waited. Rob did not know what she was waiting for, other than the food. Soon enough it arrived, as though produced by a replicator on board the federation Starship Enterprise.

She began to eat immediately.

"What are you doing here in Bangkok, working in a go-go bar? Where are you from?"

Jam loaded another mouthful of rice and vegetables into her mouth and eyed Rob over the top of her spoon.

"I'm from Had Yai. Do you know it?"

"Only by name. A friend of mine said he passed through there on his way to Malaysia on the train once."

"Is he with you now?"

'No, he's back home in Australia with his wife. Do you have brothers and sisters?"

"I have three brothers, two older and one younger. My older brother lives in town. The other two on my parent's farm, about thirty kilometres out.

Their conversation was routinely punctuated by chewing and swallowing. Rob was warming to the task when an angry voice arrested everyone's attention, yelling rapidly in Thai. Jam stood immediately and apologized to Rob as the angry man, who Rob now recognized as the same surly character who had poked his chest on the landing back at Lipstick advanced to their table. Rob stood too and grabbed Jam's arm.

"Wait a minute," said Rob. "What's going on? What's he saying?"

Before she could answer, the man snatched Jam from Rob's grasp and dragged her away. A chair was knocked over, a table shaken. People were yelling. Rob was sweating, riled, his blood boiling. He leapt to catch the man and break his hold on Jam. The latter's response was to pull a knife out. Jam screamed and Rob backed away, raising his palms. He insisted the man calm down.

It was an injunction to a cool heart, but the fire of the man's rage blazed away and he lunged at Rob. Searing pain piggybacked the blow and when Rob glanced down at his arm a copious flow of blood had already begun. Shocked, he was momentarily consumed with the injury, the terrible pain and the blood. However, he had been wronged, and Rob Archer was not going to accept that. The man, blinded by anger which seemed without cause, struck at Rob again, but Rob moved inside the blow and latched onto the man's arm. In one motion he pulled down as hard as he could and the man was flung face first into a table and rendered unconscious.

Jam was crying, mortified by the explosion of violence. Rob put his arm around her shoulder and walked her back inside to their table. He apologized to everyone along the way, trying to ignore their stunned expressions. Rob sat Jam down and returned his attention to the store front, where the whine of a siren preceded the arrival of a policeman on a motorbike. Dressed in a tight fitting brown uniform with aviator sunglasses, the officer wore a stony mask as he listened to the report of the store owner. Meanwhile, the irate little knife wielder lay prone on the footpath.

"Jam, what was that all about?"

“Your arm is really bad. You're bleeding everywhere."

Rob collected a handful of napkins from the dispenser on the table and pressed them against his wound. He placed his elbow on the table and pointed his hand at the ceiling. He felt faint.

"Tell me what happened?"

"Are you crazy?" she said.

There was no time to answer Jam's wide-eyed, shrieking demand as she rushed from her seat and begged him to follow her. She spoke to the officer, who nodded gravely several times before waving her away. She stepped to the curb and waved her arm. A blue taxi appeared, at which she gesticulated madly for Rob to hurry up and climb aboard.

Rob apologized to the driver as he got in, wincing and moaning the whole time until he was able to settle and elevate his arm again.

"So we're off to the hospital. Can you now please tell me what the hell he was so upset about?"

"I'm not supposed to leave the club without permission."

"For that I had my arm damn near chopped off? Bit of a bloody overreaction wouldn't you say?"

"I don't know what you're saying now. Too fast and I don't know the word overreaction."

"I feel sick. How far is the hospital?"

A quick exchange with the driver ensued, after which he lit a cigarette and swerved violently to avoid hitting a motorcyclist. Much horn tooting added to the aggravated atmosphere.

"Five minutes," said Jam. "If the traffic stays good."

"If the traffic stays good? We aren't moving! That's not evidence of anything good. Damn it, I'm bleeding to death here."

Jam clamped her hand over Rob's mouth. "Shut up!"

Rob heard more horns, felt the vibration of the engine and the crisp air from the air conditioner, but he didn't sense any motion. "Maybe we should walk. Are we close enough?"

Another quick exchange with the driver followed as he blew a lung load of toxic smoke out of the car window which he had wound down a few centimetres.

"A few hundred metres, he says. Can you walk?"

Jam paid the driver off and exited the cab before assisting Rob out and on to his feet. They had barely advanced. Rob fancied that if he looked back down the road he would be able to see the *raan* from where they had come and the cop still standing there nodding gravely, taking notes on his microscopic notepad. The fact was, Rob could barely stave off unconsciousness and the last thing he heard was the door of the taxi slamming shut, followed by Jam screaming again.

Chapter Four

"Let me ask you a question, Sabeen."

"Okay."

"If I commented on how lovely you always look and how I can't make up my mind whether I prefer your face with or without glasses, would you be offended? Would you think I was being sexist? Or harassing you?"

Sabeen smiled. "Are you trying to sweet talk me to wiggle out of addressing this complaint?"

Shane leaned back and stared at the ceiling to collect his thoughts. He was still recuperating from the near heart attack he'd suffered when Sabeen had announced that a student had complained about him. Her denial of his quite natural, automatic assumption that it was Melisendra, had yet to bring him any relief.

"Not at all," said Shane. "I think the complainant is a know-it-all whinger. I think he's frustrated by the fact he has to attend a language class which he feels is beneath him, in order to receive his government support. He doesn't know how long it will take until he can get himself into university and study to have his dentistry qualifications recognized so he can practice here in Australia. He's frustrated and he's scapegoating me."

"Fair enough," said Sabeen. "You know him, but he says you pay more attention to some students than others, and that you allow some to talk more often and for longer whereas you are always shutting him down."

"I refute that. His perception is coloured."

"He says, in particular, that you spend more time helping the ladies in the class than the men."

Shane leaned forward and half-heartedly slammed the table. "Outrageous. That's a terrible and unjustified attack on my professionalism. As if I would want to be as close as I could to beautiful and intelligent women for as long as possible, instead of getting cosy with less appealing and more masculine students who present greater olfactory challenges."

Her laughter was just what he had hoped for, though he had spoken the truth about preferring the company of women to men. His mock outrage had struck exactly the right chord and he was clearly off the hook. Shane did have favourites. He liked hardworking students as opposed to sloths, motivated and enthusiastic students compared to sloths, intelligent students with excellent memories rather than sloths. And he definitely had a weakness for attractive ladies while sloths left him cold, but favourites among the good students?

"Now," said Shane. "What about my previous question?"

"You are clearly a sexist pig, and if you ever say anything to me about my appearance, I will sack you."

Shane heard something other than an authoritative and angry warning in Sabeen's tone, and saw it in her eyes. "Understood," he replied, as he saluted.

Sabeen rose from her seat. "I'll speak to the client and explain to them that I spoke with you at length about the issue, and that you have promised to address it in earnest."

He nodded, then as Sabeen left the room he quickly added, "You have very nice calves, boss."

Without turning around, she replied; "final warning, Shane."

The phone rang and pilfered his opportunity to delight in the afterglow of that amusing exchange with Sabeen.

"Angie, baby. How are you?"

"I've decided we should go for it."

"What are we going for?"

"Our own business. Our own language school. We'll talk more tonight, okay? What time will you be home?"

The excitement in his wife's voice boomed down the line but was not quite strong enough to overthrow the nagging doubts he had about whether this project was even advisable, let alone viable. "Usual time. Around five. See you then."

The metaphorical horns of a dilemma were possibly the least comfortable position in which a man could find himself in. Shane shifted in his seat. Wollongong Language College may have underpaid, undervalued and overworked him, as well as all their teachers and administration staff, but they did pay the same amount each fortnight, and on the same day. They also paid for him to have a holiday, and to stay in bed if he was sick. They did also send students to fill the classrooms, and efficiently took care of all the administrative headaches. WLC were the ones who had to worry about the bottom line. Shane simply came to work and did his job, then went home. He had responsibilities sure, but as a P.A.Y.E employee, they paled into insignificance compared to the burden the company bore.

Angela was consumed by the idea, infatuated with the romance of being her own boss and doing things her way. Her excitement was infectious, every time she so much as sneezed a detail of her grandiose plan, he caught a cold. But he was happy to bear the temporary infirmity because her energy invigorated and inspired him, despite his doubts about the wisdom of the plan. Shane was not ambitious. The, 'go get it' gene had bypassed his entire family. His mother, Maureen, was a contented, assiduous housewife. His father, Alan, a conscientious company man who had graced the floor of the same saw mill for the fifty year duration of his working life. Shane admired diligence because he saw that it brought rewards without risk. As children, Shane and his brother Rob never went without, but neither did they experience the luxury of a fishing cruiser or an overseas holiday. Even interstate travel was a little far for both his parents; too overwhelming and way beyond their budgetary muscle.

The phone rang again. At this rate, what with his procrastination and the constant telephone calls, he would never get his paperwork finished for the day.

"G'day Shane. It's Rob."

"What the hell?" Shane said. He feared bad news, especially in the form of a request for money because his profligate brother had blown it all in Bangkok.

"I'm in hospital."

"No shit. Are you all right?" Rob Archer was a magnet for misadventure.

"Some lunatic slashed me with a knife."

"What for?"

"I don't know."

"You don't know? Some random person attacks you...with a knife...hang on, you were with a girl, weren't you?"

"Yeah, so?"

"Mate, when you get out of the hospital, go get yourself a T-shirt printed up that says; 'I'm a moron'."

"I'm thinking of a word that starts with s, and means to show concern, to express sorrow at someone's misfortune."

"You're a bloody idiot. You think you're the unluckiest bloke on the planet but the truth is, you ask for it. This girl was a dancer in one of the clubs, right?

"A table friend, actually."

"What the fuck is a table friend?" said Shane, then quickly added; "don't tell me."

Shane paced his classroom, cursing loudly inside his head. This conversation was pretty much like every other dialogue he had with his brother; a bizarre journey into the fantasy world which Rob inhabited. Where victimhood was worn like a badge of honour and where his troubles were always someone else's fault. No matter how hard Shane tried to crack Rob's shell of personal responsibility aversion, it was always the same story. Vitriolic abuse would bounce between them, and one or the other would hang up. Shane sucked all the air in the room into his lungs in one violent inhalation and then let it escape very slowly.

"You're going to be okay, right? What'd they do? Stitch you up?"

"Ten stitches, mate."

'Good for you Rob. I've got work to do. I'll talk to you later." He cancelled the sound of his brother's questioning voice with a firm press of the end call button. The phone slipped out of his hands and onto the carpeted floor. It was a poignant metaphor for the state of his relationship with his little brother. Twenty months separated them in age, plus nearly seven thousand kilometres in physical distance. The awful reality was Shane and Rob lived in different galaxies. He sighed as he picked up his phone.

"Everything all right? You seem a little worked up."

Shane flicked his hand from his side into the airspace beside his head. "Just family stuff, Sabeen. You know?"

She smiled. Shane looked at her, waiting for her to declare the reason for her reappearance. Not that he minded. A distraction was required and this vixen certainly provided one.

"Yeah, families," she said, hitting just the right note of sympathy. "They say you can choose your friends, but you can't choose your family."

Shane groaned inwardly and deducted a point from Sabeen's scorecard.

"Anyway," she said, cautiously. "If you want to talk about it, maybe we could get together for a drink?"

Shane and his beautiful boss shared a very weird and very long gaze, during which time he was seriously considering accepting her invitation. He feared Sabeen might mistake his protracted silence as a sign he was thinking about saying yes, even though that's exactly what he was doing. *Why the hell not?* Nanoseconds later another more authoritative voice overrode the pusillanimous one, and reminded him of the fact that he talked about these kinds of things with Angela. There was very little chance that Sabeen was merely inviting him for a drink and a friendly chat.

"Thank you, but I need to finish up here and get on home." He looked away as he spoke, then glanced back to catch her reaction.

"Sure," she said, still beaming, as though she had not just been brushed off. "Maybe some other time."

"Sure," replied Shane, even as he hoped she would never ask again. Next time he might say yes and Sabeen probably knew that. This dialogue was excruciating and he wished she would depart with alacrity.

"I'll leave you to it," she chirped. "Let me know if you change your mind."

Shane changed his mind immediately, as though her words were enchanted, but he kept his mouth shut until she was gone, then he allowed himself to breathe.

Rattled and baffled by his behaviour, Shane slumped behind his desk and stared at the blank computer screen. It logged him off every five minutes unless he showed it some affection. It was annoying, but stacked against his ridiculous flirtations with Sabeen and his childish obsession with Melisendra, it was a trifle. Why was he playing with fire? Who had flicked his pyromaniac switch? How was he going to escape this burning building when he was so entranced by the flames? Though they seared his flesh, Shane liked the pain and was lining up for more. *Bloody idiot!* He was no better than Rob. And there it was. The reason he was so intolerant of his brother's aberrant and often abhorrent behaviour; he was the proverbial pot calling the kettle black.

He dialled Rob's number and waited.

"I didn't think I'd hear from you so soon," said Rob without rancour.

"Sorry mate," replied Shane. "I..." He trailed off, his eyes roaming the room, searching for the words which had vaporised on his tongue. There was no help from the other end of the line. "I overreacted. I'm sorry. Are you okay? What's happening? Tell me about the girl."

"She's something else."

Shane quickly suppressed a snide comment. "Yeah?"

"So I'm at this place called Lipstick, in the Nana red light district."

"The Nana red light district? Are you kidding?"

"It's bigger and better than Patpong."

"Anyway, you were saying about the girl?"

"Her name is Jam."

"I bet you made a lame joke about her name, didn't you?"

"Uh-huh."

"Did she get it?"

"Nope, a waste of good material. Anyhow, the waitress at Lipstick is bugging me about doing something more than just sitting around slamming Mekong's, and I finally cave in and ask her what tablemates are. Because I've never heard of them, and I've been around."

Snide comment number two successfully repelled.

"To cut a long story short, my table friend comes over and slides in next to me, but she's shy, really shy, like she's a newbie, and she makes me feel all awkward, and I'm not awkward, especially not when I'm tanked. I'm smooth."

Snide comment number three beaten off with a large stick.

"Still a pretty long story, bro... I really need to knock over this paperwork, otherwise I'll never get home and Ange won't be amused."

"I spent the night with her then went out for breakfast the next morning, and this guy from the club marches in and starts going off his brain in Thai. Apparently Jam needed permission to leave the club, and who was I to be dining out with one of his girls, like she was mine."

"So it was a property dispute."

"That's a crude way to put it."

"Those girls are commodities mate, not people."

"They're treated like commodities."

"Whatever," Shane said dismissively. He reckoned he had done very well to last this long, but his forbearance was being stretched once more. "You going to see her again?"

"Hell yeah. She's not going back to Lipstick. She's coming to stay with me."

Chapter Five

"Are you happy, Jam?"

She frowned as a crescendo of manic, hospital busyness engulfed them. Rob wasn't sure whether her expression was a response to his question or to the noise. Bumrungrad International Hospital was a multiple specialty medical centre on Sukhumvit road, *soi* three. Jam had babbled on about the history of the place as they waited for a doctor to see him, her way of dealing with nervous tension, no doubt.

Built in 1980, it was reputedly the largest private hospital in South East Asia, and still young enough not to have had its shine eroded by disease, neglect, or the polluted atmosphere of Thailand's sprawling capital city. Given the number of cleaners hovering around, Rob understood why the hospital had retained its radiant visage. He had questioned Jam about how Thai people afforded to be treated in a place like this and she said most of them couldn't.

They walked down a gleaming corridor before turning into another one. Rob's arm was numb from the pain-killing injection the nurse had given him. He still felt fuzzy as well. His conversation with Shane was still fresh in his mind, though distant and fragmented. He had told his brother that Jam was his girl and that she would be leaving Lipstick and moving in with him. Now he wondered what Jam would think of the idea.

"The doctor did a nice job with the stitches," said Jam.

"They're staples actually, but yeah. It should heal nicely."

"It will leave a mark."

"What's another scar?"

Rob Archer had spent a lot of time in hospitals, much more than your average twenty four year old, excluding stuntmen, thrill-seekers and those with chronic or terminal diseases. Rob was a cut above the regular once or twice a lifetime hospital patient. He laughed at his own joke.

"Why are you laughing?"

"Nothing," Rob lied, preferring not to go to the trouble of explaining his private joke to her. "Have you been here before?"

"I came with a friend once before, like now with you. But not as a patient."

"You've never been a patient?"

Jam shook her head.

"What about when you were born?"

"I was born in my house, on the floor. The hospital was too far away and I was impatient."

Rob laughed but then suffered the theft of his good humour, courtesy of the tidal wave of humidity which struck him as they exited the hospital through automatic doors. He felt beads of sweat lining up in all his pores, chomping at the bit to run free over his skin. A number of taxis sat in a disorderly queue at the front of the hospital with their engines idling. Some of the drivers were out of their cabs, smoking cigarettes and chatting to one another. Once settled on the back seat of the first taxi, Rob waited for Jam to give the driver directions and then he seized the moment.

"Are you *happy* Jam?"

She looked at him thoughtfully, as though she suspected he was trying to trick her. "Yes."

"Really?" said Rob, locking his eyes on hers. "You like doing what you do, working at Lipstick? It doesn't seem like you like it. You didn't seem to be having a good time last night. Not at the table anyway. Not even in your room. You seemed uncomfortable."

He waited, wondering if she understood his outburst, if she felt his passion, his urgency. She *couldn't* be happy. There must have been some reason why she was stuck in this shitty degrading job. She clearly was not lacking in intelligence, so there had to be some hidden compulsion. Many of the girls in the go-go bars of Bangkok's red light districts probably enjoyed what they did, poor girls earning big money simply by selling their bodies. Many of them may have harboured serious ambition and looked upon the provision of sexual services as a necessary means to an end, as a fast way to get what they wanted, their own businesses perhaps, or a new life in another country. It was also likely that some of the girls were slaves, some of them were under age as well, sold by their families to wicked traffickers, dealers in human misery. Rob shuddered and shook his head. Jam was speaking to him.

"What?"

"I think you are too interested in me," said Jam. "Don't worry about me. I do my job and I make money, and when I have enough money, I will leave."

"So you have a choice?"

"Not really."

"What do you mean?"

"Never mind."

Rob turned away to stare out of the window of the barely moving cab. They were virtually paying for a nice cool place to sit and talk, rather than for transport to wherever they were going.

"Where are we going?"

"I'm going back to the club, and you're going back to your hotel."

Every woman Rob had ever met, or had anything to do with, had certain things in common with each other, certain universal characteristics; enigmatic, capricious and therefore infuriating. He thought things were going well with Jam, that there was some chemistry happening between them. He reckoned he had a reasonable sense of her disposition, that her flirtations were more than professional playfulness and she was opening herself up to him. With two terse sentences she had slammed the door in his face. He decided to knock for permission re-enter.

"Have I done something wrong?"

Silence.

"Jam? What's wrong? I thought we were friends."

"Sure. Because that's why men like you go to clubs like Lipstick, to make friends, right?"

Surprised by the spiteful edge to her voice and by the accusation which, if truth be told was slicing very close to the bone, Rob simply stared at her. She glared back for a few moments then looked away. Rob became aware of the vehicle's movement and soon, through several fits and starts, they arrived at their destination.

Jam indicated to Rob that he should pay the driver and added, "Unless you want to keep going?"

Rob had a couple of hundred baht notes in his hand which were en route to the driver's waiting hand. To Jam, Rob said; "do you want me to keep going?"

"Up to you. The club's closed so you can't come with me."

"The club is always open."

"*Buy ru my buy woey,*" muttered the driver impatiently.

"Hold your horses."

The bemused driver replied, "*A-ry wa.*"

Rob pushed the notes into his hand and exited the taxi. Jam had already started walking away. Her determined stomping was very cute, but Rob was genuinely puzzled by her behaviour. He stood on the footpath, deliberating for a minute or so.

Dizzy, he stumbled to the nearest wall and leaned against it. The sensible thing to do would be to return to his hotel room and get some rest. Ordinarily Rob wasn't especially rational, but prudence won the day and he commenced a short walk to the Ibis Nana where he had a two week booking. Fairly commodious and acceptably clean, it was all Rob needed given that he mostly only used it to sleep and shower. It had air conditioning, a mini bar and satellite television. A few dirty marks on the walls and a small blood stain on the top sheet were insufficient grounds to deny the Ibis its three star rating. When Rob finally entered his room, he collapsed on the bed gratefully and slept.

A while later, dry mouthed, Rob woke slowly and reluctantly. While studying the ceiling and the walls, pain reacquainted itself with him. He looked at his arm and noticed some blood had oozed through the gauze covering the wound. His tongue was fuzzy, matching his brain.

He had come to Bangkok fifteen days ago, having accrued both adequate savings and leave from his job at the pharmaceuticals company, Hamilton Green. He planned not to return. The job itself he was happy to leave behind, his workmates not so much, but being absent from them wasn't exactly breaking his heart. He did not miss, nor could ever imagine missing his cantankerous boss, Bobby Chase. Rob smiled at the recollection of the short and portly man cruising around the finishing floor, barking orders; curses hissing through gritted teeth. The others in his crew he mostly liked: Felix was the youngest of the general hands and he imagined that his biceps were larger than they actually were. There was Steve, a terrific bloke who would do anything for anyone, and who happened to be a bisexual with a pornographic mind and an obscene sense of humour. Houdini was the most senior general hand and the man who would be king. He disappeared when the line became too busy or when anything difficult had to be done. Then there was Paul, who wore a wig because no hair would grow on his head after his scalp and face were severely burned in a house fire. The Johnny-come-lately of the team was Sullivan, a mild mannered Satanist who fancied himself as a ladies man.

Rob rolled over on to his side and sat up on the edge of his queen bed. His workmates now seemed like caricatures, and he pondered the strange ways of the mind when it projected memories. He stood slowly to avoid vertigo and carefully stretched his back. His arm began to plead for his attention, begging with the only voice it knew; pain.

He turned the television on as he made his way to the bathroom and the discordant voices of some television game show filled the room, vanquishing the isolation he felt. Rob fumbled in his pockets for the tablets the doctor had given him. There were only four left as he had forgotten to take the prescription to a chemist on the way home. He would need to go out later. He wanted to go out later, back to Lipstick.

Jam too, like his workmates, was being summarised by his mind. It was funny how easily a complex human being could be reduced to a snatch of well-chosen adjectives.

Rob splashed cold water on his face and examined himself in the mirror. His face looked a little drawn, his eyes were red and puffy, his hair a bloody mess. He pictured Jam and saw only large almond eyes, a cute button of a nose and a flawless complexion. He wanted some other descriptors for her, besides the disparaging ones with which he tarred all women and had done so to Jam in the heat of the inexplicable rupture in their relationship. Unpredictable sounded better than capricious, and mysterious was a marginal improvement on enigmatic, but Rob could not overcome the mountain of infuriation. There was no question in his mind that he would have to return to Lipstick to find Jam and pursue her. There was also no doubt it was probably an ill-conceived venture which would ultimately prove futile. Oh well.

His mates would think him heroic, in an alcohol fuelled idiotic kind of way, while his brother would just call him a goose. Although Shane had seemed fairly sanguine when Rob had mentioned his plans during their last conversation at the hospital, it was unlikely he would ever approve of anything Rob did.

Therein lay the crux of the problem. His most significant, most meaningful and longest lasting relationship was stuck in a perpetual cycle of dysfunction. He and Shane had fought often as boys, always competing with each other and never knowing where to draw the lines. Without active refereeing from both their parents and their teachers, the two brothers may well have killed each other. Rob and Shane Archer personified sibling rivalry. All through their younger years and into adulthood the enmity persisted, even though they would have deemed the use of such a word to describe their tempestuous relationship as overly harsh and inaccurate.

Rob urinated, flushed the toilet and took another long look in the mirror. He wanted to blame Shane, as the elder brother, for fostering the competitiveness which frequently injured them and those around them, but he knew he was equally responsible. What he did not know was how to reverse the trend. He had been trying for some time now to mend the broken fence, but Shane had been strangely recalcitrant. He continued to belittle Rob at every opportunity and criticize his decision making abilities. Condescension had been transformed into art, derision into sport. Rob realized that he had left for this big holiday of his, in no small part, because of Shane. They had been too physically proximal, too often forced to interact with one another. Rob had become extremely sensitive to the heat and had consequently decided to take the advice of the anonymous sage and get out of the kitchen.

He liked Thailand. Why not stay, he mused, as he returned to the bed via the mini bar. Why not start a new life here? Maybe distance would finally heal the fractured relationship with Shane. Maybe Jam could play a leading role in the resurrection of Rob Archer. *Maybe*, he thought, as he cracked open a bottle of Singha and guzzled half of it, *I am exactly the good for nothing loser my big brother Shane reckons I am.*

Chapter Six

With large natural breasts and big hair to match her huge personality, Angela Archer was more than most people could handle. Always bubbly and energetic, she either exhausted others or carried them on her shoulders as she sped along the highway of life. Resistance was futile. Her charm and passion were overwhelming, and for those reasons she left folk both awestruck and dumbstruck. She, like Shane, was a teacher, so one could add creative and intelligent to her list of outstanding qualities. Like, loathe or love her, one could not help but admire her. Shane Archer was in the category of those who loved her, despite his wandering affections.

She was in the kitchen still dressed in her uniform when he arrived home from work. Shane found her irresistible and quickly slid in behind her, wrapping his arms around her waist. She squealed then twisted around inside his embrace to face him and plant a long wet kiss on his lips. When her eyes opened, he kissed her again and moved his hands down onto her buttocks, squeezing and stroking her flesh through the thin material of her tight fitting skirt.

"Is dinner nearly ready? I'm hungry."

"It needs to simmer for ten or fifteen minutes to let the flavour deepen."

"I love it when you talk like that."

Shane stepped back and released his wife from his lusty clutches. He reached for her hand and led her out of the kitchen, down the hall and into the bedroom. Frantic clothes tugging followed, with strings untied and buttons virtually torn off. Arms up, arms down. Feet up, feet down. Bend over. Stand up. Urgent kissing between each action of undressing.

"We could have saved time and done this in the kitchen," said Angela, before Shane snatched away her words and her breath with a violent embrace. His hands, firm and desperate, ravaged her nakedness. Her hands joined the battle, as they fell onto the bed and wrestled each other into ecstasy. A few minutes later it ended with an explosive orgasm, and Shane, sweaty and breathless, rolled off his wife who appeared to be in shock.

"Are you okay?" he asked.

Angela eyed her husband from beneath drooping lids. She smiled. "That was different."

"Good, different or bad, different?"

"Good, but I don't know if our wardrobes could stand up to too much of that sort of different, and you were a bit rough with my breasts too."

Angela was still smiling but Shane couldn't help feel that she was forcing it, to allay his concerns that he had overstepped the mark, gone too far, pushed too hard.

"I'm sorry, baby."

"What's going on? It's porn, isn't it? You've been looking at porn and you thought you'd try it out on me."

"No."

"None of those trollops have got it over me, Shane." She gestured with both hands to her nakedness, from shoulder to thigh. "And it's all mine, natural; no surgery. It's mine and I only offer it to you. This body is exclusively yours, to look upon, to lust after and to touch."

A knot was tightening in Shane's stomach as Angela ramped up her emotional attack.

"I'm not putting it out for a multitude of desperates to masturbate inside their stained track pants as they sit in darkened rooms staring at computer screens. Panting and drooling over disgusting and degrading images of women being used and abused, women who think so little of themselves that they spread their legs and insert foreign objects into their vaginas and feign untold pleasure."

Shane had no choice but to accept Angela's tirade, although clearly her hyperbole was off the chart. He would not be saying anything to her about how she was generalising, nor that many of the women who posed nude felt empowered by it, and earned some money. No time to mention choice, or the ways in which pornography benefitted some relationships, enhanced them even. He would keep his mouth shut about the difference between high quality and beautiful, artistic imagery and cheap, nasty sleaze. Shane's trap would remain firmly shut even though she was wrong on a number of accounts, especially about him using pornography.

"What hurts me most," said Angela, with tears now brimming in her eyes, "is that I am apparently not good enough for you. Who were you thinking about when you were making love to me? Although I hesitate to call *that* sexual frenzy love-making. Who were you thinking about?"

Ironically, there'd been times when other women *had* floated around in his head and danced before his eyes during foreplay, just occasionally. He could have been thinking about Sabeen or Melisendra when he made love to Angela. He might have indulged in a fantasy featuring them individually or in combination. It was possible and Angela's question was not therefore unreasonable, but the truth was on this occasion he had not been thinking of anyone but her. Angela. He loved her and he felt ashamed for mistreating her and upsetting her, and for every time he had made love to another woman, albeit only inside his head.

"No one," he ventured, moving carefully closer to her. "I wasn't thinking of anyone, and I don't look at pornography. I haven't done that since my teens."

Angela sat up, evading his approach, resisting the physicality of his attempted apology. He touched her back but she reacted by standing and hurrying away to the en-suite, where she shut the door and ended the discussion.

Shane fell back onto the bed and stared at the ceiling. Angela's insecurity was perplexing. They were happy together. Their friendship was strong, their love for one another deep and genuine. Shane had not given her any cause to doubt him. Her accusation about him and porn was unjustified and the suggestion he had brought other women into their bedroom, imaginings wrapped in the translucent veils, was offensive. Why did she doubt him? She was enough, more than enough, and yet he had spent the day at work fantasising about both Melisendra and Sabeen. Was she somehow psychically detecting his guilt? Was there an aroma of mental unfaithfulness and remorse clinging to him? The whole situation was an impenetrable confusion.

While Shane waited, his mind wandered. He saw Melisendra, in class, calling him over to her table to mark her writing. He leaned in over her shoulder, resting his hand first on the back of her chair then placing it lightly on her back. A little work, some encouraging words, all followed by a gentle caress. No reaction. He stopped. She looked up at him, smiling, inviting. *Stay here*, she whispered, *stay close, touch me, check my work but keep your hand on me. Breathe in my ear. Move closer.*

The en-suite door opened suddenly, startling Shane. He jumped, bending forward to conceal his inappropriate and poorly timed erection. *Shit!* What a hopeless case he was.

"I'd better get back to dinner," said Angela. "I wouldn't want it be ruined as well."

"Angela?" Shane called after her. "Angie, baby."

Shane had a shower and, unable to stop thinking about Melisendra, he masturbated in order to banish his tumescence. As he dressed, he hummed a tune which popped into his head. At first he didn't recognize it but then it came to him; Run to You by Bryan Adams, a classic rock song about adultery. Even though he didn't believe in supernatural stuff, Shane began to suspect that he was possessed, under attack by a demon of lust. What other explanation was there for the derailment of faithfulness and the collapse of his discipline? The Winchester boys had a lot to answer for. That episode of Supernatural called, 'Seven Deadly Sins' wasn't the first time he had heard about demons of lust, greed and sloth, but he had never seen a more potent representation of them.

When Shane finally made it back to the kitchen, Angela had finished cooking and had already served his meal. She had poured him a glass of wine and one for herself. Her plate was there accompanying his, but her person was absent. He looked around and saw her standing in the living room, staring out the front window. He watched her for a moment, noticing her motionless rigidity.

"Ange," he said softly. "Are you coming to eat?"

He waited. "Ange?"

"Coming," she said, as she turned and walked towards him.

Shane allowed her to sit first, studying her, searching for a sign she was all right, that *they* were all right. She said nothing.

"I'm really sorry I upset you. You're wrong about the porn, and I only think of *you* when we make love. I only think about *you* when I think about making love."

She looked up from her plate. Their eyes met, hers still showing flickering remnants of anger and pain.

"Don't *make love* to me like that again, okay?"

Shane understood her emphasis on the words; *make love*.

"Yes. I'm sorry."

"I only want to make you happy. If I don't make you happy you should just tell me. Don't go looking for happiness somewhere else."

"Are we still talking about sex?"

"Sex and general happiness, I'm not having a miserable marriage like my parents did. All that pretending, they faked their way through forty seven years until dad died of a stroke. He cheated on her in their first year of marriage and kept at it for years. He used to go out most nights; sometimes he said it was for work, though it never truly was. While at other times he just went out without telling my mother where he was going or with whom. I never understood why she put up with that. I despised her weakness, and I despised him for hurting her over and over again. They played at happy families but there was always an undercurrent of bitterness, of contempt even. It was dismal.

"He screwed around for twenty or thirty years, and by that time mum was locked in and unwilling to break out. She endured it for the sake of me and my sisters. In order to maintain an outward bliss and an internal sanity, we upheld the facade. We all played our designated parts. It was a fucking joke actually."

Shane knew all this. When he had proposed she'd said no and given him this long dissertation about the pathetic falseness of marriage, and how she didn't want to play that soulless and humiliating game. Love never surrenders, and Shane had eventually convinced her one bad marriage could not be used to denigrate the whole institution. He had used his own parents as an example and, as she got to know them over time, Angela found a shiny new model of marriage to which she could easily aspire.

"We are not your parents. Nor are we my parents. We are Angela and Shane Archer and we are an awesome couple who will undoubtedly enter the annals of all-time great matrimonial engagements."

Angela smiled, thus finally and thankfully breaking the non-ambient oppression. They ate with more gusto and chatted, and the conversation turned to the big news of the day. This had probably been uppermost in Angela's mind when Shane had returned home from work. She had likely imagined Shane would shower and change, then the two of them would sit and discuss it all over dinner.

"What are we going to call it?" he said. "The new business?"

"Speakeasy."

"Wasn't a speakeasy an illegal drinking venue during the prohibition in the U.S.?"

"Yeah, but that was like eighty years ago or something like that, wasn't it?"

"I'll Google it." Shane grabbed his phone and launched the app, before entering *speakeasy* into the search box. "Here we go. The Prohibition period lasted from 1920 to 1933, and during that time it was illegal to manufacture, sell and distribute alcoholic beverages throughout the Unites States."

"What a dumb idea," said Angela. "Banning things only creates black markets. Imagine if they banned cigarettes."

Shane put his phone down. "It will never happen. Not that I care. I don't smoke. I'm more concerned about the heroin issue. They should lift that ban and legalise it so I can enjoy some heavy duty relaxation."

Angela laughed.

"Seriously, think of how much crime is associated with drugs. I mean, I know heroin is not in vogue these days, but the illegality of certain drugs makes their manufacturer and distribution a financially attractive proposition for businessmen with a propensity for criminal activity. Most thefts are drug related. All the bloody shootings, in Sydney especially, but around the country and around the world are drug related. Governments spend shitloads of money in the war against drugs, but continue to make little impression on the power and insidious spread of black markets. It's simple economics. If there is a demand, it must be met, and it will be met; legal or illegal. What difference does that make?"

"Have you finished grandstanding, Mr Archer? Can I put the soapbox away now?"

"Right, I'm thinking speakeasy may not be the best choice. What about Easyspeak? No references to nefarious boozing dens implied there, either explicitly or implicitly."

"Easyspeak," said Angela. "Easyspeak…" Angela said it a few more times, tossing it around in her head and observing it from different angles, allowing it to communicate with her, to touch her. Shane watched with amusement.

Her final pronouncement was not unexpected. "I like it."

"Let's drink to it," suggested Shane as he raised his glass and tilted it towards Angela's.

"Easyspeak. Easy to say, easy to remember."

"Perhaps not so easy to establish though, right?" Shane's doubts popped out again.

Angela sipped her wine thoughtfully then laid the glass carefully on the table. "I'm not kidding myself, Shane. The mountain of paperwork required to receive accreditation as a Registered Training Organisation is going to consume most of my time, then we need to find a building, register the company name, hire staff and advertise for clients."

"It's a massive job," added Shane.

"Yes, but it'll be worth it." Angela gave him a penetrating look, clearly intended to test the strength of his resolve. "Won't it?"

"Absolutely it will, and there is no woman in the world better equipped for the challenge than Angela Archer. Intelligent, ebullient, determined, and on top of all of those impressive qualities, a woman of rare and exquisite beauty."

"You really excel in crapping on."

Another clinking of wine glasses preceded the exchange of encouraging smiles, and a kiss for good luck.

"Angela," said Shane in an earnest attempt to convince both of them. "I do believe in you. You are awesome and I am with you one hundred percent. I will do whatever it takes to ensure your success."

"*Our* success," she corrected.

"Whatever it takes to achieve *our* success."

Whatever it takes; it was a promise with frightening implications, and Shane regretted the words the moment they escaped his mouth, leaping from his tongue and into the ears of his beloved wife.

Chapter Seven

It was déjà-vu for Rob Archer as he entered the same dark, crowded bar as the previous night, the night he had met Jam. The night when his libido forsook him in favour of gallantry or what he supposed was at least some shadow of that concept, when he had felt something akin to sympathy, a protective impulse. He had not eaten since breakfast, but was remarkably uninterested in food. He felt dizzy. His mind was as furry as his tongue. After he'd found a table and ordered a soft drink, he lit a *Klong Thip* and realized his folly. It would need to be a very short night out, but hopefully long enough for him to see Jam.

Wisely avoiding alcohol of any variety, Rob sat, smoked, and searched the dimly lit interior of Lipstick for the woman he wanted to rescue. Human shapes floated before his eyes, heat rose on the surface of his skin. There were swirls of colour, blurry lines and indistinct patterns, skin, clothing, smoke and intermittent lights of myriad hues. Nausea surged. He should have left and returned to the refuge of his room at the Ibis, but Rob stayed and kept scanning the room, now hoping beyond hope that he would spot her. He checked his watch.

Then there she was, in his ear; "What are you doing here?"

"Looking for you."

"*Ay ba*!"

"I know it's crazy, but I wanted to see you again."

Jam stayed close and Rob could feel the air which bore her whispered words rustling the hair in his ears. "If Pee Lek sees you here, he'll give you a matching knife wound. He's still angry, spitting mad about yesterday."

Rob grabbed Jam's arm. "Has he touched you?"

"Get out of here."

"I'm not leaving until you talk to me. You went all weird. We have unfinished business."

Jam frowned and pulled her arm free of his grasp. "I don't know what you are talking about and I'm working anyway. I don't have time for this, for you."

"I'll buy your time. Long stay plus the bar fine. No problem. I just want to talk to you, all right?"

Rob's focus intensified, drowning out the noise, blocking the visual assault. He leaned in, projecting desperation .While Jam was thinking, the angry little man with the knife was looming behind her. He approached with alacrity, unhindered and driven by murderous intent, if the look on his face was any reflection of what might be going on inside his head. Jam was about to answer when Pee Lek pushed her aside and grabbed a handful of Rob's shirt, yanking him to his feet. The dramatic and unexpected change in altitude was too much for Rob. He slumped, sliding from the other's man's grip on his way to the floor.

When Rob opened his eyes, he saw nothing but the purposeful pattern of the watermark on the ceiling. He heard voices that were speaking in Thai. One of them was Jam's, the other unknown. Attempting to tune in to grasp a sliver of comprehension proved too difficult, as the pounding throb in his temple affirmed. The conversation ended and Jam's face appeared, a motley crew of emotion painted there.

"You were lucky you fainted when you did."

"What time is it?"

"Nearly three o'clock."

Rob rubbed his temple, trying to massage the pain away so he could think straight. "Not even an hour ago."

Jam smiled. "I told Kim you had paid for long stay before you passed out." Reading Rob's show of confusion, she added, "I helped myself. It's all paid."

"Good, thank you."

"You wanted to talk and we have all night, but I think maybe you should just listen and save your strength. Sleep if you wish. *Jai yen yen na ka*. Be still. Be calm."

"Can you get me a drink? I'm really thirsty."

"Sure. Is it time for more pills?"

"Not yet."

Jam stroked his hair, before rising to go and retrieve some water. It was a strangely tender gesture and it made Rob feel like crying. He suppressed the urge.

She returned promptly and handed Rob a large glass, inside which ice cubes clinked in the joyful embrace of cold water. Sitting in a chair beside him she looked around the room and then back to him, searching his eyes, delving and prying. "You want to know all about me," she said. "I am twenty one, already an old woman in this business."

Rob wasn't sure if she was telling the truth. Most men who used the services of sex workers in Bangkok's red light districts preferred young girls. He knew the girls all lied about their age and could do so because of their genetic quirk which meant they almost always looked much younger than they actually were. Clients wanted under-eighteen year olds at least. Sixteen year olds were even better. The real sickos liked children. Rob gagged at the very idea, hoping to God at the same time that he had never unknowingly molested anyone. Jam was not trying to win Rob's affection so she had no reason to lie to him. But he was nonetheless suspicious.

Rob was overtaken by a compulsion to reach out and touch her face. She was so pretty.

"You don't look old. You are very beautiful."

Jam smiled before continuing her narrative. "I think we were talking about my parent's farm in Had Yai when Pee Lek interrupted us."

"You have quite a gift for understatement."

"I was forced to work on the farm like my brothers. No school past year four, which the monks taught at the temple because my parents couldn't afford further education for any of us, except my brother, the eldest. He did well, graduating from Ramkhamhaeng Open University after completing school in Had Yai. He works at Thai Farmers bank in town now."

"So he's doing all right financially."

"He makes about fifty thousand baht a month. It's okay."

The tiredness Rob felt was subsumed by the magical tone and cadence of Jam's story. His questions were crude intrusions which he decided to cease.

"My father arranged a husband for me and made some arrangement with the man's father with regard to property. I was to be a good Thai wife in due course, when I turned twenty, and I was to care for my husband and bear children for him. I had other ideas, and despite the fact I loved and respected my father, the rebel in me pressed its claim. Ambition burned in my bones. I wanted to go to school like my brother, so I tried to convince my father to let me go. Good provider and loving though he was, he steadfastly refused to allow me the freedom to make my own choice. So, I ran away.

Distracted by an invisible fascination, Jam's vacant stare matched her melancholic expression. "I fled to the bright lights of the big city; the city of angels, Bangkok. I was determined to get a job and pay my own way through university. A dream I shared with thousands of other country girls from all over Thailand, with whom I also shared the crushing disappointment and the shattering reality. Low paid menial jobs with no prospects, I earned barely enough to feed myself and have a roof over my head. I couldn't afford anything more. Not even the tiniest of luxuries like shampoo."

Rob took hold of her hand without thinking. "Why didn't you go home? You would have been happier."

A rueful smile appeared on Jam's face, "Pride."

"The original sin."

Jam's brow furrowed. "I was unskilled, unhappy, unsatisfied and alone, but too stubborn to return to my family, who would have told me straight to my face had I not run away, that I was doomed to fail."

"How'd your English get so good? You said you didn't go to school."

"I read a lot," she said, casually gesturing to a pile of books on the table which Rob had not previously noticed. "And I work with a lot of *farangs*."

Rob released Jam's hand and she stared at it, as though he had left a curious stain.

"It's the best way to practice, speaking with foreigners," said Rob. "Go on. Tell me more."

"My last job before I started here was selling cigarettes. It's funny how *farangs* buy individual cigarettes because it's different. They all comment on it unless they've been here before."

"It's a novelty."

"A what?"

"Never mind."

"I was so bored and sick of the rudeness of customers. Men would ask me if I had any unusual ways to smoke them, and they laughed at me because I didn't know what they meant. Some would even come straight out and ask me how much I cost. I found them disgusting."

Rob noticed her cute little nose wrinkle as she said the word.

"One day, a very polite man who had a pig for a friend, told me I was beautiful and I shouldn't be wasting my time on the street. He said I should get a job in a bar, as a hostess. I didn't know what he meant, but I thanked him for his advice and wished him a good day."

Rob laughed. "You're a real character, Jam."

Jam was once more staring wistfully into empty space. Her voice was softer when she next spoke. "I made some enquiries at Lipstick and was offered a job. I remember my skin crawling as the manager undressed me with his eyes. I was so embarrassed. And I was afraid he might not be satisfied with just looking. I've been here for three months and I haven't written to my family since I started. I've tried but I can't."

"They'll be very worried about you."

She nodded. "This is the life I have chosen."

"What do you want to do? If it were possible, if there was nothing to stop you?"

The question carried ominous poignancy. It bounced around in Rob's head as he watched and waited for Jam to answer. It was a question he had never asked himself. His life had just rolled through season after season without direction, and he had never stopped to reflect. He felt every milligram of the pain and frustration against which Jam was wrestling. Her battle in some ways mirrored his own although this was the first time he had seen himself in combat.

A gecko shimmered across the ceiling, surefooted and purposeful despite being inverted. Rob would have fallen. He shook his head. He would not have tried such an audacious adventure, he was timid and insecure. He was a weary traveller, hiding behind a mask of juvenile masculine bravado and trudging through the days of his life, who had now found something of a kindred spirit in this beautiful young Thai woman.

"A nurse."

"What?"

"I would like to be a nurse. I think I would be good at it."

"I think you are doing an outstanding job with this patient. I'm feeling better already, a bit hungry and not so dizzy."

They looked into each other's eyes for a few moments and Rob could sense the bond between them solidifying. An affinity had prospered in such a short time, an understanding, a merging of destinies.

"Rest now," she said. "I'll get you some food."

As wise as it would have been to sleep, Rob was unable to switch his mind off. His thoughts, like bubbles of soap, sailed forth into the air and lingered uncertainly, before vanishing with a silent explosion. He could take Jam back to Australia. Marry her and get her into school. As a new migrant she would have access to free language classes, not that she really needed them, but they would be useful in preparing her for further study. She was probably intelligent enough to pass the bloody IELTS exam and get into university, where the government would happily fund her education. And once she passed and graduated with a Bachelor of Nursing, then she could work. There was always plenty of work for nurses, and everyone knew more were needed. More doctors too, maybe she could be a doctor.

With Jam's future sorted, Rob turned his attention inward. What was *he* going to do? March back onto the finishing floor at Hamilton Green and continue his old job? That wouldn't be so bad. They boys would be happy to see him. The boss would be typically and inexplicably apoplectic. Maybe if he worked hard and hung around long enough, he could take that leading hand's job off the cranky old bastard. It wasn't the most exciting job in the world, but it was a good company and the pay was pretty good for unskilled labour. He and Jam could get a place in Cronulla, close to the beach, in a new apartment. Eventually maybe even have children.

The door opened suddenly. Wonderful aromas burst into the room, preceding the bearer of the culinary wonder. Jam could cook for him, serve him and make him laugh. He may as well ask her right now, he thought, as a diabolical combination of hunger, pain, and fantasy pushed him into delirium.

"Jam," he said. "Will you marry me?"

Chapter Eight

"It's much more complicated than you might think," said Angela.

"Everything usually is." Shane accepted the complexities of life as a matter of course. The unstoppable movement from the simple to the sophisticated was an inevitable outworking of evolution. Biological entities were trans-mutated through a series of micro genetic adaptations to increasingly complex organisms, and that was reflected in every aspect of civilisation. Governments started small and were quickly corrupted by power, automatically embarking on reproductive activities to ensure their survival and the retention of their utility.

"There are a number of different visas for international students," said Angela.

She seemed to be suggesting they focus on them as opposed to migrants, which was the group he had assumed would be their target. They both worked with migrants, those newly arrived and studying English courtesy of the Adult Migration Education Program, and those who had been settled for some time. Neither had ever worked in Australia, or slaved away for decades and found themselves on the employment scrapheap, courtesy of downsizing. Bereft of the necessary language and literacy skills to find another job, the latter group were a tragic mob, frequently pensioned off with work related injuries, back problems mostly. They were the least likely, of all the students that Shane taught, to re-enter the workforce, aside from the fifty and sixty year old women who no longer wanted to work.

He allowed her to continue, albeit with a question to prove she had his attention. "How many visas are there?"

"Seven of them, visa 570 through to 576."

"There aren't really hundreds of different types of visas are there? Talk about a bloody administrative nightmare."

"I don't know. They might be like American house numbers; three houses in a dead end street, numbered 1001, 1205, and 1460."

"Why do they do that?" Although Angela was about to answer, Shane silenced her, fearful of a long winded diversion down an unhelpful path. "Don't tell me. Stick to the visas."

"You're a real party pooper, Shane. You know how much I love my trivial tid-bits." She smiled.

"I prefer trivium to trivia, so if we could get this train back on the rails."

Angela nodded and sipped her wine. "The only one that is of interest to us is subclass 570 – E.L.I.C.O.S."

"English Language Intensive Courses for Overseas Students. Yes, they want to get into university courses but they have to pass I.E.L.T.S exams to qualify."

"Or they are already enrolled and are struggling to keep pace in the course with native speakers, because of deficiencies in language skills. Not proficient enough."

"That's cute. Maybe that should be our slogan: Deficient in proficiency? Easyspeak can help."

"A bit too cute, don't you think?" Angela finished her wine and picked up the bottle. She tilted it at Shane who shook his head, and refilled her glass.

"Technically, the visa 570 is for international students undertaking a stand-alone course that leads to certificate level award, or non-formal award."

Shane grew impatient with the details, choking on the minutia, wondering where Angela was heading. "Whatever," he said. "That's where we come in, right?"

"We have to properly consider what services we offer, what courses. I was talking to a colleague today and he knows someone who is on an advisory panel for the national health practitioner's regulatory body, A.H.P.R.A. Have you heard of them?"

"No."

"It was born out of the push for national accreditation standards for health professionals. There are serious shortages across all professions but especially doctors and nurses. That's why we have to import so many. Australian high school graduates are choosing lifestyle degrees in the arts as a means of avoiding the reality of professional and permanent employment, rather than medicine. The problem is our professional standards are usually higher than many other countries from where doctors and nurses might be brought in. And there was no national benchmark. Uniformity is coveted now, but what happens when you try to bring all the states in line is that you have to bring everyone else up to spec with the highest. You can't go to the lowest common denominator."

Shane fidgeted as a creeping numbness stole across his buttocks. If Angela detected his discomfort she neither acknowledged it nor took a breath. Once she was wound up and released Angela could spin for an eternity. He had read about this issue somewhere, but as with all irrelevancies, it found no purchase on the slippery slopes of his memory banks. He really hoped she would finish soon.

"Now," she continued, after pausing briefly for another toke of claret, "We've got lots of foreign doctors whose first language is not English, and the number of complaints about 'communication issues' is rising. I mean, how much faith can you place in a doctor who can't explain himself properly? He might be a brilliant doctor, but it means diddly squat if he can't ease your mind with an easily-understandable justification of his proposed action, right?"

Shane nodded and stood up, wondering if such an obvious and impolite gesture would snatch his wife's attention. Trance like, she ploughed on, even after he left the dining table and casually strolled away to the kitchen. A noticeable increase in her volume was the only sign that she recognized his absence. He nearly told her to shut up for a minute, but demonstrated the sagacity of a much older husband by restraining himself. He loved Angela but she could be a human avalanche on occasion.

"And that's to say nothing of how he or she communicates with other doctors and the nurses," continued Angela.

"Are you aware I am no longer sitting at the table with you?"

"So the Health minister decides, after exhaustive consultations, that the rules regarding the registration of overseas trained professionals from non-English speaking backgrounds have to be tightened. The minister is aware of I.E.L.T.S and is advised that despite the intentions of the creator of I.E.L.T.S, which is that the test be used strictly to determine the suitability and competency of a candidate for further study, it would be the perfect instrument to measure whether or not a candidate was good enough, in terms of their English language skills, to do the job for which they had trained."

"Fair enough," said Shane. He noticed Angela had swivelled her chair around to face him in the kitchen. He wondered if even being out of sight would prevent her continuing to talk to him. Would she follow him to the toilet and stand outside the door, yapping away while he took care of business?

"The problem is," she went on, "that the I.E.L.T.S exam is not an accurate reflection of English language proficiency."

"Really?" countered Shane as he headed out of the kitchen. "I thought it was the gold standard. I mean, all the universities use it to vet potential students."

Shane walked down the hall towards the bathroom and smiled as Angela's voice pursued him. Either she had raised her personal volume or she was chasing him.

"Consider this. A woman sits the writing exam. She is given a random topic and a limited period of time to write on it. The woman loves gardening and science and as she goes in she's hoping and praying the subject will be something she knows, and better still, something which interests her. She sits down and finds a question asking her to write about Australian sporting heroes."

During the pause, Shane closed the door, lowered his pants and sat down on the toilet. He picked up his toilet book, Time Flies by Bill Cosby, and started to read.

"Firstly, she's not an Australian. In fact she's only been in the country for a few weeks. Secondly, she not only doesn't know anything about sport, she hates it. Now tell me how is she supposed to demonstrate her writing skills? How could she possibly write anything? She scribbles out a heavily padded paragraph about sport and how many people like it, although she does not, and how in fact football is seen as a religion by many people. Soon, she hits the deadline and a truck load of despondency simultaneously. She's crushed. She's thinking about how much better she will have to do in the other macros to pull up her average. She needs 6.5 to be accepted into the engineering course she wants to do. It's a master's degree. She's already earned a Bachelor of Engineering. The more she thinks about it, the worse she feels. She feels certain that her lack of knowledge of Australian sporting heroes is going to cost her dearly."

Shane kept reading. Cosby was talking about how he was always losing his glasses. Shane laughed, because although nowhere near fifty years old, he could well relate to losing things. The laugh sounded too raucous so he tried to rein it back in. Sadly, it was too late.

"What's so funny?" asked Angela.

"Nothing."

"You laughed," said Angela calmly, in a tone teetering on condescension. "Either you are a heartless dick or you are reading that damn book and not listening to me."

Shane chased his thoughts around the big vacant backyard inside his head, trying desperately to bring them to heel. He needed something.

"The test isn't a fair reflection of a person's ability. I get it. It's bloody unfair, but what's your point?"

Shane resumed reading once more as he waited. He chose non-fiction books to read in the toilet because he didn't usually spend much time in there, thanks to daily doses of Ryvita wholemeal crackers and green apples. Non-fiction was often more palatable in bite sized chunks. There was no chance of losing the thread of the narrative because there wasn't one. Nor was there any real danger of being sucked in by a particularly engrossing tale, and feeling disinclined to leave the toilet.

"I think the test is unfair and inaccurate, but I do acknowledge the need for some benchmark," said Angela. "Finding a truly objective measure of English language proficiency is virtually impossible, so we have to use a flawed system and, let's face it, defective systems work brilliantly with imperfect people. It's like democracy."

Shane continued to read. Cosby was now talking about how he frequently enters rooms but forgets what he is doing there. Again, Shane understood.

"Who was it that said; democracy may not be the best system but it's better than all the others?"

"Miley Cyrus?"

"You're an idiot, Shane. Why can't you take me seriously?"

Shane reluctantly closed Time Flies and replaced it in the magazine rack. "I do, baby. It's just that we are having a conversation through a door whilst I'm emptying my bowels. Maybe there could be a more appropriate time."

"Do you know who made that quote about democracy or not?"

"If I tell you, will you let me finish my business in peace?"

"All right."

"I think you're referring to Winston Churchill, who said and I quote; democracy is the worst form of government, except for all the others that have been tried."

Silence.

"I'll be out in a minute," said Shane. "And then you can tell me what on earth you have been rambling on about."

After washing his hands, Shane left the bathroom and was on his way back to the kitchen when he noticed the bedroom light was on. The door was ajar. He entered cautiously. Angela was lying across the bed staring at the ceiling. The slight creak from the door announced his arrival and she turned her head to face him.

"I really feel like we can do some good here," she said, "by helping people who need to pass the I.E.L.T.S exam. Did you know, candidates are sometimes required to achieve a minimum score in all four macro-skills, and missing out in just one invalidates all the other results which means they need to sit the whole exam again? It's not like if you bomb out in speaking, you only have to repeat the speaking exam. You have to do the whole thing again, and you have to wait to book another test date. You also have to pay the full fee again; three hundred and thirty dollars each time. If you cancel a booking they charge a cancellation fee. It's a goldmine for the examination industry and a possible blackjack table for candidates."

Shane lay down on the bed beside Angela and draped his leg across her thighs as he cuddled into her. She showed no resistance to his display of affection. With his nose pressed into Angela's neck, he inhaled her scent; vestiges of Butterfly lingered on her soft skin.

"That's what I think we should do. Offer I.E.L.T.S preparation courses. The system really sucks, but if we can't change it then at least we can do our best to ameliorate its impact."

"That is an excellent word, Mrs Archer," said Shane as he lightly caressed Angela's stomach. "Have I ever told you how much it turns me on when you use big words?"

She turned and kissed him suddenly, then licked his lips with her tongue. "What do you think of my idea?"

"To be honest, right now my brain function is severely impaired by a dramatic rush of blood to another part of my anatomy."

"Sorry to disturb you."

"No need to be sorry," said Shane. His hand wandered from Angela's stomach to her right breast. Her nipple hardened at his touch. "I actually think it's a great idea, and who says we *can't* change the system."

"Thank you," she said, before kissing him again.

"You're welcome, but if it's all the same to you, I think I've got a much better idea which requires our immediate attention."

"Sure," said Angela. "I agree, but slowly this time, okay?"

Chapter Nine

Genuine and heartfelt retractions functioned as apologies for hastily spoken or deliberately vituperative words, but there was no way of taking back those words, no means of removing them from reality. They left a lasting impression; a stain or a scar. They would be remembered, and perhaps even be transformed, resurrected into retaliatory taunts. Accompanied by mealy mouthed clichés like, *I didn't mean it*, or, *please forget I said that*, words were much more potent than most people realized.

Rob's proposal not only resulted in the loss of his dinner, and the smashing of the plate bearing it, but also in striking Jam with profound muteness.

They both stared at the mess while Rob searched for something else to say. A non-sequitur would have been useful but none presented itself. How had his amusing little adolescent fantasy exploded to life? Should he attempt a retraction? Dismiss it as a joke? God, he wished he could read Jam's mind. Knowing how she felt would have made it much simpler to plan his next move, to respond to her. This was a classic demonstration of the minefield of human relationships, the success or failure of which depended so heavily on good communication.

Jam finally knelt to begin the retrieval. She did not look up but she spoke softly, apologetically, "I'm sorry. I'll get some more."

"No, I'm sorry," said Rob. "I didn't mean to say that." As he watched Jam he hoped to catch her eye, to at least be able to attempt to read her expression. He wasn't sure if he meant what he said. The idea of marrying Jam was not remotely distasteful. Quite the contrary, but his delivery was clumsily timed. There was no chance she was expecting him to propose, and likewise, little chance she had been thinking along the same lines. True to form, Rob had acted rashly. What now?

Jam completed her task and left the room without saying a word.

Rob fell back on the bed. "Shit!"

Momentarily forgotten, the nagging ache of his slash wound returned to add to his misery. What should he do or say when Jam returned? What could he salvage from this awkwardness-inducing faux pas? Rob was always unsure of himself, constantly second guessing his actions and the motives behind them. Covering his insecurity with a veneer of brash confidence may have convinced others, but his pockets were always full of the loose coins of self-doubt. He thought back to the circumstances surrounding his decision to come to Thailand.

Swallow Rock in Grays Point was a quiet place which Rob frequented to escape the tribulations of life, and to think. He usually fished for mullet from the dirty sand which bordered the Hacking River. He rarely caught anything, but neither was he frustrated by the taunting leaps of the fish above his lead-weighted hook. Fishing wasn't really about the fish. Not for Rob anyway. A keen fisherman friend of his, Trevor, agreed that the actual fishing was a secondary activity. The social aspects held higher appeal; time to spend catching up with his mates, or with his family. It was with the mention of family that Trevor started to lose Rob during his ebullient lauding of fishing. Trevor was older and obviously had different priorities. Without a family, Rob was mystified by the attached romance. Trevor lost Rob completely when he talked about spending time with God. Trevor liked to go fishing by himself and talk to God, and he attributed his relatively calm and laconic nature to these quiet times with his creator.

This sounded like arrant nonsense to Rob because he could not perceive of the necessity for God. There was no purpose. No reason to believe in something he could not see, and time by himself was not usually terribly peaceful. Serenity was more often found in a bottle of whiskey.

One particular day, as Rob sat on the sand loosely holding a handline, his thumb and forefinger tensioning the line and anticipating movement, he had an epiphany. He was not the fisherman, nor was he the fish. He was the bait; the only element in the fishing scenario which had no choice about its involvement. He was the prawn on the end of the hook, at the mercy of fate, dead and soon to be consumed and annihilated. Rob recalled releasing the line slowly and theatrically, consciously letting go and liberating himself from the expectations of others, throwing off the shackles which bound him.

To be free, he knew he needed to escape. The suffocating proximity was not conducive to his happiness. With every word, deed or inaction, Rob found himself subject to scrutiny from his parents and from Shane, who had metamorphosed from his older brother into an additional father figure. When Shane married Angela, she joined the party. He didn't need to be so frequently reminded of the drift which characterised his life. He resented the wolf of criticism which they presented in the sheep's clothing of encouragement. He knew he could be happy if they simply let him live without foisting their ambitions on him, and without poorly disguised insinuations regarding his laziness and lack of drive.

Rob smiled as he remembered the strong tug on the line which had arrested his musings. He'd pinched the nylon between his thumb and forefinger and then began to wind it slowly around the plastic reel. He waited breathlessly for a second jerk, and when it came he yanked the line, winding it quickly. He had one. It was a sign. The unmistakeable weight on the end of the line as he wound it in confirmed he had caught something of a good size, a keeper. His prize eventually appeared on the sand, thrashing wildly in fits and starts as Rob continued to wind it in. It was dying already, struggling in vain to disengage the hook which Rob could see was protruding beneath its unblinking eye.

When the fish was close enough he placed his foot on its body and twisted the hook out of its head, before quickly snatching it up and dropping it into the bucket which sat beside him. During the catch Rob had felt powerfully thrilled, a masterful predator executing instinctive hunting rituals. Mercilessly taking the fish from its home and extinguishing its life for his pleasure. With the fish flopping around inside the bucket, dancing its final throe of death, Rob realized he didn't care about it. He felt pleasure untainted by remorse, and again the metaphor stamped itself on his consciousness. Looking to the water from whence the innocent mullet was wrenched, Rob imagined blood flowing in the current; a tiny ribbon of claret in the muddy river.

Whilst waiting for the fish to take the bait and be hooked, he felt like the bait. With his prey snared, he felt a primal satisfaction. If he left his family, if he left the country, he could rule. He could call the shots with neither compunction nor fear of retribution. That was the moment he made up his mind to go. He would start with a vacation, but as he had enough money saved it could easily turn into an indefinite stay.

Thoughts of fishing at Swallow Rock reminded him of better times with Shane too. A lump formed in his throat. Misty eyed recollections always made him feel sick. The past was to be trampled and left behind, not eulogised and clung to in pathetic reminiscence. Whatever good it held, or was believed through the distorted lens of hindsight to have held, was better left alone, as it could not be relived. Neither could its accompanying emotions be re-experienced. It was gone. History. Rob loathed history. He was deluded of course, cognizant of the deception. His antipathy towards the past had no power to limit either the frequency or the strength of its impudent intrusion into his thoughts.

He needed to prepare for an awkward conversation when Jam returned. He could only inculpate himself for the situation. For his carelessness with words, his errant timing, the deficit in his ability to think before acting or speaking. It was his fault entirely.

"You were joking about marrying me, right?" said Jam, clearly wanting that to be the case.

Rob surrendered to the lie. "Yeah," he said, conjuring a weak laugh for support. "Must be the drugs… I mean, you are beautiful and intelligent and I'm not saying if I did want to marry someone that she would not be someone like you, but we barely know each other."

Jam placed his plate on the bedside table and squatted. Rob noticed two spoons and two forks.

"You'll have to sit up," she said. "Can you manage?"

"Sure."

Temporarily distracted by the aromatic invasion of lemongrass and oyster sauce, Rob's mind cleared and he prepared to eat. It looked wonderful and his hunger, dormant during the last half hour of fleeting insanity, renewed its demands. He sat and swung his legs over the edge of the bed.

"I'm sorry for making you drop the last plate," he said.

"I'm sorry, I thought you were serious. You really surprised me. I've had a few drunk *farangs* tell me they loved me and wanted to marry me, and I've always played along, secure in the knowledge that drunken tourists don't marry the go-go girls they have sex with. The younger ones, boys really, barely men, they want to marry virgins, or at worst girlfriends who may have had only one or two other partners. When their brains are saturated with alcohol they only think about their dicks. Sobriety forestalls concupiscence?"

Rob shovelled a mouthful of rice and stir-fried chicken into his mouth and chewed slowly. Where the hell did she learn to talk like that? He also wondered whether to openly correct her naivety. In which universe did men only think of sex when they were drunk? Maybe booze disinhibited the actions they took to alleviate the slow burn of lust, but if most men were like Rob, then sex was never far from foremost in their minds. He decided instead to focus on her extraordinary language.

"Where on earth did you pick up a phrase like, 'sobriety forestalls concupiscence'?"

"I don't remember," said Jam dismissively, as she concentrated on the food. "Some book."

He stared at her. "Some book?"

She nodded.

"Something you stumbled across while perusing the shelves of the local library?"

"I used to go the university library and pretend to be a student. I wouldn't have dared try to join a lecture but I felt safe enough in the anonymity of the library. I asked for a borrower's card and they gave me one. I made up a student number which they obviously didn't bother checking."

Rob swallowed and smiled. "Very sneaky."

Jam continued eating. Was it shame, bashfulness or something else which kept her silent? Jam was marvellously enigmatic.

"Do you have any beer?"

"Just water."

"Anyway," said Rob. "You were talking about how at first you thought I was serious then you quickly realized I wasn't. How'd you know?"

"I already told you. Men like you don't marry women like me."

"I'm sure they do sometimes."

"I'm sure it never lasts."

Her certainty was laced with cynicism. "Why?" She kept her eyes down, chewing thoughtfully whilst toying with a piece of capsicum on the plate. He pressed her. "Why couldn't a man like me and a woman like you live happily ever after?"

She laughed, slapping him with such an unanticipated reaction that he wondered if she had heard him correctly or was responding to another invisible source of mirth.

After recovering herself, she drank a mouthful of water then said, "You believe in fairy tales?"

"Sure," said Rob without thinking, "Why not?"

"Okay, I'll marry you."

The same piece of capsicum Jam had casually stabbed now lodged in Rob's throat. He coughed, then coughed again and grabbed the water, throwing it down his throat, attempting to flush the offending vegetable fragment. His eyes watered as heat suffused his face. Finally he recovered, and said in a croaking voice that was barely recognizable as his own, "now you want to marry me?"

"Sure. I'll quit my job and move in with you. Are you staying in Thailand?"

Rob was speechless.

"Probably not," said Jam. "Eventually you'll go back to Australia. We'll need to start taking some photographs and writing letters to each other, to prove our relationship is genuine for my residency application. Should we get married here first?"

He continued to stare at her.

"Okay. It'll be cheaper, and you won't have the extra expense of all your relatives. Invite your parents of course, but otherwise it will just be my people. Church or temple? Are you a Christian? I guess not, right?"

"That's enough, Jam," said Rob. "You made your point." He was mystified by her sudden vehemence, angered by the sarcasm.

"Do you have enough money to pay for the wedding and the dowry to my father? A plane ticket? Visa application fees? What's your place like? A small bachelor pad with no food in the fridge and clothes all over the floor? Shall I stop taking the pill now, or do you want to wait? Why wait? Let's start now. I want to have four children. Two boys and two girls."

"Stop it!"

"Okay, I'll go and have shower and put on my teddy, then we can have sex all night, and in the morning I'll make you breakfast."

"I said, stop it, Jam!" said Rob, yelling at her this time. "I wasn't serious about marrying you. Not that it would be like that anyway."

He stood and walked to the window while the sound of her muffled sobs followed him across the tiny room. He resisted rushing back to comfort her. His body twitched as he fought the urge to wipe away her tears and hold her in his arms. He was angry and confused, and she had gone too far. He hoped her sorrow was guilt because guilt could be a tool positively employed. She deserved to feel bad for that unwarranted assault. Her presumption was outrageous, most likely without logical foundation, and painfully insulting. Rob maintained his posture of rejection, even as she crept closer to him.

"I'm sorry," she blabbered through tearful sobs. "I shouldn't have said all that, but you know we can't get married. It won't work."

Rob turned, and keeping her close with one hand around her waist, he used the other to lift her chin. Her tremble filtered through him and her chest heaved as she battled the depth of her feelings. Her eyes met his.

"You're wrong, Jam, and I'm going to prove it to you."

Jam's lower lip fluttered. She inhaled sharply and shuddered as she released the air in a jagged rush. "How?"

"I'm going to hang around and romance you. I'm going to win your heart and show you fairy tales can come true."

Even as she fell into his arms, he doubted she believed him. He wasn't sure he believed it himself. It sounded suspiciously like commitment.

Chapter Ten

Any joke was perpetually on the verge of being carried too far, of crossing the boundary from fun to ridicule. When one of the participants in the banter found themselves the butt of the humour, laughed *at* instead of laughed *with,* then the acrid stench of trouble would fill the air; the revellers standing at the precipice of social disaster, incognizant.

Abu el Temeemi was a likable, albeit occasionally irritating man. Overtly friendly and good natured, he often talked at length on topics of little interest to others, and usually of similarly retarded comprehensibility. He was a poor listener, which was why in Shane's opinion his English was not improving, and was not likely to improve. Health issues contributed to Abu's communication deficiencies, as did the heavy painkillers he took to deal with them. Nonetheless, he was an asset to the class because he made people laugh and was able to laugh at himself. Self-deprecatory humour always won friends, relaxing the tense and thawing the frosty. Abu could take a joke, most of the time.

"You don't say that to me," growled Abu, as the joke officially went over the edge. "I hit you. The woman not say to me like that. If my wife say to me like that..."

His hand was drawn up behind his ear, poised, the gesture unmistakeably hostile. Shane stepped in and grabbed Abu's hand. Abu glowered at the woman who had made herself his enemy by laughing just a little too long, and by adding a comment which pierced the fifty year old

Iraqi's pride. Maribel was a sweet and harmless Filipino who had inadvertently stepped on a lion's tail.

Shane resisted the force as Abu's hand sprung forward, catapulted by rage.

"Take it easy, Abu. We're friends here. She didn't mean it."

Suddenly Abu turned his fiery gaze on Shane as he wrestled his hand free of its restraint.

"She not say to me like that. Call me stupid."

"I'm sorry," said Maribel, her voice quavering.

"She didn't call you stupid," said Shane.

"Bullshit, Mr. Shane. You nice man with bad ears."

The air was thick with apprehension, the silence surrounding the combatants heavy. Maribel's pretty face edged on collapse, fear and regret threatening to break her. Shane stepped between them, and noticed as he did that Melisendra had left her seat and was approaching.

"Come on Abu," she said in a devastatingly placatory tone. "Sit down. It doesn't matter. You're not an idiot. We all love you."

Abu's hands rocketed toward the ceiling. "Bullshit!"

Melisendra looked crestfallen, shocked that her charm had failed. Shane wanted to comfort her, to tell Abu to leave and then offer solace to Melisendra. He smiled at her in the vain hope of conveying something meaningful about how he appreciated her valiant efforts. Melisendra turned away, oblivious, and resumed her seat. Abu stormed out of his own accord, and with him now departed Maribel's defiance crumbled and she began to cry. A sensitive classmate wrapped a soothing arm around her shoulders.

The dissipation of the ruckus left Shane in a quandary. He looked at the clock on the bottom of the computer screen. There were still ten minutes remaining in the session but was it worth pressing on at this point. Could he resurrect the lesson, refocus eighteen minds and infuse the turgid atmosphere with some tranquillity? He couldn't even remember how it had begun. It seemed wise to break early, which is exactly what he did by dismissing the class and inviting them to relax.

Slowly the students rose and left their seats, before exiting the room. Some headed for the kitchen next door, to join the queue for the microwave. Others headed down the hall towards the front door and the promise of fresh air and warm sunshine. Smokers and shoppers both comprised the latter group. Abu would be out there as he was both. Maribel smoked as well. Shane sighed. This kind of drama was unusual in his classroom, and he did not feel as though he had handled the situation particularly well. Perhaps if he had been more focused on the issue and the people involved in the conflict, he may have been a more effective mediator.

When everyone had left, Melisendra approached Shane's desk with typically silky movements. This was not a good time for her to visit. He wished he could pull the blinds and pretend he was out. Proximity to a seductress was definitely not what he needed, weakened as he was by the fracas between Maribel and Abu. There was no doubt he would inhale one whiff of her perfume and have to start battling to keep his lustful imagination under control. He crossed his legs and winced as she arrived and said, "Teacher, can I talk to you?"

Only if you sit on my lap and kiss my cheek. "Sure."

"I just wanted to say I thought you handled that situation very well." She smiled.

I just wanted to say that if you don't go away there is going to be another, infinitely more perilous, situation, over which I am unlikely to have anywhere near the same amount of control. "Thank you," he said. "You're very kind. You helped too."

Melisendra shook her head in slow motion like she was a model advertising shampoo. "I didn't do anything."

Shane glimpsed a sliver of her breast between buttonholes. She leaned very close and the aroma punched him in the stomach. He squirmed as she spoke, her sweet breath tickling his skin.

"I think Abu is an idiot," she said. "And a dangerous one."

The earnest look on Melisendra's face, coupled with his own extremely awkward embarrassment over his physical reaction to her, caused a laugh to burst from his mouth like machine gun fire.

Melisendra jumped back. Her features collected into a demonstration of hurt. Mutual mortification resulted.

"Sorry," Shane gushed. "He's not dangerous." *You are the hazardous one. You should wear a sign to warn people about your temptress superpowers.*

Apparently believing it was now safe, Melisendra leaned in once more. When her arm touched Shane's a thrill shot through his body. He reached his hand behind her and rested it in the small of her back. With no reaction to prevent further incursion, he caressed her, quickly and casually. His heart galloped but Melisendra moved away with inoffensive deliberateness.

Two minutes after she walked away, Shane was still attempting to discern the meaning of her parting look. *Nothing. It's nothing*, he chided himself. *That's just the way she is. It means nothing.*

Shane snatched up his phone and accessed the directory to find Rob's number. Angela was the other person he wanted to call because he was curious about how her meeting had gone, but he was afraid to speak to her in case she detected guilt in his voice. Angela was sharp; perspicacity personified. She would smell something in his uneasy pauses, of which there were sure to be many. It was too risky. Rob was safer.

He was about to press send when the touchscreen exploded to life, presenting a lovely photograph of his wife. His finger which had already been on the button to call Rob, now accepted the incoming communication from Angela. Shane swallowed hard, probably a dead giveaway in itself.

"Shane, are you there?"

"Uh-huh."

"What's wrong? Did I catch you at a bad time?"

Shrivelling ensued. "No, no. I was just about to call Rob when your call came through. It startled me."

Angela did not hesitate, which was a good sign. "It's all good, baby," she said. "Green lights all the way. I'm going to register the business name this afternoon, now in fact. Well, after I get off the phone, of course."

Shane relaxed and rolled over on to his back to float leisurely in calm water. "Of course."

"I think we should set a start date and start advertising straight away."

"We don't even have premises to operate out of yet."

"What? Oh, I forgot to mention that. There's a place for lease on Crown Street, just a few minutes' walk from the train station, next to Dicey Rileys."

"That's handy. We can duck next door for liquid lunches every day."

"Don't be ridiculous."

"Okay, just once or twice a week then."

"Shane." Angela's voice struck exactly the right register, somewhere between irritation and reluctant amusement. "Can you meet me there after work to have a look?"

"Yes, but you've already made up your mind, haven't you?"

"Please honey. I just want you to see it. It's perfect."

Shane cringed at the sound of the, 'p' word. There was no such beast as perfect. "All right, I can be there by quarter past four. I presume you can tee it up with the agent?"

"No problem. I'll see you then."

Angela rang off the way she always did once she was finished, with an abruptness which bordered on discourtesy. Shane said goodbye to a dead line. He glanced at the clock on the computer and realized he still had time to telephone Rob. Although the urgency had dissipated and taken with it the need to speak with his brother, he still felt like a quick hello wouldn't be such a bad thing for fraternal relations.

Rob sounded grumpy.

"What's up with you? Another hangover?"

"Jam and I just had a fight."

"An argument?"

"Uh-huh."

"What about?"

"I sort of asked her to marry me. I…"

"You what?" Shane could not possibly have heard that correctly. He listened to the strained silence as his students began filing back in for the afternoon session. "Did you say you asked her to marry you?"

"Uh-huh."

"Shit Rob. I just rang you for a quick g'day and you drop this bomb. I don't have time, but I want to hear all the pathetic and gory details. I guess she said no right, and that's why you argued?"

"It's not that simple."

"It never is, mate. It never is. I really have to go. I'll call you later okay?"

"Uh-huh."

Abu el Temeemi's failure to return to class after the break brought manifest relief to the other students. Shane was still off balance, distracted by the earlier events and more so by the brief conversation he'd had with Rob. Shane had planned to start a new topic for the class, but opted instead to set a writing task so as to give himself some time to chill before beginning his red pen death march around the room. No matter how hard he tried to assuage the paralysing effects of red ink phobia, some students still failed to understand that his corrections, or more specifically the number of his corrections, were not necessarily a sign of failure. Failure was making the same mistakes over and over again. A preponderance of red symbols on a student's written work might simply mean they were trying, experimenting.

Despite causing stiffness in his back from all the leaning over, the red pen death march allowed Shane a physical intimacy which may not have been deemed acceptable in the outside world. Aside from the odd bout of halitosis, this class was odour free; a model of personal hygiene.

Melisendra finished first, but her impressive alacrity masked an over confident carelessness with her work. Capital letters, full stops, and simple spelling errors plagued her writing, together with some clunky syntax. Shane arrived at her side as soon as her head turned to catch his eye.

The task was to write a movie review. Melisendra had chosen 'Olympus Has Fallen', which she had recently seen on DVD. He was surprised to discover she was a fan of violent action films. As he worked on her review, adding the symbols of the editing code where required, he could feel her warm breath on the back of his hand. She craned her neck to see what he was doing as he was doing it and this brought them even closer. The hairs on the back of his hand tingled, causing him to linger under pretence of thoughtful deliberation.

"Yes," she said. "I thought that was wrong but I couldn't think how to do it. How can I fix that?"

Shane straightened and her eyes followed him upwards. Her gaze was captivating and exhilarating. He felt as though they were alone, and that it was what they both wanted. *You can fix it by allowing me to hold you tightly, then lay you down carefully on the table and make love to you.*

"Adverbs of manner almost always follow the verb. You need to move the adverb, and actually I'm not sure *lazily* works there."

"Adverbs of manner?"

"Words that describe how something is done. Such as slowly, and quietly. Or beautifully." *And lustfully and voraciously.*

Somehow Shane tore himself away from the prison of Melisendra's robust sexuality. With incredible strain he disciplined his mind, rebuking himself with harsh reprimands about the need to maintain professionalism. *Don't cross the line. Don't go too far. Stop touching her. Stop flirting with her. Me teacher, you student.*

He tended to the other students, marking their work, suggesting improvements, answering their questions. He overstayed at Ling's table, authorising her blatant hogging of his time because he fancied her as well. He lost count of how many instances of accidental contact there were, and tried in vain not to recall an earlier conversation with her in which she revealed she and her husband had broken up. When the clock rolled around to two thirty he was exhausted, overwhelmed with sexual frustration and drained by its relentless assaults upon him. Angela? Angela was in danger again.

Thankfully, he would be meeting her in a public place; an empty office complex attended by an estate agent. He would think about it though. He could visualize the tightly woven threads in the tapestry of his mental purity being plucked asunder.

After disinterestedly farewelling his students, Shane collapsed onto his office chair which surrendered to the unexpected intrusion with a loud hiss. He picked up his phone and dialled Rob's number. When he answered, Shane wasted no time.

"So you asked this good time girl who you hardly know to marry you, and she said no, and you reacted badly which led to an argument."

Rob sighed. "Do you want to hear this story or not?"

Chapter Eleven

The relationship between Rob and Jam continued for many weeks. His bank account was still full enough for him to stay longer, and even if he had not met Jam, he may still have stayed. The idea of returning to Australia, and work, was becoming increasingly loathsome. However, his money would not last indefinitely, despite the exchange rate giving him the buying power of a king, and at some point he would have to make a decision about returning.

In the meantime, he devoted himself exclusively to the patronage of Lipstick, and studiously avoided irritating Pee Lek while he was there. The expectation that he was to drink and to use the services of the female members of staff, proved no hardship for Rob, who enjoyed the shows, as lame as most of them were, and also the kaleidoscope of humanity which twirled around the confined space in ritualistic dance.

Having long since overcome the crass and cringe-worthy name, Lipstick, he came to appreciate it as a professionally run establishment which offered a good range of services and reasonable prices. He was frequently disturbed by raunchy visions of other Lipstick patrons pawing his sweet and innocent Jam, but she assured him every time they were together that she was only available as a table friend, and no fellatio. Rob was never able to explain to Jam how minutely this reduced his discomfiture about what she did. Nor was he able to explain why she chose to stay. Money was patently an imposing motivator, but with all that he offered her, her insistence on staying was unfathomable. Why wouldn't she simply run away with him? Why stay when he offered something so much better?

There was no escaping the fact Jam was an object of lust, nor the equally callous reality that he didn't like it. She had a job to do. She was a professional who had improved her prick teasing skills remarkably since Rob had first met her. She evidently took pride in her performances, playing the part of *friend* with precisely that right level of cool detachment. Rob watched her at work sometimes, when she was nearby, and marvelled with morbid fascination; unable to take his eyes off her, like a jealous lover or a depraved pervert, but hating every minute she was with another man.

"Mr. Rob," said Pee Lek, who materialised in Rob's periphery and approached his table. "You come. No play with the girls. Just sit and drink and smoke and watch. You like to watch?"

"What do you want?"

"Make you happy. Make money for my boss. Simple."

Every unfortunate time Rob had to suffer the company of this weasel of a man, he fought the impulse to punch him. His sadistic little vision involved a blow to the stomach, then one to the head, then a blade, its edge glimmering with menace, slicing into Pee Lek's flesh.

He sat down uninvited. "Why you hang around? Look like..." He scratched his chin, pulling at a couple of the long hairs which occupied it. "*Seu si-at*. You know *seu si-at*?"

Rob shook his head and sipped his whiskey before lighting a *Klong Thip*. "Anything else I can help you with?"

"Like you look okay, but not okay."

"Fuck off Lek! You're boring me."

A threatening finger was thrust towards Rob's face. He sat calmly, safe in the knowledge the weasel would not do anything. Not inside the club. If he tried anything outside, Rob was confident of putting the punk on the floor just as had done at the *raan* when he cut his arm. Rob reminded himself to be careful of the knife though. After briefly staring him down, Rob turned away as though Pee Lek had already left the table.

Rob also functioned as an unofficial personal bodyguard, watching for signs that clients may be overstepping. Lipstick had its own security, naturally, but they were safeguarding all of the girls and their mission parameters were less well defined. With only so many pairs of eyes among them, they could not prevent all trouble, not even notice their genesis. The management of Lipstick would have gone off their collective brains had they known what was going on between Jam and Rob, and as much as Rob detested Pee Lek, he was grateful for his silence. Regardless of what nefarious motive may have underpinned Pee Lek's discretion, Rob appreciated it.

An uneasy agreement existed between Pee Lek and Rob and both Rob and Jam were careful not to make waves. Their *Pax Romana* was something they both valued, although for different reasons, especially after the heat they had drawn on the night Rob collapsed and had to be taken upstairs. The necessity for prudence did not altogether eliminate opportunities for Rob and Jam to spend time together. Many men had their favourite girls at Lipstick and would often return for nightly visits. However, they had both acted in ignorance of the house rules on that first morning when they went out for breakfast. Contact with customers outside the club was expressly forbidden. Jam could have been fired for that misdemeanour but instead, Pee Lek had intervened on their behalf.

Without doubt, Pee Lek was up to something. Rob doubted he had an altruistic bone in his wiry body, or even that he grasped the concept of selfless action for the good of another. Rob didn't know the man that well, but certainly well enough to recognize a cruel and greedy man with evil intentions.

As with most of the seedy businessmen and women who operated Bangkok's go-go bars, the head honcho at Lipstick was not likely to be a fool. They all realized their greatest asset was the girls. The nicest, most luxuriously appointed club, with the cheapest and the widest range of shows, services and fringe benefits could not compensate for a lack of female talent. A fine selection of beautiful young ladies whose only desire, ostensibly, was to bring joy into the lives of the men who visited the club.

These *good* girls, as they were referred to by their glorified pimp masters, were highly valued employees, though neither highly paid nor respected. They were slaves. Locked into unfair work agreements in which their only rights were to food, shelter and pretty good cash, they worked for as long as the boss wanted to keep them working. As long as they remained fresh he would retain their services. Once their use by date had expired, they were cast back out on to the streets from whence many of them came. If the manager was not making enough money out of a particular girl, he would simply get rid of her and bring in a replacement. Rob had heard there were long waiting lists.

Jam too, would eventually find herself tossed on to the scrap heap, another worn out hag. Perhaps that's why she refused to leave, though he persisted with his attempts to persuade her to do so. If she considered the brevity of her career as a table friend, and the money she could put together, she probably deemed it worthwhile. She was still young and attractive, and therefore popular. Last time they spoke she had mentioned she was planning to ask if she could dance more and serve at tables less. Rob was repulsed by that idea as well, but Jam was a single minded woman who would not consider him as part of her decision making. The mutual destiny Rob dreamed of for them was not on Jam's radar. Maybe he should have told her that his offer of marriage was genuine. He shouldn't have retracted the proposal. That was a huge mistake, and he felt like a bloody fool.

Suddenly Rob felt sick, nauseated by the whole situation. Unable to accept himself as a pitiful pseudo or wannabe boyfriend of an independent and successful sex worker, he decided to leave and not return. Angry at his weakness and beginning to drown in disappointment, he threw down the last of his Mekong then stormed outside.

Sukhumvit *soi* 4 in Nana Red Light district throbbed with late night energy, the humid air peppered with bursts of raucous laughter. Taking in the lust, lights, and the livid stench of alcohol, along with the blasts of music and sirens in the distance, Rob surveyed the scene. He perved on the women, taking care to avoid eye contact with any men and his anger simmered, though if anyone challenged him or goaded him he knew he would boil over in a flash. He played a game of spot the lady-boy to amuse himself and to restrain his seething emotion before someone interrupted him.

"Lipstick no good, hey?"

A woman held Rob's arm and breathed on his cheek. She was thin, wraith like and moved like liquid as she pulled him to a seat where she began to massage his crotch. Rob was on the verge of grabbing her hand and telling her to take it easy because he didn't fancy the idea of ejaculating in his pants, but she stopped.

"You like drink first. Fuck later, hey?"

Rob's heart was pounding with febrile desire. This girl was a frightening predator who had singled him out and was working him hard, both figuratively and literally. She was staring at him now, her pretty face hovering in front of his, her perfume inebriating him, casting a black magic spell.

"Up to you," she said, before placing her index finger in her mouth and sucking on it slowly.

"Let's go to my place," said Rob.

A siren screamed, stabbing into his dream and wrestling Rob from slumber. He turned his head slightly so that he could see out of the window. The flashing red beacon easily climbed the walls of the building to reach his apartment on the third floor. It reflected and rebounded off the walls, refracting through the windows, pulsating like a living creeping thing. Rob shuddered in the half way house between sleeping and waking. Disquiet settling on him like a wet sheet.

His partner was oblivious. She lay on her side, decorating the white pillow with her flowing black tresses. When she awoke her long stay would be over.

The siren's wail escalated, painfully loud, forcing Rob to cover his ears with his hands. He squeezed his eyes shut, tried to fight the fear as the noise intensified, blotting out everything else. Suddenly it stopped. His eyes flicked open and furious blinking followed. His breathing came in rapid, short, sharp breaths. Eventually, Rob realized the siren was his alarm clock sounding, even though he didn't remember setting it. It was eight o'clock. His visitor, roused by the alarm, rolled over onto her back then back on to her side before reaching out to switch the alarm off. The sheet fell away, revealing her body which, unless his eyes were to yet functioning properly, was nowhere near as skinny as it had appeared last night. The sense of disorientation he felt was palpable.

She looked at him and smiled. "Time to go. I shower, then go, hey?"

“Uh-huh."

As Rob watched her walk to the bathroom, her naked buttocks glowing like light globes, he tried to remember her name.

"Actually, I need to pee first," he called to her back.

Scrambling to his feet on the assumption she would understand and allow him to use the bathroom first, he almost walked into her as she stood and fiddled with the shower taps.

"I need to pee," he repeated.

"Okay."

Rob looked at his penis because she did, then he urinated whilst watching her in the shower. She had lost interest in him and was preoccupied with the task of lathering herself. He stared at her for a few moments then left.

Two weeks earlier he had left the Ibis after deciding that staying in one place for too long was too much like living there, and he wanted to maintain the freshness, the sweet fragrance of variety. Was that why he dragged a hooker home off the street? For something different? What about Jam? As he thought about her, needles of accusation punctured his flesh.

The apartment Rob found was in a building called the PM Mansion, although it lacked refinement or opulence, despite the attempted conjuring of its name. It was not as comfortable as the hotel but significantly cheaper. He had looked at other premises which were misleadingly called apartments; one square metre rooms functioning as both bedroom and living room, with a tiny balcony where two people could squeeze together to stand and admire the view of the neighbours whitewashed wall. A bathroom adjoined the balcony and was appointed with a shower, a sink, a floor level tap and a squatty potty. The tap was used to fill the laundry bucket and the toilet flushing bucket. All very functional, it was easy to use and easy to clean. You could shower while squatting on the toilet, if you wanted to.

Rob inspected a number of these so called apartments and decided they were a little too snug and simple for his tastes. At twenty-five baht a week they were a bargain, but Rob wanted more salubrious surroundings, and so his search had finally brought him to the PM Mansion, and it was worth every satang of the extra fifty baht per week he paid for it.

His guest exited the bathroom wearing a towel. She said nothing as she grabbed her clothes off the floor and skilfully attired without revealing her nakedness, as though she were modest. Rob smiled at her, but she was unmindful of him. Her inattentiveness was underpinned by the fact that her job was done and her fee had been paid. Ignoring Rob, she finished dressing and returned the towel to the bathroom by tossing it through the door. Finally she looked at him, smiling coyly as though she was surprised to see him there. She rummaged through her handbag then slung it over her shoulder.

"Have a good day," she said, before kissing him on the cheek.

Stupefied, Rob stood rooted to the spot and watched his guest leave. He felt like he had just been fleeced by a smooth-talking and unscrupulous vendor at a weekend market.

Rob recovered his senses, shaking off the feeling he had just been used and discarded. Hunger imposed itself, so he quickly showered, changed and left his apartment. Was this how prostitutes felt? At least they got paid. Rob had shelled out fifteen hundred baht for the privilege of sexual satisfaction, a soft body to share his bed with and an affectionate kiss good-bye. Was this what marriage was like, excluding the exchange of cash? Was this what he could have had with Jam, omitting the impersonal detachment? Was that what he wanted with Jam? What would a life shared with her look like? Was it even possible anymore?

When Rob opened his door to leave, Pee Lek was standing there grinning maniacally.

Chapter Twelve

Dicey Riley's was an Irish style pub with an appropriate adjective in its name and a mostly inappropriate, yet friendly and welcoming clientele. A chalkboard message announced that God had invented beer so the Irish would not take over the world. Beside that was a poster promoting the upcoming gig by some gothic looking metal band called Wrench. Authentic posters of ancient beer advertisements further adorned the facade of the hotel which boasted of being the only true pub in Wollongong. Shane walked past it on his way to meet Angela, safe in the knowledge that Dicey Riley's was a place where he belonged; a haven for him and many others, and it would remain so for many years to come.

Angela materialised behind the glass door as Shane was about to push it open. "I was just coming down to look for you." She kissed him hard on the mouth then beamed hot sunshine all over him.

Shane looked at his watch. "I'm only a minute late."

"Whatever. Let's go!" Angela grabbed his hand and dragged him up the stairs two at a time. He stumbled on the landing when she stopped suddenly.

"Office," she said, pointing at the door directly in front of them. "Lunch room, classroom, classroom, classroom..." Each introduction was accompanied by a flowing, open-palm gesticulation.

Shane followed her hand, quickly taking in the four other doors set along the wide landing. So far, so good, although the stairs might be a problem.

"Access issues," said Shane. "Stairs only."

"Negative. There's an elevator at the other end of the landing." She pointed enthusiastically again. "Anyway, our clients are going to be young people who will take stairs in their stride."

"Very funny." Shane normally deliberately avoided encouraging her terrible jokes, but he had to grudgingly admit it was a pretty good pun.

Angela pushed open the office door and invited Shane to enter first. The estate agent was standing by the window with her mobile phone glued to her ear. She turned as Shane entered and smiled at him. Shane hoped he returned the smile with equal sincerity.

He looked around, slowly surveying the spacious and brightly lit room. A multitude of power points and phone jacks decorated the lower walls. It was clean and didn't smell old, wet or dead. More than satisfactory was how Shane would have described it and he could easily appreciate Angela's ebullience, even though he had not yet seen the rest of the rooms.

The two exchanged a lingering look, which to Shane's mind projected a tantalising message; *damn shame the estate agent is here, because I would love to have a quickie on the floor right now.*

"Great so far," said Shane, as he frantically fobbed off images of him and Angela writhing, naked, in a horizontal folk dance. "Let's see the rest of it."

Angela glanced at the agent who was still nattering away, then back at Shane. As he neared her, she stepped close and whispered in his ear. "The rooms have locks on them, you know."

Shane grabbed two handfuls of her delightful buttocks and squeezed. "You are a very naughty woman, Angela Archer."

"Come on," said Angela. "She just shot mc a suspicious look. I reckon she'll follow us around like a lost puppy now."

"Just as well. I don't think I could have possibly resisted your relentless allure."

"You have a very nice way with words, Mr. Archer."

"I'm smooth all right." Angela turned away and Shane was pierced by a knife of guilt. He wondered how she would react if she knew how he demonstrated lascivious generosity by exercising his dubious talents with any beauty who caught his eye. His tongue lavished flatteries indiscriminately. He was an obsequious flirt; vapid and shameless.

"Are you coming?" said Angela.

The rest of the tour was perfunctory. Angela gushed while Shane flushed. She spouted and he doubted, mustering enthusiasm and suppressing the tide of serious reservations. Somehow through it all he maintained the outward manifestation of calm and firm commitment. He heard the conversation between the agent and Angela as he exited room five and wandered along the landing. He pictured himself in this space; teaching, explaining, elucidating and wrestling with paperwork, as he marked, filed and wrote reports. He stifled a monstrous internal yawn.

As a distraction, he invoked a memory long consigned to a dark shelf in his mind. It was of woman he'd known and loved after he met Angela, but before he had married her. A woman who had very nearly became Mrs Archer instead of Angela, an altogether different creature who now existed only as a mythical goddess in his discreet recollections.

Yan Ping was a Chinese national who Shane met for the first time when he conducted a pre-training assessment with her. PTA's were needed, at least back when Shane began working in the Language Literacy and Numeracy Program, to determine the class level into which the client should be placed. Nowadays it was also being used to ascertain the highly subjective '*capacity to benefit from training*', which was in turn being used to discriminate against job seekers and migrants with very low literacy skills.

Yan Ping was very pretty, with large almond eyes and minimal cosmetic enhancement. Thin yet femininely contoured, she had a colourful and flamboyant dress style which did not match her personality. Shy and quietly spoken, it was a difficult assessment for Shane because of her reluctance to say much more than was necessary. Most of his efforts to encourage her to open up proved fruitless. Such bashfulness had often been a source of annoyance, but he found Yan Ping intriguing.

It was at that time Angela had ended her relationship with him, saying Shane was moving too fast and was planning too much and she didn't want to think too far ahead. Shane had not even proposed. The mere suggestion of the possibility of marriage had elicited Angela's surprisingly disappointing reaction, a mystifying overreaction. The timing of Yan Ping's arrival into his world, with her seditious coyness and deferential politeness, was unfortunate for both Shane and Angela in terms of a possible reconciliation.

Shane had always favoured good students; attentive and diligent students, especially, but not exclusively, attractive female students. Adding to this perfect storm was the fact Yan Ping was single. In a very short period of time, Shane fell in love with her, and when he was satisfied she also felt something for him he invited her to lunch. So caught up in the giddiness of the pursuit was Shane that all thoughts of Angela were banished.

The love affair was pure and beautifully innocent, as weeks passed into months and Yan Ping blossomed. Shane had a strange falling out with his libido. They did all the things that lovers do, they held hands and kissed, but lightly and playfully, not passionately. Shane never tried for anything more. He never pushed the physicality of their relationship, even at her home when they were alone. It wasn't that he didn't want to but he inexplicably didn't feel it was right. It was as though they were two teenage virgins in their first serious relationship, enjoying all the benefits of their friendship without the suffocating pressure of expectation.

Shane began to feel he had found *the one*. Yan Ping was not frightened off by theoretical discussions of marriage. She was ambitious and hoped to resurrect her career in the IT customer service industry once her English had sufficiently improved, but she didn't see work as her primary reason for existence. As she waxed lyrically about the importance of good relationships, and how nothing else mattered if you didn't have someone to love and to love you, Shane was mesmerized. He planned an elaborate proposal, but before he could execute it, Hurricane Angela rampaged back into his life.

She was remorseful, she missed him, and she had pleaded during the course of several very long and ardent phone calls for Shane to forgive her and take her back. In the midst of that emotional turmoil, as his feelings for Angela recuperated rapidly from their dusty exile, Yan Ping announced she was returning to China indefinitely. Her mother was ill and she needed to be there to care for her because her father could not manage alone. It was her duty and although she cried from the heartbreak, and Shane felt metaphorically eviscerated, there was nothing to be done. She had to go, and she left almost immediately.

"Shane! Hello?"

Despite finally registering the sound of Angela's voice and the use of his name, Shane continued to stare out of the window, numb from the sedative of melancholy. Regret was dangerous when one dwelled on the past and played sliding doors. Would he change what happened if he could? Did he miss the best and settle for second best with Angela? He loved her, and Yan Ping rarely entered his consciousness these days, but he had never again felt the same ethereal love as he did for her. What benefit was there in thinking like this? What did it achieve?

"Shane? What's wrong?"

Angela was behind him, then beside him, her arms encircling his waist. Her head pressed into his chest.

"We've got a lot of work to do, but you're right. This place is perfect. I'm sure Easyspeak will be a great success."

She squeezed him tighter.

Shane watched the world outside the window as Angela talked about the purchasing or leasing of equipment, advertising, hiring administration staff and giving notice. The estate agent interrupted her, breaking into the chaotic swirl of her thoughts and rescuing him. Angela had once broken up with him because she thought he was moving too fast. The shoe appeared to be firmly on the other foot now. The commensurate alacrity with which Angela's grand plan was being assembled made Shane dizzy. It was too late for him to raise his concerns. The car was already hurtling across the Great Victoria Desert, on its way to the destination but neither close to it, nor the starting point. Are the brakes okay? Is there enough fuel in the tank? Water in the radiator? What if the answers to these questions were all negative? It's an eight hundred kilometre stretch of nothing. If you don't start with a full tank you won't make it, but there's no point worrying about that when you are halfway across. You just have to press on and hope.

Similarly, there was no point in Shane telling Angela that he was worried about the risk and about the two of them living and working together. He had concerns also about how much harder they would both have to work, and how, in all probability most of the additional burden would fall on Angela's shoulders. He couldn't say anything about how he foresaw an inevitable domination of work over home life. How unbalanced life would become and what catastrophic effects this would have on their marriage. And these issues merely scraped the surface. The elephant in the room of their relationship was the question of raising a family. The last time they had discussed it Angela had shut him down by warning him against attempting to control her, and that had made him so angry he called her selfish and made her cry.

The significance of the desert metaphor tumefied, enlarging and expanding in Shane's mind as they finally left the office, accompanied by the impatient gaze of the estate agent.

"Damn," said Shane. "I'm so thirsty I could drain a swimming pool."

"Let's duck next door for a drink then. Nothing slakes a man-sized thirst better than a pint of Guinness."

"No argument from me,' replied Shane. *Not about the beer anyway.*

Chapter Thirteen

"What do you want?"

Rob's question was answered with a sudden lunge towards him. It was the knife he noticed first, the glimmer of the blade thrust by the hand of Pee Lek who had clearly not come for a conversation.

Rob dodged the initial attack then reversed quickly. He fell back onto the bed and Pee Lek pounced. Rolling to his right to evade his aggressor, Rob found himself on the floor with Pee Lek flying towards him once more. He lifted his arm to block the blow, prepared to sacrifice some skin and shed some blood to buy some time. Hoping to achieve a firm grip on Pee Lek's arm somewhere, Rob latched onto his wrist and diverted the knife parry to the right. Pee Lek collapsed on him, which allowed Rob to toss him off on to the floor and scramble to his feet.

Breathing heavily, the two men stood face to face. Pee Lek waved the blade with menace as if trying to frighten Rob into submission. Rob was not scared, but concerned lest he be forced into a position of weakness by the other man's lightning fast movements. He needed to control the pace of the battle and use his strength. That was where he held the upper hand.

He watched Pee Lek carefully, simultaneously studying his posture, feet and hands, watching in an attempt to predict his next move. Pee Lek leapt forward, springing in to the air to a ridiculous height before descending behind the point of the blade. Rob reached for the knife wielding hand fastened again on to his wrist and pulled hard much like he had done at the *raan*. This time he swept Pee Lek by his side, swerving his body out of the way as he did so. The smaller man hurtled into the television headfirst, shattering the screen on impact and knocking it off its stand.

Rob spun around as Pee Lek regained his feet, slowly unfolding himself. As he did, Rob kicked him in the stomach then sprung on him with a fast short punch to his chin. Rob grabbed the knife and wrestled it from Pee Lek's grip, staring at it as he contemplated the wisdom of using it to finish the fight. Instead, he tossed it away behind him and challenged Pee Lek who lay dazed and vulnerable. Hauling the small man to his feet, he shook him and yelled at him.

"What are you doing here? What do you want?"

Pee Lek mumbled so Rob punched him in the gut again, doubling him over whilst still clutching one handful of his shirt.

"The boss want you to stay away from Jam and Lipstick."

"Why?"

Pee Lek shook his head.

Rob lowered his voice, downgrading the yell to a growl. "Why?"

"I don't know. I just do what he say."

"And what did he say?" asked Rob, maintaining his grip.

"He want you understand. Not welcome. Jam not your girlfriend."

Rob stared at the angry little man, so weak now and totally at Rob's mercy. What message should he send back? Considering he had become fed up with the whole situation anyway, perhaps he should not bother. Waiting around for Jam was demoralizing him. Was she worth it? Was she worth *this*?

Unknowingly, Rob had relaxed his hold on Pee Lek a little, and the other, sensing an opportunity to break free, seized it. Liberated, Pee Lek stood unsteadily at a distance, his chest heaving. Rob looked at him, suddenly shocked by the bloody mess he presented, and tried to guess whether he would be foolish enough to resume the assault. Anger still blazed an unmistakable warning on his face.

Pee Lek glanced furtively around the room, his eyes darting here and there searching for the knife. He jumped when he saw it. Rob saw it and registered the danger but again was too slow to stop it, and in a flash, Pee Lek was armed once more. He wielded the knife with renewed menace and Rob swallowed hard and steeled himself. A fatal conclusion to this conflict seemed imminent.

Pee Lek launched himself at Rob who concentrated on avoiding the edge of the knife, swerving then ducking. Rolling and springing to his feet, he faced his adversary once more. Pee Lek's face was contorted, his grip on the hilt of the knife, white knuckled. He pounced, slashing wildly while Rob blocked the strikes as best he could. Lightning bolts of pain struck him, igniting rage within. Without taking his eye off the knife, Rob ran at Pee Lek, simultaneously grabbing the arm with which he held his weapon and wrapping his other arm around Pee Lek's waist, hitting with his shoulder and driving with his legs. The smaller man slammed into the wall with a thud and a whoosh of air from his lungs.

Rob stepped back while maintaining his grip on the dangerous hand, then threw a precise punch to Pee Lek's face. A loud crepitus preceded a fresh rush of blood from his nose. Rob shook his hand then tried to extend his fingers. He gasped.

If a broken nose was going to be an impediment to the perpetuation of their battle, Pee Lek was showing no signs of any capitulation. He wrenched his arm free of Rob's grip and slashed Rob across the chest. Rob staggered back. Pee Lek advanced, the flood of claret from his nose apparently inconsequential. He lunged. Rob swerved. He slashed. Rob ducked. Slowly retreating across the room as Pee Lek waved the blade, Rob kept his eyes on the knife as a batsman watches the bowl all the way from the bowler's hand to his bat. He concentrated. He blocked out everything else. He staked his life on his speed and skill, his hand eye coordination. He waited.

The knife was propelled, his hand moved to intercept, his eyes devoured it on approach. Rob latched on to Pee Lek's wrist and yanked forward and down as hard as he could, directing the other man's face to the unwelcoming hardness of his knee. Pee Lek cried out and dropped the knife, before crumpling to the floor. Rob fell on him, securing him with a headlock before dropping his body weight on the back of Pee Lek's neck.

A sudden and dramatic limpness ended the battle. Rob released the ragdoll body of Pee Lek and rolled on to the floor breathing heavily and painfully, experiencing the adrenalin surge abated as it was subsumed by pain and exhaustion. The excoriations on his arm and chest screamed for his attention. A torrent of agony overwhelmed him as he lay on the floor beside the lifeless body of Pee Lek. Rob shuddered and quivered as he turned stiffly on to his side and vomited.

Somewhere deep within the maelstrom of frantic emergency messages being delivered to and from his brain, Rob encountered dread fear. Coherent thoughts queued to add their voices to the cacophony of condemnation in his head. Other more helpful and sympathetic mumblings struggled to be heard. Rob was hurt; bleeding from multiple knife wounds and bruised from violent collisions with furniture and walls. His physical suffering comprised not even half of his problem though. What if Pee Lek was dead? He did not know for certain that he was, and Rob's irrational reasoning rushed to the crime scene. Maybe he had not killed him. Perhaps that awful snap might not have been his neck breaking. There was a chance he was mistaken. How would he know? Rob turned and stared into the wide eyed death stare of Pee Lek and instantly dismissed every previous thought as to the question of the severity of the man's injuries. Rob turned away.

A paralysis of fear and indecision anchored Rob to the floor of his apartment. He needed to move, to rise and do something. His wounds required treatment and his thirst was demanding. There was a dead man lying beside him on the floor. Rob had killed him. The words kept repeating in an endless and heartless loop of accusation.

Finally Rob moved, and a fresh wave of torture and vertiginous nausea crashed on him. He stumbled to the bathroom, and with both hands on the basin to steady himself, he looked into the mirror at the face of a killer. He stared into his eyes desperately searching for himself, for remorse, for humanity, for any sign he was still Rob Archer. In an inferno of violence, his life had been inverted and turned inside out.

Carefully he released his grip on the edge of the basin and turned on the tap. He splashed water onto his face, then onto his arms, inspecting the cuts as he washed the blood away. None had bit deeply into his flesh. He had been lucky. Rob tried to breathe normally, deliberately slowing down and centering himself. He removed his shirt and tossed it aside. The slash across his chest was also superficial, but the wounds stung and the rigidity and relentless ache of overextended muscles combined to make him feel weak and battered.

Rob threw some water down his throat before remembering the tap water was not potable. He spat it out and went back into the living room and to the fridge, from where he extracted a bottle of cold water. He drank half of it in one greedy guzzle whilst studiously avoiding the sight of Pee Lek's corpse on the floor. The recuperative power of the water soon enabled Rob to assemble his thoughts. He considered calling Shane for advice, but dismissed the idea as he did a similar notion of trying to contact Jam. The police might have been a viable and certainly more sensible option if it were not for the fact Rob did not trust them. After scanning and assessing every possible candidate, Rob concluded he would have to run away, tell no one of his crime, and hope for the best.

With his thirst slaked from the demolition of the bottle of water, Rob poured himself a quarter glass of Mekong and topped it with ice. He sat staring at Pee Lek, wondering what he would do with his body, as the whiskey deadened his pain and rebalanced his cognitive processes. He noticed the dead man's eyes had closed and was momentarily perplexed.

He raised the glass and tilted it towards the dead man. "What the hell was your problem, little man? Why did you come after me? Why were you such an arsehole?"

Chapter Fourteen

"Are you all right?" said Angela, peering at Shane over the rim of her coffee mug. "You seem unusually quiet."

Shane smiled. Faking enthusiasm could be extremely debilitating. Each time he stood before the class and began the lesson, or introduced a new topic, or commenced some direct instruction, Shane felt as though he were performing. Like an actor on the stage when the curtain was raised or a film star when the director called action, Shane played a role for his class. He had to be bright, cheery and energetic enough to impart zeal to his students. Would they come on the educational journey if he failed to make it sound exciting, or at least interesting?

"I'm fine."

"No one who ever says that is really fine."

"Sure they do," said Shane, breaking eye contact under the pretence of rescuing a sweet lump of plum conserve from falling to the table. "I mean, what else would you have people say if they are fine? Are you okay? I'm fine. What's wrong with that?"

"You're not fine."

Angela's insistence irritated Shane. His annoyance was, however, not really anything at all to do with her. He was lying and she knew it, but he couldn't admit that because a confession would necessitate an examination of the cause of his lack of all-right-ness. Shane wished that either he was better at deception, or that Angela was less insightful.

She continued to stare at him, inviting a revelation, but Shane resisted. Instead, he wolfed down the remaining toast, following it with orange juice and then left the table without saying anything except; "time to get to work."

Angela called after him, "You're not fine, Shane. We can talk about it later if you like."

"What if I don't like?" he muttered as he entered the bathroom and took his shaver from the drawer. He continued talking to himself as he removed the overnight growth from his cheeks, chin and throat. "What if I don't want to tell you how worried I am about this new business and how generally dissatisfied with everything I feel, and how even our sex life, which is good, is apparently not good enough to stop me sleazing on to other women?"

Shane's hand stopped on the point of his chin, struck by the word *sleaze*. Was he a sleaze? Did Sabeen think he was grubby? Did Melisendra think he was slimy and sordid? He thought it was fun, harmless, flirtatious banter. Sure he fantasized about having sex with them, but he never honestly thought it would come to that. He never truly imagined sexual activity of any degree with anyone other than Angela. He was a moral person, a faithful husband. The lusty thoughts which rampaged through his mind were generated by his masculinity, by testosterone, maybe even by the devil. It wasn't his fault.

He kept shaving, pondering the word *sleazy*. He would really hate it if anyone thought he was a sleaze. He hoped no one did, but how would he know? He could ask them. He could speak directly instead of dancing around the issue with obscure ambiguities and euphemisms. What harm could it do? Shane stopped shaving again, this time lowering the shaver.

"Sabeen," he began his little practice session. "Do you think I'm a sleaze?" Cue awkward silence, the shuffling of feet and the averting of eyes, an impatient heart pattering.

Shane laughed. What was she going to say? Yes? Then she would have to deny flirting with him. Maybe she wasn't flirting. Perhaps he should ask her if she was flirting with him and clear that bit up first, before tackling the weightier issue of his moral grubbiness. Or lack thereof, depending on how Sabeen addressed the issue of flirting. Things would be so much easier without the games people played. Relationships would be simple. *I like you. If you like me, let's get it on.* He winced at the phrase; *get it on.*

"What's that, baby?" said Angela as she passed the open bathroom door.

"Huh?"

"Did you say something?"

"I said, let's get it on."

Angela entered the room and ran her hand lightly across Shane's back and down onto his buttocks, where she finished with a playful squeeze. She kissed him on the back of the neck which caused him to shiver as his arousal manifested physically.

"As much as I'd love to," she said, already distancing herself from the alluring tease. "You know I like to do things properly, and not rush. Tonight, okay?"

Shane switched the shaver back on and mumbled to himself. "Sure. Tonight, after we've finished dinner and cleaned the kitchen and talked about our day a little and about our big plans a lot, your big plans, and brushed our teeth and showered, and read in bed and switched off the lights. God forbid we should inject any spontaneity into our lives."

"Sorry Shane. I can't hear you."

Just as bloody well, thought Shane.

As he was applying deodorant under his arms, Angela came to kiss him goodbye. It was a prim peck which he received with affectionate indifference. What the hell was happening to them? To him?

When Shane was ready for work, he decided to call Rob. He had tried the previous night but failed to get through, which caused the latent protective concern to emerge. Rob always answered his phone. Even if

Shane forgot or ignored the time difference and caught Rob at some ridiculous hour, he always answered.

His growing anxiety reminded him of that one day when Rob had not come home from school on time. Shane was in his first year at Caringbah High School, while Rob was still attending Caringbah Public. The latter being much closer, Rob usually arrived home first most days, except for Thursdays which were sport days. On Thursdays Shane arrived home first and waited for Rob so they could hang out, play cricket or footy in the yard, or go for a ride on their bikes. One Thursday, Shane was still waiting for Rob to get home half an hour after school finished.

Thursday was also the day his mum visited his grandmother in the afternoon, so it was just him and Rob until dad came home from work around four-thirty. Shane fretted for Rob, worried for him and for himself if any harm came to his little brother on his watch. Shane was trying to prove he was responsible and earn more trust so he could have a little more freedom. An incident of this kind would not help his cause.

At half past three, Shane ran to the school and upon his arrival found a mob gathered under a large tree near the northern edge of the playground. His pace intensified when he glimpsed Rob in the middle of that crowd, and in evident danger. When he reached the group of jeering school children, he ignored them and whatever they were chanting and pushed through into the centre where two boys occupied a makeshift ring. One boy stood over the other with his fists clenched and his face florid. The boy on the ground with blood coming from a cut on his lip was Rob.

Shane charged at his brother's assailant and knocked him to the ground with a shoulder to his chest. Others joined in and, with much flailing and jostling, the youngsters expended their energy before quickly becoming bored and dispersing. Once they had all left, Shane helped Rob up off the dusty ground.

"What was that all about?"

Rob shrugged. "I don't know."

"Sure you do, but you don't want to tell me right?"

Shane put his arm around Rob's shoulders and guided him off the playground and back along the footpath towards home. "What are we going to tell mum and dad?" he said.

"We don't have to tell them anything, do we?" said Rob.

"What about your lip?"

"Just say it was an accident, you and me and farting around. It's happened before."

They stopped to check for traffic before crossing the street.

"I think if I'm going to lie for you, you should at least tell me why you were fighting."

Silence.

"That guy who hit me is a dickhead, so I called him that when he was harassing me and he called me out, challenged me to fight him after school."

"That's so primary school."

"Whatever."

As they approached their house, they slowed. Shane looked at Rob and asked, "Are you okay? Was it just the one punch to the mouth?"

"Nah, there were a few others. That was the only one that drew blood, and I got a few in as well."

Shane tousled Rob's hair to which he reacted with typical rancour. "Next time why don't you just keep your mouth shut. It's easier to overlook an insult than to go into battle over it."

"I don't like him," said Rob, "and I don't see why I should have to pretend I do, or even try to get along with him, especially when he always hassles me."

"Are you talking about bullying? How often does he do that?"

"I don't know. It's not bullying. It's just annoying. Just shut up about it okay."

Shane retrieved the key from his pocket and unlocked the door. Thankfully, their parents had not arrived home yet so Rob had time to clean himself up.

"You know," said Shane. "Sometimes, it's better just to walk away. What's he saying to you so bad you can't just ignore it?"

"Ignoring shit doesn't take the smell away."

Shane shook his head, marvelling at his little brother's turn of phrase even as he wondered how much more trouble, or how much *worse* trouble that attitude might propel him into.

The timing of this memory was ominous. Rob had gone on to become frequently embroiled in schoolyard drama, and he honed his craft through many skirmishes, most of which he initiated. When he left school, he used his dubious skills to start fights in pubs. He became one of those guys who smashed himself with booze all weekend, then hammered the faces and bodies of people who bothered him. He was especially aggravated by jealous boyfriends. The losers he hung around with all encouraged each other in this rabble rousing lifestyle, even boasting of their exploits whenever afforded the opportunity. They were best avoided when on the piss and on the prowl; sloshed, boisterous and dangerous.

Shane finished dressing then called Rob again. There was no answer. He tried a second time in the car, and once more when he arrived at work. After that, his personal business assumed secondary importance. As the hour neared to begin the show otherwise known as his English language class, he forgot about Rob, consigning his anxiety to the sideline in the hope his foolhardy and trouble seeking little brother was okay.

Chapter Fifteen

There is a particular species of invisible fog which settles on people when they are engaged in activities that demand everything they possess. The world shrinks, and that which it contains is magnified and exaggerated. The senses are keener, the urgency unremitting and the desperation ravenous. Nothing exists outside of the bubble and the immediate need to satisfy its desires. When something just has to be done, there is no time for pontificating or remorse, no room for vacillation.

The confusion and panic which Rob had felt lifted when he made the decision to run. A sudden clarity descended and infused his actions with purposeful efficiency. He first packed his bags. A small suitcase and a carry all contained everything he needed, his life condensed into two pieces of luggage. The suitcase… Did he need the suitcase? Was it going to become a burden, or worse, a genuine liability? Rob checked the contents of his carry all and determined he could make do without the suitcase. He could not leave it here though, could he? What message would it send to the police who eventually came to investigate the source of the stink emanating from the decomposing corpse of Pee Lek?

Rob shook his head. It was too much trouble to second guess what conclusions might be drawn by criminal investigators. He didn't know anything about how they worked or what they thought. The fleeting notion that a suitcase left behind might indicate the eventual return of its owner was crushed by the illogicality of leaving a dead man lying on the floor. If he moved the body to the bathroom it would not make any difference. It was a small apartment and even a cursory examination would fully disclose whatever secrets it hid. He looked at his watch. Nearing eleven now, he realized his overnight guest had left over three hours ago. Why had he brought her home? What was he thinking? He quickly dismissed the errant and immediately insignificant thought.

Rob found his mobile phone and switched it on, not remembering why he had turned it off. He never did that. Once the system booted, a string of missed call notifications appeared on the screen. He recognized Shane's number, but did not want to call his brother and explain what was going on. Shane would call him an idiot again, and pepper him with sarcastic taunts. Shane; his big brother and protector who, despite his professed and demonstrable love and concern for Rob, always managed to make him feel like shit. Even as adults, Shane's moral superiority was not only a badge he proudly wore but one which he thrust continually in Rob's face.

The phone rang as Rob sat staring at it. Shane's number came up again but Rob declined it with a swipe of his index finger. Shane's persistent attempts to contact him might indicate something was wrong at home, with Angela or mum and dad? Someone hurt maybe. It had to be bad news. In a knowledge vacuum, the human mind had a propensity to think the worst, to imagine disaster. Rob figured Shane was not calling about Rob. How could he know anything of what had just transpired? He may have shown glimpses of apparent omniscience or at least prophetic vision on occasions, but he wasn't a god. He could not possibly know anything.

Despite his closed-eyed, peaceful expression, Pee Lek accused Rob from the floor, somehow still radiating vengeful wrath. Rob turned away and with a couple of taps on the screen of his phone he called Shane. As he listened to it ring he inhaled very deeply then slowly released the air. He noticed his hand shaking.

"Where the hell have you been?" said Shane, dispensing with the formalities. "Why didn't you answer your phone? Are you all right?"

"Yeah, I'm fine."

Rob winced at his use of one of his brother's least favourite expressions. Shane had always shared Angela's theory that the words, *I'm fine,* almost always meant exactly the opposite, and he wondered if Shane would let it slide this time.

"Really."

Minus the inflection, Rob knew what Shane was saying and he regretted making the call. It was too soon. Rob had very recently survived a death match by virtue of murdering his opponent. He was about to take off and seditiously forget to report the death to anyone, in the hope he could get far enough away to elude capture. In the back of his mind he clung to the hope that as Pee Lek was a scumbag, the police might not care too much about his demise and might therefore not show any diligence or enthusiasm to pursue his killer.

"Rob?"

"I said I'm okay."

"No, you said you were fine. You're not fine are you? What's happened?"

Rob stood up and paced the limited available floor space of his apartment. Shane was in Blue Heeler mode, nipping at Rob's heels, and he was not going to let him get away with half-hearted reassurances. Soon, he would grab a mouthful of Rob's pants and shake ferociously until he surrendered and confessed. He had to say something without telling him anything.

"Jam and me had a fight and I pissed off from the club and hooked up with someone else. She stayed the night and I feel bad about it."

"Really."

Again, not a question. "I told you, Shane. I love Jam. It was stupid to run off and fuck someone else just because we had a fight. What does that say about me?"

"That you are mentally impaired."

Safe, thought Rob. *He's buying it.* "You know me well. My whiskey soaked brain is capable of nothing better than accidental competence."

"So what are you going to do?"

The opportunity for truth was refreshing, so Rob seized it. "I'm going to see her and make up. Apologize or whatever."

"You might want to work on your sincerity there, mate," said Shane.

"Anyway, I'd better let you go. You're at work aren't you?"

"I'm just on a break. Your timing's good."

"Lucky. Is everyone all right? Anything happening? Any news?" asked Rob.

The pause was uncharacteristic.

"Yeah. Angela found a place for the new language school. We're looking to start it up next month."

"Cool. Maybe you can give me a job." Rob didn't want to work with Shane, but the glib suggestion befitted the moment. Unfortunately for Rob, it promoted a new line of inquisition from his big brother.

"Planning on retuning some time then, are you?"

Rob considered the question. He could not remain in Thailand. It was unlikely Pee Lek's death would be ignored. How would a *farang* hide in Thailand? The police would find him. Clearly he would have to return to Australia, but he wanted Jam to come with him.

"We'll see," he answered, noncommittally.

"I'll hold a cleaner's job open for you, unless you want to get back to school and finish the education you recklessly abandoned," said Shane.

Ignoring the jibe, Rob answered with a farewell. "I'll talk to you later, Shane."

"Keep that bloody phone of yours switched on will you? I was worried about you."

'You're so sweet."

"Piss off!"

"See ya."

Rob's stomach housed the world's largest collection of insects, crawling and buzzing around, inducing nausea. The awkward conversation with Shane was out of the way and unintended revelation of actual calamity had been avoided, so Rob resumed his mission. He checked his bag one last time and then grimaced through a quick shower. As he exited the bathroom, there was a knock on the door. He froze.

The knock came again, no more urgent, nor less. Rob waited, speculating as to who might be at his door this time. His last visitor was now stiffening on the floor after apparently having his neck broken. Rob realized it was probably his neighbour at the door. El came home from work at the hospital around this time two or three days each week, and she usually brought him something to eat. Rob had never been able to figure out whether this gesture was merely neighbourliness, or something else. She was cute, and handy to have across the hall because of her medical training, but Rob did not have time to talk to El right now, and she would immediately see his wounds and probably glimpse Pee Lek's body on the floor. That was all way too messy.

Waiting a minute after the third round of tapping on the door, Rob relaxed back from extreme stress to a heightened level of stress. He looked around the room, observing the disorderliness which had resulted from the scuffle with Pee Lek. Scuffle? Disorderliness? He had not touched anything, nor did he think he should. Investigators would readily conclude an altercation had occurred and the dead man had died as a consequence. Questions as to the whereabouts of his assailant, or the possibility of additional victims would ensue.

Rob slung his carry all over his shoulder and opened the door slowly. He listened carefully for sounds of hall occupation, for other doors opening or closing, for anything posing a threat to his surreptitious departure. Once satisfied the hall was clear, he poked his head out and looked right, then left, before stepping out and pulling the door closed behind him as he hastened down the hall to the stairs. He skipped down the stairs two at a time, descending three flights to the ground floor where he shifted to a less conspicuous perambulation.

A man entered the lobby but did not look at Rob. Fortunately, the desk clerk was submerged behind the counter so Rob was able to exit the building without being noticed. That was a bonus. The police would knock on every door in the building asking if anyone had seen the *farang* leave on such and such a date, and only one man would be able to answer in the affirmative. With any luck, he might not even remember seeing Rob, or even better, perhaps he was blind.

Out in the *soi*, everyone watched him suspiciously and furtively. The street vendors, the shoppers, the diners, the loiterers all regarded his passage with abnormal interest. Rob thought about catching a motorcycle taxi to Lipstick but decided it was too risky. When he reached the rank at the head of the *soi*, the riders, all dressed in high visibility vests, leather gloves and aviator sunglasses, smoked cigarettes and eyed him dubiously. He hurried along, while attempting to not look as though he was rushing. The club was three blocks away, and at his current velocity under the cruel glare of the midday sun, he would arrive in fifteen minutes, dehydrated and dripping with sweat. What would Jam make of his sudden arrival and his appearance? Would she notice anything? Blood? He had cleaned and dried all his cuts and as they were relatively superficial the dressing he had applied staunched the flow. In spite of his best efforts to normalize the way he looked, Rob realized he still showed signs that he had been in a fight. If Jam was still angry with him for vanishing without saying goodbye, his sudden return in a state of bruised wretchedness would most likely exacerbate her wrath.

Sweat stung his cuts and his breathing became laboured. His muscles ached. Needing to cool off, he entered a mall and luxuriated in the frosty air for a few minutes. He bought some water and drowned his thirst. The patrons and sales assistants stared at him as he wandered around pretending to browse. He felt the heat of their accusations on the back of his neck, despite the air conditioning cooling the rest of his body and drying the perspiration on his skin. Someone touched him. He jumped.

"Can I help you, sir?"

A fresh-faced, male sales assistant beamed at him. This punk would remember his face. He was writing the detail of Rob's features into his memory as Rob stood there mutely gawping at him. He felt the colour draining from his face, slowly removing the strength required to stand. He swayed.

"Are you all right, sir?"

Rob attempted a smile then mumbled, "Yes, I'm fine. Just cooling off a bit. I'm on my way to visit my girlfriend."

"Girlfriend?"

Regretting his lack of discretion, Rob backpedalled. "Just a friend really."

"She might like a gift," suggested the sales assistant. "Some perfume? Some jewellery?"

This conversation was of interminable and unacceptable length. In his weakened state, Rob had talked about a girlfriend and thus implicated Jam in the unavoidable manhunt which would follow the discovery of Pee Lek's body at the PM Mansion. This young man had been studying Rob's face for a good two to three minutes already. He would probably never forget him and would happily provide an explicit description to the police.

"No thank you," said Rob. "I need to get going."

"What about some chocolate? Does your friend like chocolate?"

Rob admired his cheery persistence but he needed to leave and Jam didn't like chocolate as far as he knew. "No. Thank you, I really have to go."

Back out on the street, the sickening humidity assaulted Rob again and he feared he would not make the short distance to Lipstick without keeling over and passing out. A long detour via the hospital might be on the cards. Nevertheless he pressed on. Sipping water and convincing himself he was only suffering from a mild dose of queasiness, he finally made it to the club where everyone gathered out the front to welcome him with distrustful countenances.

Rob stumbled through the door and walked past the bar as he headed towards his favourite seat. The frigid air inside the club began to revive him as he sat and caught his breath. A waitress materialized before him and asked what he wanted, to which he replied that a glass of Mekong would be superb.

"Mekong. Yes sir. Come soon, okay?"

"Hey!" called Rob.

She stopped and turned around, slinking her way back to his table.

"I want to see Jam. Can you tell her Rob is here?"

The waitress's smile inverted as her eyebrows collapsed together. Rob found the expression amusing. "Do you know Jam? A girl, Jam? I need to see her."

She smiled again but it was one of those famously enigmatic Thai smiles. Rob switched to Thai which he should have done before, instead of frittering away time with a game of charades. This time she nodded, but sadly she did not know Jam. She was new, but she would ask at the bar. As she sauntered away, Rob was blindsided by a shocking realization. Pee Lek had probably told someone at the club where he had gone that morning, and certainly his boss would have known because he would have most likely given the order. As soon as anyone recognized Rob, they would put two and two together and they would pursue him as well. Even the waitress posing the question at the bar would arouse suspicion. Rob cursed his stupidity. Coming to Lipstick after slaying one of its employees was an atrocious error of judgment.

Rob sprang from his seat and hurried away to the door leading to the upstairs rooms. The dancing girls and the lustful drunks all noted his departure. He bounded up the stairs then raced down the hall to Jam's room. If she was there, he would tell her to pack her stuff and come with him immediately. If not, he would wait for her.

He knocked once and pushed open her door.

Chapter Sixteen

It was a mystery worthy of Agatha Christie's - Hercule Poirot. An enigma of such depth that if one descended all the way to the bottom in search of a satisfactory explanation, they might very well find themselves the victim of a heinous and gory demise as the pressure inside their craniums expanded to bursting point. It was a riddle to perplex the sharpest wit, and the question? Why would a man with everything, hunger for more? Why would he endanger that which he possessed and those who willingly belonged to him, in some sense, by stretching his jaws beyond their capacity in an avaricious attempt to consume an ever increasing bounty?

Shane watched Melisendra snake into the classroom exuding nonchalant sensuality and he wondered why she was here. Why was he forced into the irresistible presence of beautiful and intelligent women? Where were the grandmothers, the middle aged hags, those that had been intellectually dulled by a combination of the lack of mental stimulation over many years and the ravages of dementia? Not that they were ugly. Their pulchritude was of another sort, one which did not cause embarrassing changes to his anatomy. And what of the men? How he wished for more male students. There was no chance of him ever falling in love with any of them, irrespective of how charming, attractive or witty they might have been.

Greetings flew back and forth as students filed in and took their seats, marking their territories with strategically placed belongings and protecting adjacent seats from undesirables while simultaneously reserving them for their friends. Shane watched the ritual and smiled contentedly. People were marvellously entertaining.

Once all were settled, Melisendra vacated her seat and approached Shane's desk. He squirmed stealthily as he tried to keep his eyes on her face. She arrived with a rush of perfume and leaned down towards him.

"I have to leave early today, teacher."

"Okay. May I ask why?"

Shane smelled cinnamon on her breath. He gulped.

"Why?" said Melisendra, as though his question was overly personal and offensive. Her pause was an invitation which Shane declined. "I am busy," she said. "I have many things to do."

Please fit me into your busy schedule. Squeeze me in anywhere at all. Please. "Okay," said Shane, "but you understand I have to write something on the roll. I can't just write *busy*. That isn't acceptable. The admin department are really hard line, you know."

Melisendra leaned back, pulling Shane with her by the force of gravity. He almost stood up.

"Hard line?"

Hard. You know like my penis right now. Shane wanted to slap himself. "It means strict."

She smiled and walked away. Her behaviour was maddening, so erratic and capricious it *had* to be calculated. She must be deliberately attempting to render him insane. He was her amusement, her plaything, an interesting and harmless diversion. Shane knew if he weren't in such a state of dilapidated morality, he would be safe. As it was, and from whatever miscreant and devilish well his condition had sprung, Shane was in terrible peril. He was already rehearsing lines to deliver into the warmly receptive ears of Sabeen after class. Lines which she might think sleazy and highly inappropriate, but which he would imagine as smooth and seductive, and not only appreciated by Sabeen, but yearned for.

This was the vicious ensnarement. No sooner freed from the temptation of his delightful students, he would encounter the allure of Sabeen who would certainly pop in to see him, as she always did. Why could she *not* pop in? That would be preferable. Two Shanes engaged in a ferocious war inside his head. One Shane wanted her, the other one didn't. Lustful and reckless Shane wanted *her* at any cost, and he was not concerned with who *she* may be. Any *her* would do. Sabeen was the immediate cynosure of his obsession. Righteous Shane flew the flag of purity and faithfulness, proudly waving it even as the tornado of wanton desire ripped it to shreds.

"Let's get started ladies and gentlemen," said Shane, commanding his thoughts to discipline and order. "This morning we are going to continue with our work on phrasal verbs from yesterday."

With wry amusement, Shane watched the vacant looks and listened to the confused mutterings of many of his students. Yesterday was such a long time ago, they had forgotten all about it and failed to recall their teacher's admonition to bring the phrasal verbs handout with them. He raised his voice slightly to ride above the rustle of paper as they valiantly searched for the handout in question.

"Does everyone have that handout from yesterday?"

There followed blank stares and glutinous silence, awkward wriggling and nervous foot tapping.

"Hand up if you need another copy of yesterday's handout."

He repeated the query several times in the same tone until all the students who obviously should have lifted their hands, finally did.

"Okay," he said, before counting the hands. "I'll be right back."

The class was supposed to commence at nine o'clock but Shane allowed five minutes for settling time and stragglers. After which he handed out the individual attendance sheets, rifling through the collection in his hand, seeking faces to match the names and removing sheets without corresponding bodies to the bottom of the pile. Each time he finished this tedious ritual, any additional latecomers would either stroll or hustle inside and he would repeat the process, collecting completed attendances even as he doled out their incomplete counterparts.

Shane wandered down the hall towards the photocopier room which in similar fashion to the library was grossly misnamed. The former was more accurately an alcove, and the latter a cupboard. In no hurry to return, he ambled, in the hope that Sabeen would spring from wherever it was she always sprung and titillate him with her existence. When he reached the alcove, the first thing he noticed was her calves, low and horizontal. From the crease behind her knees, Shane's eyes roamed onto Sabeen's buttocks which were neatly encased in a grey skirt.

"Problem?" he asked, by way of announcing himself.

Sabeen turned and smiled. "Isn't there always a problem with this copier?"

"I don't suppose you could get us a new one. This one clearly can't cope with the workload. Whole forests are disappearing to support the educational needs of my students, you know."

She stood and smoothed her skirt down, first over her bottom then down her front. When she lifted her eyes to meet Shane's he made sure he was there, and not focused on where her hands had been.

"I'm afraid you'll have to make do," she said; "we've ordered a new part and it will be serviced then as well."

Perhaps I could service you in the meantime. "Never mind," said Shane. "Can I use it now?"

"Give it a go."

Sabeen gestured for him to come and test it, but did not move out of the way. Shane invaded the narrow space between his boss and the photocopier and felt her at his back. The heat flushed his face. Her eventual clearance necessitated her front brushing his back. It was slow and deliberate. Shane stopped breathing as she settled beside him. He watched for the anticipated successful operation of the machine, but he was no longer thinking about photocopying. Fearful that even the slightest adjustment in his stance would result in an electrification of his body courtesy of her smoking sexuality, Shane did nothing.

"Are you waiting for an invitation?"

"An invitation to what?"

Sabeen gave him a friendly shove. She was too close and Shane was convinced her proximity was going to ignite a conflagration of desire. With her eyes now centred on him, and her thoughts apparently manifest in her actions, Shane bit the bullet. Overcome by the smell of her perfume, he placed his hand on hers as it hovered over the copier control panel. Her hand remained, relaxed under his, as power was transferred, flesh to flesh.

"I'm not sure if that's necessary," she said.

"I think it is. Maybe it's time to get off the sideline and into the game."

'What game? It's only a photocopier."

"Maybe we should talk about this after work," said Shane, as he peeled his hand off Sabeen's and fixed her with his warmest and most seductive look.

"Talk about what? The copier?"

Shane turned his whole body to face Sabeen who did not even attempt to retreat. Smiling, she continued to tease him with her disingenuous naiveté. His hand ventured forward led by his fingers, reaching for her.

"I'm talking about the game."

Sabeen raised her eyebrows then allowed them to crash into a frown, before permitting revelation to show on her face. "Oh," she said. "The game."

Shane opened his mouth to speak but his words were vanquished by the sudden appearance of Min. If she was cognizant of the hormonally supercharged drama upon which she had stumbled, she gave no indication.

"Is it working?"

Her business like question obliterated the sexual tension which saturated the atmosphere in the alcove. Shane and Sabeen exchanged final glances, nodding with their eyes, agreeing they would have to pick this up again later and confirming that Min suspected nothing. That was what Shane imagined transpired in the nanosecond of ocular connection which preceded her departure.

"Yes," said Sabeen. "It's working."

Shane asked Min for a minute's patience so he could finish what he had started, even though he had not actually managed to start anything other than a bushfire of illicit passion which would probably scorch him and leave permanent scars.

Walking back to the classroom, he wondered how long he had been gone. He looked at his watch but could not remember what time he had left. Now completely disoriented and unable to concentrate, he staggered to his desk and sat down heavily. He was staring at the mess of paper which littered his workspace when a voice pushed into his inertia.

"Teacher? Are you all right?"

Although he registered the sound, he could not identify the voice.

"Teacher? Shane?"

Danijela was a beautiful Croatian in her late thirties; reserved and refined, she was a serious student with a dry sense of humour which she often held in check. She was a regular attender, a diligent worker and a considerate person, another of the extraordinary women in his life. It was she who had spoken.

"Shane. What's wrong?"

He met her concerned and probing expression with a smile. Danijela was married and that was sufficient restraint on Shane's unprofessional interest in her. A wedding ring worn by a contented woman was not always an adequate disincentive, but with Danijela it was. Shane often wished he could talk with her and tell her how he felt. He wanted to bring her into his confidence and perhaps use her as sounding board for his wayward and often abhorrent thoughts. Her steadiness may have provided an effective antidote.

"Nothing," he said, because a lie was more convenient than the truth. "I'm fine."

He nearly choked on the words. In his mind, he pictured himself walking towards a precipice, peering over into the frightening dark depths, and wanting to jump.

Chapter Seventeen

"Rob!"

The sound of his name pierced the muddled hazy slumber into which he had drifted while waiting for Jam.

"What are you doing here? You look terrible. What's happened?"

The obvious answer, the honest and full disclosure Rob wanted to provide, was trapped in a net of doubt. He worried about Jam's reaction. He worried she would be afraid of him and seek to not only escape his company but report him to the authorities. Could he trust her? God knew he wanted to. He needed to trust her. What was he doing here if he didn't trust her? Was there any way to soften the blow of the shocking news he had to deliver? Could he say something else? Not tell her? Lie to her?

"Rob?" She came closer. "You're scaring me. What's wrong?"

Rob sat up on the bed slowly. "I need to go, and I want you to come with me."

"Go where? Why?"

He demurred, keeping his eyes on the floor.

"Answer me. I'm not going anywhere until you tell me what's going on. I can see you've been in a fight. Why won't you look at me?"

Rob swallowed, inhaling sharply before releasing the air. "It's Pee Lek. He came to see me at my apartment this morning. He had a knife and I had to defend myself."

"Where is he now?"

"I left him on the floor?"

"On the floor? Is he all right?"

"Not really."

Jam yelled at him. "Stop being so evasive!"

"I just had to get away. It was self-defence. He was trying to kill me, Jam."

Her mouth fell open and she sagged under the weight of the obvious truth he implied. An interminable silence enveloped them. Rob's thoughts dissolved as fast as they materialised inside his turbulent mind, and regardless of his attempts to unearth words of solace, he remained mute. He watched a single tear scar her cheek.

"Come with me, Jam. I love you."

Her vacant stare suddenly achieved focus, her watery eyes mining the cavern of his heart. She whispered, "You love me?"

"We'll be okay. Pack your stuff and we'll leave."

Jam pressed her palms against her eyes. "And go where?" She stared at him. "You killed a man. The police will come after you. Where are you going to run to?"

"Where are *we* going to run to?" said Rob as he stood and placed his hands on Jam's shoulders. "I need you."

Rob hugged her and although she did not resist him, her body was rigid; coldly passive. He might have been hugging a tree as he wondered if she was considering his proposal. She had rejected his offer of marriage, and now he had dropped the magic words on her as if they would eradicate the severe and disturbing reality of the situation. He knew flight would at best be a temporary solution, and at worst, an act which may exacerbate the case against him. For a moment he reconsidered staying and confessing, pleading the self-defence line which was true, but a declaration of guilt was a declaration of guilt. He had killed a man.

After gently breaking the embrace, Rob lifted her chin with his forefinger and gazed into her eyes, pleading. It would take an almighty delusion for them to flee in the belief that distance would save him, but Rob could not conceive of any other saviour. "Will you come with me?"

Jam's tears evaporated into stony coldness. There was an edge to her voice when she finally spoke. "Tell me where you think you can go to get away? To another city? Another province? Another country? In case you have forgotten, you are a *farang* and you stand out. You can't simply blend into the crowd and disappear."

"We have time before the body is discovered. That's why we have to go quickly. Can we go to your father's place? And from there maybe go to Malaysia and then to Australia."

She pulled away from him, turning her back, answering his suggestion unambiguously. "I don't have a passport."

"You don't need one to enter Malaysia, do you?"

"I don't know, but I *will* need one to go to Australia and that's assuming I even *want* to go to Australia."

Half way towards her, Rob was stopped in his tracks by that slap in the face. Was she saying she would not go with him? He had to persuade her. He would rather stay and face the consequences of his actions than leave her behind. Within the maelstrom of emotions and thoughts swirling in his mind, that one was a beacon of clarity. Rob needed Jam. He saw her as the key to unlock a new life, a second chance. A brighter future beckoned if somehow they could struggle across this raging flood swollen river.

"Please Jam."

Jam kept her back to Rob while he stood and wondered what to do. Waves of dizziness washed over him. He swayed and looked back towards the bed. Exhausted and in increasing pain, Rob was not sure he had sufficient strength to continue to argue his case, let alone follow through on the ill-considered plan. He sat and waited.

"I'll take you to my father's place and we can talk about what to do next later, but you will have to go on from there without me."

It was a start. "Thank you. Pack your stuff and we'll go as soon as you're ready." As she had agreed to come with him, there was no point arguing the details now. With instant obedience, Jam went to the cupboard and extracted a backpack before assembling her belongings.

As she worked, she talked. "I'll tell the boss I need a few days off, or a week."

"Don't tell him anything."

"You aren't thinking. It will be suspicious if I just leave. If I tell him I am quitting that may make him wonder too. He'll want to know why. If I say I have a personal issue, but that I intend to return, he will be more likely to believe that."

Rob nodded, but she wasn't looking at him.

"Do you understand?" she asked.

"Yes."

She finished packing then told Rob to wait until she came back. As an afterthought, she asked, "What time did Pee Lek arrive at your apartment?"

"A little after eight."

"It's already been too long. The boss will be wondering what happened. Be ready to go as soon as I get back."

The door closed on his reply, leaving him to soak in anxiety. He searched Jam's room for some whiskey and finally found a half empty bottle buried beneath some clothes. He did not know who had drunk the first half. It may have been him or another of Jam's visitors but it did not matter because he desperately needed some, for medicinal purposes; an anaesthetic for the pain and courage for his flagging spirit.

Rob leaned against the wall, sipping his whiskey and reflecting. Once, he had believed all Thai women were desperate to escape Thailand and were consequently, solely engaged in the business of finding a rich *farang* for themselves. The falsehood still persisted that all foreigners were wealthy and would carry them away to a faraway land and treat them like princesses. His experience, limited though it was, refuted the myth. There were women who found themselves in unhappy and distressed circumstances, and sought salvation in the arms of prosperous tourists and foreign businessmen, but most did not, and why would they? Especially the middle and upper classes; well educated and well-travelled people, hard-working and materialistic, like people in many other countries of moderate to extreme affluence.

Gold digger fairy tales circulated freely in society but most people were still troubled, shocked even, by the idea that someone would marry for money and security rather than love. Perhaps that was only Rob's opinion. Maybe he was a member of the dwindling tribe of romantics who believed in happily-ever-afters. Possibly, people were reluctant to let go of the romance, afraid of a loveless dystopia where relationships were merely business arrangements. Whatever the case, Rob had never met a gold digger. The girls he encountered in the relatively tiny universe of Thailand's sex industry were professionals, who did their jobs and received due recompense. He had never been propositioned or interrogated with respect to his future and the role a young woman might be able to play.

Rob stood carefully, trying not to panic at the vertigo. He sucked more whiskey from his glass like a sleepy infant suckling its mother's breast.

"Let's go," said Jam as she entered the room.

"What did he say?"

"He said okay, and made me agree on a fixed return date but he did not really press me for any other details. He seemed distracted. As I was leaving he asked if I had seen you. He doesn't know your name so he didn't use it, but he did use a very distasteful nickname instead."

"No surprise he doesn't like me, although I still don't know what his problem is exactly."

Jam slung her carry bag over her shoulder and faced Rob. "Do you want to go and ask him *exactly* what his problem is? Maybe tell him that his plan to get rid of you failed and he needs to find a new henchman?"

Rob was surprised by Jam's sarcasm. Most of her behaviour and her words lately, and especially today, had jarred against the image of her he had built in his mind. There was a hard cynicism lurking beneath her pleasant and sanguine facade. He had always felt endangered by her sexuality, but now a new threat arose; a ruthlessness which he had not previously detected.

"You can stand there ogling me or we can go," she said.

"You sound angry."

"Really?"

Jam moved to the door and opened it. She stuck her head out and looked up and down the hall, motioning for Rob to wait. After she beckoned him to follow, she turned suddenly and hissed at him. "I have a right to be angry, don't you think?"

She slipped out into the hall with Rob in tow and hurried along to the stairs. They saw no one else as they descended and left the club through the back door. It would be the last time Rob saw Lipstick. He followed her along *soi* 4 to Sukhumvit Road where she hailed a cab, and they climbed aboard. Jam directed the driver to the Southern Bus Terminal in Borommaratchonnani Road, Bangkok Noi.

To Rob she said, "There's a first class coach leaving for Had Yai at five pm. We're going to be on it hopefully. Can I use your phone?"

Rob stared out through the window of the taxi as it crawled along Bangkok's choked arterial roads. His mind fell to a recollection of a conversation he had with a young American drifter at the Rainbow Four club in Nana. Over beer and peanuts they chatted about their aimless, hedonistic lives, and the adventures they had along the way. Rob had found the man to be a kindred spirit with whom he shared a love of sport, seventies rock music and girls. His name was Mike and he had told Rob a story about the time he was almost hooked by a gold digger.

"I was living in an apartment block called Sunshine. I'd only been there for a few days when a young lady came knocking at my door. She introduced herself as Jit and said she lived in the building. She handed me a bag of sweet breads and a carton of sour milk, and wished me well for the day. Weird, huh?"

Rob swallowed a mouthful of beer then said, "Thai people are pretty friendly."

Mike shook his head. "They can be, when you are in their bubble, when they are providing some service or when they need to interact with you, if you know what I mean. At other times, you could be invisible, and let's face it in most parts of town it's hard for us *farangs* to be imperceptible."

"That standoffishness might just be shyness," suggested Rob.

"Anyway," said Mike, before taking some beer and laying his glass back down on the table. "I should have suspected something was up with this girl, Jit, but at the time I guess I was just flattered by her interest, and she was pretty and she wasn't a hooker."

"How'd you know?"

"She told me she was a maid at the Oriental."

"Well if you're going to lie, do it in style, eh?"

Mike laughed. "She was telling the truth. I checked her out once I started to, once *we* started to get more serious."

"So she knocks on your door and gives you some food and tells you to have nice day. Then what?"

"It became a bit of a ritual. Two or three times a week she would visit and deliver some food, and we would stand in the doorway and make small talk. Her English wasn't great but good enough, and I just accepted her neighbourliness prima facie."

"You must have thought about inviting her in, and I'm going to go out on a limb here and suggest you may have had the odd lurid fantasy about her."

"Of course, bud. A man is not a camel."

Rob laughed. "Where did you hear that expression?"

"From one of you crazy Aussies."

"That's about drinking, not sex. You say it when you're thirsty and you want someone to get you a drink."

"Whatever," Mike said. "It works. You can be thirsty for sex, am I right?"

"Not really. Anyway, how long did the polite and friendly neighbour thing go on between you and Jit?"

"A few weeks, then one morning she lingered. Now understand that *she* always ended our conversations. I got high from standing so close to her, and her soft feminine voice was so delightful to the ears that I could have talked to her all day."

"You're a bloody poet mate," said Rob. "Delightful to the ears, that's beautiful."

Mike resumed the story, overlooking Rob's taunt. "So this day she was hanging around, and an awkward silence led to the shuffling of feet and forced smiles. Eventually I took the hint and I invited her in to share breakfast with me. In hindsight, Jit was desperate not to appear pushy. She hammed up the whole young and innocent thing and was immune to my subtlety. I thought it was sweet, and it made her more desirable. Now we're getting to the part about lurid fantasy."

"Another beer?" said Rob, holding the glass at an angle above the table between them and shaking it slightly.

Rob caught the attention of a busty but plain looking waitress who scurried to their table and advanced her best assets into Rob's arm as she took his order. The two men exchanged wry, knowing looks, before Rob invited Mike to continue his narrative.

"We ate in companionable silence and then I told her I really needed to take a shower because I felt dirty and a bit seedy from the previous night on the tiles. She frowned and stood as though she was going to leave.

“I better go now,” she said quietly, as if afraid of intruding on my privacy.

"I won't take long. There's no need to leave. Would you like to watch some television?"

"I need shower too. I just come home from work. I dirty too."

"I seized the opportunity. 'So we both want to have a shower.' I drew out the last syllable of shower and added an unusually high inflection for effect. I didn't want her to misconstrue my intentions. I realized in that moment we were either at the terminus of our friendship or the beginning of something else. I watched for her reaction, knowing I would detect it in her eyes first. She remained silent, playing dumb although I wasn't cognizant of that at the time.

"I continued, 'and we both need to have a shower, and we are here together.' I used the exaggerated inflection again, despite how stupid it sounded in my ears the first time.

"I had a full woody by that stage and when I stepped closer to her, my heart pummelled its way from my chest into my mouth. Jit froze. 'Would you like to have a shower with me,' I said with a friendly smile as I reached for the top button of her blouse. With her arms by her sides, Jit authorised the continuation of my advances. There was no question now as to where we were heading. My senses sharpened and I could smell her perfume waging war against her body odour even as my own musk was beginning to offend me. After I had completely unbuttoned her shirt, I led Jit by the hand to the bathroom where we quickly undressed ourselves and dived in under the cool water as it rained down on us."

"I'm serious, Mike. You should write erotic fiction. You're giving me a hard on."

"Don't talk to me about your penis. I am not now, nor will I ever be interested at all in the exploits of your member. Got it?"

Rob had laughed.

~ * ~

Jam shook Rob's arm, speaking urgently to him. "Where were you Rob? I was trying to talk to you and you were miles away."

Rob looked at Jam, studying her face, noting the new edge to her formerly soft features. There was a hint of a scowl there. Perhaps it was simply stress causing her uncharacteristic tone but he resented her intrusion into a pleasant memory. He had some good times with Mike, and he really could spin an entertaining yarn. The girl, Jit, had Mike completely hooked and before long she was asking about America, and soon after, requesting that he take her there. Mike didn't want to marry her and he was pretty happy living large in Thailand so he dumped her. Jit went off her brain, swearing and yelling at him, mostly in Thai so he didn't understand the words. Not that he needed to. The day after Mike ended the relationship, he had a visit from some angry little man claiming to be Jit's cousin. If his harsh and threatening words were insufficient evidence of his intentions, the little knife he produced proved the case beyond doubt. Luckily for Mike, the guy was full of hot air and when Mike shirtfronted him, he ran off. If only Rob had been so fortunate. Pee Lek was an altogether different little beast, and Jam was not a gold digger. She had however, demonstrated a darker side to her personality which Rob would never have believed.

"What's your problem?" he asked, too abruptly.

"Do you have cash for the taxi and the bus fares?"

"I'm carrying about five thousand baht."

"That will do," said Jam flatly. Then she turned away from him.

Chapter Eighteen

At stake was the credibility of Angela's claim that accountants were endowed with the characteristics of divinity.

"Leo is a good bloke, and he's good at what he does," said Shane. "But he doesn't have a crystal ball. Economic forecasting can be as dangerous as predicting the weather."

Angela stared at Shane as though she expected an instant retraction. "You sound like a doom booster. Why are you going all negative on me now?"

"I'm just saying that although I trust Leo's judgment and advice as it pertains to financial matters, he is not a prophet. If we place all our eggs in this one basket, he can't say for sure that the bottom of the basket won't wear out, or that the hens won't stop laying."

"What the hell are you talking about?" demanded Angela.

Surprised that the logic of his argument had not proved convincing, Shane opted for a tactful retreat. "I'm just saying a modicum of caution is not altogether unreasonable in these circumstances."

"He who hesitates," said Angela, rising from her seat abruptly, "or *she* who hesitates, is lost."

Shane recalled meeting Leo at a party for teachers and their partners. He was easy going, warm, and a good conversationalist. He had the uncommon knack of actually listening and interacting with his interlocutor rather than talking at them like many people did. The attention span of revellers, especially inebriated ones, was the same as a hyperactive three year old, so Shane always found party conversations obsequious and annoying. He measured his enjoyment of whatever celebration he found himself immersed in on the scale of delightful dialogues. There were two categories. The first was intimate ear shouting with aromatic angels, which might be about anything, but was essentially sustained by the pure joy of feminine company. The second was serious discussions about issues. He also liked hearing people's personal stories.

Leo had told him he liked to read professional journals, and had done it in such a way as to suggest there was something wrong with that. Shane had told him that while he didn't share his passion for work related reading, he could certainly understand its appeal. They both laughed at that fabricated attempt at solidarity and then switched to a discussion of novels which Leo did not read. With effortless ease he demonstrated his craft, by allowing Shane to ramble, and to refill his glass of wine, then prompt him for more information about a topic which probably bored him. Shane, who possessed commensurate conversational skills backed off before his literary monologue irritated Leo and outwore its welcome.

"Do you want to help me with dinner?" asked Angela.

Shane looked at Angela and noticed she had not waited for his answer. He had still not determined whether she meant to take his obedience for granted, trusting Shane to discern the strong request hidden within the question, or whether she did not care and merely asked for the sake of asking. It was her modus operandi and Shane realized he probably should have figured it out by now.

"No, thanks. I'd rather watch TV."

Angela tossed a careless *okay* into the air and carried on with her business. Shane presumed this meant she did not want his help, but if he was wrong he would find out in due course. He walked to the living room and arranged himself on the recliner before switching the television on. Soon he was staring through the screen and the sharp images it displayed, his thoughts wandering back to Leo and his lack of omniscience. This humble and hardworking accountant had become the cynosure of Shane's nagging doubts. He simply could not shake the feeling something was going to go wrong, despite Leo's confident assurances. Shane envisioned more precipices, long fragile tree limbs towering over the earth, rumbustious rivers overflowing their designated boundaries. Rickety bridges, wobbly ladders, fraying ropes.

The telephone startled him with Ozzy Osbourne's voice calling *all aboard* at the beginning of Crazy Train. The coincidence struck him over the head and rendered him incompetent to respond. He fiddled with the screen lock as Tony Iommi's riff kicked in. Finally, he successfully dragged off the lock.

"Shane speaking."

"Hi Shane. How are you? It's Yan Ping."

Without doubt, Shane had misheard. He must have.

"Hello?"

He recognized her voice as though he had been speaking to her for hours every day since she left. How long was it now? Some number of years? It resonated a thrilling warmth; an unspeakable joy verging on relief, and a shock which paralysed his vocal chords. Yan Ping? He saw her face, the faint freckles decorating her cheeks, her engineered eyebrows astride those dark almond shaped eyes which embodied her magnetism.

"Hello?"

From the ceiling Shane heard another familiar voice. "Come and help me with something please."

Angela and Yan Ping were talking to him simultaneously, each unaware of the other and both bemused by Shane's silence.

"Just a minute, love," said Shane to Angela, as he belatedly lowered the phone and covered it with his hand. "I'm on the phone."

Removing his hand, Shane jammed the phone against his ear. "Yan Ping?" he whispered loudly. "Yan Ping?" He looked at the screen and saw the call had either dropped out or she had hung up on him. Perhaps she panicked and thought she had dialled the wrong number. Why didn't he speak? Why was she calling him? Why now? He propelled an expletive into a pillow and traipsed off to the kitchen. He would check his call history later and hope to God she wasn't using a private number. Yan Ping? Damn. As if he didn't have enough to deal with at the moment.

"What's wrong?" said Angela. "You look upset. Bad news?"

There had been numerous times when Shane wished he had the gift of poker face. Having an expressive countenance and wearing one's heart on his proverbial sleeve was a bloody nuisance more often than not. What should he say now? Why did every word have to be the subject of an internal committee meeting? Diplomacy and tact were exhausting occupations.

"Someone tried to call me but the line dropped out or something, I could hear them but they couldn't hear me."

"Who was it?"

"I don't know." A lie.

"Did you recognize the number?"

"No." A variant of an untruth. He had not actually looked at the number. Angela had not asked about his suspicions, and he was thankful for that because deceit was also physically debilitating.

Angela lost interest in his mystery caller and changed the subject. "I think we should target health professionals who are trying to get registered with AHPRA."

He watched Angela carry on with her meal preparations as though he was not present. She had called him for some reason which was apparently no longer of any import. Suddenly, she looked up and said to him. "Please get the large bowl down from the top of the cupboard."

"Did you ask me to do that already?"

"That's why I called you, silly."

"Actually you didn't ask me to do anything."

Without taking her eyes from the onion that was being professionally dissected on the wooden chopping board beneath her Miracle Blade knife, she said, "Didn't I?"

Shane reached up above the fridge, opened the cupboard and lifted out the bowl Angela had requested. "You know those English language proficiency rules are really discriminatory."

"Are they?" she said.

"Yes, and I've told you before the IELTS exam wasn't even designed as a benchmark for occupational proficiency. It is supposed to be used to determine the ability of a candidate to undertake further studies in English. Not of English, in English. If someone wants to do a Master of Engineering for example at an Australian university, they need more than just a Bachelor Degree, and even the degree may not be recognized. They have to prove their English is good enough to undertake a course of study in a foreign language. That's why the test is difficult. It's meant to be. But for people who have already completed degrees, and have had those degrees recognized by Australian tertiary institutions, the issue of language proficiency cannot be fairly settled by IELTS. It is not only unjust but also inaccurate."

Angela stopped chopping, much to Shane's relief because he was certain the noise level had risen as he spoke. Ignoring her disapproving look, the one which told him she really was not in the mood for one of his soapbox sermons, Shane continued.

Angela stared at him. "You realize I've already heard this lecture, and I don't like it when you talk to me like this."

"Like what?"

"Like you're raving; speaking in a raised and angry sounding voice with a stiff aggressive posture and finger jabbing!"

"I'm sorry," said Shane, taking a few steps to close the gap between them. He wrapped his arms around Angela's waist and nuzzled her neck. "I'm really sorry. I get carried away you know, and I can't stop myself. You agree with me though, don't you?" A kiss on Angela's neck and a suggestive slide of Shane's hand chased his question.

Taking obvious care to avoid breaking their embrace, Angela turned in his arms. He could recognize the signs of her arousal and smelled them on her hot breath. Her hips swayed, causing a pleasant friction between their bodies.

It was not that Shane stopped caring about this issue, but rather at that moment he was mightily distracted by the sexual energy which promised to delay dinner. Food also fell into a neglected hovel. Everything faded away as desire overtook them. As unlikely as it might have been, their kitchen had once more proved to be a venue of serious seduction. The fire burned so fast on this occasion they were unable to resist it and ended up entwined on the floor. It was awkward and uncomfortable and over very quickly. Shane shuddered through the final throes of his orgasm with his leg shaking uncontrollably, as Angela lay panting beneath him with her clothes atypically arranged on her body.

After a few post coital moments, Angela said, "I guess I'd better get back to making dinner." She smiled and kissed him.

Shane withdrew himself and grabbed a clean tea towel from a conveniently situated drawer.

"As long as I haven't injured myself in that mad little romp," she added. She took the tea towel out of Shane's hand and pressed it between her legs. "Just a quick trip to the bathroom and I'll get back to work."

Although surprised by her afterglow attitude, Shane kept his peace. There was an inevitable risk attached to his attempts to use words in unusual or embarrassing moments. When Angela left the kitchen, Shane stood and pulled up his pants, making a few adjustments before zipping closed another satisfying love making session. He went back to the lounge room and resumed his seat in front of the television. Having finished her ablutions and adjustments, Angela called to him again from the kitchen.

"Dinner will be a little late, honey. Sorry. There was an unforeseen interruption."

Hopefully not an unwelcome one though, Shane mused as he felt a smile lift his cheeks. "No worries."

Shane's phone sat patiently on the coffee table, blinking intermittently at him as if trying to send him a Morse code message. He looked at it, but could see nothing except an image of him and Angela on the floor in the kitchen. He smiled again, releasing a contented sigh.

He finally picked up the phone and unlocked the screen before selecting call history. The last call had been Yan Ping. The quickening of his heart rate, the sudden onset of a strange angst and the aridness of his throat as he looked at her telephone number and imagined talking to her, all screamed of the immortality of his affection for her. A succession of mental pictures followed, displaying selected vignettes of the Yan Ping days; those delightful, enchanted days. He felt hot as he navigated out of call history back to contacts. When he found Rob's number he dialled it and then concentrated on mollifying his apprehension before he spoke to his brother.

"G'day Shane," said Rob. "What's happening?"

"Nothing. Usual stuff. I just banged my wife on the kitchen floor then told her to make me dinner."

"She's in a different room, isn't she?"

"Uh-huh."

"You're a dickhead," said Rob. "That's no way to talk about my sister-in-law. Keep your shit to yourself, will you?"

"Just jokes, mate," answered Shane, feeling sheepish in the aftermath of Rob's rebuke. "Just jokes."

"If you want to tell me you have a healthy and satisfying sex life, just say that. You don't have to be so bloody crass."

"Point taken. How are things with you?"

"I'm in Had Yai. I mean we are in Had Yai. Me and Jam."

The sport report came on the television with the lead story about the successful reclaiming of the Ashes by the Australian cricket team, courtesy of an easy victory in the third test. Shane was torn at this point. Even though he knew the result and had seen the pictures, he was a cricket tragic and would never tire of watching Australia achieving and celebrating victory.

"Where's Had Yai?"

"South."

"What are you doing there?"

"I'm going to meet Jam's dad and brothers. This is her hometown."

"Shit," said Shane. "That sounds promising. Does this mean she's said yes, you persistent bastard? You wore her down, did you?"

"Well, not exactly, but yes, close enough to yes."

"Okay. There's more to this story. Problems?"

"No. Everything is fine."

Shane said goodbye to Rob and disconnected. Something *was* wrong. Rob had used the word *fine* again, too easily, automatically. In an unnerving confluence, Shane felt a similar thrill of apprehension as he considered his brother's potential disasters and his own inexplicable philandering, which itself was borne out of discontent and was equally likely to end in calamity. Something was definitely wrong.

Chapter Nineteen

Rob Archer, laconic and fearless traveller, soldier of hedonism, aimless wanderer, and ne'er do well, approached the meeting with Jam's father with great trepidation. This was the man whom he hoped to one day address with the familiar and warm epithet; father. The current circumstances were far from the ideal ones in which he imagined offering himself as a prospective son-in-law to a man he had never met. With each kilometre rolled over by the wheels of the coach, Rob's discomfiture festered.

He recalled the tragic tale told him by another of his casual bar room buddies, a fellow foreigner who had crumbled under the severe inquisition of his mother-in-law to be. The woman had drilled him so mercilessly that he literally scarpered, taking flight as if his life was under threat. Needless to say, that relationship was quickly terminated. The poor bloke was too disturbed by the thought of not only marrying the girl he loved, or thought he loved, but also her dragon of a mother. Either that or the girl herself was disappointed by the way her man disintegrated under pressure and decided he was patently not the right man to sweep her away. Her search for a protector was probably continuing in vain.

His last conversation with Shane had also been awkward. His brother would probably have seen through the charade of his forced positivity, but had nevertheless played along. The future of his relationship with Jam was fog bound at best, despite what he had said. The topic of marriage had not been raised and in the current climate of seething hostility, Rob could not see how he could bring it up again. In fact, he was afraid to.

"Do you want to stop in town first or go straight to the farm?" asked Jam.

"Why stop?"

"Just asking."

"Are you mad at me?"

Jam glared at him. "Why? Because you wouldn't go when I wanted you to and now you've got me caught up in a murder? Plus the fact you are forcing me to face my father and his questions about what I have been doing, and why I have been out of contact. He'll want to know what sort of trouble I'm in and why the hell I brought a *farang* home for dinner. And that's only dad. My brothers will want a piece of the action as well. I don't want to be here. I'm not ready, and that's your fault. I mean it's your fault I am here before I wanted to be here."

"You said that."

It slipped out like a bar of soap from the hands in the shower, a lame attempt to defuse her burgeoning rage. He snatched at the vacant airspace and watched his words clang against the glass door.

Jam swore explosively in Thai, before suddenly mastering her emotions. Rob observed her shoulders sag as she pushed angry air from her lungs. She stared straight ahead.

"You know there is one good thing about my career," she said coldly.

"Pulling dicks and spreading your legs is not a career, Jam!"

She swore again, but this time *at* him. The subsequent self-calming procedure was enacted once more before she continued.

"I have learned how to pretend. This will be a performance worthy of an academy award, and my family will not suspect a thing. I'll lie as easily as I breathe. Do you think you can match me? Can you be as convincing as me? You'd better be."

Having twice disgraced himself and exacerbated Jam's animosity toward him, Rob was afraid to answer. He simply could not trust himself to refrain from spitefully responding to Jam's condescension. It infuriated him that she described prostitution as a career, but only because he was jealous. Her icy demeanour had now been eloquently justified but that did not make Rob feel any better.

"We have about thirty minutes until Had Yai. Then we have to change to another bus for the ride closer to the farm. That's another hour after that. We have plenty of time to get our story straight."

Rob fidgeted and sipped from the bottle of water resting in his lap. "What are we going to say?"

"Let's keep the lie as close to the truth as possible. That will be safer, don't you think?" Jam's tone was almost flippant, which was astounding given her seething temperament not more than five minutes ago.

"I'm not sure any lie is safe."

"Not helpful," she said. "I'm going to say I was working as a barmaid at one of the big hotels." Jam played with her lip as she pondered. "The Oriental."

"Sure. Why not aim for the top? It's where all the good gold diggers go."

Someone on the coach opened a jar of fermented fish and began to consume it with oblivious relish. Rob looked around briefly and wondered why no one else seemed bothered by the rancid smell which violated the air. He was also more than a little bemused by the person's decision to eat twenty minutes from their destination.

"What do they pay bar staff at the Oriental?" asked Rob, rubbing his twitching nose.

"I don't know. More than they do at Lipstick."

"Wouldn't you be better off pretending to be a maid? That way there will be no suspicion about extra bar services."

"I know bar work," said Jam. "I don't know maid work."

"What's to know? You make beds, tidy and clean, stack shelves and mini bars. Here a scrub, there a scrub."

"*May dong ma ha ruang!*"

Rob threw his hands into the air, surrendering immediately. "I'm just saying." He wasn't attempting to fight with her, despite her accusation to the contrary, nor was he deliberately goading her, but he didn't need to try. The conflict was effortless.

Turning away from him, with a jerking motion that might easily have caused an injury, Jam ended the conversation emphatically. "Well, just stop saying."

The coach slowed as the driver veered off the highway and into the bus station where crowds buzzed around street vendors. Rob was curious about Had Yai, but Jam's persistent ill humour forbade any questions for the time being. He knew Had Yai was quite a large city and had a sister city called Songkla. The two were often thought of as twin cities due to their proximity. He also knew everyone who was heading south into the Thai peninsula and from there on to Malaysia and beyond, regardless of which mode of transport they favoured, came through Had Yai. The gateway to the predominately Muslim south of Thailand, this thriving city had become an increasingly frequent target of terrorists who were fighting for separation from the Kingdom of Thailand.

Rob climbed down from the coach, stiff from inactivity, and immediately searched for a toilet. The crowd carried him for a while until it thinned and released him. He turned to see Jam right behind, impassively shuffling in his wake. The leadership role thus his by default, he took hold of her hand and veered back away from the street to the terminal building. Finally spotting a toilet, he made directly for it. Jam followed him as far as the entrance, where he squeezed her hand lightly before letting go and handed the attendant a single baht coin.

When he left the amenity, his expectation that Jam would be waiting for him was replaced with fear that she had deserted him. Childhood memories of imagined abandonment rushed back to strangle him as he stood and searched desperately for her. He was always getting lost as a child, and consequently always worrying the life out of his mother and frightening himself half to death. The noise intensified as he shrunk into the milling crowd, alone and increasingly distraught. The melodic and vociferous cries of street vendors rolled over muttered conversations, swamping Rob's panic stricken inner dialogue. How would he find her? Why had she left him? What was he supposed to do now?

"Rob!"

He felt the ripple of her voice reaching for him and froze, fearing the next step would separate them once more.

"Rob! What are you doing over there?"

Jam's hand crawled inside his, inviting an affectionate and reassuring response. With the connection re-established, he breathed again, albeit slowly with quavering inhalations.

"Where did you go?" he asked.

She lifted her free hand to display two cola filled plastic bags with straws protruding from them like the antenna of translucent beetles.

"You could have told me you were going to buy drinks, or waited until I came out."

Jam's eyes narrowed in investigation. He felt foolish and looked away from her. That voice was the voice of a frightened child, petulantly blaming the parent for careless neglect. It was the same whiny tone of disapprobation he always delivered to his mother when she finally found him after he had wandered off. When he turned to face Jam once more, she had lost interest and was scanning the sea of people beyond him.

"What are you looking for?"

"I'm looking for the man who travelled here on the bus with me."

"Wow, that was bitchy!"

"Come on," she said as she turned and began to walk away.

Rob stood for a moment and watched Jam go, before hurrying after her. People invaded his path continually, frustrating him as he attempted to keep pace with her. The crowd seemed indifferent to his needs and wholly consumed by their own, as the bustle persisted. Despite his most sedulous efforts, Jam eluded him again. In the hope of bumping into her when she stopped, Rob maintained his path, fixing his gaze on the sign which said; *mini bus tickets.*

When he eventually caught up with her she was queuing, and he could not resist asking the question which he decorated with spite. "Are you *trying* to get away from me?"

"Not hard enough apparently," she replied.

"Fuck you! I'm sick of your smart arse comments," said Rob, before spinning around and surging away from Jam. Not caring how far away she became, or whether she was following or where the hell he was going, Rob stormed from her presence. People who fell across his path now experienced his wrath; violent and unforgiving. He forced his way through them and out of the terminal with livid determination. His rage demanded victims.

Rob surged away, furious with Jam and himself simultaneously. Clearly, she was going to hold this against him; an ever present threat hovering within a whisper of his flesh. An unwilling subject to her caprice, Rob would forever be on edge, fearful of her burning anger and uncertain of his capacity to ameliorate her resentfulness. Despite his acceptance of his fate, Rob fantasized it away, downgrading the hurricane of her retributive outbursts to a passing shower of disenchantment; a disappointment from which she, and their relationship, would recover. His love stood firm, undiminished by the reality of Jam's increasing emotional frigidity.

He stopped suddenly and stared through the thinning crowd as far down the road as his vision could reach. Pain began to leak from his eyes in unabashed streams of grief and frustration. He had stumbled headlong into a spider's web and now felt the masterfully engineered arachnoid threads entombing him. How had it come to this? He was on the run for taking the life of a man, now fleeing from the only person who could help him. Rob sensed the hopelessness as it crept into his bones, exchanging his strength for weakness.

As dizziness assaulted him, a voice broke through. "Are you okay, sir?"

The human tide ebbed and flowed around Rob as he stood and fumbled in his mind for words to respond. He was not okay. He felt sick, nauseated by despair and dehydrated by the merciless humidity.

Slowly, Rob turned to meet the gentle enquiry, but he found only a sea of dispassionate faces. He looked back towards the bus station and wondered if he should return. What was he going to do by himself? He needed Jam. He needed her help and her person, not the miserable bitch she was morphing into, but the sweet and caring girl with whom he had fallen in love. That was who he wanted. Surely she remained, imprisoned within the walls of her own body which was possessed by a nasty bovine demon. After finding a water vendor and purchasing a drink, Rob drowned his thirst with it immediately and headed back to the bus station.

They almost collided en route; Rob dressed in despondency and Jam wearing what he imagined was frantic concern. When they met, silence spoke first, before their minds attempted telepathy through searching eyes.

"What are you doing Rob? Why did you run off?"

"I told you why," said Rob. The recalcitrance in his tone hopefully matched hers. Perhaps they should have stuck with telepathy because the conversation was already decaying on the acidity of their tongues. He wanted an apology, but she refused to say anything.

"You said you hadn't tried hard enough to get rid of me."

"It was a joke."

"It wasn't funny."

More sullen, wordless staring followed. Rob was unsure what she expected from him and equally uncertain how to defuse the bomb which waited, hovering in the awkward quiet. Jam's volatility worried him. She had him on the defensive again, feeling apologetic, and he was thoroughly sick of it. She used her patience as a weapon, alternating between protective and offensive deployment. Rob knew he could not outlast her. He was already wavering and verging on surrender simply for the sake of movement, of some activity, something to break this disturbing stalemate.

"How many times do you want me to say I'm sorry? I already feel like shit. Can you cut me some slack?"

Jam frowned. "You feel bad and you want me to do something about it. Is that it?"

Rob nodded. "Yes. I need you."

He watched the pressure of an expletive building behind her lips, felt the intense struggle within, tarried in breathless anticipation. She exhaled a jet of air and dropped her head into her hands. She held the pose for a few seconds before lifting her eyes to again meet his.

"You think this is all about you?"

"I'm the guy running from the law because I killed someone."

If Jam had wanted to abandon him she would have already done so. It would have been easy for her to alert the authorities in Bangkok or to at least tell her boss who would have done the reporting for her, or perhaps metered out his own justice for the life of Pee Lek. If she had truly wanted to cut herself free of this entanglement she could have. Rob took a quantum of comfort from these thoughts but was nonetheless disquieted by Jam's demeanour. It seemed as though, having decided to help him escape the consequences of his actions, she was now determined to punish him herself. That did not make any sense. Not to him anyway.

"I'm the woman," said Jam finally, "who has trapped herself because she wanted to help."

"You still want to help me, don't you?" His beseeching tone sounded pitiful.

"I'm not sure that I do."

Rob studied Jam's face for any trace of humour but found none.

Chapter Twenty

Most people want to live peaceful, simple lives. They want to love and be loved, they want to feel as though they belong and are connected to other people, and they need to have a sense of purpose. Despite this yearning, and the earnest efforts to do everything possible to achieve these personal and relational goals, most people are afflicted with the symptoms of their brokenness. They live in the discordant tension between how they want things to be, and how things actually are. This dissonance is unbearable, especially for those souls with a propensity for self-reflection. The search for contentedness is invariably in vain.

With Sabeen's expectant face exploring his, Shane sat uncomfortably in the torment of his narcissism, as though it was a dentist's chair. A fracture had occurred in his relationship with Angela and he had not even seen it coming. He did not know when exactly it had occurred, but it was widening rather than healing with time. His life was going to fall into the inevitable chasm that would be formed, and he was powerless to prevent it. It should have been as simple as a metaphorical slap in the face, to rouse him from his torpor and force him to see his life and its little problems in perspective. It should have been as easy as reminding him to be thankful for what he had, but his discontent was like a cancer; too lately diagnosed and now untreatable.

"Tell me what you're thinking about," said Sabeen. She moved beside him and leaned close, breathing into his ear and robbing him of his power of speech. Her hands worked him over; one stroking his hair, the other rubbing his crotch. She kissed him and he felt dizzy. His body responded to her. The demands of his mind, the rational, sensible voice of reason were ignored. He pressed his lips hard against her. He sucked her tongue and then fell on her neck like a vampire. His fingers fumbled with her buttons, pausing to feel the flesh of her breasts within the cotton, her erect nipples. Amidst their heavy breathing came a knock on the door.

Then there was another knock, which they heard simultaneously and froze. It came again. They stared at each other. Air rushed into Shane's lungs, thrust violently by the interruption and the resurgence of sanity. He looked at the door and glanced back at Sabeen. They hadn't moved as their breathing slowed harmoniously, and in due course they extracted themselves from the web of lust as an awkward silence filled Sabeen's office. Whoever had been at the door had left on the assumption Sabeen was not there. Shane struggled to ascertain his feelings. Although recognizing guilt should have been one of them, he could not find it. What was it that he felt? The overriding emotion was disappointment. Yes, but was he disappointed with himself for leaving the relative purity of flirting and diving into reckless passion? Or was he frustrated that they had been interrupted? Thwarted. The moment had certainly passed. The flames had been extinguished but still no words passed between them. For God's sake, they should have simply stuck to a conversation about the photocopier.

When Shane finally found the courage to look at Sabeen, she was smiling at him.

"You think this is funny?" he asked.

"Pretty."

"We nearly got busted."

"We got cold feet."

Shane searched Sabeen's eyes for meaning. She was gorgeous and shiny and even now desire stirred once more, easily and carelessly, as though there was no difference between having sex and eating a sandwich. He bit his tongue, suppressing the compliments with which he wished to sprinkle her. There was no danger here of her misconstruing his intentions, mistaking his flattery for pleasant chit chat or unwanted attention. It was wanted. She had been in the process of giving him what he wanted and taking what she wanted. She smiled and he smiled back, as unspoken words rode the waves of light which joined their eyes. Shane adjusted the crotch of his pants.

"Don't you think it was a warning that we shouldn't be doing this?" said Shane.

"Someone knocked on the door and freaked us out for a second. That's all." Sabeen stepped closer to Shane and wrapped her arms around his waist. "There are no signs or omens or whatever, just bad luck, bad timing. Whatever. Let's get back to business."

He accepted her kiss, participated in it fully, albeit momentarily before breaking the embrace and gently pushing her away. "I need to get going."

"Why?"

Shane looked at his watch. "I have a class to prepare for."

"True," said Sabeen. "What a shame."

"Is there any lipstick on my mouth? Are my pants straight? Zipper up? Check."

"We didn't get that far. A real shame as I said. Maybe you should see me after class today. Can you work late?"

Shane's hand was on the door handle, turning it to effect his escape, but he stopped. Could he work late? Did he want to work late? His chest felt tight and his head pounded. What was he doing? He was a madman flirting with disaster.

"Shane?"

He left without answering her and hurried down the hall into his classroom. In the relative serenity, he attempted to calm himself down while also admonishing his folly. Why was he so weak? Why was it so effortless to fall into the arms of a temptress? Why had he allowed himself to be seduced? Though it was a question based on an erroneous assumption that she had seduced him. That wasn't true. What a relief that at least he could be honest with himself. He had hunted Sabeen, preyed on her, and although she had not resisted him, she was not as much to blame as Shane himself. He would shoulder the burden of guilt. He should. He was to blame. Was it greed? His head hurt; a searing pain right across his forehead, as the questions piled up and the answers were absent and beyond contact. He needed to talk to someone else. Another voice was required to join the battle.

Wretched and confused, weary from the inner turmoil, Shane slumped in the chair behind his desk until nine o'clock when the first of his students arrived.

"Teacher? What's wrong?"

Shane looked up to greet the concerned countenance of Melisendra. The transformation from pulsing siren to doting mother figure was astounding. Pouring out maternal care seemed so natural and genuine coming from her, that Shane found it impossible to reconcile this persona with the vixen who drove him insane almost every time they occupied the same space.

"You look very tired and sad," she continued. "No sleep? A fight with your wife?"

Why did she have to mention Angela? What was it about Angela that satisfied him in every way but still left him hollow? Was it her fault or his?

He shook his head and lied to get rid of Melisendra. "I'm fine, thank you. It's nothing."

While Melisendra interrogated him with her huge hypnotic eyes, he thought about Rob. Saying the words, *I'm fine,* triggered the fraternal anxiety which he had felt when Rob used them. He would have to call him again and not just to check on his welfare but also because he needed to talk to another man; someone he trusted, someone who knew him, about the near catastrophe with Sabeen and the ongoing barrage of inappropriate thoughts. Meanwhile, he held Melisendra's gaze, refuting her accusations with every blink and twitch. He marvelled at the immunity he suddenly possessed, and wondered why it invariably deserted him when he needed it most.

"I'm fine, really. Take your seat please."

The class expected the lesson to begin but Shane could not motivate himself. Five minutes after everyone had entered and sat down he had still not handed out the attendance sheets. The odd impatient whisper fluttered in the silence. He speculated how long it would be before someone said something to him. How far could he extend their collective forbearance?

"Ah, Mr. Shane," said Walid. "Are we do work today?"

Shane looked at Walid's beaming visage and appreciated his enthusiasm and his forthrightness. *We bloody well better get on with it*, he thought. "Of course. There's no slacking in this class. You know that."

A few of the students exchanged perplexed looks as the meaning of *slacking* eluded them. The evident bewilderment of others was due to the fact his words were in sharp contrast to his actions. There was movement outside in the hall and Shane glanced in time to see Sabeen waft past and throw him a lazy wave. He told himself to focus. He had wasted enough time grappling with intemperate fantasies.

"Let's get these attendance sheets filled in then we are going to do a writing task. Recount writing; one hundred word target. Tell me about your weekend. Remember to use past tense verbs, joining words and time words. Even if you did nothing on the weekend, I want you to tell me all about your nothing. You know, you can't actually do, *nothing*."

Groans and gasps intermingled in the aftermath of his instruction but there was nothing new there. Most students continually underrated their own abilities, and many liked to complain for the sake of solidarity with the few who really did struggle to meet Shane's demands. Those who lacked confidence needed prodding, and those who didn't needed discipline. There were always babblers who imagined their communication skills at higher levels than reality and who loved to talk but not to listen. The best speakers, the clearest, the most efficient communicators were excellent listeners.

Likewise, the best writers were diligent and thoughtful readers. Good listening was far more important than most students realized, even those who had frequent difficulty in not only comprehending oral texts, but in hearing them, isolating morphemes and discerning how they combined to make words. To reproduce distinct sounds you first had to be able to hear them.

Shane made another circuit of the room to gather the completed attendance sheets and provide encouragement for those who had not yet begun the writing task. He perceived an increasing reliance on the no preparation, minimum supervision writing task. For at least half an hour he could sit at his desk and work, or pretend to work, until the first writers finished and requested the intervention of his red pen.

He knew who he would be visiting first, the usual suspects, the faster workers like Melisendra and Danijela. If they were his only two students he would not have been at all displeased. Aside from the obvious attraction of their femininity, they were nice people and hard-working students. To be close to them, inhaling their perfume, drinking deeply of their undivided attention, touching them and teetering on the brink of harassment was so enjoyable that at times he felt he didn't deserve his wages.

Melisendra reproved him for his tardiness at the beginning of the class before allowing him to mark her work. He accepted the rebuke with good grace and deliberately pressed in a little tighter to her than usual. There was no reason to do that but he did anyway, and when he finished marking her work he placed his hand lightly on her shoulder and left it there for way too long. Danijela intercepted Shane next, and he treated her with exactly the same distorted reverence, even pointing out the tattoo she had on her am which he had not seen before. She quickly tried to cover it, and in so doing, her hand collided with his as he withdrew it. He apologized. She apologized. It was weird but Danijela indulged him with an explanation.

"It was a long time ago. I was young and rebel."

"Rebellious."

"Yes, rebellious. I did it myself. It was stupid and dangerous."

"Everybody does, or has done, stupid and dangerous things."

Shane treasured such moments when he was invited in to visit the person who lived inside the body. "Anyway," he said. "I like it."

Danijela dismissed his compliment with an enigmatic smile.

He was on his way back to the desk when the telephone rang. He didn't recognize the voice which responded to his greeting.

"I'm sorry, who is this?"

"Chris. I'm a paramedic. Your wife has been in an accident. We are taking her to Wollongong Hospital."

"Is she all right? What happened?"

"She's critical."

"What does critical mean?"

"Come to the hospital. We have to go now. I'm sorry, Mr Archer."

With an elevated heart rate, escalating blood pressure, tightening in the chest and breathless anxiety, Shane tried to hang up the phone but missed the cradle. He addressed the class as calmly as he could, the effort of restraining his fear causing his head to throb and each word produced as though a painful extraction. "You can all leave. I have to go now."

Questions flew at him from all directions but he ignored them as he quickly snatched up his belongings and rushed out the door. He slammed into Sabeen as he left the room, knocking her to the floor.

"God, Sabeen, I'm sorry, really sorry. I have to go."

Shane left her on the floor, dazed.

Everything was blurry; flashes of light, smudges of colour, muted fuzzy sounds. A voice yelled at him, insisting on reckless alacrity. The menagerie of thoughts and feelings with which he was battling were now of no consequence at all. Angela was critical, and nothing mattered except getting to her as fast as humanly possible.

Chapter Twenty-one

The odds of acceptance by Jam's family were heavily stacked against Rob. He mulled over his situation as they traversed Had Yai in a clapped out, noisy mini bus. Jam's only words were the occasional comment on something of interest outside the bus, or soft words of encouragement about how it was not a long trip. Fortunately, she had calmed down, as had he, but the atmosphere was still tense. They raced through the heart of the bustling city but Rob scarcely noticed anything, paying lip service to Jam's intermittent travel guide commentary. Children played, young men stood around and smoked cigarettes, street vendors plied their trade, haggling and bartering. There was an occasional suit, and a uniform here and there. Lots of people moving backwards and forwards with disguised intent. Narrow alleyways exchanged their cargo and detritus with the main arterials, some spillages occurred. Life hummed. At one point they had to reverse out of a *soi* because it was blocked by a small herd of water buffalo, evidently on recreation leave from their labour in the rice paddies outside the city. Loafing and chewing their collective cuds, the beasts of burden had forced the driver to employ an alternative route.

At no point during the journey had Rob been able to convince himself he would be welcomed with open arms. The forty five minute minibus ride out of Had Yai into the countryside was followed by a long walk along an unforgiving dirt track and a detour along a ribbon of flattened grass to the edge of a pregnant stream.

"It's too small to be called a river, Jam. It's a stream at best, maybe even only a creek."

Jam slapped Rob's arm and guided him down the embankment to a tiny and pathetic jetty. "Call it what you want," she said. "Its name is Pattani, and it's a river. Get in." She pointed to a small tin boat with an outboard motor attached.

He surveyed the length of the river in either direction, noting it was consistently narrow for as much of its course as he could see. Rainfall had churned the bed and turned the water into chocolate. Although it looked dirty, Jam assured him it was clean apart from the mud. Eventually, with more prodding from Jam, he inserted his frame into the bow end of the tiny vessel.

"Sit still," she said, as she nimbly hopped into the stern and began to fiddle with the engine.

Despite appearances to the contrary, it soon sputtered to life, albeit reluctantly. Jam smiled as she gripped the throttle and issued a final warning: "Hold on!"

After Rob domesticated his initial panic, he relaxed somewhat and submitted himself to fate.

Aside from the fact that Rob was a *farang*, an outsider and a Christian, nominally if not practicing, Jam was her father's only daughter; his princess. Furthermore, Jam's mother had died giving birth to her, a fact only very recently revealed to him. Her father and three older brothers were fiercely protective of her, and while that was understandable, it was also intimidating. These facts did give rise to the question as to why they had allowed Jam to leave home and fend for herself in the City of Angels. He'd asked her about it.

"I don't know really," she replied. "Pride probably. They said if that was what I wanted they wouldn't stop me, but they thought I was very foolish."

"And they didn't come after you? Once the emotion had gone, once everyone had settled down a little?"

"I don't know if they did or not. I haven't had any contact with them since I left. Pride stopped me from reaching out to them as well, I guess."

It was lamentable and Rob's sadness carried over to thoughts of Jam's mother, and how horrific it must have been to fight for her life as her womb yielded the child it had housed since conception. How afraid she must have felt. How desperate to safely deliver her unborn alive and healthy into the world of suffering. How tormented her thoughts. And what of Jam? The guilt she must have experienced, surrounding her and smothering her when she emerged from the cocoon of childhood. Until she was old enough, her father and brothers had concealed the truth from her, saying only that her mother had died when she was very young and that was why she had no memories of her. They did not have any photographs and any mention of her ignited awkward silences. Rob had asked Jam about not having any memories of her mother, but she had dismissed the question by saying it was not possible to miss something which you never had. Rob understood then where the hardness he had seen in Jam had had its genesis. It made perfect sense.

Suddenly the engine cut out and Rob turned around to see Jam sitting at the helm unperturbed, still guiding the tin boat around the bends of the Pattani River. When the vessel ran out of momentum, she steered it into the embankment where another worse looking tinnie sat forlornly. Jam demonstrated her agility again by leaping from the boat before it reached the bank. She landed softly and quickly grabbed the bow, pulling it with a sharp jerking action. Rob fell backwards into the boat when it came to an abrupt stop. With both sound and movement now quelled, a monumental quiet enshrouded them. Jam pulled him from the bottom of the boat and out onto the embankment. He looked around. Nearby, a house squatted in the tall grass.

"I thought you said your family home wasn't far out of town."

Jam smiled, almost condescendingly. "Not even two hours."

She began to walk slowly towards the house with uncertainty in every step. A thick mud of trepidation sucked at her feet, retarding her progress. Rob watched her briefly then joined her. When he tried to take her hand, she shook it loose.

"Not acceptable here," she said, by way of reprimand. Then, as though instantly transformed into another person, a little girl; "I hope daddy's home." The buoyancy in her voice juxtaposed the caution in her gait.

The land around the house was flat and denuded of the long grass which encircled it. As they stepped into the clearing, Jam stopped. A few seconds passed before Rob realized Jam was no longer beside him. He turned back to see her face manifesting her anxiety. Her angry sniping at Rob had probably been her method of dealing with that which now faced her. A home coming she must have thought about on countless occasions and fretted over endlessly, always attempting to push it to a dark corner of her mind, but never quite succeeding. Perhaps she needed Rob's support more than she would willingly admit.

"Jam?"

"They'll be out in the paddies at the back of the house. They start at sunrise and come in for an early lunch."

Jam spoke dispassionately and remained rooted to the spot where she had been frozen by the proximity and nostalgic atmosphere of her home. Rob wondered what he should do. The tumultuous emotions with which she must have battled were beyond him, and he did not know how to help her.

"Do you want to go in and wait for them, or go out to see them now?"

She took a few hesitant steps then stopped again. Rob studied the house. It was elevated by dozens of posts providing just enough headroom underneath the floor. A crude kitchen occupied the western side of the space underneath the house with a stainless steel bench, a sink, a gas stove, a wok and some utensils hanging overhead. A large earthenware jar stood adjacent to the stove and there was a rectangular table with six chairs in the centre. Constructed entirely of wood, it looked worn and neglected, the timber greying with age. A staircase led up from the ground and spilled onto a veranda which extended around the perimeter of the house. Steeped, sloped twin rooves adorned it and evenly spaced square windows punctuated the walls. The house looked old and uncomfortable. Rob searched for evidence of electricity but found none. Jam's family led a primitive lifestyle; basic, simple. He was eager to survey the interior of the house, and therefore moved towards the stairs without further reference to Jam.

"Wait," she called. "Let me show you around."

"I can pretty much see all there is to see apart from inside the house. It looks small though."

"Four rooms," said Jam. "One for the shrine of the house spirit and the spirits of our ancestors, the others for sleeping. I used to have my own room. With my eldest brother now living and working in town, the other two probably have one each, and the other one is my father's."

As they began their ascent, a baby cried. They looked at each other.

"*Mee kry you may ka?*" called Jam.

"*Ka,*" was the response to her question as to whether anyone was home. To which was responded with a question in return, about who was asking. "*Kry ma pood?*"

They kept walking as the conversation continued. Jam, having established there was an adult present with the child, identified herself and entered the second door she came to. Rob followed.

A young lady sat on the floor cradling an infant on her lap. Her hands left her child to form the wai; palms pressed together, fingers pointing skyward, her forehead lowered to touch the fingertips, as she greeted Jam formally and welcomed her.

"We weren't expecting you," she said, returning her attention to the baby who had started grizzling. "I am your sister, Ohn, the wife of your brother, Som. And this," she looked back down at her child, smiling, "is my son, Noy, your nephew."

Jam fell to her knees beside them and wept. Rob stood awkwardly, trying to figure out what to say or do, or where to look. He felt like an intruder. He watched Ohn console Jam by stroking her back as her shoulders trembled. Perhaps he should have left, but he stayed. Ohn looked up at him and asked him in Thai if he was a friend of Jam's. This was a gesture to break the ice, and an obvious effort on Ohn's part to include him. Although he and Jam were more than friends, he decided not to complicate matters by correcting her assumption.

"I am."

"You are welcome here," she said. "The men will return soon for lunch which I must prepare now." She stood gracefully, lifting her son as though he were physically attached to her. Rob averted his eyes when he noticed that the baby was still suckling her breast. "Come down. Have some water."

"Thank you."

Jam cried her eyes dry and eventually the tremor of emotion abated. She was able to stand, and as she wiped her face she looked at Rob and smiled. They followed Ohn downstairs and sat at the table. Jam took Noy from Ohn and held him as though he was the most precious thing she had ever held in her arms.

Rob silently watched the domestic scene still disoriented by the nagging feeling he was an outsider. The conversation between Ohn and Jam floated in and out of his attention, but he managed to follow the gist of it as much as he wanted to. His mind was on Jam's father and the imminent reunion. The discovery of a sister-in-law and a nephew had been pleasant, but what would Jam's father make of the sudden reappearance of his only daughter. Rob had questioned the wisdom of Jam not giving some advance warning of her arrival. Perhaps she could have contacted her elder brother in town, gone to see him first and found some way to soften the blow. The shock of seeing his daughter for the first time in three years, and meeting her *farang* boyfriend at the same time, might be more than the old man could handle.

With confidence, Jam had assured Rob that her father was not some frail old codger with a weak heart who might keel over from astonishment. He was not yet seventy years old and strong of body and mind, at least the last time she had seen him. She spoke of him with such obvious pride and affection that it was hard to imagine why she had left.

When a pause presented an opportunity, Rob inserted himself into the dialogue with a question. "Aren't you worried being here by yourself? We could have been strangers who meant you harm."

Ohn smiled. "Your accent is interesting and a bit funny."

"Thanks."

Ohn laughed before returning her attention to food preparation. Miffed at having his question dismissed and piggybacked by a direct statement which could easily have been seen as an insult, Rob decided he was better off talking to Jam. He asked the same question, albeit slightly rephrased.

"There are no thieves and no strangers. Not any who are dangerous. If visitors come, and they very rarely do, we welcome them. If there is no one here, they wait for us outside the house, or they move on. We trust them to do the right thing, to behave properly and to not take advantage of our hospitality."

"That's very quaint."

"What is quaint?"

"Old fashioned," said Rob. He watched the baby sleeping in Jam's arms and thought how becoming the scene was, how motherhood suited her, how he would like to have a child with her. He smiled at the innocence of the baby, at its lack of understanding and knowledge about the cruelty of life. How it was completely dependent on his mother and other family members and wholly trusting without even being aware of it.

"I wouldn't feel safe in a place like this, and I would feel lonely," said Rob.

"You're used to having people around; neighbours, friends, and a large cast of extras."

Rob laughed. "A large cast of extras. That's funny. But even with neighbours nowadays, people are less interested, less involved, maybe even less caring. Immediate family and immediate needs, stay out of other people's business. People don't want trouble so they keep their distance."

"People are still lonely even when surrounded by a large cast of extras," said Jam.

"Stop saying that."

The isolation felt surprisingly safe. It seemed no one came to this house, and if they did it was by accident, not because they were looking for someone or something. Rob was satisfied by the relative security this place offered and increasingly sanguine about his chances of escaping the authorities and the consequences of his crime. They had not discussed it. There was nothing else to say. Rob stood and wandered to the back of the house while Jam and Ohn continued chatting. Maybe Jam's father and brothers would be as friendly as Ohn. Perhaps they would embrace him and his relationship with Jam. He could only hope that would be the case. The alternative was rejection and the subsequent possibility of Jam being compelled to choose between her family and him. He paced as he wondered, eventually ending up where he had begun. A break in the conversation allowed him to ask a question on a non-threatening subject.

"Tell me about the house Jam. Did your father build it?"

Jam opened her mouth to answer, but the words evaporated as her eyes widened and flooded with tears. She was looking behind Rob, and he did not require any genius to know who had just arrived home.

Chapter Twenty-two

Wollongong Hospital was a twenty minute walk from Shane's workplace. He had his car parked three blocks away, beyond the thievery of council parking meters, but he did not stop to think about whether it would be quicker to drive because he was not thinking about anything. He ran. His bag slapped his thigh as adrenalin pushed his legs to carry him along the most direct route. From Burelli Street to Crown Street and westward, the footpath disappeared beneath his feet as people, cars and buildings flashed past, wrapped intermittently in distorted sound bites. His breathing resonated loudly in his ears. He was too slow, and would be too late. Angela was going to die without him because he could not run fast enough. He couldn't save her. He would not even be there to say good bye.

The, *don't walk* signal at Victoria Street was ignored as Shane sprinted across the line of stationary cars waiting at the lights. A horn blared, startling him and causing him to stumble as a car skidded to a halt and bumped him off balance. He scrambled to his feet and continued, oblivious to any injury he might have suffered. Certainly, there was no diminution of power, although his muscles burned from exertion.

Shane could see the hospital looming before him, resplendent in orange and purple panels. He dodged a white sedan as he leapt from the curb on the southern side of Crown Street and crossed into and through the Seven - Eleven car park, between two cars waiting for the green signal on Loftus Street, up and over the fence, along the footpath to the entrance to

Accident and Emergency. The automatic doors were sluggish and he bumped his shoulders against their edges as he pressed through the opening they reluctantly provided. At the triage counter, he ejaculated his query.

"Angela Archer?"

The nurse looked down and studied the computer screen.

"She was in an accident. A paramedic called." His words came in staccato bursts as he struggled to breathe. "She was brought here. Not long ago."

"Are you family?"

"I'm her husband. Where is she? I need to see her!"

The nurse gestured to the side of the triage counter and said, "Please come in."

Inside the accident and emergency, another nurse appeared and took hold of his hand. When he finally looked at her, she said, "Come with me please, Mr. Archer."

She led him past a number of cubicles which he noted were empty. Here and there, there was a doctor, more nurses, an ethereal hush and equipment beeping. Finally, he saw Angela lying on her back. Her eyes were closed and surrounded by a dark wine bruise. She had been intubated and a pulse meter was attached to her finger. She looked so small and frail, not the energetic, larger than life woman he knew and loved. He looked at the machines, then back at his wife, then at the nurse who was standing beside her bed. Questions assembled, eschewing an orderly queue in favour of a disorganized crush. Angela.

"Angela?" He leaned close and kissed her forehead. "Angela?"

To the nurse, Shane said, "Can she hear me?"

The nurse nodded. "Probably, keep talking to her."

"When will she wake up?"

"She's been unconscious since she was brought in. We haven't been able to rouse her. We just have to wait."

A sudden weakness dragged Shane to his knees. His head fell on the bed in the narrow space between Angela's prone body and the edge of the mattress. Hot tears scorched his eyes, erupting from the back of his throat, drowning him. He felt a hand on his back, gentle strokes. His head threatened to explode as his heart was ripped in two. Angela. His head pounded.

"Mr. Archer?" A male voice penetrated the fog of his grief. "Mr. Archer, can I speak with you?"

Shane turned his head and squinted through bleary eyes at the speaker. He recognized the coat and the tone. "You're a doctor? What's wrong with her? What happened?" The questions seemed pathetic, sounding lame and inconsequential. The only one that counted was whether she would wake up. Would she survive? He saw them kissing each other good-bye that morning, recollected the brightness of her eyes, the hopeful and positive attitude she carried into every day. *See you this afternoon*, she said. *Have a good day*. Monstrous sobs wracked him.

"Doctor?"

Even as he asked the question, he feared the answer.

"Angela was hit by a car while crossing the road. The impact broke her legs and threw her to the side of the road where she hit her head. The resulting skull fracture caused a subdural hematoma. Thankfully it resolved itself. That is, the bleeding stopped, but she hasn't regained consciousness and we don't know why. She also has some internal injuries."

Shane consumed the doctor's report with all the clarity he could muster, but the bottom line was she could remain comatose indefinitely or... "Will she die?"

"It's possible. I'm sorry. We need to operate on her legs and we're attempting to determine the extent of her internal injuries."

A nurse entered the curtained treatment room and presented the doctor with X-ray and ultrasound pictures. Shane watched as she strung them on the backlit panels on the wall. They meant nothing to Shane and he turned away to stare at Angela's peaceful face. Such tranquillity seemed almost obscene given the circumstances. Unaware of her dire situation, Angela rested; passive and calm, while Shane was assaulted by waves of emotional turmoil. He wanted to be strong for her, but his tank was empty and he was far away from a petrol station. He didn't know how to toughen up. He didn't think he would even be able to stand. Feeling so weak and useless only added to his horror and misery.

"Faarrkk!" he shouted before crumpling to the floor. He grabbed his head in his hands and tried to crush it, his hands balled into fists, banging against the floor.

"Mr. Archer, please."

Hands covered him, resisted him, pulled him, pushed him and pummelled him. Shane allowed a gush of sorrow, of grief and guilt to flood the room.

"Shane. Shane."

He scrambled to his feet certain that Angela was calling him. He stared at her, waiting for her to speak again but she was still. He surrendered to the serene strength of others, and eventually the storm passed. As he was lowered into a chair, he kept listening, straining his ears. Who spoke his name? It sounded like Angela. He looked at the nurse.

"Did she speak?"

The nurse shook her head, pity etched into her features.

"Someone called my name," mumbled Shane. "Someone was calling me."

"Let's get her to theatre now."

"Who?" said Shane, confused and frightened by the violence of his behaviour.

"We need to take your wife now."

"Don't take her!"

"Mr. Archer, your wife needs to be operated on. She needs surgery."

"Can you save her? Please save her. Please."

"Let's go."

"Please save her! Bring her back! Angela!"

"Come with me, Mr. Archer. I'll take you to somewhere you can wait. Do you want us to call anyone? Does she have other family?"

It was only the nurse's hand on his arm, holding him, guiding him as they walked together that anchored him to reality. An awful numbness descended on him. He was vaguely aware of responding to her questions, incognizant of time, unable to feel anything. They entered an elevator where he fixated on the stainless steel panels and the image of the shattered man they reflected. The doors opened and they walked down a hall and into a small waiting room where he sat down heavily and stared at the floor.

The whole world carried on around him, indifferent to his pain, unconcerned about Angela's desperate plight, careless. Time was robbed of purpose, even as life itself seemed pointless. It was in this morose state that he received visitors; Angela's parents and her sister and his own parents, Bill and Maureen too. They were close now when he needed them, as they always had been. They sat and whispered hope to each other to dissect the silence and to dispel the forlorn terror as they waited.

Shane became angry at himself for his meltdown in the trauma room. He had wasted what might have been his last chance to speak to Angela. He had squandered the opportunity to tell her that he loved her, and to encourage her, to plead with her to return from purgatory. He had failed to be the man she needed as she hovered on the precipice of eternity. More tears followed these thoughts and he received the comforting embrace of his mother, despite its impotence against the might of his guilt.

His thoughts wandered back through the life he and Angela had built together. Short though it was, it was loaded with wonderful memories and he felt a weak smile crease his face as he pictured her laughing, her eyes sparkling with joy. Joy? Dissolving, crumbling. If she died he would never forgive himself for those times when he petulantly and avariciously imagined himself with other women; Melisendra, Danijela, Sabeen,Yan Ping. He had betrayed Angela, was cheating on her right now as he allowed those women into his mind, inviting them into his anguish although it was nothing to do with them. He had not had sex with any of them, but he had wanted to. He wanted to expel them from his mind and devote his energy to Angela's recovery. He should have been praying incessantly for his wife, not thinking of himself and his infidelity, the objects of his illicit desire. She needed him to fight for her, to be her champion.

The door of the waiting room opened slowly and the doctor entered the miserable desperation wearing a look of infinite sadness. All eyes were upon him, but he only met Shane's and delivered the news in a sombre tone. Shane's heart stopped as he watched the doctor's mouth open and he heard him say; "We did everything we could but she died. I'm terribly sorry."

A plethora of lunatics and bible freaks had been predicting the end of the world ever since it began. Shane was with the masses who believed the world would never end. People were ephemeral, their lives fleeting, but humanity would continue to propagate along with the cycles which saw babies born in the same moments that people died. Despite the inevitability of death, people lived as though the end would not come, even as they shelved thoughts of how exactly they would deal with it when they faced the grim reaper. Shane had never given it much thought, but now with the revelation that Angela was dead, he understood his world *had* ended. From this moment forward, everything would be tarnished by her death, her absence. A hole had been torn in his heart which would never be repaired. Nothing would make sense, and nothing would matter.

"Can I see her?" asked Shane softly.

The doctor nodded. "Come with me, please."

The sight of Angela lying still, much as she had done when he had last seen her, had surprisingly little effect on him. He walked to the side of the bed and studied her lifeless face. Her soul had been evicted from the vessel of her body. Did he believe she lived on in some form? Was there an afterlife? His mum had always told him so, and it was a part of what he thought he believed but now he wasn't sure at all. Death itself was certain, but for those left behind it caused cruel insecurity. Was she safe and happy and well? The answers to these questions seemed simultaneously significant and inconsequential. People always expressed vague hopes about their loved ones being at rest and looking down on them from Heaven. Perhaps Shane had never truly believed any of it and even now when he desperately wanted the succour such faith might provide, he could not muster any belief. Angela was dead, gone.

He stroked her hair and kissed her lips, lingering millimetres above her, longing to feel one last puff of warm air from her lungs. Trembling, he straightened without taking his eyes from her face, knowing it was the last time he would ever see her. He would never hear her voice again, never hold her, laugh or cry with her. Shane stood, swaying against the impulse to fall, crying quietly so as not to smash the reverent silence, until the nurse entered and executed her final duties for Angela Archer.

Chapter Twenty-three

Rob did not know what reaction Jam expected from her father, but he was certain she would fall apart at the sight of him, and he was right. She cried before she spoke, before she even moved. The old man slowed as he approached, realization dawning. Clearly unable to accept the evidence of his eyes, he said her name, the inflection not indicating a question but expressing surprise, a wonderful surprise.

Jam stood and walked towards her father, then fell to her knees as she made the wai and bowed her head to touch her upward pointing fingertips. Cautiously, he reached for her with a shaky hand and placed it upon her head. Rob was spellbound by the unusual simultaneous display of respect and deep affection. He knew Thai people did not generally hug one another and he always felt their greetings were stiff and ceremonial, rather than warm-hearted. This demonstration was incredibly moving. When her father bid that Jam rise from her feet, her brothers rushed in, minus the circumspection of their father. Jam attempted to forestall their excited advances with the appropriate greeting, but they smothered her in a warm communal embrace.

Not a single word had been uttered by anyone. It was as though there was a collective fear that words could stain the poignancy of the occasion. Rob marvelled at this dramatic reunion.

Ohn broke the silence. "What are you all standing around for? Lunch is ready. Wash up."

Rob sat still as though he was an invisible spectator. He felt like an outsider, or worse an intruder. Jam caught his eye and shared with him an encouraging smile, as Ohn's husband, Som came to her and touched her cheek before gazing love-struck at his son. Ohn introduced the two men. Unable to discern the marriage of the other man's facial features, Rob decided to accept his greeting on its merits without trying to investigate what feeling may have lurked beneath.

Conversation swirled around him as though he was a flower in a windswept field. He smiled whenever anyone looked at him and nodded where he guessed he should be agreeing or at least agreeable. Much of what was said was beyond his comprehension, due to the rapidity of their speech and the fact they were using the local dialect which was similar to Thai, but not the same. Although Jam floated near on occasions and proffered a reassuring glance or even a word or two, he felt increasingly disconnected; pushed further to the periphery of this family reunion. Rob expelled a disconsolate sigh. Life was happening without him. He tried to steal Jam's attention but her brother's monopolized her, while her father watched with a strange expression of melancholy on his face.

Finally, they came together to eat, with each taking assigned places at the table as though there had never been an interruption to this ritual. Aware that Rob had been excluded, Jam shuffled along the bench seat towards her younger brother who protested the nudging but moved nonetheless. Rob sat carefully, mindful that even the way he positioned himself at the table would be under intense scrutiny. He ached for some examination, some analysis. For some interest in him; an acknowledgement that he was present and concrete. The silence which accompanied his descent to the bench was not encouraging.

Determined not to be overwhelmed or overlooked, Rob seized the opportunity to speak. Albeit it with a couple of tonal misfires, he spoke in Thai and thus injected himself.

"It is very nice to meet all of you. Thank you for welcoming me to your home."

The younger brother said something, causing Som to laugh and Jam's father to spit a rebuke which silenced them. He spoke in Thai, addressing Rob directly for the first time: "All visitors are welcome, and on this occasion of the return of my only daughter, I must thank you for bringing her home safely." He bowed his head slightly then lifted it to smile at Jam. Rob felt Jam's hand brush his thigh out of sight, a secretive gesture which suddenly imbued Rob with renewed confidence. Finally a door had been opened to him.

"I want to tell you a story," said Jam's father. "Jam first heard this story when she was twelve and about to begin high school. I decided to tell her the truth. Waiting until then was my decision and I had my reasons. I had to be sure Jam could not only understand what happened but also that she was emotionally mature enough to deal with it."

Rob quickly became lost in the narrative, literally, so he looked at Jam and sent a request for assistance via a version of eyebrow Morse code.

Jam asked her father to pause, to allow her to translate for Rob. The younger brother chirped another apparent witticism before again being silenced by the old man. He continued. "I also needed to give myself time to heal. I was angry and my boys were too. It was easy to direct that blindly ignorant rage towards Jam even though we knew it was not her fault. I was ashamed of myself too. For a long time, I could not make sense of any of these feelings, but eventually the agony subsided and my thoughts clarified. I came to see Jam for what she was; a beautiful little girl, the daughter I had always wanted, my wife's parting gift to me, a lasting legacy of the love we shared.

During those dark times, in the first few years, I was morose and insensible. I sent Jam to stay with her grandparents because they were worried I might neglect her or even hurt her. It was with tremendous relief and deep humility that I arrived at their home to beg their forgiveness and ask to be allowed to take Jam home with me where she belonged. Reunited we may have been from then, yet the terrible secret remained, interred beneath the veneer of our resilience. Jam knew nothing. It seems stupid now that we concealed the truth for so long, that we hid it at all. Maybe it would have been easier on everyone if we had have faced the painful reality and the crippling grief which accompanied it. At the time, it was hard to think straight, and the human heart has great capacity for deception. Running provides the illusion of escape, but you cannot elude the consequences of your actions indefinitely."

Jam's father looked at Rob with a heart stopping unspoken accusation. Rob held his gaze for a few seconds before his eyes began to water and he had to look away. Did he know what Rob had done? How the hell could he know? It was disconcerting to be the victim of such perspicacity, even if it was only Rob's guilty conscience fuelling his imagination. If Jam detected anything, she kept her own counsel as her father continued speaking.

"When we finally told her that her mother had died giving birth to her, she accepted the fact as though it was no more prescient than an announcement of dinner being served. I wondered if she had already somehow figured it out for herself, or perhaps her grandparents had told her. In any case, her reaction made me feel like an idiot. I did not realize of course that she faked her stoicism, and was actually enveloped by an awful turmoil which eventually resulted in her announcing her plans to leave us as soon as she was old enough. I forbade it of course, and warned her of the potential catastrophic consequences of her foolhardy plans. We derided her scheme as delusional and mocked her in the hope it would dissuade her, but when she turned nineteen, she left. That was more than three years ago."

He looked at Jam with such tenderness that Rob felt weak. He desperately wanted to take her in his arms, as he could feel her quavering beside him, wracked with emotion. Clearly, Jam still blamed herself, and adding to her guilt was the realization that her attempts to deal with her guilt over her mother's death had caused her family to suffer, especially her father. It was obvious she blamed herself for the misery of her family, and it was a putrid stain on an otherwise pure white sheet of her character. The tragedy of the situation struck the dinner party mute.

Rob felt that regardless of what was said it would have been an intrusion, an insensitive and unwelcome guest, and yet someone had to say something. He had an agenda which although he recognized as being of lesser significance, was nonetheless salient to him and to Jam, and by extension to the whole family. How would he broach the subject? Should he even try? Would it not be better to let Jam lead the way?

"Anyway," said Jam's father with an explosive sigh. "That is in the past and though we are indebted to the past, and inextricably linked to it, we are not its slaves or prisoners. We have choices and we live with the consequences of our decisions, whether good or bad, right or wrong. Our destiny is to some extent always in our hands, though we remain ever vulnerable to the whim of fate."

Appreciative of the philosophy, Rob smiled at the old man and raised his glass. Although he did not appear to understand the gesture, he returned the smile. A tangible dissipation of tension resulted from that exchange as though the two men had communicated an unspoken camaraderie. It was no doubt an exaggeration for Rob to think they were now allies and confidantes, but that was what he desired. He loved Jam as well. Obviously not as deeply as her father did, but he too wanted her highest good. He felt sorry he had involved her in his crime, but not that he had brought her home. This was a victory to be celebrated. Any negative repercussions Jam may have imagined had not eventuated. There was no calamity.

Jam stood suddenly and pulled Rob away from the table as her family fell into good humoured badinage. When they were out of earshot, she said, "Thank you for bringing me here. I can't believe how light and happy I feel. They haven't asked what I have been doing or why I was gone so long or why I did not keep in touch with any of them." Her eyes glistened. "They are just happy to see me. It's like I never left. I really can't believe it."

Fighting the urge to wrap protective arms around Jam, Rob settled for a quick, light touch on her arm. "Did you think they would be angry, that they would reject you?"

She thought for a moment, staring into the distance behind Rob, into the darkened fields bathing in moonlight. "They would have been right to do that," she said, "because I rejected them."

"Obviously that's not how they see it."

Jam nodded and leaned in towards him. "I'm tired, really tired. I'm sorry I've been such a bitch."

Again, Rob was forced to resist his instinct and refrain from embracing her. It was what she wanted from him, what she was begging for even, as he comprehended the reason why displays of affection were not appropriate.

"What do you do for fun around here?"

She laughed and playfully slapped his arm, before clasping it and leading him back to the table.

"Private conversation?" said the younger brother, who was the only thorn in this garden of roses. His tone was accusatory and Rob wanted to respond by telling him to mind his own business in much less polite terms than that.

Jam, to her credit, ignored the loaded question.

For almost the entire time, Rob had been peripheral to the reunion scene, floating around the edges, there but not really necessary. He felt the disconnection most definitively, through the language which Jam's family naturally used. However, more than the language, there was the undercurrent of shared history and the bond of blood. There were esoteric jokes and flashes of behaviour which only made sense contextualized in familial attachment. Something happened when Rob and Jam returned to the table. If the exclusion had been discomforting, then the calculating and threatening inclusion which followed had no lexical equivalent. Som's directness was alarming and it caused a severe contraction of Rob's stomach muscles.

"What are you doing here?" he asked.

Assuming that Som was asking why Rob had come to their home, this question required one of two possible straight forward answers. Firstly, he had simply come to visit the family of his girlfriend. Was this presumptuous, provocative? Perhaps, but it was honest nevertheless. Would Jam find that answer acceptable? He turned to her, lowering his voice. "Can I say you are my girlfriend?" The question was painful and awkward and he worried about having to ask it, because surely if he had to ask then it meant the answer was doubtful. Just because he had asked her to marry him and they had spent time together, did not necessarily mean they were in a relationship. That had never been formally acknowledged by either of them, and yet it must have been true.

"Just say friend."

"Friend?" said Rob, in a louder voice, as he tried to ignore the scrutiny of the others. "Just friend?"

"Don't be difficult! They'll figure it out anyway."

"Then why not say it?" His voice lowered to a whispered outburst.

"It's not a trick question," said the younger brother. Everyone laughed and Rob felt himself redden. If he told them he had killed a man and was on the run from the police that would shut them up, and he desperately wanted to silence their ridicule.

"I'm just visiting the family of my good friend."

"Really?" Ohn chimed in with resounding scepticism. She looked at Rob then at Jam, who smiled.

Rob braced himself for more, but mercifully Jam's father changed the subject. "My grandfather built this house with the help of my father."

As the man was looking directly at Rob, he felt obliged to respond. "It's a beautiful home."

"It's run down to shit," said the younger brother who was immediately punished with a verbal spray from Som.

"It's all right," said the father. "It's an old house. It does need some work."

"Don't we all?"

Rob's quip elicited an expression of astonishment on the old man's face. He stared until Rob felt himself withering, and eventually nodded slowly, thoughtfully.

"We all need some work," he said. "Yes. We all need some work."

The celerity with which dinner was concluded was stunning. No sooner had Rob begun to truly relax and luxuriate in his improved status with Jam's father – a conclusion he drew based on their exchange on houses and work –when everyone rose and hurried away, leaving Ohn and Jam to clean up. Rob sat in deep consideration of the permutations of this inaugural family dinner and it caused an aching nostalgia to creep into his bones. He missed his family. Suddenly and surprisingly he felt homesick, so he excused himself and went to a secluded corner of the compound where he tried to call Shane.

There was no signal. He was alone.

Chapter Twenty-four

Water has often been used as a metaphor for life, to describe its movement and progress through time. Adages like smooth sailing and calm waters, stormy seas, rough seas. Given the choice, most rational people would like to spend time near tranquil water because it is peaceful. Tsunamis are relentless and destructive, raging rivers are dangerous, water rapids suggest trouble and rips in the ocean suck people out to sea. Marine predators lurk beneath the surface and yet we like water. We love to swim and play in it, to soak in it, to bathe in it and we like to look at it. We like the sounds water makes; gurgling, bubbling, trickling, crashing waves, the pitter-patter of light rain, the cacophony of a waterfall.

Shane sat on the soft sand beside the Hacking River at Swallow Rock and stared at the water. Light faded from the sky as the final few boats were docked or beached and winched on to trailers. Four wheel drive vehicles towed them away through the car park and up the steep hill to the only road out of Grays Point. Quietness descended as dusk fell and the curtain was drawn on daylight.

One week had passed since Angela's death; the slowest, most tormented week of Shane's life, as he'd sifted through the ashes of his former happiness. He came to this spot each afternoon and adopted the same forlorn position on the sand, numb and stricken by a pall of grief which he could not shake. His thoughts were lumpy like badly made porridge; thick and lacking consistency of texture. There was no coherence or sense. He would get stuck on one idea and wallow in it without even feeling it. He couldn't feel anything. He moved only when it was necessary.

He went through the motions of life, maintaining routines because they were his only link to sanity, the only anchor to reality, and every night he went to bed and waited for Angela to join him. Every morning, when he awoke and touched the emptiness beside him, he wandered into the kitchen expecting her to be there making breakfast. The house was quiet, devoid of Angela's footsteps, her humming, her banter, and she no longer called his name from other rooms, because she was gone. Each day he sprayed her perfume on their bed and around the house, to maintain the illusion she had merely left a room, rather than departed the world. Every photograph reminded Shane of what had been stolen. He roamed the empty house like a zombie, moribund and mechanical. He prepared food and ate it but found no pleasure in anything that passed his lips. He uttered very few words, and wept periodically.

Reassured by close friends and family, especially his mother, that his behaviour was normal, Shane did not attempt to resist the tide of misery. He allowed himself to be pushed and pulled by the ebb and flow, like detritus which found itself dumped on the shore and left to wait until the tide returned to lift it and carry it away once more. There was an endless inertia, a lack of purpose which characterised Shane's life. His trips to Swallow Rock, which once were times of beautiful solitude and quiet contemplation where he could reflect on his life and engender gratitude, were now times of heightened mourning. There was no utility in whatever he did, it served no benefit and yet he continued, robotically.

He saw Angela everywhere. Her face appeared in his mind, on walls, in mirrors, and she materialized in crowds, always walking away from him. He told himself she was dead, kept repeating it coldly as though the repetition would magically empower him to move on, to get over her, but he was stuck. The rut wore deeper and his world grew darker.

Thinking he was alone now at Swallow Rock, Shane began to talk, at first to himself, then to Angela. In the midst of his monologue, other voices entered. A car door closed, then another. Engines trilled with faster revolutions before ceasing. Tyres crunched gravel. People were returning. He stood and looked towards the car park but it was empty. He was still alone. The noise had been an echo of those who had left to return to their homes. Shane imagined them all, happy and together with their family and friends, laughing and content, trading stories of the day's activities, building memories. Shane would not be able to build any more memories with Angela. His recollections of her were all that remained. There was nothing tangible, nothing real, just his thoughts and memories. Even objects that belonged to Angela contained nothing of her, and her photographs were not her either. She was gone.

Shane collapsed on the sand, buried his face in his hands, and cried.

Chapter Twenty-five

Crisp morning air carried sunlight through the countless gaps in the walls of the house, waking Rob gently with a warm caress. The sounds of life wandered in and out, swirling in the vacuum of his inactivity. What would this day bring? He rolled onto his back and stared at the ceiling. Jam had slept in her father's room, refusing to share a bed with Rob on the grounds it would anger her family and insensitively confirm their suspicions about the nature of Rob and Jam's relationship. She used the word *relationship* as though it carried an undefinable weight of meaning, not casually or carelessly but as though she was certifying their status. That was encouraging. The burnished wooden slats glowed in the sunshine and he experienced a commensurate lifting of his spirits, although he had no right to be happy. Not really.

After breakfast, which consisted of rice soup, fried eggs and spicy sausages which Jam called *guncheon*, Jam's father and her brothers went to work in the fields. The conversation had been safe and Rob took comfort from that, allowing himself to experience fragments of a sense of belonging.

"Go and feed your baby," said Jam to Ohn. "I will clean up."

"I like your dad," said Rob, as he watched Jam work.

She stopped for a moment to fix him with a curious look which might have suggested she was pleased with his comment, or just as easily that she did not believe him. Jam was like a mirage which kept fading in and out, blurring and dissembling as he approached it. She returned her attention to the clearing of plates and wiping the table.

"I think maybe he likes me too. Do you think?"

"I don't know what my father thinks of you, or me, or anything."

"Didn't you talk last night?" Rob was troubled by her tone. "Before you went to sleep?"

"My father keeps his own counsel."

Rob had not thought the old man particularly taciturn. Neither was he extravagant with words, nor in how he lived, that much was clear. Austerity marked his life, but he was polite and evidently willing to participate in conversation. "He must be pleased to see you."

"He must," said Jam flatly.

Rob stood and walked over to the sink where Jam was standing with her back to him, her hands in soapy water rescuing plates and utensils from the debris of breakfast. He closed the gap between their bodies gradually, until a static charge brought them together. She gasped.

"What are you doing?" she whispered, frozen and stiff like a pole inside his arms as they enfolded her, one around her waist, the other across her chest.

"What's wrong?" he asked.

She trembled.

"Jam?"

"I don't belong here anymore."

"What do you mean?" he said, as he turned her gently around to face him but kept her close. Even as he waited patiently for her to answer, no longer just holding her but upholding her in his arms, Rob sensed the tearing disconnect she must have felt. It must have seemed like she possessed the baggage of two lives and could not find sufficient room for both of them in her trunk. The engine was running and although she was prepared to leave, she couldn't depart until the trunk was closed with her lives safely stowed within. Her pain and her joy, the sum of the experiences which had fashioned her, defined her. She pushed and pulled and wrestled with the puzzle of how to accommodate them but the result was exhaustion and exasperation. Rob could feel her wilting from the heat of her internal conflict. Past malefactions haunted Jam, robbing her of strength, frightening her into a submissive reluctance.

"You know what I mean," she said. Her liquid eyes leaked confused desperation, pleading with Rob for understanding. "Don't you?"

"They've welcomed you back. Last night it was like you had never left. They didn't seem to care where you had been or what you had been doing or why you had been gone for so long. They seemed happy just to have you back."

A strange, jolting laugh supplanted her tears. "You have a lot to learn about Thai culture."

Rob released Jam from his embrace, but she clung tenaciously to his arms, holding on as though she might lose him forever if physical contact was terminated. "What are you saying?" he said. "That they were faking affection? Pretending?"

"So much pain can easily be concealed."

That the mirth and lively banter of a family reunion could be part of an elaborate, even if subconscious plot to bury truth, was an atrocity. Rob felt his composure evaporating as invidious thoughts marched triumphantly into his mind, as though they belonged there and were simply reclaiming territory which was rightfully theirs. He suddenly felt angry, disappointed and hopeless, and he would have soon found a way to personify those feelings with action, except for the unexpected appearance of Noy.

"Take your hands off her!"

Noy stormed towards Rob with his right fist cocked. He covered the distance between them in the blink of an eye. Jam screamed as he leapt. Rob swerved and the angry blow cut through empty space. He spun around and reloaded his weapon, but this time struck out with his foot. Caught off guard as he sat in expectation of a punch, Rob received the hit to his stomach and collapsed, winded. He looked up to see Noy descending upon him. He heard Jam scream again.

"Stop it! What are you doing?"

Rob raised his arms to protect himself and once the weight of Noy rested on him, he locked on and twisted the man's body back into the air. Flung to the ground in an arc, Noy hit the dirt and rolled against one of the thick pots which supported the house. He grunted. Both men scrambled to their feet and faced off, before Jam stepped between them.

"Stop it, I said!"

Irate now more than frightened, Jam held her ground in the middle of the tempest. She looked quickly from Rob's face to her brother's and back again, casting a warning, pleading for an end to the violence.

"What's wrong with you, Noy? Why did you attack Rob?"

Breathing heavily and rubbing his side, he seemed more willing to continue the skirmish than to talk. His truculence incited Jam to further rage. "Answer me," she demanded.

Finally and with great effort, Noy calmed himself sufficiently to speak. His words were nonetheless suffused with bitter animosity. "I came back to talk to him, and tell him he was not welcome here and he should leave."

"He *is* welcome," said Jam.

Rob felt the tension dissipate as he listened to the conversation which was *about* him but excluded him. Noy did not look at him. He was having trouble maintaining eye contact with Jam, and Rob appreciated his difficulty. Jam could be ferocious. Tempestuousness was clearly a family trait.

"He is not welcome by *me*."

Jam turned her back on Rob, allowing him to retreat. "Who made *you* master of this house?"

Noy had no authority and he knew it. Clearly, he was not claiming to speak on behalf of his brother or father. For whatever reason, he was antagonistic towards Rob and had taken the opportunity to abscond from his duties in the field to deliver a personal rejection. Thus effectively rebuked by his older sister, he lapsed into sullen silence.

"Well?" demanded Jam. "What gives you the right to insult my guest, and a man our father has already welcomed?"

"Why did you come back?"

The question was a venomous hiss and Rob saw Jam's mouth drop open in response. The implied denunciation in it stunned her, wounded her.

"You don't want *me* here either?"

"I didn't say that," replied Noy, softening his tone.

"You didn't have to say it. I can see it in your eyes and hear it in your voice. You haven't forgiven me, have you?"

The long pause which preceded his answer made his words redundant. "I can't forgive you."

Jam turned away and stumbled towards Rob as though Noy had slapped her face. He stood to catch her as she fell, grief stricken into his arms. Rob kept his eyes on Noy while he consoled Jam, absorbing her tremors and allowing her tears to soak his shirt. He had never seen such an expression of anguish, and although it harrowed him, it also fostered intimacy. Noy stood for some while, paralysed by the acidic exchange with his sister, before finally trudging away back towards the rice fields. He had only taken a few steps when he turned and said, "You have only ripped off the scab by coming back, Jam. Blood is flowing again."

Rob wanted to charge at Noy and cause copious quantities of *his* blood to run, but Jam was fastened to him, and Noy's final taunt had sent her crashing into a fresh paroxysm of sorrow. The promised haven was not to be. Although the family had appeared happy to have Jam home and equally pleased, albeit somewhat reluctantly and suspiciously at first, to welcome Rob, an insidious duplicity had been revealed. If any of the others felt even a fraction of the acrimony which had fuelled Noy's recent behaviour, then Rob and Jam's position would become intolerable for everyone, if it wasn't already. When Jam recovered her composure they would talk, and Rob knew she would be disinclined to leave, despite the toxic atmosphere. Leaving under such circumstances might well slam the door shut and bolt it, locked forever. If they could not be fully reconciled now, then when could they be? Time had not healed anything and the scabrous facade was so thin it had been easily and irreparably torn. Rob recognized the vile potency of un-forgiveness, and it caused him to reflect on his relationship with Shane and their parents. He was hiding from them, trying to avoid their judgments and criticism because he perceived it as antipathy, when in fact it was more likely to be clumsily expressed love.

He needed some soothing words for Jam but everything he rehearsed sounded lame, trite and condescending, so he held his tongue.

Jam whispered into Rob's chest, "I shouldn't have come here."

Rob couldn't argue with her at this point even though he wanted to. He was not without blame, having implicated her in his crime by association, after which he had compelled her into an impossible dilemma. Although she had chosen him, and he had been grateful to a greater extent than his words could describe, her choice had evidently caused her significant pain and was continuing to torture her.

"I don't belong here. Too much has happened. I'm not the same. I'm not a part of this family anymore."

"Don't say that," said Rob as he gently pushed her away from him, and looked into her watery eyes. "Noy is not speaking for the family. He is speaking for himself. You saw how happy your father was last night. How relieved he was."

"My father keeps his own counsel."

"You said that before. Do you mean you think he's faking it? That's contemptible!"

"No." Jam detached herself from Rob and settled on the bench, staring at the ground. "I don't think he's pretending but I don't think he has forgiven me either."

Rob sat beside her and took her hand in his, studying her mournful countenance in profile. "Forgiven you for what?"

"For leaving him, for running away."

"But you explained why you had to go, didn't you, at the time? And they understood and accepted your right to live your own life and make your own decisions. Didn't they?"

She turned her tear stained face to Rob. "You make it sound so simple. You make everything sound so straightforward." She waited in vain for him to respond before saying, "I need a bath. I feel disgusting."

"Is there a bath here? Where?"

Jam smiled and it was as though nothing was amiss. All wrongs righted, all pain removed, all fear obliterated. "Wait here a minute."

He watched her hurry away and marvelled at her recovery. Her improved disposition did nothing however to alter the uncomfortable reality, but it did inspire him to hope maybe something could be done. Maybe there was remedy.

Jam returned wearing a *pa-ka-ma* and carrying another one which she tossed at him when he was within range. "Put this on."

He wrapped the *pa-ka-ma* around his waist, folding it back around the front and gathering the ends before tying them together. He reached underneath to unfasten his pants and carefully lowered them to the ground. Jam handed him a bar of soap and said, "Let's go."

She led him by the hand through some tall grass to a small pond, then into its cool inviting water. When she released his hand and began splashing water over her body, he took the cue and removed his shirt. He tossed it on the bank of the pond and wet his body. Jam was using a bowl which she handed to him.

"This is a bath?"

She lowered herself underneath the water, then rose, dripping, glistening streams rolling along her perfect skin. Rob's curiosity had worn off, and he became aroused watching Jam wash herself. He moved closer to her. Her *pa-ka-ma* was expertly tight across her chest, covering her breasts, and he wished she had the same dearth of skill which led to his coming loose as a result of the encouragement of the moving water and his erection. She allowed the invasion of her privacy as he tugged at the knot holding her *pa-ka-ma* in place, then kissed her nipples each in turn. She sighed as they melted into each other and made love standing in the cool water. The sun blessed their connubial intercourse. It was the first time but it didn't feel like it. Jam showed no reluctance to surrender her body to him.

When they finished, they embraced, standing in beautiful silence in the harmonious solitude of physical intimacy. After a while, Rob lifted his head from Jam's shoulder, opened his eyes and saw Noy watching from the other side of the pond.

Chapter Twenty-six

To say Shane's first day back at work was awkward would have been like describing the Pacific Ocean as a sea, or the Grand Canyon as *big*. It was going to have to be the greatest performance of his career, perhaps even of his life. He was going to try to convince everyone, his colleagues and students that he was okay, when he knew he was far from okay. Knowing he had to, at some point, return to work and attempt to resume normal transmission had not made it any easier. He only took two weeks because he could not see any point in taking more. Fourteen of the worst days in his life had him desperate to get back to work, to find something else to focus on other than his unending misery. He had tried distancing himself from things which reminded him of Angela, including taking the difficult decision to sell the house and move. His job was a reminder as well, and it was not safe either, not for any number of reasons, but he could not leave until he had somewhere to go. Easyspeak was dead in the water. He buried it deep in the earth with Angela's corpse. Shane was in the process of reinventing himself because it seemed the only logical way for him to move on. Nothing could possibly stay the way it was, but he had no intention of making any rash decisions. That wasn't his style.

When he arrived at work, he went straight to Sabeen's office and knocked on the door.

"Come in," she said. He entered and she added, "Welcome back. How are you?"

Shane smiled. "Fine, thank you." And with those words it began, his attempt to resume the normal conduction of life, to get back on the saddle. He continued, "I'm ready to get back to work."

Sabeen looked at him with all too familiar pity. "I..."

He helped her by not waiting for her to finish her sentence. "I know. Thank you."

She smiled weakly and he excused himself.

Opening the classroom door brought with it an automatic reaction of preparedness, of duty and his readiness to do his job. He surveyed the room and found everything exactly as he had left it, aside from the students. There would be questions from some of them too and expressions of sympathy. How would he deal with them? Would he be tolerant?

Grief was a universal emotional process which no one could escape. As certain as death, was the assurance that those left behind, the loved ones remaining in this life, mourned the dead. Everyone reacted differently but within a framework of stages of grief. A range of emotions might be experienced with varying degrees of intensity, and for longer or shorter periods of time. There were no rules for how long these stages took but psychologists posited some generalities. Shane had heard them talked about before in the abstracted isolation of films and other people's lives and he had seen it in people he knew, but he had never experienced it himself. Death had not touched him. None of his friends had been stolen by tragic accidents or disease, and his parents were still alive. His grandparents had all passed in his early childhood. He wondered why he had been left untouched. Why were some people victims of tragedy and misfortune while others escaped unscathed by the reaper's scythe? Why were some untouched by the arrows of calamity and unaffected by the dark depths of misery?

"Hello teacher," said Melisendra, floating into the room as her words wafted in Shane's direction. "Welcome back. How are you?"

How many times would he be asked that question? How many times had he been asked that question? Sometimes, *how are you,* was a de facto hello - a rhetorical question functioning as a greeting. Melisendra, among other marvellous attributes, was a genuinely caring person and she would not bother with the question if the answer was of no consequence. Shane summoned a smile with a misery binding incantation. '"Okay, thank you."

Melisendra smiled with precise empathy and left the conversation without requiring more of him. He blessed her for that.

Other students rolled in and took their seats amid the usual hum of perfunctory greetings and the allocation of bottoms on seats and bags below them. A few threw cautious glances Shane's way as though afraid of more commitment. Many of them would have experienced pain at least the equivalent, or in a number of cases, way beyond his own. Some were refugees from war torn countries; Akote, for example, forced from his home in Burundi into a refugee camp in Kenya, and from there finally to Australia more than four years later. Losing family members at each stage of his journey to freedom and safety, his loved ones falling away, like Autumnal leaves tossed to the ground by merciless winds. Scarred for life, with deep psychological wounds for which a lifetime of relentless compassion might perhaps provide inadequate healing. Healing, maybe some injuries never healed and victims simply had to learn to live with pain.

"Morning everyone," said Shane. "Welcome to Monday and another week of learning. Are you ready to have your minds expanded? Are you ready to learn?"

There were mumbles here and there, fear flickering on some of the faces and edgy uncertainty with the embedded question of what they were going to have to do today. It was no doubt worse this particular Monday. Shane had been off work for two weeks on compassionate leave and his absence had been explained to the class by Sabeen, with his permission. It was better to talk about it. Death was a part of life, pretending it wasn't or that it would not come, or that a person could be unaffected by the sting of its tendrils was foolish.

"I've been away," said Shane, who surprised himself with the sudden realization he wanted to talk about Angela's death. He had not planned to do that. In fact, he had decided he would certainly *not* do that, but the words were bubbling on his lips even as his heart rate jumped. "My wife, Angela was killed in an accident on the day I had to leave class suddenly. She was hit by a car and suffered fatal head injuries. I didn't get to say goodbye to her although she might have heard me speaking to her when I sat by her bed and watched her sleep." Unable to continue, because the word *sleep* seemed to have such dreadful poignancy, Shane looked around the room at the faces of his students and registered their surprise. Some had followed his normal speed oratory and among that group there was an awkward unspoken understanding. Others had clearly been left behind as Shane raced off down the road to disclosure without bothering to strap them in for the ride. He realized then that he was not speaking to them anyway.

"Anyway, life must go on. We must go on, so let's get to work." With those words, Shane pulled the plug on the tension and there was an immediate repose for everyone, himself included. "It's Monday, and on Mondays I like to hear about what you did on the weekend."

It was a motorized call to language acquisition, an automatic instruction which Shane had delivered more times than he could remember. Routine was the ultimate safe haven from emotional distress. As the words rolled off his tongue, liberated from the chokehold of sentiment, he felt control returning triumphantly. He could do this. He could carry on, immersing himself in his work, diving in to teaching and encouraging, and even the disheartening threat of paperwork promised to help Shane move forward. He knew how much he needed to escape the grip of depression which had taken residence in his mind. Death on Two Legs was a wonderful song by Queen, not a description of himself with which he could abide.

With a flurry of activity, the class began their writing task. Sheets of paper were removed from the scrap paper box and dictionaries removed from the shelf. Shane wandered around to ensure everyone was on task and offered some encouragement for the reluctant writers, before returning to his desk where he settled into a reflective frame of mind. His mother came to mind instantly, and in particular the conversation he had with her at the wake following Angela's funeral.

"Have you said anything to anyone?" asked Maureen.

Shane shook his head.

"When was the last time you spoke?" She took hold of both of his hands and implored him with her eyes.

He met his mother's worried look and decided to abruptly end the vow of silence he had taken that morning. "I spoke to myself in the mirror this morning when I was debating whether or not to speak today."

"I see."

Maureen Archer was a wizard with words, equally competent with succinct verbal punches as she was with verbose wrestling, whatever was required. *I see,* was one of her jewels. Never were two more powerful words uttered than these from his mother's mouth. *I see* had many possible meanings, and often it was left to the hearer to determine which of them was most applicable in any given situation. Here, Shane guessed it meant that his mother thought his behaviour was childish and inappropriate and that he should grow up and deal with his feelings like a man.

"You need to talk about how you feel," said Maureen. "And I don't mean making inane conversation with yourself in the mirror."

Shane looked into his mother's eyes and then at the ground as she continued. "How you feel is completely natural and normal, and you know of course that you aren't the only person to have ever lost someone you love. Accept your feelings. Don't fight them. Don't bottle it all up inside. It's a miracle you didn't explode at some point today from the pressure of faking composure." She glanced at her watch. "There's still time for that, I guess."

"I'll be all right, mum."

Maureen's eyes widened in despair where Shane had hoped to see something else. "This isn't a beer commercial, Shane. You can't just raise a stubbie to the sky and wink at your misfortune as though it were piffle."

"Good word, mum."

"Stop being flippant."

"What do you want me to say?" Shane's posture stiffened. "That I'm sad? Heartbroken? Miserable?"

"That would make a good start."

"What's the point of stating the obvious?"

Maureen grasped Shane's hands again and squeezed them. "Because what lies beneath the obvious is the crux; the heart of the matter. When the heart is laid bare the depths are plumbed and real healing can occur."

Shane groaned. "God, mum, you're not going to run me over with platitudes, are you?" He heard the words *run over* echoing around inside his head like the thunderous booming of New Year's Eve fireworks among Sydney's skyscrapers.

"It's not a platitude," she said, "And don't use God's name in vain, especially when He could help."

"Don't start."

Maureen's hands shot up in surrender.

"And don't tell me God understands my pain, or that time will heal my wounds. What if I like this pain? What if I deserve it?"

"What?" Maureen's outrage took Shane off guard. "Why would you deserve to suffer? Angela's death was an accident. God forbid you should even think of blaming yourself. Why do you think you deserve to suffer?"

"It's nothing. Forget it."

When she grabbed his hands again, he pulled away in petulant anger.

"I won't forget it," she said, "I won't allow you to beat yourself up. Tell me why you won't let go."

"Let go of what?" Shane hated the anger in his voice but it seemed to be operating independently.

"Let go of Angela. Let go of yourself and your anger, your sorrow, your bitterness. Yes, you sound bitter as though you have been inflicted with some cruel justice. Let it all go. Let it out. That's what I mean by talking about how you feel. Inside your head, your thoughts can be tyrants. Your doubts, your fears, your unanswered questions can become horrible monsters which bully and maul you. Speaking about them disarms them. It strips your negative thoughts of their power.'

"Now it's psychology one zero one."

"I'm going to forgive your lack of respect because I know you are not yourself, and I am going to state it again, very clearly; let it go."

A rush of anger erupted from Shane. "I don't want to let the pain go!"

"Why?" Maureen placed a comforting hand on Shane's shoulder. "Why won't you let the pain go?"

Shane refocussed his eyes when he realized he was staring at the computer monitor. He glanced up and around the room to see the students working in silence. He snatched a nearby pen and scribbled on a scrap of paper in front of him. *The pain is all I have left.* He had thought about the conversation with his mother many times since, replaying it over and over again, until it felt as though it happened seconds ago rather than nearly two weeks ago. She had been right of course, to push him, and correct in her assertion that he needed to release his emotions rather than battle to suppress them. It was plainly stupid and counterproductive for him to cling to his suffering as though he needed it to survive. Nevertheless, he had carried on with his morbid self-destruction, believing he lacked the strength to say good-bye to Angela, to finally accept her death and the deep piercing of his soul as facts which would persist. Immutable truths could not be denied because along that path lay insanity. He was not dead, and it was about time he stopped acting as though he was.

When the morning tea break arrived, he first staved off Sabeen's attempts to engage him in some kind of first session back debrief, then telephoned Rob. There was no answer and Shane felt a jolt of anxiety. It seemed like a long time since he had last spoken to Rob, too long. He had said he was fine and Shane had left it at that, a decision he now regretted.

Chapter Twenty-seven

"I just saw Noy. I don't know what he saw. Maybe he came after we had finished, but still it would have been pretty obvious what was going on."

Jam froze. "Where is he?" She turned quickly, looking all around. "I don't see him."

"He's gone now. Probably off to let your father know."

Her eyes found Rob's and she smiled. "Oh well."

"Oh well?"

"I'm not a child. If I want to make love to my fiancé, I will. There's no law against it."

"Did you say *fiancé*?"

Still water enveloped their naked bodies to waist height. There were no other sounds besides their breathing as Rob searched her face for confirmation. Her eyes widened, sparkling, reflecting the sunlight which frolicked on the surface of the pond. "Did I? Oops."

"I don't understand."

"Let's get out of the water now."

Rob gently took hold of Jam's arm to prevent her escape. "Jam, are you accepting my marriage proposal? Did you mean to say fiancé? I mean, since we arrived here you have been pretty coy and I thought we were playing the friend card not the boyfriend one, and certainly not the fiancé one. What's going on?"

She took his face in both hands and kissed his lips softly. "I think I love you and I want to marry you."

"When did this happen?"

"When did what happen?"

"You love me? You've never said that before, and to be honest I hadn't seen much if any evidence of it, until just now."

Jam waded out of the pond and on to the embankment. Rob followed and watched her as she secured her *pa-ka-ma* across her chest. She twisted her long hair in a thick knot and squeezed it, before flinging it about to dry. Countless drops flicked against Rob as he stood and waited for her to respond.

"Where's yours?" she asked. Following Rob's blank look she delivered a more precise question. "You aren't wearing anything. Where is your *pa-ka-ma*?"

She sat while he went to retrieve his missing garment. "I've been confused," she said.

Rob wound the saturated *pa-ka-ma* around his waist and tied it off before sitting beside her. The sun felt pleasant but that would not last. "Go on," he said, as he worried about the potential transience of her newly discovered love for him.

"I did not expect to fall in love, and I don't think I recognized it when it first happened. It was something new and baffling. It was pleasurable and painful, and it still is but I guess I thought it would all be beautiful and sweet and romantic. It has been but it's been awful too. When you asked me to marry you, I really thought you were stupid and a part of me wanted to tell you that, but another part of me was flattered, and that part did not want to hurt your feelings. I didn't really know what to do with the situation or how I felt. It was all so new and unexpected."

"So you stalled, you put me off?"

Jam looked straight ahead as she spoke, staring as though she was reading an autocue floating on the surface of the pond. "I thought if I waited, you would either change your mind, or get sick of waiting and just leave, or I would get more comfortable with the idea of caring for someone other than myself. I wanted someone else or something else, some external event to make a decision for me. My world, until I met you, was about me and my needs. My need to survive, to make money and to...I didn't know what I was doing. Leaving here was a selfish decision. I see that now, and I understand it was wrong."

Rob wondered why Jam had waited until now to share her heart with him. Since he had killed Pee Lek and fled to her for help, he had not thought about anything except escaping. He loved Jam and wanted her to not only help him but come with him. Nevertheless, he had not really thought their relationship was going anywhere. Even the word *relationship* suggested something more than what he perceived existed. Rather than warming to him and the idea of marrying him over time, Jam had seemed to drift further away, and her sarcastic acrimony whipped him with every word she uttered. Could she really be saying what he thought she was saying? After so long, and with so much to suggest otherwise, was she going to give herself to him and accept his marriage proposal. He forced himself to breath. Having sex was surprising enough, but her radical change of heart stretched credulity.

"I really don't belong here," continued Jam. "I'm not the innocent young girl who left with high hopes and fanciful dreams. I'm different."

"Everyone changes."

"My family haven't changed," replied Jam. "Apart from Som marrying Ohn and having a baby, they live how they used to live. Maybe that's why Noy is so angry. Maybe I remind him of what he sees as imprisonment."

"Why doesn't he leave then, if he's so unhappy?"

"Obligation," said Jam. She patted him on the thigh and stood up. "Let's go."

They walked through the long grass in silence, hand in hand, as the sun strengthened to intimidating heat and pounded upon them. Rob felt like returning to the pond.

"Maybe," said Jam, picking up the thread of conversation as though they had been interrupted. "It wasn't until I came back that he saw his own predicament. While I was gone and out of contact they may well have imagined the worst..." The salience of her words dumbfounded her. Her voice cracked, her emotions choking her once again.

Rob squeezed her hand but said nothing.

"He might have felt justified in the assumption that me leaving was dangerous and stupid and would not end well, but when I came back and he saw me healthy and happy, it tore down the foundation of his belief. I was, without meaning to, slapping him in the face saying to him; *see you were wrong. You were wrong about me and wrong about this life.* Perhaps that's why he is so angry."

"And then there's me," suggested Rob. "No doubt my presence is not helpful. He's alone. Som has Ohn, and you have me. Even though we didn't say as much, they must have figured it out, and I think our little marine romp proved it beyond a shadow of a doubt. He doesn't have anyone. Maybe it's simple jealousy that he's expressing."

"Maybe." Jam stopped and turned to face Rob. "I do love you, and I'm sorry for being such a bitch."

"Apology accepted."

They embraced quickly, furtively, as though they were doing something illicit and perhaps being watched. They walked on and Rob said, "So what now?"

"Now I tell my family I am not staying and that you and I are going to get married."

"That won't make anyone happy."

"We'll be happy and that's all that matters."

It was difficult for Rob to keep pace with his changing fortunes. His thinking had been short term for some time now, restricted by his circumstances and by his unwillingness to commit to anything beyond the immediate. He considered marriage and was instantly hit with a barrage of questions; who would marry them, and where, and when? Where would they live? What would he do? What would Jam do? Answers were as scarce as koalas in Thailand's imported eucalyptus trees. Next, he pondered his future on the run from the law. More questions rushed upon him; were the Thai police coming after him? Were they looking for him right now? Would they track him down wherever he went, to the ends of the earth? What punishment would he receive? Jail? Certainly. Death? Did they have the death penalty for capital offences in Thailand?

"Rob?"

"Yes?"

"That's all that matters, right?"

He managed a weak smile which was a stinging indictment of his misgivings. "There are a few other things we need to think about."

With characteristic perceptiveness, Jam received his unspoken message and the optimism drained from her face.

They arrived back to find Ohn reclining on a cane lounge under the house. A string joined her finger to a hammock in which lay her son and she tugged it gently every so often to rock him.

"Have you been for a wash? You were gone a long time?"

Rob answered quickly, "We were very dirty." He laughed at his joke first, then at Ohn's bemused expression. "We're all clean now."

"We're going to get dressed then we're going into town. We'll be back for lunch," said Jam.

"Are you going to stay?" asked Ohn.

The question threw up a wall in front of Jam, stopping her in her tracks. She looked at Rob, then at Ohn, before slowly walking back towards her. She squatted beside her sister-in-law.

Ohn said, "You don't need to answer me now. You already have."

"This isn't my home, anymore. It's yours. You belong here. You're happy here, aren't you?"

Ohn smiled; "very happy. But what will you do?"

Rob kept his distance and listened.

"The truth is we can't stay, even if I wanted to. We have to go. Rob has to go and I want to be with him."

"So we're finally dropping the charade are we?" She raised her eyebrows and glanced towards Rob.

"What charade?" asked Jam.

A slightly embarrassed laugh escaped Jam which Ohn fortunately joined. "Okay," said the latter. "Your secret is safe with me."

"Actually," said Rob. "It's not that much of a secret anymore. Noy saw us at the pond."

"Bathing?"

"You could call it that," replied Rob.

"Ayy!" exclaimed Ohn as she playfully slapped Jam's shoulder. "Ridiculous!"

"You know he'll run off and tell father straight away," said Ohn. "He's like that. Father won't be impressed."

Jam stood, stepping back away from Ohn and glancing at her nephew. Rob knew exactly what Jam was thinking; if father knew what she had been up to for the last few years, he would think nothing at all of a naked romp in a secluded pond. All those men and all those favours, he would be mortified, and Rob hoped to God he never discovered the truth. He didn't need to know. Jam had not been hurt or abused, impregnated or infected. She had been very lucky. He had heard horrible stories and seen the evidence of cruelty and depravity with his own eyes. His desperation to rescue Jam from Lipstick was infinitely much more than mere prudishness. She caught his eye and smiled knowingly.

"Father will have to accept I am not his baby girl anymore. I am a woman."

A brief silence intruded, during which Rob moved towards the stairs with the intention of dressing. Ohn's next question to Jam halted his progress, though it was the answer which interested him more.

"Are you going to marry him?"

"I am."

Jam skipped over to join Rob at the foot of the stairs and took hold of his hand, pressing it to the side of her face. "I am," she repeated. "I will. I do."

They changed in separate rooms because that's where their clothes were, and Rob knew it was just as well because he doubted he would have been able to resist throwing Jam on the mattress and making love to her again. He tucked the evidence of his arousal inside his underpants and pulled on a pair of shorts, topping it off with a clean white T-shirt with the Singha beer logo on it. He headed back down to wait for Jam and discovered Ohn feeding her baby. He maintained a respectful distance but did not wish to squirm in feigned invisibility.

"He's a beautiful baby."

"Thank you," said Ohn. "Will you have children with Jam one day?"

Rob was taken aback, despite the obvious naturalness of the question. He had honestly never considered being a parent. Although of course it was assumed and customary and perfectly in order, it had never crossed his mind that he could or would father a child.

"It's not a trick question."

"What's not a trick question?" said Jam as she joined them.

"I asked Rob if you and he were going to having children and he seemed to struggle to answer."

Jam took hold of Rob's arm and squeezed it gently. "We'll probably have dozens. We might even have made a start in the pond."

"Oo- bart!" scolded Ohn. "Get out of here before you embarrass us even more."

"I'm not embarrassed," said Jam.

"See you for lunch," said Ohn, before returning her full attention to her son as he suckled at her breast.

The journey back to town was significantly quicker than the trip in but that was always the way. Perception coloured reality but did not alter it. Rob was sanguine about his prospects, *their* prospects, now that Jam had committed herself to him. Uncertainty loomed ominously on the horizon like thunderclouds, but Rob felt confident that together they would survive whatever storms may assail them.

Once in town, they quickly found a *raan* and Rob took a seat as Jam ordered food for them. She came to the table with a can of Coke and a glass filled with ice cubes. She sat, opened the can and poured Coke into Rob's cup before filling her own glass with water. She sipped it and smiled at him. A newspaper lay folded on an adjacent vacant table and Rob grabbed it absently, even though he could not read Thai. He amused himself with the pictures while Jam babbled on about how nice it was that Som had found a wife, and how lovely she was and how beautiful the baby was, and how she would love to be a mother one day. Rob listened carelessly, nodding where he felt it appropriate. Leafing through the pages, he was again astounded by the graphic photographs of the victims of crime which were published. Horrible, disturbing images which made him think of Pee Lek. Had his body been discovered, a photograph published, and a manhunt for his murderer commenced? Were they coming for him while he sat casually enjoying the company of his fiancé in relative safety and anonymity?

Their food arrived and just as he was about to fold the paper and lay it aside, a face in the newspaper grabbed his attention. His mouth dropped open and his eyes popped.

"What's wrong?" asked Jam.

"My photo is in this newspaper."

She snatched it from his hands and placed her finger on the text as though it would help her read faster.

"What does the headline say?" he asked.

Jam lowered the paper and fixed him with a grim stare. "It says, *wanted*."

Chapter Twenty-eight

Having broken through the pall which desensitized him and obscured all goodness from his sight, Shane cruised through the remainder of the day. Instinct took over and he revelled once more in the dynamic of teaching, riding the lows of frustration to the highs of achievement. It was as though he had never been gone and had not suffered a cruel and debilitating bereavement. The facts had not changed, past circumstances were fixed forever now but Shane experienced a lightening of spirit for which he was grateful and to which he clung as though his life depended on it.

Sabeen came in to see him after class. She carried a novel awkwardness with her and it pervaded the room as she cautiously approached Shane's desk. Less afraid now of the inevitable irritation arising from the predictable question, Shane smiled at her and eased back in his seat.

"You look happier," she said, pausing before adding, "That's good. I take it your first day back in here went okay."

For some reason, Angela's death had also killed the lascivious nature of his relationship with Sabeen. He still recognized and appreciated her beauty, but the desire to flirt with her and to push the envelope of propriety had gone. That, in Sabeen's own words, was *good.* On reflection, he realized Melisendra had not disarmed or disoriented him either, the way she so carelessly and effortlessly had done on numerous occasions.

Naturally, he could not continue with his flirtatious and unfaithful ways even though now he would only be intellectually and emotionally cheating on Angela's memory. Death had parted them. It no longer felt right or even necessary to carry on philandering, and it had never been justified in the first instance. He was wrong, and despite the fact Angela was dead and he could not apologize to her, and more than likely she no longer even cared about him, or remained cognizant of his existence, Shane felt righteous. He had won a hard fought battle, but it had cost him dearly.

"Shane?"

He shook his head theatrically. "Sorry, my mind drifted away."

Sabeen smiled sympathetically. "Why don't you leave early today?"

"I have some work to do. Leaving it for tomorrow won't make it disappear."

They held each other's gaze for a moment and Shane wondered what else she might say. He was finished and wanted her to leave. "See you tomorrow then," he said, hoping it did not sound rude. Sabeen did not deserve impoliteness, but she did have the right to know and understand things had changed between them. The referee had blown the full time whistle on whatever game it was they had been playing.

Sabeen nodded. Her eyes still searching Shane's as the message sunk in. "Okay. See you tomorrow, and again..." she hesitated, strangely unsure of herself, almost sheepish, "It's good to have you back."

Shane removed his eyes from her the moment she turned to leave, and he ignored her exit altogether. His thoughts returned to Rob, so he picked up the phone and dialled his number.

"I have some bad news," said Shane, when Rob answered after only two rings.

"I know about Angela," he said. "Mum called me. I'm so sorry, mate. I've been trying to call you."

"I've been off the air. Off the planet actually."

"Of course," said Rob. "Listen, I'm coming home."

"You don't need to do that."

"Actually, I do."

"Seriously, I'll be okay."

"The world doesn't revolve around you mate."

His brother's voice was edgy, lined with tension. Shane was aware of the need to tread lightly in order to avoid aggravating Rob and forcing him to clam up and hang up. "Sorry. Sorry."

"Talk about bloody narcissism. Is that your photo in the dictionary under the word narcissist, is it? I thought I recognized you."

"Calm down. I said I was sorry. What's going on with you? Why do you need to come home?"

Rob's silence shouted down the line.

Shane continued. "Last time we spoke you told me you were fine when I asked, but you're not fine, are you?"

"Not exactly," admitted Rob.

"Do you remember that time when dad grounded you because you were being a smartarse?" said Shane.

"Yes," said Rob after a mystified pause.

"You were a smartarse, but that's beside the point. You had lined up a meeting with Jantra I think, or Debbie, and you told me when dad was out of earshot you were going to go, grounded or not grounded, with permission or without it. I told you that you would get into even worse trouble but it was your call, and you said?"

"I'll see you later then."

"Yeah, then you left, but not before making me promise not to tell mum or dad where you were going."

"And you didn't tell them," said Rob.

Rob laughed suddenly as though Shane's cute little boyhood story had severed the ropes which bound them in discomfort. "You know I ran down the street as though Dad was chasing me. I really thought he would know I had gone and would come straight after me, and I reckoned I could outrun him, but I still kept out of sight as much as I could as I headed down Ultimo Street. Ducking in and out of people's front yards, always looking over my shoulder, expecting dad to come rumbling down the road towards me at any moment. My heart was pounding. Shit, that was exciting! When I made it to the train station, I was still convinced dad was in red hot pursuit and would eventually catch me, so I went in to the ladies' toilets and hid in a cubicle until the train arrived."

Although the story was an old and oft repeated one, the two brothers laughed together like it was the first time they had heard it. It was the first time since Angela's death that Shane had laughed, and as he staggered out of the mirth, struggling to compose himself, he felt the stench of death dissipate. The filth of his grief was purged from his mind. Release had come so unexpectedly that it was frightening, and a flicker of guilt flashed through him.

"Anyway," said Rob. "Is there a point to the retelling of this little story? Don't get me wrong. It's as funny as hell but were you trying to say something?"

"I can't bloody remember."

More laughter followed.

"You're an idiot Shane. Fair dinkum."

A burst of sobriety hit Shane and he felt ashamed for being flippant, and for laughing and having fun as though the world was all as it should have been. As though he had not lost that which was most precious to him, and as if his brother was not embroiled in a major situation which he was refusing to disclose. "Tell me what's going on, Rob. You can trust me and I want to help if I can."

Another long, disquieting pause ensued.

"Shane, I have to go. There's a cop outside. He just pulled up out the front, I have to go."

"Wait Rob. Wait!"

The line went dead and Shane stared at his phone, wishing the screen could come to life and transmit images of his brother, so he would not be forced to sit there and imagine the worst.

Chapter Twenty-nine

"Let's go, Jam."

Rob hung up on Shane and stood and grabbed Jam's wrist, all in one smooth, albeit alarm stricken movement. The table reacted with displeasure to the jolt it received from his knee, and Jam nearly fell with the force. His hips hit shoulders and more tables on his way out of the *raan*, and murmurs of disapproval clung to his back like beads of sweat. The policeman was still sitting on his motorbike and looking straight ahead when Rob and Jam catapulted themselves into his field of vision. Rob stared at him waiting for the unavoidable flash of recognition and the hot pursuit which must ensue, but the cop remained oblivious. Rob was too hyped to slow down now, even though the immediate danger had passed, if in fact it had even existed.

"That was a bit of an overreaction, don't you think?" said Jam, as they scuttled off down the street away from the potentially problematic policeman.

"My fucking face is in the newspaper."

Jam halted suddenly, jerking Rob to a stop. "Don't talk to me like that."

"Sorry, but seriously. If I held any delusions about the authorities forgetting my murderous action and just chalking Pee Lek's demise up to another Bangkok lowlife death by misadventure, then I was badly mistaken."

Jam frowned with incomprehension.

"Let's just go. I can't stay here. In Thailand I mean. I have to go back to Australia as soon as possible. Where's that damn minibus? We need to get back to your dad's place."

"Slow down," pleaded Jam. "Please."

The bus station loomed in the near distance and Rob pressed on, pulling Jam along behind him. The crowd thickened as they approached, reducing his run to a fast walk. The smell of barbecued corn filled his nostrils and soon after that the tantalising aroma of chicken roasting on a street side spit. Food vendors were calling out to him, to anyone, spruiking the delights of the wares, even though their customers were already lined up two and three deep. The crowd condensed to a crush and a real struggle began to push through the thronging masses. Rob could feel Jam's small hand safe inside his. He assumed he was heading in the right direction and if he wasn't she would let him know.

She tugged his hand and he stopped and turned to look at her.

"Our bus is there waiting." She gestured with her free hand. "But there are two policemen on it."

"Shit."

"We can take the next one," said Jam.

"How often do they run?"

"Every fifteen minutes."

"And until then, what?" said Rob, fighting panic. "Stand around like shags on a rock. Like sitting ducks."

"What are you talking about now?"

There were times when Rob really resented having to explain his self, and although it was grossly unfair, he blamed her for not understanding whatever colloquialism he trotted out. Now was not the time for explanations or English lessons. He lacked the patience for teaching at the best of times, didn't understand how Shane could put up with it. Jam's English was good but if he strayed too far outside of normal usage, which he often did, then she got lost. Neither could she cope with alacrity of speech, he needed the occasional reminder to slow down. This was not the time for any of this nonsense and he cursed himself for wasting energy on such a trivial inner banter.

"The police are looking for me, Jam. Don't you understand? If I just stand around here, I may as well wear a sign saying; *I'm a murderer, come and arrest me*."

"What if the police haven't seen your picture?"

"Don't be so naive," said Rob, again with much less tact than he would have preferred. "Who do you think put the picture there? The picture in the newspaper isn't *for* the police. It's *from* them. They'll be talking to each other, exchanging faxes or e-mails and sending communiqués from Bangkok with a more detailed description of me. I'm screwed."

The crowd jostled around them, flowing like a river around a half sunken branch. They stood their ground, while Rob kept his eyes on the police in the mini bus. He let out his breath violently when the bus exited the station. Looking at his watch he reckoned there was at least ten minutes before another bus appeared, and if no cops showed up in the next fifteen, he would be safely away. He pulled his shirt away from his chest and back and adjusted the crotch of his pants. He could smell himself now.

"How did they get a photo of you?"

Rob shook his head. "I need some water. Do you have any?"

"Over there, closer to the bus stop. It's safe now, isn't it?" said Jam.

"I honestly don't know if I am ever going to feel safe again."

Jam pushed past him and forged on through the crowd towards a vending cart. He followed in her wake and when they reached the cart she ordered two waters and handed over a baht for each. Rob drank greedily, guzzling the cold water. Half the bottle had disappeared by the time he lowered it from his mouth. Aware of Jam's studious gaze, he ignored it and continued to survey the terminal, searching in every direction for any sign of police. He glanced again at his watch, five more minutes until the bus arrived, ten more to escape, for now anyway.

"Really Rob," said Jam. "I'm very curious about the photo, aren't you?"

Rob maintained his surveillance in silence.

"Do you remember anyone taking your photo, or you giving a photo to anyone?" she asked, refusing to let the matter drop, despite Rob's reluctance.

"Why would I do that?"

Jam shook her head. "Look. The bus is here."

Rob turned quickly to see it pull in and disgorge its load of passengers. He scrutinized every face, making sure they weren't even remotely interested in him and more importantly that none of them wore a uniform. He glanced again at his watch and sipped some more water. He scuffed the ground with his shoes as the last of the passengers exited the bus and an excited and intemperate group of people heaved towards the empty vehicle, hurrying to fill it once more. Rob and Jam joined the movement, and soon they were climbing the steps of the bus. Jam paid the driver with a hundred baht note and he asked for another one.

"A hundred each," said the driver, pointing at Rob, "One for you and one for the *farang*."

"You bastard," said Jam, snarling as she slapped another bank note into his greedy palm.

Rob was impressed with her restraint, and on any other occasion he might have insisted she take up the fight and protest harder about the driver's unethical behaviour. Unscrupulous locals often charged higher prices and fares for foreigners because they could easily afford it, or so it was assumed. However, now was not the appropriate time to make a scene.

"Don't worry about it, Jam."

"Is his dick bigger than a Thai dick?" said the driver in Thai.

The comment was aimed at her back and she lunged towards the driver, yelling vitriolic curses. Rob intervened to prevent a physical altercation while the driver laughed at his own lewd audacity. "Leave it Jam. Not now, okay." He pushed her along the aisle and into a seat, before sitting beside her.

With the temporary distraction over, Rob resumed his vigil, now concentrating on the door and occasionally glancing out through the windows of the bus. It filled quickly, but not fast enough for Rob's liking as he continued to fretfully expect the appearance of a policeman at any moment. Soon the doors closed and they were off, but even then Rob still anticipated being stopped. When the bus departed from the terminal and the driver changed up a couple of gears, Rob finally relaxed. A loud whoosh escaped his lips and he permitted a tired smile.

"Is this what it's going to be like for us?" said Jam, without looking at him. She continued to stare out through the window.

Rob knew exactly what she meant.

She turned, a film of sadness clouding her eyes. "I mean always running, never being able to relax."

"I wouldn't say *always* or *never*."

"What would you say?"

What could he say? All the reassurances in the world could not alter the reality of his being wanted by the police. Running away had worked so far, for a few days anyway, but what next? He would have to leave Thailand, which was bad enough but he would also have to leave Jam, and God only knew when he would see her again. She might be able to visit him in Australia but she wouldn't be allowed to stay, not until they were married.

Rob placed his hand on her thigh and sighed with relief when she did not flinch. "I would say that I think we should get married as soon as possible. If we were married you could live with me in Australia."

A look of wonder came over Jam's face, not for a second obscuring her pretty features but rather enhancing them. She searched his eyes, then smiled and turned her head.

"What does that mean, Jam?"

She shook her head. "You make it sound so simple."

"It is. It will be."

"It won't be!"

"Keep your voice down. What's the matter?"

"I don't have a passport, and you have probably heard of Interpol, and I'm not sure I want to leave Thailand."

"You already agreed to marry me."

"But I didn't agree to a move to Australia."

"But I thought..."

"You assumed," said Jam, hissing the words out through her teeth. Rob recognized the strain she was under, fighting to remain as calm as possible. Her anger, he had learned, burned on a very short fuse. "You like to make decisions for me, but I want to make decisions for myself. You think you are the most important person in this relationship."

Rob listened, in the knowledge that it was futile to argue with her. There was nothing he could say to mollify her and convince her that she had it all wrong, especially when she had it partly right. He did like making decisions for both of them, as though he had a right to. He knew he often put his own needs before hers, and above everyone else's most of the time. He *was* selfish. Resisting her righteous outburst was out of the question.

"You come in to my life like a typhoon of sweetness and gentleness. You show me more respect than I'm used to, or that I deserve. You treat me like a lady not a whore, and you make me fall in love with you, and now I'm stuck. I want to tell you to get the hell out of my life but I can't."

Rob watched as tears filled her eyes and her words were choked off by a sobbing heave of her chest. She whispered, "I just can't."

Rob embraced her as best he could in the confines of the bus seat and soaked up her pain. He remembered something his mum had told him a long time ago, when he was still a teenager, and the first girl he had ever loved had pulled out his heart and trampled it under her feet.

"Love is painful," she had said, as his sorrow overcame his embarrassment at crying in front of his mother. "In order to get the full benefits of love, to experience its grandeur, you have to be open-hearted and prepared to risk being hurt. It doesn't work any other way. To have love, you need to give love. To truly have someone else's heart, you must be ready to surrender your own."

Rob had gruffly replied. "I suppose you have to keep doing that over and over again."

His mum had nodded. "And do you know what's even worse?"

He'd shaken his head.

"The ones you love the most hurt you the most, even when they don't mean to."

"God, that's a bleak picture you're painting mum."

She'd stroked his hair and said softly. "That's life, my son."

Thinking about his mum caused a lump to form in his throat and it lead to other thoughts about love and suffering, and in the midst of his crumbling, Rob had an epiphany. Love was the only truly invincible addiction, and only the hard hearted were not afflicted.

"I'm sorry," he said to Jam. "I'm sorry but I can't help loving you. I didn't plan to meet you either, and it's way too late to think about life without you. I see no one but you in my past, present and future. I can change for you. I can be less selfish if you help me and are patient with me."

Jam shook her head against his shoulder and kept sobbing quietly.

Chapter Thirty

Shane stood slowly and wandered towards the front of the classroom. Absently picking up the whiteboard eraser, he cleared off a collection of words, phrases and arrows in an assortment of colours. New words and phrases appeared as quickly as he removed the former occupants of the board. Names; Rob, Jam, Angela, Sabeen, Melisendra and Yan Ping. Phrases; in trouble, how to help, why am I thinking about her and I am no longer infatuated with her? What should I do? What next steps? Where am I going? He leaned in close to the board and smelled the ink. The world seemed to have taken on a sharper focus. He heard the air conditioner fan adjust itself automatically. Everything seemed much more vivid and real than it had this morning.

His phone rang so he hurried over to receive the call. Without looking at the screen, he swiped to answer.

"Hello Shane, this is Yan Ping."

Shane's heart stopped as all his energy focussed on the question of whether to hang up or not. *Make a decision, quickly.*

"Shane?"

"Hi."

"Hi. I thought it was going to be like last time. Can you talk now?"

"Uh-huh," said Shane as he struggled for the right words, the right tone of voice. He did want to speak to her, but he didn't know what to say. As she had called him, he decided to let Yan Ping do the talking.

"I'm back in Wollongong now, in a new apartment."

"I see."

'Yes, I'm going to come back to English classes."

"Still no job, eh?"

"My English isn't good enough. I hope you can teach me again at the library like before."

Shane remembered how excruciating those private lessons had been. Yan Ping had paid him for his time, but he had loved every second in her presence. He'd taken every opportunity to invade her personal space, to catch her scent, to touch her hand, to look into her eyes. While she didn't know how he felt, it was nearly impossible to restrain himself and inconceivable that, not only did she sense his desire for her, but also that it was reciprocated. At times, he had felt as though he was taking money from her under false pretences, and he doubted whether her English improved at all. His reminiscing caused no stirring of emotion or arousal.

"Sure.'"

"Can you come and visit me. I bought you a present from China."

"Okay."

Shane was cognizant of the wariness in his voice and the brevity of his responses, but he could not summon any enthusiasm. Yan Ping was inviting him to visit her which is something she would not have done if she was not interested in renewing their relationship. Surely, that was presumptuous, wasn't it? He felt overloaded, overwhelmed and fuzzy headed.

"Can I call you back later tonight?"

"Okay."

Unsettled by the bizarre conversation with Yan Ping and the timing of her re-emergence into his life, Shane hurriedly packed up his stuff, switched off the computer and air conditioner and left the room, determined to walk off the haze. Out on the street, he turned away from the direction where he had parked the car and made towards the hospital as if pulled by an invisible force. With every step he knew where this path would take him, and he argued furiously with himself about the sanity of visiting the spot where Angela had been smashed into the coma from which she never awoke. It would be his first time there since the accident. He had even changed his route to work to avoid the area, and yet he walked on.

He walked past Woolworths and crossed Burelli Street, and up to Crown, turning right after the cinema. A man was standing at the front of the cinema, on the corner, handing out little cards and trying to talk to disinterested and busy people. Shane did not want to stop either, but the man's words arrested his attention and brought him to a sudden stop. He held out his hand and received the tract from the other's hand, as he pondered his answer to the question; what do you think happens after this life? Shane felt uncomfortable under the man's scrutiny, although he sensed nothing malicious about it. He fumbled in his mind, in the secret drawers of his worldview and beliefs, everything he had learned so long ago in Sunday school, but he found nothing. He had no answer, and right now, it seemed impossibly important that he find an answer. He wanted to know where Angela was now.

"My wife was killed in a car accident just over two weeks ago."

The man's face fell. "Oh my God, I am so sorry." He placed a comforting hand on Shane's forearm. Under normal circumstances he would have shrugged it off as an unwanted invasion of his personal space, but he could feel warmth and caring seeping into his arm.

"That's terrible," said the man. "Awful."

Was this all that the street preacher had left, adjectives in a commiserative tone of voice? Where were his words now? Shane needed some words? Shane looked at him and saw genuine compassion in the man's eyes. Why should this guy care so much?

"I have been trying to figure out why?"

The man raised his eyebrows slightly to encourage Shane to continue.

"Why she died? Why did God allow that? Why would God allow that to happen?"

During the pause before the man answered, Shane sensed a rising sadness and feared he would lose control in public. He was about to leave, to break free of the man's loving concern as though it were a prison instead of a healing balm, when the other tightened his grip, and said. "Death is a part of life. Do you want God to keep everyone alive forever? He could save everyone, but would you want him to do that? Think about what that means. To save everyone, God would have to control everyone. We, his children, would be reduced to robots, or puppets. Do you really want God to control everything, to save everyone?"

Shane liberated his arm with a violent wrench and stared at the man. "I would have settled for him just saving one life, just one."

Throwing the piece of paper at the man, Shane turned and stomped away. He was angry but not stupid, and the man's words plagued him all the way up Crown Street, haunting each step. As hard as he tried to erase them or refute the logic, it was not possible.

As Shane neared the scene of Angela's accident, his pace slowed and he felt darkness closing in and a suffocating fear. He did not know exactly what he was afraid of, but tight apprehension enveloped him. He was closer now; at the corner, on the road. An image of Angela's stricken body flashed before his eyes. He stumbled as he moved towards her. He reached for her.

"Careful mate!" a voice yelled at him, and simultaneously yanked him away from the curb as a rush of air slapped his face. He looked up into a concerned face which said, "Are you all right? What's wrong?"

Shane was unable to answer the man, but he managed to nod and smile with sufficient conviction so as to persuade him that he did not need any further assistance. He did, but he did not want to impose on the charity of a stranger. The ‘good Samaritan’ lingered momentarily before nodding and releasing Shane's arms. That was the second time today a stranger had held on to him. He may not have been wearing a sign announcing his desperate helplessness, but there were evidently some incredibly perceptive people coincidently crossing his path. Either that or there were angels floating around. He scoffed in the knowledge that the existence of angels and their legendary benevolence was just another one of his mother's fairy tales.

He shuffled back away from the curb towards the shopfront and leaned against it, concentrating on breathing. Dizziness still disoriented him, and worse than that was his bewilderment about what had happened. There was a dream like quality to the afternoon's events, and he could not fully convince himself that he was not dreaming. When finally he felt composed enough to move, he left without looking again at the road. He determined in that moment to no longer avoid the spot because by doing so he had infused it with a power over him that it should not have had. He must take control, and maintain it. Hell, he had nearly had been decapitated by his wistfulness. If not for the unfamiliar, but thankfully not uncaring soul who had pulled him back from the road, he would have had an instant reply to his outstanding query about the afterlife.

Shane reached into his pocket and extracted his phone. He needed to speak to someone, anyone familiar, and safe. He tapped on the call history icon and again on Yan Ping's number which, although he did not recognize, he knew to have been the last call he received.

"Hello?"

"Is it still okay if I come and see you? You're in Wollongong right?"

"Yes."

"What's your address?"

Shane filed the number away in his memory, he already knew the street. It was only a five minute walk from where he now stood, buzzing with renewed energy and a sprinkling of apprehension.

"Are you alone?"

"My flatmate has gone out."

"Your flatmate? What about your husband?"

An awkward pause; "Didn't I tell you my husband died?"

'What?" Shane stopped walking. Did he know that? Should he have known that? "No," he said. "When? What happened?'

"He had a heart attack on a golf course in Sydney last year."

Walking again now, Shane processed this new information; Yan Ping was single and here in Wollongong, and she wanted to see him. Now seemed like the perfect time to tell her about Angela but the words were stillborn on his tongue, and when he finally did speak, all he said was; "see you soon."

In no time, Shane arrived at Yan Ping's apartment building and buzzed the intercom set on the wall beside the all glass front door. When the door clicked, he entered and proceeded to the lift which he rode to the seventh floor. Completely oblivious to his surroundings, Shane focused on rehearsing his lines. He often ran through what he planned to say to people and anticipated their responses, planning his subsequent answers. It never turned out the way he thought it would, but it seemed to assist in calming his nerves. On this occasion, when he knocked on Yan Ping's door and stood dry mouthed and dizzy, it did provide a modicum of stability.

"Hi," she smiled, and he nearly fell over. She had changed but not unrecognizably. Her hair was shorter, not just bundled as she often used to like to wear it but actually cut short just off her shoulders. Shane studied her, marvelling at the way her radiant beauty had been enhanced in the intervening years. She was stunning.

"Are you going to come in?"

Shane took a few tentative steps and stopped to admire Yan Ping again.

"Stop it," she said without anger. "You're embarrassing me now. Say something."

"You look amazing, so gorgeous. God, I've missed you." The last sentence slipped out. So far nothing had gone according to plan here. He had majorly underestimated the potency of her striking beauty. How could he have forgotten that awesome enchantment he felt whenever he was with her? His had a strong urge to kiss her instantly, but his body rebelled against the spontaneity. The good angel that he didn't even believe in was screaming for self-control.

She turned away, her cheeks reddening. "Would you like a drink? You look thirsty."

"Yes." He followed her into the kitchen and stood on the living room side of the counter. "It really is good to see you again. May I ask why you called? I really never expected to hear from you, though I've always secretly wished for it."

Yan Ping kept her back to him as she made a show of busyness. "What would you like? Tea? Coffee? A cold drink?"

This was so weird. All the while Shane felt weakened and vulnerable in Yan Ping's presence but she was acting as though she held misgivings about the wisdom of their reunion. It seemed she was the one struggling for words, perhaps questioning her motives, trying to find an appropriate answer to his very reasonable question. Despite how he felt inside, it was Yan Ping who was outwardly manifesting the most remarkable discomfiture.

"I lost my wife just over two weeks ago," announced Shane with no introduction.

Yan Ping immediately ceased her fussing and looked at him.

"She was hit by a car just a few blocks from here."

In the early days and weeks of their relationship, Yan Ping had not been especially tactile, preferring to avoid public displays of affection, and fraught even in complete privacy. She had become more affectionate over time, as she relaxed into their status, and an amiable and persistent peace characterised all the time they spent together. Shane watched her now, to see how she would respond. Her frozen demeanour suggested perhaps he should have been more diplomatic in the impartation of his bad news.

She took a single step towards him which he reciprocated. He wanted her to hug him, he wanted to embrace her. He wanted to feel her softness, her feminine suppleness within his arms. She took another step but this time he held his ground. Their eyes met and locked as Yan Ping took another step which brought her within striking distance. Shane hastily examined his motives. Was it Yan Ping he wanted? Or the substitutionary comfort she could provide? He felt arousal stirring and was appalled, but he was falling, and she was the only one there who could catch him.

Chapter Thirty-one

The train journey from Had Yai to Butterworth in Malaysia can be completed in one of two ways. Either comfortably in an air conditioned sleeper carriage, or uncomfortably; upright and hot, bombarded by noise and drenched in sweat, even at night, in a second or third class carriage. If money is not an issue, it is not a difficult choice. The only train departs at ten to six each morning, so it meant an early start for Rob. He tossed through the night, anxious about going to another public place where there would be bucket loads of people, all informed by the newspapers about Rob's heinous act, the smell of money from cash rewards making their collective nostrils twitch.

He had decided to lay low at Jam's place and allow her to do all the leg work for their departure. She had agreed to at least investigate the possibility of her going to Australia with him, although she showed no signs of gleeful enthusiasm. This necessitated a number of frustrating trips to the immigration office where she often received conflicting information, and that was if she even managed to see an immigration official before they closed for business each day. Had Jam known anyone in the office or in the local council, Rob had the financial means to grease the requisite number of palms to make it all happen as fast as possible, but she had no such connections. She needed a passport and a visa but after a week of being given the run around by infuriating bureaucrats, they agreed it wasn't going to happen, not quickly anyway and Rob could not wait any longer.

The atmosphere at Jam's house was tense. Noy still seethed with undisguised hostility. Despite what should have been good news for him, that Rob was leaving, he looked as though he would have preferred Rob to leave in a coffin, rather than on a train. As far as he was concerned, Rob should not have spent another minute in his home, let alone another night. The week had been torturous, and the burden of Noy's animosity was almost sufficient to make Rob leave to go and stay in a hotel but Jam insisted he stay; such indiscretion may have proved disastrous.

Trivial, half-hearted small talk filled the terse air as they rose and prepared to leave. Rob had packed the night before and only needed to change quickly and eat. They left without saying goodbye and the rest of the family slept soundly, at peace with the knowledge that their major problem would be gone when they awoke. It was difficult for Rob to understand the lack of acceptance shown to him by Jam's family, especially Noy. They had made no effort to get to know him.

Silence accompanied Rob and Jam through the early morning darkness until they reached the road leading into town and managed to flag a mini bus. In Had Yai they disembarked at the bus terminal and, as it adjoined the train station, moved quickly from there to the ticket office.

"When you come back, maybe I will show you around. We haven't exactly had time to relax and explore the place. There are many interesting tourist attractions."

"Jam," said Rob, hesitating to destroy the lovely scenario she was painting about a peaceful future. He knew she was not being deliberately flippant but merely trying to cope with her emotional distress, and he did not want to make a promise he would not be able to keep. The darkness of the sky mirrored the black despair in his heart. With every moment that passed, he became increasingly confident he would eventually be caught and arrested. The rosy future which Jam was trying to conjure seemed a forlorn fantasy, but he did not want to shatter her hopes, or douse the smouldering ashes of his own.

"We didn't even get to the park. It's only six kilometres from the city centre and full of beautiful flowering plants, a pond with a pavilion in the middle, and an aviary. It's a wonderful place. I used to go there as often as I could when I was young."

"Jam." Rob moved away from her physically as she spoke, easing away, carefully peeling the band aid.

"And the Tong Nga Chang waterfall is not far from here either. It is seven levels, like the more famous Erawan Falls in Kanthchanburi province. You can walk around and beside the levels as you go up, and swim anywhere you want to."

"Jam". He spoke louder this time, as though trying to rouse her from sleep. A slightly hurt look appeared in conjunction with Jam's silence, and satisfied Rob that he had her attention. "Let's not make too many plans, okay?"

Jam lowered her head to conceal her wounded expression as she fell into his arms. "Don't talk like that, Rob. I love you. Please come back." Her tearful sobs penetrated his chest, not only wetting his shirt but drowning his heart. No words would come, as hard as he tried to invoke them. A loud whistle snapped the cords which bound them in sorrow. Rob gently pushed Jam away from him and kissed her lips, before lifting his case and walking away. He boarded the train and showed his ticket to a conductor, who then escorted him to his cabin. He did not look out through the windows until he was seated, then he saw that Jam had left. His attempts to magically will her back to him with wishful thinking were in vain; she was gone. He was leaving. His throat burned and his chest hurt. Touching his shirt he felt the warm wetness of Jam's tears.

Eight and a half hours later, the train rolled to a shuddering stop at Butterworth station, creaking and groaning on every centimetre of track. Rob saw Jam's reflection in the window, a fleeting wraith, and he sighed before the image was replaced by the more disturbing sight of police officers. Rob counted five. They stood in a lazy circle facing the train, their eyes scanning every panel of glass. They must be looking for him. Someone in Had Yai had recognized him and contacted the authorities. Had Yai police had contacted Butterworth police. Jurisdictional issues seemingly overcome, they were here to arrest Rob and detain him until their Thai counterparts arrived to take him. Rob sat in breathless anticipation, running through the unavoidable scenario in his mind. He had not made it very far at all but perhaps it was better for the hunt to be over sooner rather than later. He had not yet figured out how he would cope with the strain of being a wanted man, of fearing recognition and capture, dreading the punishment.

Most of the other passengers had already disembarked and now formed part of the shuffling crush on the station. Rob lost sight of the police as the human river flowed along the platform towards the exits. He had to move. Probably should have already joined the crowd and sought asylum in anonymity. Despite his height and colour, a stoop and a tightly tugged down cap might have helped him sneak past the dangerous scrutiny of the police. It was too late now. He was about to epitomise conspicuousness, like a tall tree in a desert, or a white suit at a funeral. He breathed in, trying to suck some courage from the surrounding air then he stood up. With his bag in tow he walked down the aisle and out through the door, accompanied by the sound of his heart hammering in his chest. Thoughts of Thai prisons, the horror stories he had heard, filled his mind and rubberised his legs. He pressed on. Out onto the platform and along towards the exit. Stragglers travelled with him but he was exposed, and aware the police were still there.

Suddenly they looked in his direction and he was paralysed. They moved as one towards him. Rob stopped breathing.

"You there!" yelled one of the officers in Thai.

Another yelled something else. They were running now but Rob held his ground because he could not escape them. They were too close, and all the fight had died within him. He waited. They were closer now.

"Don't move!"

"Stop!" Guns appeared and Rob dropped his bags and then himself to the platform.

A gunshot sounded and, flattened on the platform like a lizard sunbathing on a rock, Rob flinched and jerked on the ground as he heard the crack of the gunfire. Another gunshot followed and then a third, but he felt no pain. The officers were beyond him. They overran him. They hadn't been shooting at him. It wasn't him. He was safe. *Move*, he told himself. *Get up*. It was harder than he expected to recover from the worst fright of his life. He had never been more afraid.

Finally, he stood, shaky and unsteady. He grabbed his bag and slowly walked away from the violent scene behind him, not wishing to know what had become of the criminal the police *had* come to arrest, only feeling incredibly grateful it had not been him. Death, injury; Rob was sick of suffering, his and everyone else's. The world seemed like a playground inhabited by the demons of humanities worst filth into which the innocent were lured and permanently corrupted. He hurried along the platform and out through the exit, puffing and parched.

"Taxi sir?"

"Taxi!"

A man was in his face. "You look like you need a ride and a good hotel to rest, my friend."

Rob studied the man's cheerful countenance and took some comfort from his friendly tone. "That sounds great."

Neglecting to mention the five dollar ferry ride across to Penang, about which Rob subsequently learned, the driver told him he would drive him over for only forty dollars. Still shaken from his recent near miss, Rob pulled his wallet out of his pocket and discovered he had a few five hundred baht notes. He pulled one out and the vulture like cabbie noticed and said; "You can change it there." He pointed to an American Express booth behind Rob.

After he changed all his baht into ringgit, he loaded his case into the already open boot of a nineteen eighties black Mercedes. The friendly and lead-footed driver was soon piloting the old Mercedes across the Penang Bridge at a speed more suited to an airplane.

"The Penang Bridge was designed by a local engineer," said the driver, easily slipping into tour guide mode. "It is 13.5 kilometres long and the fifth longest bridge in all of Southeast Asia. Of course it has been joined by its twin over there. The new one opened very recently. It looks the same but uses different technology, more modern."

Infected by the bubbling enthusiasm of the laconic driver, Rob began to relax as they sped along and he listened to the commentary. If there were another way across the channel it surely would not have come with such entertaining commentary. "What's the water called?"

"The bit under us is called the channel between North and South channels."

Rob laughed, and instantly plummeted into fantastic freedom. If only for a moment or two, or as long as it took to drive to Georgetown and find a hotel, he felt safe and at ease. He listened as the driver continued.

"The Strait of Malacca," continued the driver. "Before nineteen eighty-five, the transportation across the channel was only by ferry."

"That's about when this car was built, wasn't it?"

"Yes, sir. It is a classic."

"The two bridges have a total capacity of over two hundred and fifty thousand vehicles."

"And the speed limit on this fine bridge of yours?"

The driver laughed. "I can't remember."

As they exited the bridge and entered the bustling centre of Georgetown, the driver said, "Welcome to the Pearl of the Orient."

Rob took in his surroundings. Georgetown was very different to any Thai city or town he had visited. It bore the unmistakeable mark of its British colonial history with its strange symbiotic coexistence of heritage buildings and modern high rise. It was clear that, regardless of the urban appetite for space in this vibrant city, Georgetown respected her past.

After a few turns, and increasingly retarded progress through the thickening congestion, the driver pulled into the curved driveway of a hotel. "Beautiful hotel here for you, sir. Not too expensive and good location. Only ten minutes from Gurney Drive. Have you heard of Gurney Drive?"

"No."

"A world famous eating area. Fantastic selection of foods from all over Asia and the world. And also, only five minute walk to the wonderful Komtar shopping district. And the swimming pool up top overlooks the city. Swim at night. Beautiful. Perfect for you. Go and have a look. If you don't like it, I will take you to another one. If you do, then stay, and come back to give me a tip." He finished with a dazzling, self-satisfied smile. Very smooth.

"Okay, I'll have look."

Rob got out of the Mercedes and was immediately greeted by a finely dressed doorman. "Welcome to Sunway Hotel, sir. Do you have any luggage?" he said.

Deciding he didn't need to check out the hotel because it looked good enough and he wasn't staying long, Rob thanked the driver and paid him, adding the requested gratuity. Rob declined the offer of assistance from the doorman, and subsequently followed him through the shiny glass doors towards the reception desk which perched on a gleaming white tiled floor. Rob followed him, booked himself a room and trailed the porter to the elevator, which they entered after a short wait and rode to the fifteenth floor.

Inside his room, which was typically styled with simplicity and straight lines in shades of coffee, chocolate and cream, Rob made for the mini bar and helped himself to a cold Heineken. He sat on a somewhat accommodating lounge chair after spinning it around to face the cityscape which lay outside the window. Alone again with his thoughts, Jam's face materialized in the glass. A sudden and spiteful sadness fell on him with the realization he would probably never see her again. How the hell would he be able to return? Even assuming he somehow permanently eluded the police by hiding out in Australia, the Thai authorities would not simply forget about him. His face was probably being plastered all over airports and bus terminals and trains stations. There was no reason to believe he would not eventually be captured. He felt exactly how he had on that day Shane described his puerile little running away stunt when he was a teenager. There was biting certainty, a relentless anxiety which would never leave him, the heartless beast of inevitability.

He guzzled some Heineken then dialled Shane's number. As he pressed the screen, Rob realized he did not have a phone number or an address for Jam and his heart sank even further. How could he have forgotten that? How bloody stupid! The bell was tolling loudly to signify the death of their relationship.

"Hello?" said Shane.

"Shane, it's Rob. I need to talk. I feel like shit."

He croaked out the words, cognizant of how pathetic they sounded, and unsure whether he had the strength to say anything else.

Chapter Thirty-two

"Where have you been?" said Shane.

"Have you been drinking?" replied Rob. "Your voice sounds weird."

"I believe *slurred* is the word you are looking for," said Shane as he shifted from reclined to horizontal on the couch, which squeaked and groaned a little with approval. He laid his drink down on the coffee table so as to avoid any more spillage.

"Okay,'" conceded Rob. "Slurred. Rough day eh?"

"Rough fucking life mate. You think everything is sweet then it all turns sour and shit in the blink of an eye. You know what I was doing when I got the phone call about Angela?"

"No."

"Neither do I," said Shane. He laughed awkwardly. "I can't remember exactly but I was in class and I was probably fantasizing about fucking one of my students or the boss. That's how I spent my intellectual downtime; thinking about fucking other women while my wife, my beautiful wife was being sent to hell via a heavy metal collision."

"Cut it out, Shane."

"Rough day he says. Fuck yes. Thanks for asking about my shithole screwed up wreck of a life."

"Go and make yourself some coffee, you moron, and stop talking like that," said Rob.

"Like what?"

"Coffee stupid. Now!"

Shane rolled off the lounge and dropped the phone on the floor beside him. He finished his drink before picking it up and finding his feet. With a slight sway, he wandered off to the kitchen, pressing the phone to his ear as he went; "still there?"

"I'll be here until you are sober, at least marginally."

"Did you ring to rouse on me, mum?"

"I rang to tell you I'm coming home, and I was feeling pretty low myself. I needed someone to talk to and you're my brother so naturally I thought of you. I was hoping you could cheer me up but I see you're the silly bastard who needs solace."

The kettle was switched on, the coffee mug loaded with course brown granules and an unnecessarily large amount of sugar, before Rob finished speaking.

"That's a fancy word. Have you been reading the dictionary again?" asked Shane.

"You don't have a mortgage on the English lexicon, you know."

The kettle boiled and Shane filled his mug, leaning in to savour the rich aroma. "I have a mortgage on my house."

"Good for you. I heard the kettle boil. Hurry up and make your coffee and get it inside you."

"I'd forgotten how bossy you can be," said Shane, as he did what he was told.

"I think you have things arse backwards mate. I recall you, the eldest son, being the enforcer of parental regulations. Mum said this, mum said that. Dad said so, blah-blah-blah. What an angel you were. It must have been great for mum and dad to have you to keep me in line. They probably needed the assistance I guess. I *was* a bit of a delinquent. I resented you for it at the time, you know. I always wondered why you weren't automatically on my side, fighting in my corner against the injustices of parental rule."

The effect of the alcohol dissipated quickly but only partially because of the coffee. Shane realized he had been hamming it up for his audience of one. He had not really had that much to drink, and was drowning in confused misery rather than whiskey. His emotions were frazzled, and he wasn't thinking straight but the booze had neither hindered nor helped him.

"Well?" said Rob.

"Well what?"

"Why weren't you on my side against mum and dad?"

Shane sipped the coffee, delighting in its sharp bite. "It was your destiny. Your insignificant rebellion was always going to be crushed by the empire."

Rob laughed. "You're such a prick!"

"Why did you really call?"

"I'm in hotel in Georgetown."

"Malaysia?"

"Yep."

After a second sip from his steaming mug, Shane walked back to the living room, and sat down. "What next?"

"I haven't booked a flight out of KL yet but I will tomorrow. I only just arrived. I had a bit of a scare at the train station."

"Yeah?" prompted Shane, as he relaxed on the lounger and allowed the eradication of his own dismal musings.

"When I arrived, I thought the police standing on the platform were there to arrest me, but they were there after some other poor bastard, who they shot I think. I don't know. I was on the ground because I thought they were coming for me, and after they passed and I was safe, I just stood up quick sticks and took off."

"Why would they have been after you?" asked Shane. There was obviously a pretty damn important part of this story which he had not heard yet. "Enough of the bullshit, Rob. What's going on?"

In silence he waited for his little brother to answer, and with every passing second the grip of horror tightened around his chest. He had spent his whole life anticipating disastrous outcomes for Rob's countless misadventures. His brother had been right to suggest he was their parent's ally. He had worried for Rob, as they had. He had laid in his bed waiting for Rob to return even as either mum or dad, usually mum, sat in the living room trying to pass the anxious hours with some pathetic diversion like knitting or a crossword puzzle. He had stood beside mum when those frequent late night calls shattered the fragile calm of their home. He had lived with the terrible apprehension, and seen the toll it had taken on his father in particular. Mum seemed imbued with some special extra power of resilience which enabled her to continue to love and show her wayward son mercy, despite Rob withholding even the faintest whiff of gratitude. She called it *grace*, and Shane had always thought of it as a kind of magic superpower given to people in times of need.

It was grace that kept the door permanently unlocked for Rob to re-enter whenever he saw fit. It was grace that kept mum sane through so many sleepless nights, and grace that armoured her and anointed her for the role of mediator in the brutal verbal stoushes which inevitably occurred between Rob and Dad.

"Did you hear me?" said Rob.

"It sounded like you said you killed a guy."

The absence of a denial is invariably taken as a sign of confirmation and Shane's heart skipped a beat. Rob had survived his teenage rebellion and become a relatively law abiding citizen, if not exactly a model one. He found a job, a string of jobs in fact, which enabled him to stay home and avoid the eviction dad promised him if he was going to attempt to make a career of idleness. Shane recognized that Rob was a beast behind bars. An incurably wild animal trapped by forces which he did not understand nor respect. Every word which formed in Shane's mind sounded pathetically wrong. As fast as he could assemble his thoughts and marshal his emotions, another firecracker would go off, scaring and scattering the contents of his mind. He didn't know what to say. Had he heard correctly? His brother was a killer?

"Fuck," said Shane finally. "Maybe you should save the details for when we see each other, but I just want to know why you didn't tell me before. It didn't just happen right?"

"No."

"What makes you think the Malaysian police know about it?"

"I made the newspaper in Had Yai, so I figure they have worked out where I'm heading and are sending word ahead to all their brothers in arms to watch out for me."

Shane leaned forward in his seat and laid his coffee mug on the table beside the empty whiskey glass. "Two things," he said. "Is there any chance the guy wasn't dead, just unconscious?"

"No. What's the other thing?"

"Is it possible you are overrating your own importance? It wouldn't be the first time." Shane regretted the insult which Rob fortunately overlooked.

"I considered that. It is possible and you are right about me, but Shane, I killed a man. Even saying it sounds wrong and impossible, like I'm talking about someone else. You know what I mean?"

Surprised by Rob's uncharacteristic humility, Shane demurred and drank some more coffee, in the hope his brother would continue. He had of course been the victim of frequent surreal experiences, and he was therefore able to grasp something of what his brother might be feeling. But murder?

"I can't escape the feeling that I won't be able to get away. They'll get me eventually. I've even thought about turning myself in, but it feels like I should have done that immediately, and my running away has not helped with any proposed self-defence argument I might like to throw at them."

"Uh-huh."

"Is that all you've got?"

"I just wish you'd trusted me with this from the start. Why have we been living such disconnected lives? You killed a guy and you're just telling me about it now, a week later. We're brothers Rob. I knew something was wrong when you called one time and told me you were fine, because you never say that. You always make a joke about other people saying it and how it's a dead giveaway that if someone says they are fine, then they are definitely not fine. I should have pushed you then."

"Mate, don't try to load any of this on to yourself. You don't need to carry the flag of martyrdom for mum's sake."

"Shit, does she know anything?"

"Of course not. She doesn't even know where I am. She doesn't know what I've been doing and she doesn't know about Jam. I've kept her in the dark."

"There's been way too much fucking darkness in this family, Rob."

"Yep."

"And what about Jam? Is she with you?"

"No."

"You left her behind?"

"I *had* to leave her behind. She doesn't even have a passport, and there was no time to organise anything. We tried, but the wheels turn so slowly, and although we thought we had some time, we didn't think it wise to push our luck. I mean before I saw my picture in the paper, I thought we had plenty of time, but boom! All of our plans went out the fucking window."

Shane finished his coffee and wondered what else to say. What do you say when you learn that someone you have known your whole life, your brother, has murdered a man? He must still have been in shock to even be able to ask the question himself. The muscles in his stomach ached from tension, and with the coffee gone, he decided to switch back to whiskey.

"What's your plan?"

"I am going to stay out of sight as much as possible, purchase a plane ticket and fly home."

"And then what?"

"I don't know."

"Call me when you have the flight details and I'll pick you up at the airport."

"Thanks," said Rob. "Shane, are you okay?"

"No."

"Apart from the obvious contribution I've made, what's up?"

"Do you remember Yan Ping?"

"Yes."

"I nearly had sex with her tonight before I came home."

"So what? You're upset because you didn't, or because you nearly did?"

"Angela's only been gone for a couple of weeks."

Silence.

Shane spoke next; "It just feels wrong, like it's too soon. Like Angela would be upset."

Out of the next pause in the conversation, Rob's voice struck him like a slap on the cheek. "Until death we do part. Remember that bit of your vows? Angela's gone so stop being so hard on yourself. Go and root Yan Ping, if you want."

Shane hung up and ignored the next few minutes of repeated ring tone as he sipped whiskey and imagined himself in the arms of his lover.

Chapter Thirty-three

On the plane, Rob felt secure. It was a flying haven which afforded him an unassailable advantage, unless the Thai police dispatched the air force to hunt down their most wanted. Was he now on Thailand's most wanted list? Everything seemed so idyllic and peaceful on board. Rob was not quite able to forget his troubles, but they didn't seem to carry quite the same ominous weight.

On the ground, an entirely different feeling overwhelmed him as though the rarefied atmosphere of the sub heavens evaporated in the harsh climate of earth. Also deserting him on terra-firma was hope. He trudged off the plane and through customs with a heavy dread weighing him down. He was glad to be seeing Shane, but he really wasn't sure if he would make it that far. Although he didn't bring his suitcase, he had a vision of it making endless lonely laps on the baggage carousel waiting in vain to be picked up. He might as well have been that lonely piece of luggage because his predicament was identical. No matter where he roamed, it was the same circle and the authorities would be waiting somewhere to snag him.

A mutton headed security guard waddled around the corner in front of Rob and startled him. Rob tried a wan smile but the guy looked right through him. Invisibility, he mused. Now that would be handy.

"Excuse me sir?"

Rob jumped, and turned despite his apprehension. "Yes?"

"Could you move please? You're blocking the way," said a polite young man in an airport service uniform.

After mumbling an apology and shifting himself as requested, Rob wondered if he was set to be permanently on edge, and if so, how could he live such a precarious life? He wandered along towards the exit, drifting, occasionally looking around for Shane and continuously watching for any sign of the enemy.

"Rob!"

A familiar voice rescued him and he saw Shane, the two brothers shook hands and embraced warmly with the obligatory three pats on each other's backs.

"You look like shit, mate. Rough flight was it?"

Rob shook his head. "Let's get out of here."

They hustled through the exit and along the wide footpath in the direction of the car park, where they rode the escalators to the second level and found Shane's car waiting quietly.

"Are we going to your place?" said Rob. "I don't want to see mum and dad yet. I didn't even tell them I was coming home. Did you?"

Shane dropped the boot lid and looked at his younger brother. "You didn't say not to, but as it happens I didn't. Why didn't you want them to know?"

Rob moved to the passenger door, pulled it open and climbed in before answering. "I have been so on edge for so long now, I just can't think straight. I'm totally swamped, mentally. If I'm not peering over my shoulder and sneak peeking around every corner wondering where they are and when they're going to get me, I'm stricken with this massive sense of loss. Leaving Jam ripped my heart out, and I can't stop the bleeding."

The engine was running and Shane had his hand on the gear lever but it had become stuck there. He stared at Rob. "Have I ever told you what a bloody drama queen you are?"

"What do you mean?" said Rob while concealing a smirk. "And can we please get out of here."

"Do you really think they, whoever the hell they are exactly, are that hot on your tail?"

"Just humour me."

They corkscrewed their way out of the car park and into the rudely vivacious morning sunshine. Rob sneezed as his sinuses made a quick adjustment to the brighter light.

"How long are you going make me wait to hear the whole story? The full catastrophe?"

"You got booze at your place?" answered Rob, obliquely.

"Is the pope catholic?"

"How about we spend the drive with me listening to you and trying to stay awake, as you regale me with what's been happening here?" suggested Rob.

Shane turned his head and unloaded a rebuking glare.

"What?"

"I'm sure the day will come when you give a shit about other people," said Shane, "but I'm not holding my breath until then."

Thus admonished, Rob turned to look out the side window and allowed Shane's wrath to subside. He was tired, exhausted actually, but he could not keep using that as an excuse for every infraction of manners. His big brother was right of course, he was as narcissistic man as God had ever put breath in to. Jam had begun to heal his self-absorption, not with any deliberate action but with subtle enticements and gentle manipulations. He hadn't even known what she was doing until much later when the depth of his emotional entanglement had become a disease from which he did not want to be cured. Every fibre of his body wanted to defend against Shane's outdated perceptions of him, but he bit his tongue and permitted the falsehood to linger. In timc hc would dcmonstratc how he had changed. How he had been transformed by love. God that sounded soppy. He would never try that sentence on Shane. It was better to exist in the shadows until he was brave enough to face the light, or until the right circumstances presented themselves.

When the silent drive to Shane's apartment ended, and they were safely ensconced inside, on the lounge in front of the television and fully armed with a couple of cold Super Dry's, the real conversation began.

"I've been struggling since Angela died. Most of the time, I have felt like a bloody zombie, and the rest...like I'm about to explode. Everything tastes like shit now. Everything is shit. I keep trying. Then I'm alive enough to attempt it, to kick my arse into gear, but I'm bogged down in misery."

Rob drained the bottle with a purposeful scull, and laid the dead soldier on the coffee table. "What happened to us?"

"Life happened to us."

"Life's a bitch."

"So they say."

"You don't think so?"

Shane finished his drink and stood up. "You want another one?" and after Rob nodded; "The truth is I don't want to believe that. Life has been good to me, very good until Angela died. I don't want to say she was taken, or maybe I do."

"Go and get the beer you babbler!"

Strangely, Rob knew exactly what Shane had been trying to say. He sensed the unpleasant and impersonal disconnect between the world that was and the world that he, and probably everyone else on the planet, wanted it to be. It wasn't quite right. Something was wrong but he wasn't able to put his finger on it.

"I think I want there to be a God," announced Shane as he re-entered the room. "I think God existing would be useful."

After hopefully managing to remove the look of incredulity from his face, Rob said, "I'm not sure I want to hear this but by all means, brother, speak on."

"If there is no God," Shane said slowly, as if he had forgotten how to put a sentence together, "then I wonder, what exactly, is the point of this whole thing?"

Rob mimicked his gesture of waving both hands. "What whole thing?"

"Life."

"Life is a string of absurdities; an ill-advised curiosity."

"I'm trying to get serious here, and you're quoting Don Quixote?"

"Do you know," said Rob, leaning forward as though he had suddenly acquired the requisite sobriety, "I have not read another book since I read that? It kind of ruined the experience of reading for me. Not in a bad way."

"How is something ruined in a good way?" asked Shane.

"I mean, it was so good that I doubted whether anything else I read subsequently could match it, or even get anywhere near it."

"It's a bit like your first true love, right?"

Rob nodded sagely. "You never quite love someone the way you loved her. You never seem to be able to find the same sort of love, the same intensity. You tell yourself it's possible and when you find something like it, you fool yourself that it's at least as good if not better, but somewhere deep inside, every woman who comes into your life, and stays for any period of time, is always subjected to the yardstick of the first love. The bar is set very high. So high it is virtually unattainable, so everyone compromises because most people don't get to keep their first love. It doesn't last even though you want it to and you try to make it last. It is as ephemeral as life itself."

Shane guzzled from the bottle of beer, apparently thinking, but who could really tell what took place inside the head of another. Finally he said, "It's true," and he raised his bottle to face height and tipped the top of it towards Rob. "You speak well, my brother."

Rob accepted the unnecessary compliment and pondered the significance of his own words. Who was his first love? And how did Jam measure up to her?

"I don't reckon school boy crushes count," said Shane. "I think your first true love is the woman you fall in love with when you are old enough to know what love is. And it doesn't have to have anything to do with sex. I thought I was in love with this girl when I was fifteen and she organized a special sleep over. She had to show me what to do. She was the same age as me but was experienced and as confident as hell. I don't know how she got like that at such a young age, but the point is I was curious and lusty and malleable, and when she was finished giving me a master class, she dumped me and moved on. That hurt. And I thought it hurt because I loved her, but I know now it hurt because she used me to amuse herself. I didn't have to say yes but who's going to say no, right? There was nothing school girl about her, except the uniform she arranged seductively on her body five days a week."

"Depends on the person," said Rob shuffling down and burrowing into the lounge chair, heading towards horizontal. "But generally fifteen year olds don't know shit about love. Even at sixteen or seventeen, maybe for many blokes, not even then."

"Yeah. So you know mine was Debbie. Who was yours? You weren't as heavily into girls as I was, even though I was younger than you."

"That experience with Leanne damaged me. I was suspicious and a little afraid of the ladies for a while after that. I focused on school and sport and pretended not to care whether I was missing out on something special or not. The girls in the magazines were much safer and much less trouble, so if I needed to unwind, I could."

"So who was she?"

Shane drained his bottle of beer and clutched it to his chest. He stared at the ceiling. "I don't think I figured myself out until a few years ago."

"A few years ago?"

"To be honest I'm still not sure. Recent events have shaken my foundations a little. I thought I knew myself and was fully reconciled to my character flaws, and had found my niche in life, my groove. Where I was meant to be, and I thought Angela was the one. But I've recently come to see that although I married Angela, and I did love her and was happy with her, I was constantly measuring her, comparing her to someone else, and now that Angela is gone and that someone else has reappeared in my life, I feel sure of it."

"This Yan Ping chick?"

"Yan Ping," said Shane sonorously as though reciting a sacred poem.

Rob finished his beer and laid it on the coffee table. "I'm empty by the way." When Shane stood, he added, "I'm confused. Why did you split with her in the first place and marry Angela and why aren't you with this chick now?"

"Stop calling her a chick."

"Woman, sheila, broad, babe, lady? Any of those work any better for you?"

As Shane left him to go and get more beer, Rob pondered what he had said about first love and about him and Debbie. They had been as thick as thieves for months and months, nearly a year. Good friends before that because they hung out in the same circle, their relationship had changed gears unexpectedly when Rob had broken up with his previous girlfriend because she wouldn't have sex with him. He had not liked her enough to keep waiting and reasoned he could do better. She had a bit of a bitch princess complex going on anyway. Debbie and he had been talking one day, as they walked home from school. He was boasting about his singing ability and she dared him to prove it with an impromptu footpath performance. He sang his best rendition of Cold Chisel's Janelle, and she never looked at him the same way again. There was a complete lack of pretension with Debbie, and the stark contrast with the bitch was what compelled him to look at her differently. There seemed to be nothing in the way of them continuing to enjoy each other's company, and allowing the natural blossoming of their relationship into whatever flower it was destined to be. It was easy and comfortable but by no means perfect. Yet, even the flaws and cracks resounded with overarching love, real, 'I genuinely want what is best for you', love.

The fateful decision made by Debbie's parents to move the family to Perth, while at first only presenting a challenge to their relationship, ultimately eroded it by virtue of the nearly four thousand kilometres which separated them.

Every relationship after that had proved fruitless and unsatisfying, even though Rob tried to love again. This girl did not have a sweet smile like Debbie. That girl did not have her patience. Another one lacked her passion and imagination. Others were deficient in all manner of characteristics and physical features. Most of them were quite beautiful, inside and out, but they weren't Debbie. Then, nearly five years after Debbie moved to the other side of the country, taking his heart with her, Rob met Jam.

"I don't want to talk about fucking woman anymore," said Shane as he marched back into the living room and handed Rob another open bottle of Super Dry. "They're fucking annoying, aren't they? I mean they mess you up. I just don't want to talk about them anymore, okay?"

Rob accepted the beer, nodding a murmured agreement, but thought to himself; *I don't want to talk about anything else, especially not Thailand and murder.*

Chapter Thirty-four

Shane remembered the night he came home drunk and vomited on the floor in the foyer, in front of his mother, splashing her slippers. It had not totally been without warning. Maureen's accusing glare had only elicited the response that he was feeling unwell. As she was suggesting Shane's poor condition was more than likely due to excessive alcohol consumption, he was being traumatized by the intense nausea which immediately precedes the disgorging of the contents of one's stomach. Maureen told him to go to bed, and also sent Rob and his father packing back to their rooms as well.

The man in the mirror smiled at Shane. "Once was enough," he said. He nodded, content with the knowledge he had never been physically ill from over drinking since that night. The feeling alone had been enough to deter him from drinking at all for several months, and coupled with the embarrassment of unloading his stomach on the floor in front of his mother, his sobriety had been guaranteed for years. Even after he trusted himself to drink moderately, he never forgot the feeling. It was exactly the same as his first foray into driving while drunk which ended almost as soon as it begun because he was frightened by the lack of control he felt, and somehow able to consider the potentially disastrous consequences of his actions. The sense of order and proprietary which was now so deeply ingrained in his character had its genesis in those seminal moments from his adolescence.

Although many years had passed, and the threads of fabric which constituted Shane Archer had been tightly woven together, there was a sense in which now, in the midst of this emotional turmoil, he was very definitely unravelling. He rubbed his arm and imagined it fraying. There was a tattered, disordered quality to his cognitive processing. He mistrusted his judgment and doubted his ability to cope beyond the next instant. Last night's late and heavy drinking session with Rob had not been helpful, though he had spent every minute of it wishing that something could save him. That some word, or phrase, a slice of wisdom, an epiphany, anything stronger than his weakness could rescue him and give him hope. No amount of unsentimental rebuttal or denial of the erroneous thoughts which dominated his thinking lasted beyond the initial engagement. Rationality was a little boy running up to an elephant and tossing a few pebbles at its thick hide, before scurrying away to hide and subsequently discover the elephant had not even noticed him.

"Got any plans for today?" he asked the inert lump which was his brother.

Rob grunted and theatrically adjusted his position on the lounge, suggesting he may have just done all the work he was going to do for the day. Shane stared down at him, wondering whether to press him for a proper answer. Did it matter if his weary little brother crashed on his lounge all day? Could he handle the prospect of someone doing nothing for such a long period of time? It was not his way. Relaxation was a luxury to be enjoyed in small, high quality doses when not standing in place as the object of one's labour. People worked to be able to rest, but seldom took enough time to enjoy their leisure. It was always over too soon, marred by the persistent demands of the grind stone.

"Make yourself at home. I'll be back just after four, unless..." *Unless what? What am I thinking of doing this afternoon?* He refused to complete the sentence even though he knew he was going to try to visit Yan Ping. All the talk the previous night about first loves had knocked a hornet's nest of emotions to the ground and was beating it with a stick. The raging swarm would drive him to Yan Ping whether he resisted it or not, and the truth was he no longer had a heart for the fight. Rob had been right in urging him to throw of the shackles of guilt and redundant loyalty, and run into the arms of another woman. But Yan Ping was not just another woman, and Shane was uncertain about what exactly it was he wanted from her. He was messed up, a walking travesty; unstable and degraded. Could he inflict his misery on Yan Ping, and expect her to be thankful and to love him despite himself? It didn't seem fair.

Shane was walking through the door hoping to leave these thoughts inside, but they jumped through the narrow gap between the door and the jam. Aware that he was talking himself out of visiting Yan Ping with every step he took, he wished he was not so bound by conscience, and wondered what the hell his conscience had to do with anything anyway. Why could he not be more instinctive and spontaneous? Why did he have to plan everything in advance and rehearse eventualities and contingencies? Why was he so introspective? It was bloody annoying.

Behind the wheel of his car, Shane imagined Yan Ping opening the door for him with that same celestial pulchritude and welcoming smile, as he strode towards her and embraced her strongly like he should have done before. Why worry about whether she might have reverted to her former non tactile demeanour? Why not simply show her that although many years had passed, there was not the slightest diminution of his feelings for her, and he expected her to reciprocate? Why waste more time with awkward and unnecessary words? He pictured her peeling her clothes off slowly and provocatively, and he hardened instantly. The fantasy steamed his mind's eye. Why not run to her and take her with the authority she had ceded to him by virtue of her invitation? She wanted him, and he wanted her. It was simple. Everything else be damned!

The phone rang, rudely wrenching him back into the present, into the driver's seat of his car where had been sitting behind the wheel in the car park for God knew how long.

"Shane speaking."

"Shane, it's Sabeen."

He waited, then started the engine and turned down the radio, trying to figure out why he didn't say anything. He seemed to have temporarily forgotten how to have a telephone conversation.

"Shane?"

"Yes, Sabeen. Sorry."

"You sound weird. Are you okay?"

"Yep, what's up boss?" He let his hand fall onto his lap after selecting drive and releasing the handbrake. It rested a moment before performing an absent minded and extended scratch.

"I wanted to talk about what happened between you and me the other day."

Shane's hand sprung from his lap onto the steering wheel where it joined its partner in a white knuckled grip. *She wants to talk about it now? Why now?* "I'm not sure now is the best time. I'm on my way to work. Can't we talk when I get there?"

"I'm not in the office today."

"Well, another day then. Is it really that urgent? I mean we had a moment of madness which was the inevitable result of some pretty intense flirting, and when we finally got to where we wanted to go, when we had reached the peak of the mountain, we were all set to jump off before we were interrupted. Said interruption brought us to our senses, and we moved on."

He drove through the streets; the buildings, signs and the trees that inhabited them, passing by as if they were inconsequential. And Shane received Sabeen's next words with the kind of calm only experienced by those who are inured to the devastation of chaos.

"The thing is I don't think I've moved on," she said.

"You still have feelings for me?"

Four blocks stood between Shane and his destination, and as he rolled along the street, he waited for her to answer with an obvious affirmative.

"I'm in love with you actually."

"No you're not," replied Shane quickly and much more tersely than was required. Why was she in love with him? That was stupid. They had just been playing a game, amusing each other with saucy repartee and snippets of titillation. What did love have to do with anything? It was nothing.

"I am," said Sabeen softly. "But perhaps you're right. We shouldn't be talking about it now. It's just been bothering me. You know how sometimes things prey on your mind and they pester you and drive you to distraction? I needed to tell you how I feel and find out if it's mutual, because if it isn't that will break my heart, but at least I'll know, and I can try to let go."

Shane pulled into the kerb and parked the car, increasingly agitated by Sabeen and strongly desiring to tell her to grow up. Didn't girls mature earlier than boys? What was with this barely post pubescent outburst? She loves me? It was all just a game!

"Shane?"

"Yes Sabeen," he said flatly, shooting for a tone which would indicate he disapproved of her behaviour and found her confession embarrassing.

"Aren't you going to say anything?"

"What do you want me to say?" He knew what he wanted to say, and he reckoned it would be a safe bet to put the house on what she wanted him to say, but he wasn't going to say anything.

"You don't feel the same way?"

On foot now, covering the last two hundred metres to the front door of the building with his phone plastered to his ear and burning it, Shane decided enough was enough.

"Why are you ambushing me with this now? My wife just died and you *love* me? What the fuck, Sabeen? Seriously. Not now, okay."

The silence on the end of the line told him he had gone too far. She'd hung up on him, and as a result, he might need to start considering a change of employment. He cursed himself, horrified by his lack of tact and self-control, mortified to think of how he had just wounded someone he cared about. Suddenly work, which loomed before him as he entered the building and walked down the hall to his classroom, seemed anathema, an abomination; an insufferable expenditure of time and effort for which there would never be adequate recompense.

A painful day passed without incident although Shane felt himself on the verge of regular and intermittent explosive episodes. His patience eroded much more quickly than it used to, apparently constructed of sand and built where waves broke with dogged reliability. He wondered if losing Angela, and the slow slide to mental chaos which had preceded her tragic death, and which now persisted through his grief, was the end of a chapter in his life. Perhaps it was time to think about doing something else, but why add more uncertainty to the tumultuous mix?

Shane called Rob immediately after work to finally satisfy his worry that his little brother was okay and had managed to avoid further trouble. Then he called Yan Ping, who authorized his self-issued invitation to visit her with no trace of doubt in her voice. It was as though she was expecting it, expecting to see him again, and if he had not invited himself then she would have. There was an irrefutable assuredness about the direction they were heading. It was becoming increasingly difficult for Shane to believe their convergent paths were anything other than a nictitating neon sign, screaming that it was meant to be.

One hour later, at Yan Ping's door, he knocked then waited in electric anticipation.

When she opened the door, he replied to her smile with a quick hello and added, "You never gave me the present you said you bought for me."

Yan Ping smiled with the same unforced coyness which had always thrilled him for some reason. "You never gave me a chance."

Although clearly intended as a humorous ice breaker, Shane apologized.

"Never mind," she said casually. "I'll get your gift. It's still in the bag. Wait here."

Imagined as a smooth flowing witty little episode of badinage, their conversation crumbled into an awkward groping for the right words, and a desperate attempt to decode that which was unspoken. By the time she returned, Shane's mood had flipped back to cautious despair. If this was destiny, then why did it feel so uncomfortable? What was hindering them? Was it him? Was it her? Was the chemical reaction he hoped for more of a fizzer than a volatile bubbler?

"Here you are."

"Whoa, it's heavy. Is it a brick from the Great Wall?"

Her laughter relieved the tension and set them back on track. Shane reached into the bag, and felt cold, smooth metal beneath his fingers. He peered inside but his curiosity was un-sated until he had removed the gift from the bag.

"It's a crab."

"Do you like it?"

"It's gold and shiny."

"I thought of you as soon as I saw it and I had to buy it for you."

Shane was afraid to ask how a crab reminded her of him. "It's very cool," he said diplomatically. "Thank you."

He had finished kissing her cheek before he even realized he had done it, and the astonishment on her face was therefore puzzling. "Sorry, I didn't think."

"That's different."

Shane lowered the crab to his side, tightly gripping its shiny carapace. "What do you mean? What's different?"

"You, doing somcthing without thinking."

They looked into each other's eyes for a long time without speaking. A flood swollen river of thoughts raged through his mind, not the least of which was the confronting irony of his current actions standing in strong support of Yan Ping's assertion. The fight between action and reflection, was fierce, it always had been for Shane. Spontaneity was a dirty word, and his ability to live moment by moment, skimming on the crest of the waves was impeded by his almost phobic aversion to risk. Despite the successful identification of the problem, Shane struggled uselessly to overcome the inertia of circumspection.

Yan Ping intervened. With the warmth of her hands and the wet softness of her lips, she conquered him, and led him away to a pleasurable slaughter.

Chapter Thirty-five

Having spent a whole day at Shane's place, doing nothing but drinking and watching television, Rob needed to get out. He had unsuccessfully tried to contact Jam, and could not escape the sinking weight of negativity which pulled him down under the water. How would he ever see her again? How could he return to Thailand? He would be arrested immediately, and locked up. That was his inevitable fate regardless of where he was, and he was fully resigned to that awful fact. He had been so low for some time now, and was attempting to soften the pain with copious quantities of alcohol. As a temporary fix it was pure genius and always had been, but in order to maintain the feeling, you had to stay drunk because with each burst of sobriety came a heavier blow of despairing reality. Shane had not said anything yet, but Rob knew he would. Hell, he had only allowed himself some moderate boozing and self-wallowing over Angela's death, and now, although a little more moribund than he remembered, was clearly on the way up a new mountain.

He climbed into the cab and ordered the driver to take him to the pub. When pressed for clarification, Rob said, "The first open one you come to, mate."

"No problem."

"I'd like to be able to say that and *mean* it," said Rob under his breath.

"What's that mate?"

"Nothing," said Rob, as he realized the import of what had slipped from his tongue. How long could he carry on this shadow of an existence, faking engagement with reality whilst simultaneously ignoring it, and wandering in some fantastic mental construction?

"Steelers club," said the driver, as he eased to a stop out the front of a fat, glass fronted building.

Rob paid him off and went inside. He went to the sports bar and bought himself a beer before taking a seat in the sparsely populated lounge. Patronage would increase significantly later in the afternoon, as workers finished their day's labour and sought the bonhomie of beer, sport and mateship. For now, it was Rob and a couple of red faced, pot-bellied pensioners, sipping beers and reading horse racing form guides. Another man who looked to be roughly in Rob's age ball park was also in attendance, drinking alone with eyes only for the large television screen which was presenting an EPL match between Arsenal and Manchester City. None of these men stood out as likely conversation candidates, which was a pity because Rob felt like talking.

Not wanting to accept his loneliness, Rob approached the guy who was watching the football match and broke the ice with a typical quip. "Arsenal cruising again, are they?"

The man turned to face Rob and offered something like a smile. "Yes, I suppose."

"You suppose," said Rob. "You're watching, aren't you?"

"No, not really."

Terrific, thought Rob. I should have picked one of the old farts and let them catalogue their health problems and tell me war stories. This guy must be on drugs. That would account for the weird smile and his lack of attention to the game right in front of his face. The question now was, having begun, whether he should continue.

"All right," said Rob after some silent deliberation. "I'll bite. What are you doing here in front of the box then? That's a beer in your hand there too. Did you know that?"

The man suddenly stiffened in his seat as though something had bitten his arse. "I get it now," he said. His face lit up with a sudden explosion of friendliness. "Here sit down, mate. My name's Chris."

Despite the somewhat absurd prelude to the invitation, Rob accepted Chris's hand, shook it, and took a seat beside him.

"Are you a football fan?" asked Chris.

"Fan might be stretching it, but yeah, I like sport. And you?"

There was another pause during which Chris seemed to spend an inordinate amount of time considering his answer to Rob's question. "I lost my job."

"That sucks," said Rob, choosing to overlook Chris' non sequitur. "So you came in to drown your sorrows and you really couldn't give a fuck about the soccer. You just want to get pissed."

"I don't get pissed. I hardly drink."

"But you're starting today because you lost your job and you feel like shit, and you don't know what else to do with yourself.'" Rob noticed Chris had nearly finished his drink, so he insisted on buying his new friend another. If nothing else, listening to someone else's troubles might alleviate his anxious melancholy. It couldn't hurt anyway, and he really wanted company. He didn't enjoy spending a lot of time by himself. It unnerved and unsettled him to be in his own company for extended periods of time. That was why the previous day of self-imposed isolation had driven him half way to the insane asylum.

When he returned from the bar, Chris seemed to have relaxed. His shoulders weren't quite as hunched and he was nestled lower in the seat.

"Okay," said Rob, handing Chris a schooner, "There you go. Tell me about your job. What happened?"

"I knew it was coming. They told us a couple of months back that the company was in trouble, we manufacture steel pipes by the way, and they were going to try to trade out but they weren't hopeful. I'd worked there for ten years and had it been the case that they were only downsizing, then my seniority might have saved me. But they were talking about pulling the pin, and no one was going to be saved from the scrapheap."

"It's not quite the scrap. You've got transferrable skills, haven't you?"

"It's a tough labour market. Jobs are few and far between, and down here, well, it's even worse. I'll apply for whatever, of course. That's my plan. I'll take anything. I've worked since I was fifteen, and at forty eight, I'm nowhere near retirement."

"Did you get a payout?"

Chris sipped his beer, swallowed it slowly then took another. "Yeah," he said. "The company did the right thing by all the workers, so I'm not destitute, and my wife works, so we'll be okay for a while. I just don't know what to do with myself. It's like I've stumbled upon a new world where I don't belong, and I can't figure out what I am supposed to do. I'm a bit lost."

Rob raised his glass and titled it towards Chris. "I hear you mate, I hear you. Let's drink to lost-ness."

Their glasses clinked and both men imbibed some more amber fluid, before Chris said, "What's going on with you then?"

Disinclined to divulge too many details, if any personal information at all, Rob nevertheless felt obligated to give Chris something in return for his openness. The man's invitation and his disclosure combined to arouse a vague suspicion in Rob's mind but he dismissed it. "I've just come back from Thailand, and I had to leave because I had a bit of trouble. I left my girlfriend there and I don't know when or even *if* I will be able to go back to her."

"That sucks."

Rob nodded. "So, I too am a little lost. I don't know what to do about anything. I spent yesterday shitfaced in my brother's apartment where I'm staying and I just needed to get out to day. I need to straighten the kinks out of my pipes."

Chris laughed. "So you've been putting a few away have, you?"

"Just a few."

"I don't want to get drunk. I don't like the feeling and I don't want to spend the money. I think it's a waste."

"Fair enough mate. As for me, I think it's a solid investment in my happiness and general well-being."

"I guess we'll have to agree to disagree."

Rob raised his glass again and guzzled the remnants of his schooner. "Time for another, your shout?"

"I'll buy you one but I don't want another. I'm going to go to the employment office soon, to register and to start applying for work."

"It wouldn't kill you to take a day off to catch your breath, Chris."

He smiled, before standing and making his way over to the bar. Rob was curious. There had to be something else going on here. There was something unusual about Chris; an unexpected calmness despite his situation, and he spoke without pretence. It was obvious he was hurting and confused, but he didn't seem unhinged by his predicament. He recognized the man's attitude as the antithesis of his own angst-wracked state of mind. While Rob felt he needed to fake casual disregard for his circumstances, Chris actually radiated peace in the face of his misfortune. He probably had not killed a man, and was not on the run or in hiding from the law, but he had his own genuine worries, and they were apparently not crippling him.

Chris returned and handed the schooner to Rob. "Can I tell you something?" he said. "It's probably going to sound a bit weird."

"Shoot," said Rob before sipping the froth crowning his freshly poured lager.

"One thing I do when I'm in trouble is pray."

The word floated in the air between them, and Chris made no effort to hurry it towards its target, neither did Rob do anything to hasten its arrival. It reminded Rob of the aggressive posturing of dragonflies, in the way they hovered in the space, threatening to attack. On this occasion it was more than mere intimidation, although Rob was certain that Chris had no intention of harming him.

"Do you pray?"

Rob wanted to tell Chris to shut up, and tell him all about his pious mother and her endless God bothering, bible-bashing ways. He wanted to say he didn't believe in God, and he didn't need God, and that religion was for weaklings, and for the intellectually feeble. He felt it necessary to remind Chris about all the paedophiles in the church and all the wars started by Christians. He was ready to unlock his armoury and hit Chris with everything he had, because he really detested this kind of sneaky preaching. Make friends, win their confidence then bam; knock them out with truth, or their version of truth. It really pissed him off, and Rob felt his anger roiling inside and his face flushing, but in spite of his feelings, he simply said, "No."

"I asked God this morning to make me useful, to give me something to do, and while I was praying I saw a picture of the front of this club flash in my mind. I've been here before but only in the evenings for the odd function or after a footy game."

Rob listened dumbstruck both by his lack of aggression, and by what Chris was actually saying.

"I came here and bought a drink and wondered why on earth God had sent me here."

"You think God sent you here to meet me?"

"Sounds crazy, right?" Chris laughed a little self-consciously.

"Yep."

"But I can't explain it any other way. And now I know exactly what I'm doing here."

Still wrestling with his internal rage, Rob forced a polite curiosity into his tone. "And what is that, mate?"

The look on Chris' face suggested that he had received a different message from Rob's question than the one the speaker had intended. "I have a message for you."

"A message for me?" Rob thrust his thumb towards his chest.

Chris grabbed a coaster from a nearby table and flipped it over, before pulling a pen from his shirt pocket and writing something on the back of the coaster. When he finished, he handed it to Rob and allowed him to read it.

Jeremiah 12:5

"What is this?"

"A bible verse. Jeremiah is in the Old Testament. Do you have a Bible?"

"Doesn't everyone?" said Rob. "But what does it say and what's the message? You're not going to leave me hanging, are you?"

A dramatic seriousness fell across Chris' face and he searched Rob's eyes with disquieting intensity. "I'm not saying you should believe me necessarily, but I would ask you to please think about it and look up the verse. I think the message is, or the heart of the message, is that you should stop running."

Rob hoped he was still standing, but he had no way of being sure because his head had achieved such unimaginable lightness it could not have possibly been still connected to his body. Was he standing now, or still sitting? Did he hear that correctly? From a bloke he had just met? Stop running? Fuck, it was spooky.

"Rob, are you okay? You look a little pale."

A voice said *uh-huh* and a hand shook Chris' hand, then the same voice said *good-bye*.

After an indeterminate length of time, Rob reconnected with his senses, and was able to take some more beer to irrigate the desert which was his throat. He stared at the coaster, and wished he had a Bible. He looked around. Would anyone have one? The bartender shook his head as he said no, in a way which suggested he thought it was an absurd request. More bodies were present in the sports bar now, and Rob noticed the volume of conversation had increased. He began to ask everyone if they had a Bible. The responses ranged from the polite; *no, I'm sorry mate*, to; *fuck off home and out of here you lunatic.* It was the latter which finally detonated the bomb whose fuse had been lit by Chris' first mention of the, ‘p’ word.

"No need to be rude, mate," said Rob through gritted teeth. "It's just a question."

"And you're just a fucking loon."

"Why do you keep calling me a loon, shit for brains?"

Soon the man was on his feet and in the face of Rob who shirt fronted him to the floor, before unloading with a few well directed punches, together with half a dozen misdirected strikes.

"Get this fucking fruitcake off me!"

Rob kept the hailstorm of punches going, pounding away at the guy until he was wrenched away by unseen and irresistibly strong hands. There was a lot of yelling, and Rob's adrenalized body twisted and jerked to break free and resume the assault. He continued to mouth off at his victim who was still on the ground, having bitten off far more than he could chew with his impolite name calling. Slivers of clear-thinking invaded Rob's rage. Blinking neon signs in his mind flashed their message with annoying persistence; *Stop running. Stop fighting. Stop running.*

Chapter Thirty-six

It was settled quickly and easily, as though no impediment had ever stood in its way. A relationship, a love affair, the greatest of Shane's life, blossomed in the fertile soil of freedom. Any misgivings Shane held were swept away like dust in the wind, as Yan Ping dedicated herself to making up for lost time. The fire of their passion consumed all the dross and stripped their love of all impurities, strengthening them and filling them with a vigorous enthusiasm for life. There was joy and purpose in every action. Shane felt completely renewed; born again.

Yan Ping even managed to find a job in a nursing home, which gave her the opportunity to use her formidable interpersonal and clinical skills, as well as providing some hope she would be able to be registered as a nurse in Australia.

There was however, a spectre of ever present disaster. Rob had not been able to find any peace and his turmoil overflowed into the lives of those around him, including, of course, Shane and his parents, who were still dismayed by being kept in the dark. Shane had made the point very strongly that Rob wanted to be left to his own devices. He did not want any more saviours attempting to rescue him, including, and perhaps especially, his mother and father. Maureen, in particular found the whole situation hurtful and beyond comprehension.

Seven days passed. Rob was drunk most of the time, and swinging wildly between cantankerous and morose. He stayed with Shane, at the latter's insistence because Shane feared for his brother's safety. He was fixed on a path of self-destruction, as though he needed to punish himself, to be his own judge and executioner. With each day, the menace of impeding incarceration faded in Shane's mind but sharpened in Rob's. He was a haunted, tormented man. Not a day passed when he did not rant about a message from God which was both meaningless and cruel. A message he said had been delivered by a stranger at a club, who talked to him, befriended him, won his confidence then wrote a bible verse on a drink coaster, and told him to stop running. The first time they had discussed it, Shane had urged his brother to read the verse and do as he had been instructed to do, deeply consider what the message might mean. Rob's resistance to anything and everything which might be categorised as helpful was baffling. Shane felt Rob was not only becoming an alcoholic but had also developed an addiction to his misery.

His failure to contact Jam tore at his heart as well, because he saw her as light in his darkness. He could not see clearly without her. Rob had explained it one day during another of his long drinking and complaining sessions which Shane was forced to endure.

"Sometimes," he said, "it was enough for me just to see her for a few minutes and say hello. The, *'see you later'* addendum promised more joy, and if I had to wait longer than I would have liked, there was still that next meeting to look forward to. There was always next time. I didn't like her working there but I loved her too much to insist she stop. I wanted her to make that choice and to make it for me, but not just me, for her own sake too. I wanted her to choose us, but in the end I failed to maintain her liberty."

He stopped as though he had nothing left to say, but Shane knew he always had more to say, even if it was mere regurgitation of all he had already said.

"I let her down because I didn't respect her and I killed that fucking prick, Pee Lek. Why was he such an arsehole to me? Why didn't he just leave me alone? Leave us alone? He came to *me,* Shane. He threatened *me*. The little shit was always trying to bully me. Why?"

His hands flew repeatedly into the air as he spoke. Shane sensed he wanted an answer even though he knew that Shane could not give him one. It was like asking a door why it hung and swung and closed, and locked. Sometimes, Shane wished Rob would seek the company of a door rather than bend *his* ear every night. Eventually he would snap and have to punch his little brother, and have him arrested or thrown into a detox clinic or something drastic. It was pathetic, and had Shane been compelled to endure Rob's misery alone, he would have lost his mind. However, Shane had Yan Ping and also his parents who, now that they were almost fully informed, were engaged, although only from the sidelines, in the battle to save Rob.

It was the same conversation night after night, Rob whining and lamenting in between bouts of railing against the injustices of the world, and Shane listening, being supportive and trying, albeit unsuccessfully, to shake his brother free of his despondent paralysis.

The Pacific Ocean twinkled as it pressed against Wollongong beach which was concealed by the high grassy dunes lining Cliff Drive. Thus obscured, the waves waged an endless tug of war with the beach, sending the soothing sounds of their battle on to the shore and into the city. Nestled against WIN entertainment centre, and adjacent to the stadium was a boutique bar and micro-brewery called The Brewery. Shane and Yan Ping sat outside, enjoying the warmth of the sun and the tang of salt carried by a cool breeze. Together they gazed out into the vastness of the impersonal ocean.

"You're quiet today," said Shane. "What's on your mind?"

Her silent reluctance suggested something was bothering her. She shifted her weight in her seat as though discomforted.

"What is it?" urged Shane.

"Do you believe we are meant to be together? That God or destiny, or whatever, wants us to be together?"

"Yes, but I can't quite believe that any distant, external thing or person is involved. It is what it is. And I'm glad. It feels right."

"I've been keeping some things to myself, Shane. Not because I wanted to but because I felt it was necessary to shield you, to protect you."

"Protect me from what?"

"It's still so soon after Angela died, and I don't want to rush you or force you, but I love you. I think I've loved you for a long time. Even when I was with my husband, I always imagined that one day, it would be you, not him. Funny thing is I don't even feel ashamed about that."

Shane studied Yan Ping's face and noticed the tense frown. Lines of angst joined her temple to her manicured eyebrow. Each word had to be wrangled and herded into a corral before she spoke, in case one was wrong or inappropriate and it spoiled the message, or obscured it, tarnished it. Fear retarded her communication, but Shane was bemused. What did she have to fear? She spoke of not wanting to push, but there had been no compulsion, not from her anyway, not that he had felt.

"I don't want to be your bounce girl?"

"You mean rebound. And you're not. Not at all.

Suddenly Yan Ping looked at him, and as the intensity of her gaze engulfed him, he sensed her hand gripping his. "I don't just want to pass the time with you, Shane. I want to make time stand still when we are together, and I want to fast forward it when we are not. And when we make love," she looked away but did not release his hand. She turned back. "And when we make love, I want you to make love to *me* not to a memory, or a ghost."

Puzzled, Shane took a contemplative sip of beer and resumed his observation of the Pacific. Yan Ping might have been waiting for a response but he didn't have one, so rather than try to bluff his way through or out of the awkwardness, he held his tongue.

"Do you understand what I mean?"

He didn't but he did not want to admit his ignorance. "You think I've been a bit selfish in bed, and you'd like me to think about how to please you more." It sounded good, and Shane was satisfied with his delivery of a snippet of something he had read in a women's magazine in some waiting room.

Yan Ping smiled as one would smile sympathetically at a simpleton. "Where did you read that?"

"All right," said Shane, trying not to appear defensive. "If when we make love I am not making love to you then who am I making love to. I am physically with you. Those are my hands on your body and my-"

"Stop it."

"Now you're angry with me. I'm just trying to figure out what the hell you are on about."

"Now who's getting mad?"

Shane raised his palm in surrender. "Okay. I'm sorry. Just cut the bullshit and tell me what's on your mind. You're making me think the phrase *beating around the bush* was coined to describe your personal and particular communication style."

Yan Ping scowled. "You don't look at me when we make love, and it makes me feel like you are imagining being with someone else, with Angela. I feel like you are using me to stay close to Angela, to hold on to her."

That's crap, was what Shane felt he should have said to immediately assure Yan Ping it was not true, but her accusation had sliced deeply into his flesh, and the sight of blood rushing from the wound made him queasy and robbed him of speech. He wasn't the type of man to use a woman. He admired and respected them. He never saw them as a collection of orifices and body parts, but as individual persons. That was why pornography had always made him uncomfortable. A sudden montage of women about whom he had fantasized ran through his mind and he felt ashamed. He had taken liberties. It was an abuse of privacy and personhood. Was that what he had been doing with Yan Ping? His queasiness escalated to nausea.

"God, Yan Ping, I'm sorry," he said. "I didn't know I was doing that. I'm sorry. Maybe you're right." Then the tears came and a solid wad of emotion in his throat choked off any further words. He leaned towards her, drawing her in to an embrace which she reciprocated with passion and warmth. Shane sobbed into her shoulder, shuddering uncontrollably. He was vaguely aware of her hand stroking his hair and her voice, soft and cool, whispering words of solace.

"It feels like the first time you have cried," she said.

Shane tried to answer but barely managed a nod. He wanted to speak. He wanted to regain control instead of making a spectacle of himself with this embarrassing display of blubbering, but the surge of grief was overpowering. It *was* the first time he had cried. Not the first time ever, but the first time since Angela died. How the hell had he managed to suppress this torrent of grief for so long?

"It's okay, baby. It's okay," said Yan Ping.

That was what people always said to placate anxiety and mollify grief, but they were just words. Shane felt hot and sick, and he wanted to stop crying. "I miss her," he muttered. "I miss her."

"I know you do," said Yan Ping. "And it's right that you do, and it's good you are finally and properly mourning her but a dawning is coming, then they'll be another day followed by another night and so on. You're alive. I'm here. I don't want you to forget her and I know I will never replace her, I don't want to. But I have to feel it's me that you want to be with now. I'm not a memory. I'm not trapped in a photograph on your shelf. I'm real, and I love you and I can make you happy now, if you let me in."

Eventually, his sobs died to whimpers and finally evaporated as he cried his tear ducts dry. An overwhelming exhaustion stepped in to take the place of his dejection, and he lifted his head from Yan Ping's shoulder and looked at her through bleary eyes. "I understand."

"I think we should not have sex for a while, and maybe see a little less of each other until you figure yourself out. You need some time to process what I've said."

It was hard to argue in the face of such merciful authority. Shane would have done anything she asked in that moment, although what she had suggested was not pleasing to him. A new wave of loss was rolling in to further erode the foundations upon which his hope was erected, and Shane had to accept the inevitability of the destruction of his castle. He had another issue which he had been avoiding for too long as well; Rob.

"Can I ask your advice before we break up?"

"We aren't breaking up, Shane," said Yan Ping, grabbing his arm, mortified. "That's why I said what I said, because I believe in us, and in our future. I told you that I love you and I do, and it's unfaltering."

"Okay," he said with a feeble smile.

"What do you want my advice about?" she asked.

"Rob."

Yan Ping's eyes rolled back and she pulled in her chin, leaving her unflatteringly adorned with an expression that Shane interpreted as antipathy towards his little brother. "What about him?"

"He's a mess and I don't know how to help him."

"Do you really want my advice?"

"Of course. Why would I ask otherwise?"

"You're not very estate sometimes, Shane."

"Do you mean astute? You're right. Anyway, I do want your advice."

"Your brother needs his arse kicked."

"Okay," said Shane. "That's blunt."

"Tell him to stop feeling sorry for himself and get on with his life. If he really wants to find his girlfriend, then he should try harder. It can't be that hard, and he needs to stop drinking and move out of your place, and he needs to stop living as though tomorrow he'll be in jail. Tell him the Thai cops have probably given up on him. Convince him he has massively overstated his own importance, and that of the man he killed. How's that for some advice?"

Shane laughed and pulled her into a tight embrace. "You're something else you know. And you're right about the police. I couldn't find anything online to suggest he is the subject of a manhunt, but he's convinced himself that he's doomed. I even tried calling the club where Jam and the guy worked, but no one knew anything, or maybe they just weren't willing to tell me. No one had even heard of Jam. Or so they said. I don't know."

"Tell him Shane." Her serious countenance wiped the smile off his face. "He is a bigger problem than you realize, and you're the only one who can sort him out."

"I just let him rage and babble, hoping he'll eventually run out of steam, but his reserves of bitterness seem to be unfathomably deep."

"Sort him out!"

Chapter Thirty-seven

"This shit has to stop Rob. I've had enough."

Shane's voice rushed Rob and mauled him on the lounge where he was semi reclined and completely stoned. Anger resonated and reverberated around the room. Clearly, his big brother had been working himself up to this moment on his way home, and had timed it perfectly to coincide with his entry into the apartment. Fight fire with fire? Why not?

"Hello to you too, arsehole. Never mind you woke me up."

Storming in amidst a hurricane of animosity, Shane was soon towering over Rob, and wagging his finger with menace. "That's exactly what you should do, mate. Wake up!"

"I am awake."

"You know what I mean."

Rob clambered to his feet and stood face to face with his brother. "I know you are pissed off about something and you're taking it out on me."

Shane's jaw dropped. "You can't be that thick."

"Why not?"

"Have you eaten anything today?" Shane walked away towards the kitchen, leaving his question floating in his wake.

"No, mum," Rob said, dragging out the word *mum* to make it sound as churlish as possible. He sat down on the lounge and scratched his head. His position as belligerent resident had been usurped, and he had now been relegated to an object of annoyance. Of course he was irritating, he did nothing but drink. Or go out occasionally and get into fights and end up arrested or hospitalised. Shane had quite justifiably reached the end of his tether, and was laying down the law.

"Here," said Shane, as he thrust a plate holding a sandwich towards Rob. "Eat this. And give me that." He snatched the stubbie from Rob's hand and swilled the remaining contents. "Eat it, and while your mouth is full, listen to me."

Rob bit into the sandwich and wiped tomato juice from the side of his mouth.

"I realize you have been through the wringer. I know you're missing Jam, and you're worried about the police coming to get you. I understand you feel like you are living on borrowed time and therefore it doesn't make any sense for you to do anything purposeful. I mean, what's the point, right? I get it. I do."

With his brother's eyes flicking between him and the sandwich which he devoured like a man who had not eaten for days, Rob allowed Shane to speak. There was a huge *but* coming.

"I appreciate how hard things have been for you but enough is enough. You and I have to sort some shit out because I'm not going to put up with this pathetic, wretched version of you for another minute."

The sandwich was very good and Rob marvelled at how expertly Shane had constructed it in so short a time, and how cleverly he had used it to shut Rob up while he delivered his sermon. He heard every word his brother uttered and received it as gospel truth. The depth of Shane's concern for him was unquestionable as was his evident commitment to helping him to get back on his feet. His tone was resolute, suggesting he had been doing some soul searching and had possibly received some advice. Most likely from Yan Ping, who on the few occasions they had met had reeked of disdain for Rob's dishevelled chaos of a life. She was a good influence on Shane; steady and focused. Although Rob recognized his predicament, the problem of how to break free seemed insurmountable. He had made a prison for himself; custom made and inescapable, and having pronounced a life sentence, he was resigned to serving it. Anyway, he thought, let Shane speak on, who knows what he and his accomplice have come up with. It couldn't hurt to listen and the sandwich was very good.

"I'm going to be really clear and logical," said Shane. "If I lose you at any point, let me know, but I'm only interested in questions of clarification at this point, and I only want them if you're sure they can't wait."

Shane was in teacher mode, but Rob tried to dismiss the condescension and concentrate on the message. "Gotcha," he said.

"Firstly, you have to dry out. If you can't do it by yourself, then we'll get you into a program. In any case, it starts now. You won't be drinking anymore tonight. I'm going to stop you and send you to bed at least half sober. I imagine you'll have a pretty unpleasant night trying to sleep whilst fighting the demon's cravings, but stiff shit. Secondly, you are going to get a job, or at least register and start looking for one, do some course or whatever. But you aren't going to sit around here all day shitfaced and indolent. When you get a job, you are going to move out. In fact it might even be a good idea for you to go home until then, to mum and dad's place, I mean."

Home was the last place Rob wanted to go. He didn't even know where it was or what it was. His parent's place was no longer his home. It had been a long time since he had felt at home. It was a nice idea, but the reality of living with his parents as a disgraced prodigal son appalled him. "Fuck no to that one, bro. I'm not moving back in with mum and dad."

Shane gave Rob a reproving look and continued as though he had not interrupted. "Thirdly, if you want to reconnect with Jam then you are going to do something positive about it rather than just whining about how you let her go and she's probably better off without you. Make some serious effort, man. You know where her family home is and where she lives and works in Bangkok, so make some proper enquiries. Find her, and tell her how you feel instead of soaking my pillows with your bloody tears every night."

Rob finished his sandwich. "Thanks for the sanger. It was good. Is there anything else?"

"One more thing," said Shane.

"To eat I mean. I didn't realize how hungry I was."

"It happens when you don't eat, you wally."

"What's the last thing on your list?"

"The Thai police have more than likely forgotten about you. We can check online again, I've already checked once, and make some discreet inquiries but I'd be willing to bet my soul they have dumped your file in the, '*never to be solved, and nobody gives a stuff anyway*' department. The lowlife you murdered was probably a pain in their arses and they were glad to see him lowered into the ground."

"That doesn't explain my face being in the newspaper," countered Rob. "They obviously made some effort. How can you be sure they aren't still looking for me?"

"The fact that you are here," said Shane, "And look, you don't even know for sure it was the police who posted that photo, do you?"

"What do you mean?"

"It might not have been the cops. That's all I'm saying. Anyway, how hard do you think it would be to find you? If they had your photo, and presumably they would have made enquires at the club where you hung out, and the hotel where you stayed. They would have been told you and Jam were an item, and they would have tracked her down, and if they couldn't find her, they would have found her family who would have supplied some information. They probably arrived in Had Yai just after you left. They would have jumped on a train, after telling their buddies in Malaysia to be on the lookout for you, and they would have been waiting for you at the station. You said you had some trouble there, didn't you? They could have snatched you there. They could have nabbed you at the airport, if not in Kuala Lumpur, then in Sydney. Am I getting through? You are here; safe and sound."

"You make everything seem so bloody simple."

"It is that simple."

Rob stood abruptly, suddenly angered by the situation, by Shane's words and tone of voice. He was irritated at being patronized and controlled, and being told what to do as though he was not mentally competent to make his own decisions. "The fuck it is, big guy."

"Why are you yelling at me?"

"Because you're acting like some fairy godmother waving a bloody magic stick around; twinkle here, twinkle there, and everything's rosy."

"What are you talking about?"

Rob palmed Shane's chest, causing him to stumble backwards. "You're going to fix everything are you? Just like that. You've got a plan for my life, to sort me out? Is that it?"

"Pretty much," said Shane, who remained calm and steady on his feet despite Rob's burgeoning hostility.

"Well fuck that totally! I'm a grown man."

"Why don't you start acting like one then, instead of being this pissy whiny little baby, chucking tantrums, because he can't have things his own way."

The first punch only connected because Shane was unprepared, and by the time it reached his stomach its power had diminished to the point of ineffectiveness. His brother grimaced and doubled over while Rob prepared the next one. His flying fist was intercepted by a sweeping block and he found himself set back on his arse when Shane twisted his other arm behind his back and thrust him towards the floor. He scrabbled quickly to his feet but Shane pushed him back down. His anger burned white hot and he swore vociferously as he attempted once more to stand. Half way up this time, he ran at Shane and tackled him against the armchair, which flipped backwards and tossed them both across the room towards the front door. More scrambling, grasping, wrestling, weak misdirected punches. Sweating, puffing and cursing.

Rob finally managed to climb on top of Shane and thus used him as a spring board to stand up. Words were lining up to be spat but he lacked sufficient energy to propel them. He watched Shane reassemble himself, smoothing down the front of his shirt, twisting his belt buckle around to its rightful position, and fixing his hair with a few casual swipes of his shaking hands.

"It's been a while since we did that, eh?" said Shane breathlessly.

"How old did you say you were?"

Laughter filled the room, displacing the electricity of violence, and causing both men to unclench their fists and wobble on legs made weary by unfamiliar exertion.

"I'm thirsty," said Rob.

Shane wagged his finger. "Nice try bro. The fisticuffs stalemate changes nothing. You're drying out."

"Yeah, yeah, water will do. Then a big glass of Coke to wash it down."

"Right."

"And another sandwich wouldn't go astray either."

"Come on you bastard," said Shane, who turned and led the way to the kitchen.

Rob sat on a stool while Shane put the bottle of Coke and an empty glass on the counter before fixing another sandwich. "Do you really think I am in the clear?"

"I do," said Shane, "but..."

"Oh shit," said Rob. "I should have known there was another *but* coming. What is it?"

"You killed a man Rob. You should be punished for that, don't you think?"

He did think exactly that. The first thought which popped into his head was Chris telling him to stop running. The truth of that statement had slapped his face so hard it still stung, but he had refused to act on it because of what it meant. He knew it then, and he knew it now. He recognized that instead of stopping, he had run faster, as though he could outrun himself and his crime and his misery. The alcohol was supposed to anesthetize him;

to dull the pain so that he could continue his absurd and futile flight. It was over now. It had to stop.

"One thing at a time, eh?" he said, without acknowledging Shane's question. "One thing at a time."

Shane studied him for a moment then nodded sagely. "Sure."

"I've got to find Jam. It'll be all right if I can just talk to her again. She was the only light in my darkness, Shane."

"Don't be so dramatic. Eat your sandwich. Then we are going to visit mum and dad."

The mouthful of bread, ham, cheese, lettuce and tomato became a wad of soggy cardboard in Rob's mouth, almost choking him.

Chapter Thirty-eight

It was with a tremendous sense of satisfaction that Shane telephoned Yan Ping to advise her of his triumph. Whilst acknowledging the significant role she had played in producing action on his part to address the long overdue issue of Rob, his sense of fulfilment at his own eventual expediency buoyed his spirits, and claimed the greater share of glory, at least in his mind. Rob's response had been surprisingly taciturn. Even though he had thrown in a few conditions, he had accepted Shane's terms and agreed on a course of action. The visit home would not be pleasant, even though everyone, at last, wanted the reunion. That mountain remained on the horizon waiting to be scaled, but first things first.

"I did it," he said to Yan Ping when she answered his call. "Mission accomplished."

Yan Ping said, "Good for you," but Shane heard, or perhaps imagined, a distinct tone of, *about bloody time,* in her voice.

"He seemed pretty bullish about his prospects all of a sudden after we had…" Shane paused to consider his choice of words, "after we had discussed it."

"Bullish means something good, does it?"

"It means he thinks things are looking up. He's feeling positive."

"And all it took was a few severe words."

Shane pondered the word, '*severe*'. God, if anyone knew how he slaved behind the scenes of his conversations, they'd be amazed. Had he been severe? It sounded too strong and yet the discussion had climaxed in to a living room brawl, so it couldn't very well be described as soft or gentle.

"Shane?"

"I'd like to see you, how about breakfast tomorrow?"

"I'm on day shift. What about afternoon tea?"

"Day shift?"

"At the nursing home."

"At the nursing home? You work at a nursing home?"

Yan Ping said, "You are ridiculous!" then she rung off.

An obsession with his inner world was most likely the cause of Shane's inability to participate properly in the present. His memory had developed sieve like qualities and his listening skills were on par with a four year old with hyperactivity disorder. Of course Yan Ping worked at a nursing home; Hammond care in Horsley. She had qualified as an assistant in nursing through the college of Technical and Further Education, and had been offered a job at Hammond care where she had completed her final practicum. There was a desperate shortage of nurses at all levels, and although she was qualified as a registered nurse in China, those qualifications were not recognized in Australia so she had to take a lower a job. It was all coming back to him now. He redialled her number.

"Sorry about that," he said. "Senior moment."

"Don't you listen to anything I say? I sometimes feel like you don't care at all about me."

"Not true at all," he said. "I do, but I have a lot on my mind and sometimes I get a little vague."

"If vague means stupid and selfish, then I agree with you."

"Ouch."

"Meet me after work at Gloria Jeans, in the mall."

"Wait," said Shane, afraid she was going to hang up again. She could be astonishingly terse sometimes. "Can't we talk some more?"

"We can talk tomorrow."

"What's with you and phones?"

"What do you mean?"

"You never like to talk to me on the phone. It's just boom-boom; business done, and hang up."

"I can't see your face, and I don't know what you are doing while I'm talking to you."

"I'm just talking to you. I can't do anything else at the same time. I'm not that clever."

There was a long pause during which Shane sensed Yan Ping reaching through the phone line with a microscopic camera, like the one used for colonoscopies, to investigate his activity and verify his claim of singular attention. Finally she said, "What do you want to talk about?"

"Well, I wanted to thank you for being straight with me about Rob and helping me find my balls."

"Don't be disgusting."

"And," continued Shane, accepting the mild rebuke, "I wanted to know if there was anything I could do for you." Before she could answer he hastily added, "I mean besides looking at you next time we make love."

"Next time?"

"Come on, don't be mean," said Shane.

A hint of repressed giggle snuck down the line. "There is something, but I don't know if you can help me with it or not."

"Ask, my love, and we shall see."

"You know I have to pass the IELTS exam in order to be registered to practice as a nurse in Australia?"

Shane thought he should probably know that, so he answered accordingly; "yep."

"I've already done it twice. I just got my latest results the day before we last spoke."

"What do you need, sevens right? A minimum of seven in each of the four skills?"

"Last time, I scored three sevens and one six point five. So I just missed out, but what's worse is I scored the six point five in listening. The first time I sat it I scored seven in listening. Previous scores don't count though. You have to get four sevens in one sitting. It's so unfair."

"Damn right it is," said Shane. He remembered having a conversation along similar lines with Angela when they had been discussing the opening of the new language school. The thought squeezed him in a bear hug; all those dreams. He could detect an echo of the trembling excitement in her voice as she had talked and talked about how great it was going to be. He was stung by a familiar pang of guilt as he recalled his lack of genuine enthusiasm for the project, and how he had played along while all the while escaping into the fantasy world of frivolous sex with students and co-workers. He could not quite forgive himself for what he saw as betrayal.

"I would like to appeal for a rule change, but I don't know how."

"You want to take on the goliath of an Australian government bureaucracy? Brave girl."

"I don't know what a goliath is, but I guess you're saying I shouldn't do it."

"Not at all. I'm saying that bureaucracies are inhumane behemoths who are notoriously inflexible, unhelpful and unsympathetic to the plight of individuals, but if you want a fight then I will armour up and plunge into the battle beside you."

"I don't know what you're saying now, Shane."

Disappointed that his fine words had fallen on unappreciative or at best uncomprehending ears, he rephrased his attempt at encouragement. "It will be very difficult to change the rules but I will help you."

"So, how do we begin?"

"Letters, emails, phone calls. We start with the regulator."

"AHPRA?"

"The Australian Health Practitioners Regulatory Authority, hereafter known as the enemy."

"The enemy?" said Yan Ping, tasting the word. "I like that."

"Leave it with me. I'll start by calling AHPRA and seeing what I can find out."

"They are frustrating and annoying, from my experience."

"No worries," said Shane. Not for a moment did he realize the enormity of the challenge he had taken on, and neither would he have cared if he did. "Now, about that afternoon tea, how about we make it today? I'm pretty sure I can't wait until tomorrow to see you."

"It's dinner time, Shane. I'll see you tomorrow, okay?"

Shane now no longer felt competent to do anything else until he saw Yan Ping again. Running through the motions was one thing, but it all felt so useless and trivial. He wanted her now. Even to hear her voice again would have been sufficient for now, just a little bit more of her to tide him over. His mind was frazzled and frayed, his concentration absent without official leave. He could think of nothing but her. It was so juvenile. He looked at the telephone in his hands as though she was waiting there for him to call her again. As if she had nothing else to do either, apart from pine over him. She had called him ridiculous, and it was true. He needed a giant boot up the rear to overcome this deadness, to move, to live independently of Yan Ping's essence. *Focus. AHPRA. Fight. Concentrate.*

"What's wrong with you?" said Rob, rudely inserting himself into Shane's love addled fogginess. "You look like you did after I smashed you around the living room."

"The man rewrites history," said Shane with a manly chuckle.

"What's up?"

"Nothing, I'm in love that's all."

"Aw, that's nice. Yan Ping is a lucky girl."

"You almost sound sincere."

"I am," said Rob, as he stepped forward and placed a firm hand on Shane's shoulder. "You're a good bloke and a good brother."

Shane looked at Rob and wondered about the future of their relationship. A new day was dawning, in which there would be some equality and respect, instead of paternalism on his part and recalcitrant rebellion on Rob's part. The time apart had healed some wounds and provided a path forward for deeper reconciliation between them. Shane began to see fresh, brighter colours being painted on the canvass of their lives and he smiled.

"I mean it. The times, they are a changin' bro. Can you feel it?"

"Yes, Rob."

What would the finished piece look like when the invisible artist stepped back from the easel to examine his work? Why was Shane now pondering life in terms of such unfamiliar metaphors? Just as quickly as the image had appeared it left, and Shane's thoughts switched back to Yan Ping and then to Angela, and to the feelings attached to them. They were finely engineered, viscerally fragile, yet impossibly strong strands of a spider's web. Yet, those strings binding him to Angela were not as tough or resilient as those which bound him to Yan Ping. She was his first love, and his time with Angela now seemed like a disruption, and that thought saddened him and ushered in a new round of guilt punches to his soul.

"What now?" Rob said. "I never realized what an interesting face you have, so readable. You must suck at poker."

"My guard is down now. I don't feel like I need to pretend with you. I used to, but something has changed. For the better I mean. Do you know how bloody exhausting it is to fake interest and enthusiasm, and worse, to pretend you are happy or at least okay?" Shane searched his brother's face, longing to see empathy but all he found was sympathy, and he knew the difference.

"No," said Rob. "I don't. And I don't understand why you've always felt you had to bung on an act for people. I've always been myself and to hell with everyone else."

"That's been your downfall."

"Rise and fall, rage and grace," said Rob with a dismissive wave of his hand. "That's life."

"Do you have to always quote song lyrics to demonstrate your wisdom or lack thereof?"

"Get stuffed. Are we going to eat tonight or just sit here and yabber?"

The mention of eating ignited latent hunger within Shane, so he dropped his philosophical dribble and focused on the immediate need. He left Rob strolling into the living room as he headed for the kitchen. A new collection of reminiscences awaited him there. He would have to learn how to integrate the memories of Angela and their good marriage with his newly reborn relationship with Yan Ping. He would marry her in time, and they would have children in due course and he would be building new memories every day with her. They would not replace the old memories, but stand harmoniously beside them in the pantheon of his experiences, hopefully. Shane was aware of the obvious conflict, but conflict was as intrinsically human as suffering. In fact the two were different sides of the same coin.

Shane stared deeply into the bright and largely unoccupied interior of the fridge, searching for inspiration. Without Angela, food had become a necessary nuisance rather than a keenly anticipated pleasure. She had always been very organized, and more than that, possessed a passion for the culinary arts. She often said cooking was more enjoyable than eating, a claim Shane had hotly disputed for the entirety of their relationship. Cooking was the means to the end of eating, and he could never see how the preparation could usurp the pre-eminence of the partaking of the product.

"What wonderful cuisine are you going to whip up for us tonight?" said Rob.

"Do you know how many meals I have cooked since Angela died?"

"None?"

"One or two, maybe three; I just can't be bothered. I know whatever I throw together, regardless of the effort I put into it, will turn out at best lousy and insipid, or at worst, inedible."

"The hungry man cares not for the quality of the food," said Rob.

Shane closed the fridge, sighed and turned to face his brother. "This hungry man feels like pizza."

Chapter Thirty-nine

There is a strange torpor which afflicts those whose hopes have been decimated by the hands of cruel reality. Many speak of the power of positive thinking, as though incantations of happy and uplifting thoughts actually possessed power to transform objective reality. Perhaps some were so gifted, but Rob Archer did not consider himself to be among the alumni of this university of aggressive optimism. When life ambushed him, or chased him across the plains before sinking its ravenous teeth into him, he failed to find any solace in wishful thinking. What good did happy thoughts do in the face of heartless truth? Life sucked sometimes. In Rob's case, it sucked often.

Shane's tirade against his withering and self-indulgent lassitude had kick started a dormant appetite for success. Rob suddenly saw how stupid it was to continue along the path of self-destruction. Swinging wildly between belligerence and depression had left him too tired to live in the quiet spaces in between. When he had opportunity to rest, he was no longer capable of taking advantage of the respite on offer.

The computer eventually booted during his musings, he opened up a browser and typed *Thai police*. He hoped to find something, somewhere about the murder case involving Pee Lek and himself. He prayed that if he did find any useful information in the labyrinth of the world-wide-web, it would be good news, along the lines of the case being dropped, or closed.

He began with the newspapers; trolling through current and previous editions of both Thai and English language newspapers in Bangkok and Had Yai. Not being able to read much Thai, he relied on the pictures, and in particular any appearance of that shot which had appeared in the Had Yai paper on that disturbing day. One hour turned into two as he continued his fruitless, and increasingly frustrating, search for any sight or mention of himself. He knew it was possible that he had overlooked something because his eyes had been wearied by straining and scanning, and because he simply was not sure exactly what he was looking for. Finally, he stood and walked away from the desk, turning his back symbolically on the computer.

His old friend, from whom he had now been estranged for two days whispered in the silence, calling him back to the fellowship of the bottle. There was no alcohol left in Shane's apartment. As part of his drying out, his brother had insisted they dispose of the temptation. Rob had thought nothing of acceding to Shane's suggestion at the time, because he saw what it represented. Now he regretted it, due to the inconvenience it created. To drink, he would need to go out. He glanced at his watch and figured he had at least three hours until Shane came home. A relapse would invite his brother's wrath, and his own guilt, but he had stopped caring when first the demon seed had seduced him, easily rendering his deliberate sobriety of the past forty odd hours an aberration. The adulteress of illicit comfort was far too great a temptress for him to resist.

There was a pub nearby, a comfortable walk into central Dapto, and once Rob had determined to pay a visit, he bounced out of the door of Shane's apartment and along the footpath. Fifteen minutes later he slid into the welcoming, if slightly dank smelling, ambiance of Dapto Hotel. He ordered a beer without thinking, and sipped it appreciatively before carrying it to a vacant glass topped bar table. Positioning himself in direct line of sight to one of the large flat screen televisions on the wall, he imbibed slowly and luxuriated in the tranquillity which it delivered.

"Rob? How are you?"

Startled, by the sound of his name, Rob jerked his schooner glass a little and splashed some amber liquid on his shirt. He turned. "Chris. G'day. Did God send you here to find me?"

"What?"

Rob was surprised by Chris' apparently genuine bewilderment. "The first time we met was at the Steelers Club and you told me God had sent you there to give me a message. Remember?"

Chris laughed a comfortable, effortless laugh. "Yes. No-no, I work here."

"Get the fuck out!" said Rob then quickly added, "Sorry."

"It's all right."

"For how long?"

"That afternoon after I left you at the Steelers and I told you I was off to the employment office to see what was what."

"You got a job that day?" Some people had unbelievable luck. Rob tried to suppress the envy, and it assisted him greatly by reminding himself he had not really tried to find a job, and that was most likely why he had not found one.

"Not quite that quickly. They suggested I do an RSA course, which I agreed to, not because I really wanted to work in a bar but because it seemed like a good idea at the time, and once I finished the course, this casual position opened up and I applied and I got it."

"With no experience?" This was cruel, almost beyond Rob's ability to bear it. He maintained a pleased and interested demeanour in order to avoid being rude, but it was a real struggle.

"Yeah."

"Shit, you're a lucky bastard."

Chris smiled and took hold of Rob's now empty glass. "I don't really believe in luck. I think God wanted me to have the job, and I'm thinking it was a reward for my obedience."

"You think God hands out rewards and punishments to individuals who attract his attention?"

"You don't have to attract God's attention, Rob. He's God. His eyes are on everyone, all the time."

"There's a scary thought."

"Or comforting," said Chris. "It depends on your perspective. I'd better get back to work. It's my first day."

Chris walked away with a string attached from his belt to Rob's jaw, which pulled the latter towards the floor with a painful yank. *First day?* He stood and rushed to the bar for another drink, unnerved by the coincidence. He wanted Chris to be an arsehole about seeing him again, to smother his words in condescension and press Rob on the issue about which they had previously chatted, the whole; '*you should stop running*', thing. He wanted Chris to be smug about getting a job so quickly and to rub it in Rob's face. If he had been a prick about it then Rob could have simply got mad and cursed him behind his back. But he was none of those things, and he hadn't tried to push anything, or to scold or to boast. He seemed happy and grateful. The second beer went down Rob's throat in half the time of the first and then he ordered a whiskey.

"Not driving mate?" said the young female bartender in an officious tone. He had not noticed her before.

Rob raised his glass and winked at her. "I'm on foot."

"Good," she said with a smile, before wandering off to serve another customer.

He could have been pissed off with her as well. Who was she to lecture him? He looked up at the glass panelling behind the bar, noticing a sign which reminded patrons of the need to drink responsibly, as well as pointing out that inebriated patrons would be refused service. *Fucking stupid!* That's what pubs were for, it was their God ordained purpose. He heard himself invoke God's name and shuddered. What were the chances of a random who Rob had met a week ago, turning up on his first day of work in another establishment where Rob was bent on drinking himself into a state way beyond mild inebriation? Rob was back running around in ever diminishing circles, as though he had never left. He sighed and sipped his whiskey, eventually wandering back from whence he had come to resume his seat. The whole bloody situation was an intolerable nag. Why? Why was he being badgered by fate? But it wasn't fate. Impersonal, uncaring and distant fate would not trouble itself so assiduously with Rob's affairs.

Rob drank, in the desperate hope the alcohol would overwhelm him and calm the storm raging in his heart and mind. The battle was so difficult and so protracted he could not believe he had fought for so long without fainting. What kept him going? The fabled human spirit which the atheists and agnostics praised in ignorance of the source of true heroism, or pigheadedness?

"Still here, then?"

Chris had sailed in from somewhere behind Rob carrying an armful of empty glasses and an indomitable cheerfulness. Rob merely raised his glass to acknowledge the question.

"Are you all right?" asked Chris.

"No I'm fucking not, mate." The impact of his schooner with the table was harder than he intended and some more beer was sadly wasted. Rob looked at what he had done, and felt ashamed. 'I feel ashamed because I spilled beer. Does that strike you as a comment by someone who is all right?"

"Yes, if that someone is hypersensitive."

"Hypersensitive? I used to only drink whiskey, and if I ever spoiled a single drop of that precious nectar I would put on a right royal show." Rob stared at Chris, waiting for some sign of appreciation, acknowledgment. When nothing was forthcoming, he changed tack. "What do you think the chances were of me, of us, meeting again? Do you know I've been dry for two days or something like that? What are the chances?"

"Very small."

Rob nodded in an exaggerated, conspiratorial fashion and waited for Chris to reciprocate. "Almost infinitesimal, wouldn't you say?"

"I might not be able to say that word, but sure." Chris looked puzzled but not worried. "I would love to hang out and chat with you, Rob, but I'm working. Do you want to get together sometime? I'll give you my number. Just call me if you want to talk, okay?"

"We don't need to make appointments or use telephones, do we?" Rob shook his head to emphasise his point.

"We don't?"

"We just meet. We're brought together when we need to be brought together. It just happens."

Studying Chris' face gave Rob no conclusive evidence about what he was thinking but had he been forced to guess, he would have identified the look on Chris' face as a mixture of compassion and panic. He appeared to be torn between his duty, and a desire to not leave the conversation with Rob in such a perilously unresolved state. After some time, which was occupied by Rob with further consumption of whiskey and by Chris hovering between staying and departing, he spoke. "Rob, I think it would be better if we talked when you were sober, but let me just say this; you seem to be suggesting, in your own sardonic style, that someone or something keeps bringing us together. I agree, and I want you to know I believe it is God. He is calling to you Rob, and he wants you to listen. The message is the same, stop running."

He laid a friendly hand on Rob's shoulder and squeezed it with a smile. "For now, you should probably go home, don't you think?"

His smile withstood the thunderclap of Rob's frustration and the offensive words contained therein. "I think you should fuck off and leave me alone. You and the fantasy you worship."

Chris left and as Rob watched him walk away, he lined every one of his steps with a whispered apology; *stupid mouth.* Maybe he needed to muzzle himself when he went drinking. That thought made him laugh, and from within the temporary fog of his mirth, the bartender reappeared and asked him if Rob wanted her to call him a taxi. Despite his irritation, he consented.

God, what he would have given to speak to Jam. As the temporal distance between them enlarged, so did the hole in his heart. It took every ounce of concentration and mental determination to think of something other than her. He craved alcohol and had given it permission for a dictatorial rule of his life, but what he felt for Jam went beyond craving. He couldn't even think of a stronger word than crave to explain the miserable compulsion to dwell in the hollow trunk of what once was, and would probably never be again. His heart ached for her and what they had lost. He wanted to be with her, but he couldn't be. That was the harsh reality. If there was some way to eliminate the sad longing which pumped through his veins in a sluggish imitation of normal function, then he would gladly have taken it. Even if a stronger pain could momentarily suppress the hurt, Rob knew only death would ultimately and completely release him. He loved her, and he wanted her, and no amount of self-talk, rebuking or loathing, could stop the tide of emotion. The heart wants what the heart wants, and his heart wanted Jam.

Shane had tried to infuse him with hope, but it was a useless, forlorn hope, like attempting to empty the ocean with a bucket. His brother was good to him, and had been good for him, and it pleased him to think of how their relationship had changed for the better. Rob felt a little lighter as he left the pub and stood on the footpath to wait for his taxi. If there was no way to forget Jam, no possibility of letting go of her, or the idea of her and the future she represented in his dreams, then he would have to forge on through the muddy swamp and trust that eventually he would make it through. To believe there was no other side was to admit defeat.

A light appeared in his periphery, which he finally recognized as being a taxi roof sign and he waved at the driver. Inside the cab, Rob greeted the driver and told him his destination, before suddenly remembering he could have walked.

"I don't know why I called a cab," hc said.

"Cause you've had a skinful and you need a ride home, mate."

"It’s walking distance."

"Doesn't matter," said the driver. "You're still safer with me than staggering along the footpath."

Knowing the infamous penchant of taxi drivers for speed and recklessness, Rob doubted the man's words but it seemed futile to comment. He studied the dashboard through bleary eyes and was jerked to attention by a sticker on the glove box which read: *This cab is watched over by angels.*

Chapter Forty

Hundreds of thousands of houses nestle in the relative serenity and safety of suburbia, perched on blocks of land, long ago divided into individual portions to satisfy the desire of the masses to dwell in buildings which have been transformed into homes. The sanctuary of home affords all men and women security, privacy, and personal satisfaction while simultaneously burdening budgets and exacerbating the already harsh demands made on their time by life. The benefits of home ownership have always sufficiently outweighed the disadvantages of being tied to and responsible for a single location. That is, for most people. Not all.

To the latter group, the concept of being permanently attached to one place, one dot on the vast landscape of the planet is anathema. Many, even those who own homes and are settled, lust for adventure and exotica beyond the familiar four walls of home, because familiarity breeds contempt.

Shane and Rob Archer walked along the concrete path which led to the front door of their family home, the house in which the two brothers were raised. They had shared the house and the yard, and even a bedroom for a period of time, despite Rob's frequent and vociferous protests. They shared meals, shared the bathroom, and even shared clothes which again left Rob miserably lamenting being forced to wear hand me downs. They shared the same space and many of the same events, but their experience was rarely identical. Everyone has their own perspective on reality, and in relation to childhood memories, everyone's glasses are different shades of rose.

As they simultaneously climbed the accommodating steps up onto the porch, Shane thumped Rob on the back. "Home sweet home, eh?"

"It's not my home," replied Rob, deferring to his older brother and allowing him to turn the knob and push open the door.

"Mum? We're here. Dad?"

"They'll be out the back won't they? Working in the bloody garden," said Rob.

"It's more beautiful than it was," said Shane. "They've had much more time to tend to it, so it has really flourished, and there's no ill-disciplined mutts rampaging around the yard trampling the flowers, digging holes and crapping everywhere."

"Were we ever able to actually play in the backyard? Those dogs were off their rockers. As soon as you moved they were all over you."

"Very loving animals, as I recall."

Rob laughed as they walked along the hall towards the back of the house and diverted into the kitchen, before exiting the backdoor and finding their parents where Shane had expected them to be. The yard was truly a garden of beauty, so beautifully manicured and organized, to demonstrate the complementary pulchritude of nature in her finest array of colours, shapes and textures. Maureen had always said that when the house was empty of boys and dogs they would renovate in expectation of large family gatherings for birthdays, and Christmas, and whatever other reason they could concoct to be together. The garden was one of her great passions and Shane marvelled at how it testified of her. Her children, her grandchildren and her family were, in her eyes, the greatest possible expression of God's love, and her garden was how she demonstrated her gratitude.

"I thought you'd have the kettle already boiled and the *lammos* laid out for us, mum," said Shane, stepping down and quickly crossing the lawn to greet his mother with a kiss and a hug. A man hug for his dad followed the obligatory firm handshake. He was reminded of the philosophy so often espoused by his father and grandfather regarding the statement a man made about himself to another man by virtue of a simple handshake. *Make it firm. Don't close early, and keep your hand at ninety degrees. Palm down tells the other guy you want to dominate him. Palm up says you are a pussy waiting to have your butt kicked.* Of course, Alan Archer never used language like that. Shane coloured the recollection to amuse himself with the irony.

"How are you, son?"

"Good, dad, good to see you. The garden looks great, but I was serious about the Lamingtons."

Alan smiled then cast his eyes beyond Shane, who turned to follow his father's gaze. Rob was trapped on the back porch, moving and perhaps even trembling, but seemingly unable to escape an invisible cell. He looked quite pathetic. Like a child who was waiting outside the headmaster's office for an inevitable dressing down and some form of punishment for his crime. Shane recognized the timid hesitancy of movement, and the furtive glances Rob threw their way as signs that his brother felt like an intruder. As Shane and Alan studied him, Maureen hustled across the grass, bounding up the steps to take Rob in her arms before he could say or do anything. Shane watched her shoulders heaving as she gripped her youngest son, as though she thought she might never have seen him again. Rob looked uncomfortable with the dramatic outpouring of affection.

"Let's go," said Alan, as he placed a guiding hand on Shane's shoulder and urged him forward. "Does your brother *want* to be here?"

It was a good question given the circumstances, and one which Shane had had plenty of time to consider previously. He understood Rob's reluctance, but did not recognize it as a sign of inner turmoil. Shane had not yet moved past the rebellious Rob, the younger brother who screamed through life with reckless disregard for others. The boy who became a man physically but suffered the affliction of persistent emotional pubescence, had always stood on the outside, lingering in the shadowy fringes of society. He did not fit, nor did he want to. Family was a foundation stone, but he had spent most of his life trying to build elsewhere. Shane did not understand his brother, but he hoped now that they had cautiously wandered into the alien territory of brotherly bonding, they might find a way to be the best of friends as brothers should be.

"Are you going to give me a turn, love?"

Maureen finally released Rob, and Alan moved in, extending his hand to his son at right angles to the ground. He had to take Rob's hand and lift it.

"Welcome home."

Rob raised his head slowly to meet his father's eyes and thus revealed the wet pain of inexplicable emotion. He seemed so unsure of himself now, as though seeing his parents had scorched his brash confidence and rendered him vulnerable and helpless. Alan pulled him close and embraced him tightly. As Shane watched, he felt a lump in his throat, followed by his mother's hand gently taking holding of his and leading him away.

"Come on inside, boys. I'll put the jug on. I've got some Lamingtons in the fridge."

"I knew it," said Shane.

Maureen squeezed his hand a couple of times as they entered the kitchen. "Sit down. Do you want tea or coffee?"

Shane had been a frequent visitor home since he left, especially in the early days when he wasn't able to cook much for himself. Apart from warming tins of assorted mush and dumping them on slices of toast, he was hopeless in the kitchen. He wasn't a fan of laundry either, so his dear mother had taken care of that for him as well. In those early years after he had ventured out on his own, he had depended heavily on her, and he knew she would rather have had him stay at home until he married and had someone to look after him. Rather than feeling slighted by her lack of confidence in his ability to care for himself, Shane simply received her demonstrations of love with appreciation. When Rob left, he slashed the apron strings with a machete. Shane's response had been to recognize his mother's attention was much more keenly focused on him. Rob had not wanted help. Not Shane's, not his parents. Not anyone's. He considered even the mere suggestion that he needed any help an affront to his independence. Rob's proud rejection of assistance drove a wedge between him and his mother in particular. While she loved him, she was nonetheless cognizant of the strong talons of pride which held him and directed his actions. He proclaimed the power of his self without being aware of the bondage that his sovereignty had placed him in.

"Tea, thank you."

"Does Rob want to be here?" asked Maureen.

"That's the same question dad asked."

"I couldn't believe it when you told me he had come back to Australia without telling us, and tried to hide away at your place. Then, when you said that he had finally agreed to come and see us..." Maureen stopped her fussing momentarily, and looked at Shane. "I feel hurt. Really hurt."

"I know, mum. I told him he was being a...an idiot, but I couldn't force him, and the truth is he was pretty messed up, and a bloody nightmare to live with."

"Has he changed, do you think?"

"I have mum," said Rob.

An awkward silence wrapped them all up in a quiet bubble for a few long seconds before Alan popped it. "Gee, it's great to have you both here. When was the last time we were all here together? Do you remember, Maureen?"

Maureen retreated to the safety of busyness and dismissed the question. "I don't know. Too long."

Shane knew that his mum knew exactly how long it had been, but had chosen to keep the information privileged. Further conversation was stalled by the sound of chair legs scraping against the floor, and the ballooning roar of the water as it rushed to a boil. With Alan and Rob now settled at the dining table, Shane joined them, pushing through the silence which followed the kettle's click off.

"We have quite a bit of news to share with you guys."

"I'm sure you do," said Alan.

Shane and Rob had discussed just how much of what had been happening they were going to share at this long overdue family reunion, and had ultimately decided to play it by ear. Shane wanted a plan, because he was a non-spontaneous person, but Rob had been angered by his older brother's attempt to control the situation. He'd warned him to try living, instead of planning. Shane did not understand how to live without planning. He and Angela had been prodigious schemers and organizers, and since her death, he had continued the tradition to honour her. He also recognized significant merit in living that way. His relationship with Yan Ping was having some impact, but not enough to draw any attention to the fact.

Soon, all four Archers were clustered around the solidity of the dining table, each with a steaming mug set before them and an empty plate which awaited a Lamington. Shane was aware of the uneasiness which clung to them like cobwebs; invisible, irritating and difficult to remove. To break the ice, he said; "This is nice, mum. Thanks."

Alan and Rob also murmured their appreciation, as words retreated from their oppressive onslaught of the elephant in the room. They were being trampled in their seats. Shane could not stand it. "The garden really looks terrific."

Maureen smiled and thanked Shane for the compliment.

"Can we please cut this bullshit?" Rob's words ripped through the disquiet. Maureen's mouth dropped open in mortification and Alan's face blanched. "This is weird," continued Rob now that he had everyone's attention. "It shouldn't be, but it is. This is my home. You are my parents and yet I feel like an outsider. I don't feel unwelcome but I do not feel as though I belong here."

"But you do," protested Alan. "You always will."

Rob held up his hand, impersonating a stern traffic cop, before saying, "Please just listen, dad, okay. I just want to tell you how I feel, and maybe explain why I didn't come sooner, why I even left in the first place. Who knows? I just need to speak my mind here, so I'm going to tell you how I feel."

After sucking in a deep breath, Rob said, "Please don't interrupt. I'll take questions at the end." His last words were delivered with an accompanying wink at Shane, who hoped his face communicated something positive and encouraging, but he couldn't be sure. The joke was completely lost on Maureen and Alan. Shane noticed how rigidly they occupied their seats, the strain evident on their faces.

"I don't know why, but I've always felt a resistance to authority. My back always arched whenever I was told what to do, and if I was told I was wrong, or my behaviour was inappropriate, unacceptable, then I took such criticism as a compliment. Good, I said to myself, you have succeeded. You bothered someone. You've annoyed someone, upset them. Why did I take pleasure in other people's misery? Why was doing wrong so much more appealing than doing right? It's a kind of darkness I guess, a restless evil and a demon which found in me a willing vessel to inhabit and make trouble."

Shane listened quietly, observing the response of Alan and Maureen to Rob's hyperbolic and poetic language. He liked it, and was pleased Rob had developed the art of selecting and employing strong language for dramatic effect. Shane would have felt pleased with himself for such a performance, and he eagerly anticipated the continuation of his little brother's monologue. It wasn't that Rob was incapable of such eloquence and lexical diversity, but he generally preferred simpler language.

"I always got a reaction from you." Rob looked at both Alan and Maureen in turn. "From both of you but especially you, mum. Shane was ignored and probably could have gotten away with murder had he the heart for it. I had all the attention from the day I was born, didn't I? A worse sleeper than Shane; worse eater and worse son, I was nothing but trouble. I probably even filled more nappies with my crap than he did." Rob laughed at his last words, whilst appearing to be uninterested in anyone else's reaction.

Rob sipped his tea, and remarkably this ignited a flurry of nervous and furtive sipping among the others. He gathered his thoughts and said, "Whatever the reason was, by the time I was fourteen, I had made up my mind I was a little devil, and I should act according to my nature, and not try to resist my immoral urges. I didn't think I would deliberately hurt anyone, but neither did I determine not to. I would be a naughty pragmatist, and as long as I felt okay, and as long as I was having fun, I was prepared to persist, and be damned the consequences. Lying came easily, as did cheating and stealing. When my sexual instincts kicked into gear, I went along for the ride. Smoking was bad, frowned upon, so I smoked. I drank because the law said I couldn't. Mostly, this was all dismissed as the rampant lunacy of a typical teenage boy who was experimenting with life and pushing the envelope. I said sorry when I got busted, without even feeling remorse. When I made you cry mum, I usually apologized and hugged you to prove my contrition, but I never felt regret. Actually, the only time I felt repentant was when my own stupidity had landed me in hot water. I could get angry at myself for a lack of criminal ingenuity, and perhaps rue some ill-considered and over exuberant exploit because it brought more grief than it was worth, but I never really felt sorry."

It sounded as though Rob was confessing to not having a conscience, but such a statement defied belief. Didn't every soul have a conscience, a built-in sense of right and wrong? Maureen had often talked about how the conscience could be damaged, seared was the word she used, by repeatedly neglecting it, or overriding it, but was it possible to so wound the conscience that it ceased to function at all? Or was Rob suggesting he was defective, in the sense he was not born with an operational conscience? Shane's mind was flooded with the rushing, turbulent water of unanswerable questions, and implications. He wanted to speak now, to stamp out Rob's apparent perfidy, to expose the lie, to challenge the implausible suggestion, but he held his peace. His brother had asked to be permitted to speak without interruption, and judging by the mortified look on the face of his parents, Shane was the only one capable of denying the request.

Surely Rob could not say anything worse than that he was a demon with not a care for right or wrong. Shane took a hot mouthful of tea, gasping in discomfort as Rob continued to lay open his hear and speak his mind with what amounted to, at least on the surface of it, a calculated verbal assault.

Chapter Forty-one

Rob was surprised, shocked even, that he had been given free rein to speak and none of his generally talkative family seemed remotely inclined to stop him, to challenge his mad ramblings. He knew he was doing the very thing he said he had always done, to speak and act without regard for the feelings of others, and yet the motivation to desist was non-existent. Quite the opposite was true; a throbbing compulsion insisted that he continue. His parents wore horrified expressions while Shane, although certainly troubled by what he was hearing from his little brother, appeared to also be slightly amused. Rob guessed the latter reaction was brought about by admiration for the theatrical language he was using.

"When I was able to leave home, I did, and I did so for freedom's sake. Then, I reasoned to myself. I could use my devious skills for more adventurously and contemptible behaviour. How much easier would it be, without needing to connive my way through family policies and procedures? I had enjoyed the challenge, but was cognizant of the fact it was time to move on. I thought I might be left alone, if I wasn't living at home, but you all kept badgering me with your patronising motherhood statements, stern warnings and the general level of disapproval. I got a job, or two, and held them for as long as it suited me. It was simple enough to bluff my way into and out of a string of meaningless and tedious jobs. I lived an uncomplicated life, and managed to save some money and make more on the side by certain nefarious means. I took my fill of whatever my heart desired whilst consistently maintaining some semblance of model citizenship. I had a plan to remove myself entirely from your collective influence."

Tea had grown despondently cold within the four mugs on the table, and Rob noticed the dearth of Lamington crumbs on the small plates which his mum had laid on the table. His mouth was dry, so he gulped the remnants of his mug.

"Thailand provided new opportunities and escapades, and all without the shadow of conspiratorial condescension which haunted my every step here at home, in Australia. In Thailand, I carried on as I pleased. I suited myself entirely and absolutely, and it was fun. Then I met Jam."

An unexpected knot of sorrow lodged in Rob's throat at the mention of Jam's name. Many months had passed but he still ached for her, bled for her. He had thought himself untouchable and unbreakable, but Jam had invaded his soul, and though physically absent and resident in an unknown abode, her memory and her spirit infected him with melancholy. He missed her. She stood as an imposing symbol of the watershed moment in his life when he realized his occupation of the earth could no longer continue in its current form; solitary, hedonistic and aimless. He had never looked for love, because he felt that even if he really understood what it was, he wasn't sure he was deserving of it. When he crashed into it, Rob had not immediately recognized its awesome transformational power. Alan and Maureen and Shane were watching him now, waiting for him to progress his disturbing narrative.

"Jam changed everything for me. Quite suddenly, I cared about something or someone other than myself. Thus exposed to the light, my selfishness sickened me but I found that love was stronger than I had previously believed it to be. It was as though I had been stumbling around blind, but had now had my sight miraculously restored. I imagined myself healed, whole. Everything looked different. I mean it was the same, but I saw it all with a radically altered perspective.

"Then, as with all things good and pure, the bliss of my new status as a liberated and cleansed man was degraded by the evil which forever lurks at the door of our circumstances. This guy, Pee Lek, who worked at the club where I met Jam, interfered with my happiness, and persevered, for whatever fiendish purpose, with his attempts to undermine it. We had several run-ins but I was never able to figure out the source and intent of his animosity. He once cut me with a knife to warn me, but succeeded only in fuelling my antipathy. He made himself my enemy, and I welcomed the opportunity to wage war against his baseless hatred. One day he showed up at my apartment, again armed with a blade and clearly with little desire for conversation. We struggled, and I feared my life to the extent I fought him as though I was possessed. And he died. I killed him."

Maureen exploded in mournful disbelief. "No!" she cried. "No Rob, You didn't! You couldn't! You wouldn't!" Great heaving sobs overcame her, battering her like storm driven waves and between them, on thin slivers of stolen breath, she protested. "You couldn't have. It isn't true. It can't be true."

Alan stood and moved quickly to his wife's side, embracing her even as his own shock at Rob's revelation threatened to fling him to the floor in appalled misery. He cast an eye on Rob, and said, "You *really* killed a man?"

Rob nodded, then quickly returned to his story as though his terrible disclosure of murder was merely another in a series of connected but otherwise unremarkable facts. "I ran, literally, to Jam, to tell her and to take her with me, knowing I must flee or be damned. I was desperate not to be flung headlong into the ignominy of exile without her by my side. That was a mistake. However, out of loyalty to me, and I hoped love, she came with me and we headed to her home town of Had Yai. She had not seen her family for many years and was extremely anxious about the reunion. Damn, I can relate to that a bit. She was also angry with me for forcing her hand, and I accepted that. I accepted whatever ill feeling she bore, and the unavoidable resentment which had to follow, because she was with me. I fooled myself into thinking I could escape, and we could be happy. I had fantastic visions of what our new life together would look like, and I comforted myself with these delusions."

He talked over the top of Maureen's muffled and anguished moans, deliberately ignoring her grief, blocking it, barring its entry into his ears and mind. He needed to finish. Shane had heard most of this sorry tale previously, but never in one long articulate and agonising stream.

"My false hopes were smashed when I saw my face in the newspaper. It was then that I knew the authorities would keep coming, and I would have to go home. There was no decision to be made, no time to debate the issue. I had to leave immediately or as soon as I could, and I would have to make my escape without Jam. She didn't have a passport and there was no time to organize one. My heart was torn out when I farewelled her at the train station in Had Yai, not least because I had no idea when I would see her again, if ever. I miss her still, long for her, but I haven't been able to find her, and unless this also is vanity, she has not been able to find me. It really hurts.

"Anyway, I called Shane and told him what had happened briefly, and he picked me up at the airport. If the police from anywhere were coming after me, I outran them, but again with the passage of time, I began to fool myself into believing they would give up on me. Why should they bother when I had taken the life of a good for nothing scumbag? I was really messed up when I arrived. Emotionally devastated and incapable of doing anything besides wallowing in my wretchedness, I drank a lot and whined in Shane's ears about how pathetic I was. I couldn't face you, mum." Rob placed his hand on Maureen's shoulder. "And you dad." A weak smile was directed towards Alan. "It wasn't that I feared the mother of all '*I told you so*', nor would anymore disapproval have bothered me, I just..."

Shane spoke next, to fill the void left by Rob's incomplete sentence. "I told him you guys would be okay, and you would forgive him, and everything would be all right, and it was better to get it over and done with rather than stew. But like Rob said, he was messed up. Still is."

Maureen sniffed into a tissue, while Rob stared at the table. Appreciative of Shane's words, he was nonetheless bereft of his own, as though he had extinguished his whole supply in one outpouring. He knew what was required, and it bubbled in the back of his throat, struggling to rise and escape his lips; an apology. This time he *was* sorry. He had felt more genuine regret in the last few months than in the rest of his life, and yet the humility required to express contrition remained elusive. How much further would he need to be beaten down before his pride was obliterated? Now was a good time to start. He cleared his throat and found Maureen's reddened eyes.

"Mum, I'm sorry." A mask of sorrow gripped Rob's face and twisted it to squeeze out the remorseful tears. Although he felt hot and close to combusting, Rob surrendered to his feelings. His head fell against Maureen's shoulder and he gratefully received the caress of her hand through his hair. He had never felt so close to his mother. Why had he waited so long to accept her love when it had never been beyond his grasp? When it had always been there, right in front of him? More idiocy; he was a grand master of foolishness.

"You know you are your own worst enemy, Rob?" said Alan.

Rob nodded.

"I have a few questions. We listened as you asked, but I want to revisit some of the things you said."

"Gee, dad," said Shane. "Maybe now isn't the best time."

Alan shook his head sympathetically. "Now is exactly the right time. This family has been fractured for too long, and I for one want to give God the glory for finally bringing us together. You don't know how hard and how long your mother and I have prayed for this day."

"I'm sorry dad," said Shane.

"What are you sorry for?"

"I haven't exactly helped the situation. I've been sort of harbouring a criminal."

Alan paused, thoughtfully. "Not really, son."

Shane nodded.

With his head now raised from Maureen's shoulder, Rob watched these proceedings and waited for an opportune moment to enter the discussion. He heard such conviction and strength in his father's voice that he could not help feel inspired, yet the nagging accusation of his stupidity persisted and rendered him mute.

"Let me start by saying how sad it makes me to hear how you have shipwrecked your life with such terrible and selfish decision making."

"Bloody hell, dad," said Shane. "Not helpful."

"Be quiet, and mind your language. Remember where you are." His words were accompanied by a wagging finger to signal a warning.

"Rob," he continued. "I'm sorry you took our loving concern and our sincere efforts to shepherd your soul as interference, disapproval and condescension. You thinking like that and feeling that way, only proves how right we were to worry and fret over you, and to consequently do everything in our power to help you stay close to God. I am really sorry you could not see that what we did was because we loved you. Can you see it now?"

Rob nodded, but said nothing.

Alan straightened in his chair, stretching his back to relieve the tension. "I understand now and I understood then, when you were a boy, your need to be free of our influence, but what I don't understand is why you never felt as though you could talk to us. It always hurt me to think that despite my best efforts to love you and to relate to you, and to model the love of God to you in the hopes you would follow Him, despite all that, you couldn't or wouldn't even talk to me. I have been in pain because of you for most of your life."

"Alan, please," said Maureen, suddenly finding her voice in the midst of her snivelling despair. "This is too much. He needs our forgiveness now. Not more condemnation. He's asking for forgiveness."

Rob observed the measured way in which his father received admonition from Maureen, but set his jaw against reducing the potency of his words. The merciful look in his eyes was strangely juxtaposed with the hard and steely features of his face. He appeared to be two men within the one, each fighting tooth and nail for control, and yet, there was no weakness present in this man, and no duplicity. When he finally spoke, it was with authority and the same paternal jurisdiction to which he had always been subject. Something *had c*hanged however.

"Rob, you need to hear these truths now, and you need to listen. Accepting the truth of what I am about to say to you is the only way back from perdition. It is the only path which you take to the light. You've heard all this before but you've never listened, have you?"

"Just because he didn't do what you told him to, what you wanted him to do, doesn't mean he wasn't listening," said Shane.

"That's exactly what it means, Shane, and would you please stop interrupting me. I know you want to protect your little brother, you've always done that, but Rob is a man now and this is his moment to stand up and face the truth."

"Pretty sure that's what all this is about, dad?"

In support of her husband, Maureen asked Shane to hold his tongue. Rob had always hated the way they stuck together, presenting a united front, one mind setting itself against him, always against him. Rob now recognized this annoying defect as a quality worthy of admiration and emulation.

"Love is painful, son," said Alan. "There is no getting away from that fact. To love someone means to suffer for them and sometimes to suffer because of them. You have hurt me and your mother because we love you, and we accept that suffering as part of life. I would rather bleed and agonise in the midst of messy relationships, than live pain and trouble free alone. Do you understand your actions have hurt other people? Not just us, Shane too, and God knows how many others. Do you understand that?"

Rob heard a minor elevation in his father's volume and a harder, more urgent edge to his tone. "Do you, Rob?"

Rob nodded.

"Look at me, son."

Rob held his father's gaze, although it was excruciating to be examined so deeply and to wrestle with the torment of guilt. He knew the words he was expected to say but even though they were the same words he wanted to say, it was extremely difficult to speak. Finally, like the very last drop of water squeezed from a sponge, the words came. "I'm sorry. Please forgive me, dad."

A single tear gouged a trench down his father's cheek. "I forgive you."

"Mum, I've been a bastard, a terrible son, a terrible person. I'm sorry. Please forgive me."

Maureen sprung from her seat and hugged Rob with such ferocity he felt they must be headed for a collision with the floor. The intense and overpowering emotion of the moment obscured any thought of what exactly this momentous family occasion meant and the possible ramifications. There was the fact that God had only been mentioned in the periphery and that was not where he belonged, especially not in Alan and Maureen's worldview. Chris popped into his head for a visit, as though just wanting to voice his approval of the proceedings, and then he left again. The warning phrase, '*stop running*', floated around in the mist created by the joy of a long held hope fulfilled, but Rob still wondered what it all meant.

While he mused, Alan joined their hug, and finally Shane weighed in with a slap on Rob's back and the light-hearted call of, "Group hug!"

Chapter Forty-two

Breaking out of a time tested routine was not as easy as people suggested. To burst out of the safe cocoon of familiarity required considerable effort, similar to what caterpillars did when they were ready for rebirth, they struggled. They had to struggle to escape the chrysalis and explode into their new life and, in fact, the struggle itself was crucial because it provided the catalyst to push the fluid out of its body and into its wings. If it did not fight for freedom, it would never fly. Shane pondered the plight of the caterpillar and experimented with it as an analogy for his own life. It was, of course, an imperfect metaphor, as most of them are, but he nonetheless felt a synergy with the lowly crawler. He knew that caterpillars grew fast, metamorphosed quickly and then went on to death with commensurate alacrity. Pointless little lives they seemed to lead.

He tried to recall a lesson from school somewhere in the distant past about caterpillars, and pictured his year six teacher, so slim and pretty with her dark skin and dark eyes. She had probably been a caterpillar too once, before blossoming into the delightful creature who enchanted silly pre and mid pubescent boys. When the image eventually cleared and he was not mesmerized by an image of her long, shapely legs poking out from beneath a red mini skirt, Shane found the right memory; Goat Moths.

Yan Ping was sitting beside him on the lounge reading a magazine, while he used the television as cover for a period of determined introspection. The cricket was on which he loved, but he was severely distracted. His sense of her presence was intermittent, as though she was a light fragrance tossed from a flower by a stuttering breeze. Shane wanted to invite her into his mind and show her, rather than tell her, what he saw.

"Ever heard of the Goat Moth?"

She dragged her eyes from the glossy pages of the magazine and studied him with an inquisitive look. Desire swelled without warning and he swallowed as though that would extinguish the feeling. "You say the strangest things sometimes."

Shane smiled. "I was just thinking about caterpillars and butterflies. You know, how the former transforms into the latter."

"Yes, I know about caterpillars and butterflies. Why are you thinking about them?"

"I feel like a caterpillar, a Goat Moth caterpillar."

Her smile said everything about why he loved her, why he had always loved her. Her curious and laconic nature, the way she was interested in things which shouldn't have interested her. The way she tempered her condescension with a thick coat of sweet affection, and thus said she pitied his aberrant mind, but loved him enough to indulge his more whimsical babblings.

"The Goat Moth caterpillar spends up to five years in its larval phase, hanging out inside a tree trunk. Or hanging around, I should say."

"What does a Goat Moth look like? Moths aren't pretty like butterflies, are they?"

"Not usually," said Shane, unsurprised by Yan Ping's sudden interest in moths. "This one is drab, grey, and quite big. Wingspan's around seventy to a hundred millimetres."

"Why would you know that?" Yan Ping shook her head but then just as she had instantly appeared on board his bandwagon, she leapt off and returned to the relative sanity of the lifestyles of the rich and famous. She had not permitted him to develop his theory out loud, about how he felt as though he was changing and how he sensed an urgency to leave the tree trunk and the pupa, to grow some wings and fly. He hadn't properly thought it through yet, and it was unlikely to have made any sense to Yan Ping, so perhaps it was better to continue the project alone. He watched her reading for a while, trying to force her to stop pretending she didn't notice, until a wicket fell in the cricket and arrested his attention. After the inevitable string of replays and analysis, Shane tuned back in to his inner world.

He reminisced about his youth, about the time before Rob went off the rails and he still had the liberty to do stupid things. He wondered why he decided to become sensible so much sooner than nature would have it. Why did he have to step up and be a model son? Why did he take that responsibility? No one forced it on him. His parents were no doubt thrilled to have at least one son about whom they did not have to fret over during his every waking hour, relieved too that they only had to fight the battle on one front. They could trust Shane to be good, to do the right thing. Why had he not resisted that? Why had he not demanded he be allowed to run amok, and be a normal teenager? He emerged on the other side of puberty as a stodgy moth rather than a free spirited and beautifully adorned butterfly. Instead of flitting from one aromatic flower to the next, he buzzed around the light globe until he became dizzy and was burned. Now, he wanted to flit.

The powerful lust he had for freedom began to suck energy from his body, or more accurately, to draw it from everywhere and centre its force in his cranium. It's pounding and booming, a fever with imaginary symptoms of some exotic affliction. He tried to breathe but could not remember how, or maybe he could but was unable to find enough strength for that most basic function. He was dead; a heart attack, a stroke? Who knew, but that he was no longer connected to the realm of the living was unquestionable.

"What's wrong, honey?" said Yan Ping. "You look so white."

Her hand was on his arm, then touching his forehead, his cheek. He could feel her, she was real. She was speaking directly to him, so he must have still existed in her dimension.

"Say something, Shane. You're freaking me out."

Say something Shane, he repeated to himself. *Say something, you're freaking her out. Say something.*

"I want to be a butterfly."

"What?" She heard him and was incredulous.

He repeated it anyway, pleased that his voice worked and simultaneously relieved he had not expired. Yan Ping punched his arm and scowled.

"I was frightened. I thought something was wrong with you."

"I'm going through some sort of metamorphosis." Shane responded to her frown with an explanation. "I'm changing. Things are changing. I feel like soon I will be an altogether different person. Different from the man you know, and different even from the man I know." He could see Yan Ping was no less perplexed, so he changed tack. "I feel uncomfortable with who I am now, and I'm aware of a need, an urgent need to transform, like a caterpillar turns into a moth."

"A Goat Moth?"

It should not have been so hard for Yan Ping to grasp his meaning. He felt she was being purposefully dense for some reason. Perhaps the thought of him changing was a terror to her, now that they had been reunited and were solidly and indefinitely together. Maybe she didn't want Shane to change because she loved him the way he was, and therefore why should she encourage him to think about becoming someone else. He speculated while Yan Ping waited for an answer, ultimately forcing her to repeat the question.

"You want to be a Goat Moth? Is that it?"

Laughter seemed essential to break the tension induced confusion, and to splash some water on the rising heat of his irritation.

"Can you answer me, instead of laughing?" said Yan Ping. "I don't see what is so funny. What on earth are you talking about? First you can't talk, then you talk shit, and now you're laughing at me."

She had stood during that barrage, and was now marching away from Shane, leaving him to battle with restraining his mirth at her over inflated tantrum. He wasn't laughing at her, and he would tell her that when she calmed down. Anger brought about temporary deafness; the inability to detect apologetic or reasonable tones. The break afforded Shane the chance to reflect on what it was exactly he had been trying so clumsily to verbalize. People changed. Relationships evolved through an inevitable series of abatement and procession, the highs and lows of the fuzziness of affection, the storms of lust and anger, the dark forests of depression. Life was movement and therefore could not tolerate stagnation. Shane was painfully aware of having almost passed through a period of quiescence, of seeing a firm rock offering salvation, on the bank of a putrid, muddy mangrove. He had been stuck, but the tide of life had shifted him, torn him from the entanglement of swamp detritus and fallen, rotting tree fragments.

His relationship with Angela had run its course and sat glumly in some corner of the past. Yan Ping and he were moving forward subconsciously, without knowledge, nor even careful thought for the path upon which they walked together. Rob and he were now closer than they had ever been, and a new sense of true friendship now permeated their familial status as brothers. Shane even felt that his parents, as they moved into the next phase of their lives and laboured for serenity and reconciliation, had become more real to him. Alan and Maureen were less caricaturized in his imagination, and consequently more solid. He shook his head as he struggled with the abstraction to which he was attempting to attach a label. No wonder Yan Ping had become exasperated. What he really wanted was an opportunity to live outside of other people's definitions and expectations; the husband Angela required, the brother Rob wanted, the son his mother and father desired.

"I'm sorry," she said, as she returned and resumed her seat on the lounge. "You just make me really angry sometimes. I don't know why."

"It's because I'm obtuse."

"What does that mean?"

"I speak in riddles and enigmas and malformed notions. I'm ungainly when it comes to self-expression. Awkward."

Yan Ping pursed her lips thoughtfully. "Awkward? Yes, that's it, sometimes anyway. Would you like to try to explain yourself again, now that you've had more time to think about it?"

"Let's take the day off tomorrow. I'll take you to a nice quiet place on the river, one of my favourite places. Swallow Rock, do you know it?"

"Wait," said Yan Ping. "You're going to take a day off work. You don't do that. You'd have to be in hospital to call in sick, and no other excuse would ever be acceptable."

"That's what I mean." Shane took both of Yan Ping's hands in his. "Does it really matter if I have a day off? I never take sick days. I'm allowed to and I want to. You can skip class. You're too good for that lot anyway. Come on."

"Just like that?" Yan Ping was still uncertain if Shane was serious.

Responsibility and reliability had always been hallmarks of Shane Archer, as had efficiency and organisation, but not spontaneity. He was not a spur of the moment kind of man. Actions needed to be considered carefully first, rehearsed and examined. Now, as he looked into Yan Ping's eyes, widening as they were with the appreciation of a fresh aspect of Shane, he could think of nothing else but being with her and of how wonderful that would be. Just the two of them, walking, talking, laughing and loving, swept up into a whirlwind of their own making, a world where there were no external concerns, no interruptions and no distractions. Thus, they would fall into each other and delight themselves in an entirely exclusive and custom built world. All the necessities and duties in his life dispatched, broomed impetuously under a rug and out of sight.

"Just like that." He confirmed, as he squeezed her hand and smiled. "Will you come with me?"

"Of course."

Yan Ping did not take time off work, or skip English classes either. She was a dedicated and determined student who not only eschewed indolence but found herself frequently angered and upset by the lazy indifference or lack of ambition shown by others. Shane was surprised she had said yes. Her more practical side might have suggested they simply wait until the weekend. There was nothing planned, plenty of time and no need to feign illness, to claim a day's pay for a day's leisure. In surrendering to a slice of wildness and impulsive decision, she had demonstrated she loved him and wanted to be with him. That was Shane's interpretation, and he felt no need to subject it to a possible refutation on her part. The excited warmth which sluiced through him was, he decided, a taste of things to come for them. Although he had not been able to effectively communicate what was going on in his mind, Shane felt confident that this deed, and many future actions of its ilk, would provide more than adequate explanation.

Chapter Forty-three

After months of fruitless searching, of teasing promises and sudden dead ends, Jam parachuted back into Rob's life. He had just about given up, when she landed behind enemy lines and crept a stealthy and cautious approach towards him. He was lying comfortably in a slouch of despondence, accompanied by a cold beer and a replay of the 2004 NRL Grand Final, when the telephone rang. He considered ignoring it, but relented.

"Hello?"

"Rob?"

Her voice was like an echo which had almost completed its reverberations through a labyrinthine network of caves, familiar yet eerie. It tickled his ears like a cool breeze. His heart stopped, from fear that its excited thudding might drown her out. He was the eternally restless wave tempted time after time by the child flirting with its powerful liquid touch on the wet sand. The child came near, the wave pounced, the child fled, the wave receded. Its desire to kiss the child's feet never satisfied.

"Jam?"

"How are you?"

Such a banal question after so lengthy an estrangement seemed absurd, and yet, what would you say to someone to whom you had not spoken for many months? Someone who you never really believed you would see or hear from again, regardless of any flickering hopes to the contrary. Anything else would have seemed ridiculous in the circumstances. *Jam.* Rob sighed and closed his eyes.

"Rob?"

"I'm here. I'm sorry. God, where have you been? I've been looking everywhere for you. I've missed you so much. Are you all right?"

The rush of anxious questions must have overwhelmed Jam because she did not answer, although she was still there on the line. It was the only connection they had enjoyed since he left and yet it was as tenuous as gossamer, and he therefore felt afraid it would snap, and he would be alone again.

"I'm okay."

"Where are you?"

Another pause increased his fretfulness, and he wished he could transform himself into a soundwave and zoom along the fibre optical cable to be with her. It was almost impossible to calm his nerves, to prevent the tremor in his voice, to halt the tapping of his foot on the floor.

"In Sydney."

"What?" Again, explosive and incredulous. "Where, why?"

"I'm studying English at a private college, and I'm going to try to pass IELTS and get into university."

All the time Rob had been scouring Thailand, overturning stones in every province from Chang Rai to Ubon Rachathanee and south to Yala, she had been here, just up the road, possibly as close as a ninety minute drive. A stampede of questions charged at the gate of his mind, rendering him dumb. He had to say something. Anger danced in the same field as elation and relief. Confusion and hurt frolicked there as well. He had to say something. *Say something.*

"That's great," he said, forcing himself to be pleased for her, to match the enthusiasm in her voice. "How long have you been here?"

"Only a couple of weeks."

A couple of weeks wasn't too bad, not as bad as a couple of months. Imagine, she had been here, virtually in his backyard the whole time he had been searching for her. It was only a couple of weeks but still he wondered why she had not contacted him immediately. Obviously she had kept his number so why had she never used it. These were questions for which he must have answers, but Rob was cognizant of the need to tread lightly. Jam had a story to tell and reasons for what she had done, whatever it was that she had been doing all this time, while he was tormented by her absence from his life. She had to have a reason. He would hear it all in time. That must have been why she had finally called; to talk to him, to explain herself, and, if he dared dream of such, to reconcile with him.

"So you got a student visa and you're staying...where?"

"Student accommodation for the college, near Central Railway Station; do you know it?"

"Of course. Can I come and see you? We need to talk, don't we?"

"I'm sorry, Rob."

His heart stopped. What was she apologising for? Did she not want to see him? Then why had she called?

"I'm sorry I didn't call before."

Rob breathed again and coached his heart to a steady rhythm. "I'm sure you have a good reason."

"Yes and no."

"Jam," said Rob, again sensing the tension along the thin threads which held them together. "I want to run and jump on a train to Sydney right now. Are you free? I need to see you. Whatever you have to say, you can say to my face, okay? That's better, isn't it?"

"Okay," she said without any conviction. The nervousness in her voice worried him. "The Edge cafe on Elizabeth Street; do you know it?"

"I'll find it. What time?"

"Come tomorrow. It's too late tonight. Nine thirty tomorrow morning."

"I won't be able to sleep a wink tonight. Jam, is it really you? I can't believe it."

"Try to sleep. I'll see you tomorrow morning."

Jam hung up before he could wish her a good night. His beer had not been touched during his conversation with Jam, nor had he moved from the lounge. His foot stopped its maniacal bouncing, despite the incessant waves of thrilling anticipation which coursed through him. After finishing his beer, he drank another and then another, before turning off the television and attempting to sleep. At some point he succumbed to a peaceful slumber.

The seven forty-five from Wollongong station was due to arrive at Central at nine-eighteen. During the trip, he googled the location of the Edge Café and was pleased to see he would make his date with Jam comfortably. Thankfully, none of the frequent and highly irritating track maintenance works had been scheduled. The buses which replaced the trains were an unpleasant necessity and an inferior form of transport. As he sat, he watched with disinterest as the tenebrous surroundings of the world passed by, resenting their occasional intrusions, struck by how meddlesome they could be and how inconsequential. Rob realized he had suffered this sense of disconnectedness ever since he left Jam behind in Had Yai.

When the train arrived, he was standing at the doors willing them to open and release him. He pushed through the slowly widening gap, stepped onto the platform and hurried along towards the frighteningly steep escalators which carried him near the surface. Through the electronic turnstiles, weaving through loafing clumps of people, he made his way to the exit and merged from the subway into bright sunshine. He was reminded of a C. S. Lewis quote which Shane had once shared with him. It spoke of how the sun not only provided light but was itself light. Lewis said he believed in the sun, not only because he could see it but because he could see everything else by it. Rob had never really understood it, although he agreed with Shane at the time with respect to its apparent profundity. He stood for a moment and allowed the warmth of the solar rays to ease his apprehension.

Following a brisk walk he arrived at the cafe, where he saw Jam sitting at one of the tables arranged on the footpath under bold umbrellas which advertised the cafe's preferred coffee supplier. As he approached her from behind, she did not see him, so he paused to watch her, trying to grapple with the reality of her existence. She had faded to become nothing more than a dream. Rob spoke her name before he reached her, and she turned and smiled. The effect of her greeting was as it had always been; faintness inducing, knee weakening.

"Hi," he said. He wanted to kiss her but he didn't, due to the uncertainty of their status.

"Hello."

She looked more beautiful than the goddess she had become in his fantasies, though he would not have believed it possible. Her features, once lined with anxiety and the turmoil of inner conflict, now radiated tranquillity. Something had happened to her. Maybe she was indeed a celestial being, elevated beyond regard for the mundane. What had brought about this ethereal transformation?

"Have you been waiting long?"

"No. I already ordered my drink. You have to go to the counter if you want something."

What he wanted was to crush the ice and steam into the open waters of disclosure. He needed answers, not liquid refreshments. "Sure," he said. "Okay. I'll be right back." He was bothered by the fact that she had already ordered a drink. Was she in a hurry? Anxious to say what she had to say, then run away? When he returned, he settled himself opposite her and asked her permission to smoke, which she gave without hesitation as if it was of no consequence. They sat and looked at each other, silently evaluating the situation, wondering how to begin, where to begin.

"You look different," he said. "Even more beautiful."

Jam lowered her head and murmured a thank you. "I guess I should start at the beginning."

"That always works best."

"Are you all right? You look well," she said.

"You've caught me on a good day," said Rob. He drew deeply on the cigarette then turned his head to slowly expel the smoke. He faced Jam once more. "The truth is I have been a complete basket case for most of the time since we split."

"A basket case is a bad thing, is it?"

Rob laughed. "God, I've missed you Jam. Did I tell you that already? I've felt so hollow-empty and lost without you."

"I'm sorry I didn't contact you earlier."

Not yet ready to extend forgiveness, Rob said, "Please tell me what's been going on."

Jam sipped her coffee and stared into the cup, as though the words she needed were floating there on the surface of the bitter brown fluid. "When you left, I wanted to kill myself. I seriously thought about it. I saw no possible way for us to ever see each other again. I guessed you would eventually be caught by the police and thrown in jail, and if not, then you would stay and hide in Australia, and I had no way of getting here. I had some money but how would I get a visa? I had no idea what to do with myself. Life seemed suddenly pointless. My future looked very black. I tried to talk to my dad but he told me I was better off without you. My younger brother foamed at the mouth when he spoke of how he would kill you if you ever came back. No one thought there was any future for us, so why pine away, agonising in vain for a hollow promise, an obscure and unlikely hope. They told me to get on with my life and they wanted to know all about my life such as it was. Can you believe they finally asked me what I had been doing, and where I had been living?"

"What did you tell them?"

"I wanted to tell them everything. I nearly did. I almost confessed my shame to them, because I was so miserable. I felt self-destructive so what further harm could it do to tell them I had been selling myself, my body, to men for sex? What difference would it make, if they knew everything? That's what I was thinking."

"But you didn't?" Rob had long ago stopped thinking of Jam as a go-go bar girl, a sex worker. That seemed like an eternity ago, another life, another time. It was the past, but had she returned to it? This troubling thought broke into his mind and settled there. How did she find the cash to come to Australia? He gulped.

"I reasoned that telling them everything would hurt them more than keeping it to myself would hurt me."

Rob nodded wisely. "Sometimes honesty is *not* the best policy."

"I was wandering around in a daze for almost a week after you left. It was as though you took with you my whole reason for living. My brain, my normal clear thinking brain, protested against my obviously ridiculous attitude but it was a quiet and ineffective complaint. Like the way a child grizzles before it falls asleep on the floor with a half-eaten biscuit in its hand. I couldn't snap out of it, and I was shocked by the experience of feeling that depressed. I've never felt like that before. I thought about killing myself but I couldn't even find enough energy or motivation to get beyond the idea of suicide. I was like a..."

"A zombie?"

Jam nodded, sipped her coffee and stared at the table for a few moments. "Anyway, one day I was in town buying something for my father, and I ran into a group of missionaries. I didn't know at the time they were missionaries, but they all wore white T-shirts with smiley faces on them. One of them played a guitar and a couple of the others sang a song, and some more of them were sort of standing around and talking to people, handing out little pieces of paper. I was really curious so I hung around and watched them for a while."

At the sound of the word, *missionaries*, Rob's stomach tightened. It was patently obvious where this narrative was heading and, as he was reminded of his two chance encounters with Chris, he was equally certain God was doing it again. Three strikes now and Rob was withering in his resolve to avoid an inevitable conclusion to this pursuit. He projected moderate interest to cover his panic, as she continued.

"One of the white shirts approached me and greeted me with a smile. I don't know how to describe her smile, I mean, you know in Thailand a smile can mean almost anything, but it was odd, different, more sincere than usual. She spoke to me in very familiar terms even though we had just met, and although initially I found that confronting, I soon relaxed and allowed her access to my heart."

"Access to your heart?" Rob was intrigued by the phrase. "You mean you opened up to her? Trusted her?"

Jam suddenly leaned forward as though she was about to deliver the best part of her story. "I had an irresistible urge to confess to her."

"Confess what?"

"Everything. I just wanted to get everything off my chest. I felt so full of misery I knew I had to release it. Like a poison. Yes, it was like I had swallowed poison and been stumbling around thinking I was sick but would recover, but then I was confronted with the truth that the poison was killing me, and I had to do something to try and save myself."

She paused, and a huge smile spread across her face, the expression of a beautiful, happy memory being relived. Rob watched, fascinated by her, and simultaneously still afraid she was leading him to the end of their relationship. Or to the demise of any hope of renewing their relationship. She was definitely leading him somewhere and the suspense rattled his bones. Despite the torrent of mixed emotions he felt, he found his voice and urged her to tell him more.

"She said Jesus could take away my guilty feelings and my sin, and wipe out my past. She said he would let me start my life again, if I trusted him. But I said I didn't understand how that was possible, because I had done too much sin to be forgiven. Then she said God's love and forgiveness was unlimited."

"You're a Christian now?" said Rob, making his statement of the obvious sound like a question.

Jam nodded with cautious enthusiasm. Rob perceived she had picked up on his negativity and was reluctant to come on too strong with him. She was right, if that was the case. He interpreted Jam's conversion as the final nail in the coffin of their relationship, and her wanting to see him was only so she could say sorry to his face and be nice, because that's what Christians did. A flash of resentment sparked in his heart, and almost as quickly was surpassed by a rising anger at himself first, then at Jam, then a general rage which seemed disproportionate to his circumstances. Confusion dive bombed into the turgid waters, and made a tremendous splash which obviously registered on his face.

"What's wrong?" asked Jam.

"This isn't how I thought the conversation would go," said Rob. "Not how I wanted it to go."

"What do you mean?"

"I was hoping this would be the beginning of a new start for us, but I can see you've changed and I don't fit in anymore. There's no room for me. I mean, how can I compete with God?"

He didn't want to sound so bitter but he couldn't help it. If he thought his rant would produce something, anything, either good or bad, he was mistaken. Jam seemed so lost in tranquility as she sat and listened to him, that he almost felt ashamed for speaking so petulantly. An apology was in order but his stupid bloody pride sewed his lips shut.

"It's not like that," Jam said.

Rob swallowed his acrimony and forced civility into his voice. "What *is* it like?"

"The biggest challenge I have faced in my life is my feelings for you. I even asked God to take them away so I could truly move forward, but..."

"He didn't answer?" *Typical*, thought Rob.

"He said it was okay for me to love you."

Chapter Forty-four

A wonderful experience can have such stamina through subsequent unpleasant ones, such power to sustain and to provide a lasting afterglow. Sadly, bad times come in waves and the might of the pounding eventually subdues the strongest delight. Three days after he and Yan Ping had jigged their respective responsibilities and indulged in a day of esoteric paradise, Shane was fuming. Sitting in his living room, he gripped the telephone so tightly he was sure he could crush it, or melt it, or bust a blood vessel. He was on hold with AHPRA, getting the usual run around, being passed from one faceless, dense secretary or bureaucrat to another, climbing an impossibly tall ladder, one slippery rung at a time. He was getting nowhere except into a heightened state of agitation.

Yan Ping was at work, in her low paying job at the nursing home, slaving away despite being overqualified for the task and underappreciated, frustrated yet trying desperately to be patient and cling to any sliver of hope which presented itself. Shane had all but promised her he would fix this situation and that he would right this injustice, it had not been a hollow promise. He firmly believed himself capable of changing the stupid and discriminatory rules which prevented qualified and experienced medical professionals from practicing in Australia.

He started by trying to find his way through the maze, the chain of command, to reach someone who was actually capable of making a decision. AHPRA itself was a monster, like all bureaucracies, especially large ones, and seemingly incapable of flexibility. The rules were in place and they afforded no loopholes, exceptions or special passes. Shane accepted the practical necessity of such rigidity, but that didn't make it any less annoying, as anyone who had ever had the misfortune to wage war against any of these behemoths of officialdom knew full well. The rules which were so efficiently applied were not the domain of the bureaucrats in the sense that they made or changed them. The politicians wrote the laws and established the administrative mechanisms to whose task it was to govern. And so it was that Shane shifted his attack to the legislators, particularly the health ministers. He learned that a ministerial council had been scheduled to discuss, among other pertinent issues, the subject of the English language proficiency rules for the registration of health professionals. If he could convince enough of them, even just a few, of the merits of his arguments against the current regulations, then they would surely be willing and more than able to go in to bat for the cause.

They proved difficult to track down however, and then to pin down. He sent letters and emails and made phone calls to press his case, but the response was less than encouraging. Some, like the Victorian minister for health, agreed with him with respect to the discriminatory nature of the rules, but frustratingly, would not agree that they should be changed. Others did not respond at all, and those who did regurgitated the history of AHPRA, the background to the development of national standards, the fact these regulations were under regular assessment and review, and they repeated the rules as though Shane was an ignoramus. He found their attitudes condescending and insensitive.

Suddenly a voice broke through the static of elevator music which he had been enduring for fifteen minutes. "You could try the national health ombudsman."

"Do you have that phone number?"

"No, sorry. It will be in the book."

Shane disconnected and swore at the phone. When he had finished venting, he dialled directory assistance and was connected to the ombudsman's office where he was greeted with an answering machine. He left a disconsolate message, expecting to have to call again tomorrow, and the next day, and so on. Following his unsuccessful efforts to gain the support of the health ministers, he turned to the media. After a long wait on hold one morning, he was able to state his case to the not insubstantial audience of the listeners to Sydney radio station - 2GB.

The phone rang, grabbing his attention, and he quickly answered without looking at the display, expecting for some baseless reason to be receiving a call-back from the ombudsman. He answered with more tension laden haste than he could hide.

"G'day, Shane. Did I catch you at a bad time?" said Rob.

"I was foolishly hoping to hear from someone else. Stuff it. No, I'm good to go. How're things at mum and dad's?"

"It sounded like the stupidest, shittiest idea I had ever heard, but mum was so insistent, I just couldn't say no. It wasn't quite the mother of all nagging jobs but it was pretty bloody close."

"So it's going okay?"

"It was pretty weird at first. There was still a lot of...tension probably isn't exactly the word but it'll do. And the circumstances were unusual, but you know what they're like, so forgiving and easy going. I should've reminded myself of that fact when I was busy avoiding them."

"They are unbelievable," agreed Shane. "I don't know how many times I've thought how much they deserved better than a couple of mug sons like us."

"Speak for yourself. How are things with you anyway?"

"I jigged work on Monday?"

"No shit!"

"Yan Ping took the day off as well and we went to Swallow Rock for a picnic. It was magical mate. That is, once I got over the anxiety of pretending to be sick when I wasn't. I didn't have to say I was sick. I just told my boss I needed the day off for personal reasons."

"That's all right. It was true, wasn't it?"

Shane sat down on the lounge, then stood again and wandered to the kitchen. Although Rob had been the biggest pain in the arse in the universe, and Shane had had frequent bouts of extreme agitation having his lazy, busted up little brother lying around his apartment using up oxygen, he missed him now that he was gone. It hadn't all been bad. They had managed some serious bonding.

"I felt surprised, and kept asking myself why I was doing this. It was so unlike me, Yan Ping too, baffling for both of us, actually. It was as though we had been possessed by a couple of free spirits, winsome ghosts of carefree lovers from the past. Eventually we talked each other out of caring about our responsibilities and we slid into a mysterious happiness, and it felt pretty comfortable. The time passed so quickly and yet it felt like slow motion. We talked and we walked and we ate and we canoodled."

Rob laughed. "Canoodled? Nice euphemism."

"It's not a euphemism. We kissed and cuddled. That's canoodling."

"Whatever."

Shane had wanted more. He had loosened up so completely during the course of the day that he had felt fearless and would have made love to Yan Ping right there on the beach, or under a tree. There was no one around, apart from the odd dog walker, so who would have cared if they'd let themselves go? Who would know if they surrendered to passion? Why not seize the moment and forget everyone and everything else? He didn't see the need for restraint and he told her so. Speaking directly while holding her hand and gazing into her eyes, he had told her he wanted to make love to her. She was uncertain, bound by inhibition and whatever other enigmatic forces controlled her. He wanted her and she wanted him. It was simple; for him, but not for her.

"Still there, mate?"

"Yeah. I'm not saying I didn't want more but we were in a public place and Yan Ping was reluctant."

"That's understandable. I take it you two are going okay?"

"We'll probably get married if we can blow away this black cloud hanging over us."

"Black cloud?"

"This whole AHPRA registration thing, she's going to have to consider going back to China."

"What? Because of her visa? Why don't you just hurry up and get married then?"

He had thought about that, but did not want her decision to marry him to be based on some external necessity. It seemed wrong. It was a laughable cliché; marriages of convenience, marrying for residency or whatever. Shane had heard some horror stories, including one particularly bad example from a former student who had got herself entangled with a much older man for the sake of getting a residency visa. He'd seemed nice initially, but had turned out to be a manipulative and controlling abuser. She would often come to class crying about her predicament and how afraid she felt, how the bastard had taken her freedom. Eventually, Shane had referred her to a domestic violence advisory service, with the result that she dropped out of English classes and he never heard from her again. God, he hoped she was okay and that she had managed to get away from the prick who took advantage of her. He wished he could have done more to help.

Rob interrupted his thoughts. "Well? It's not a trick question. What's the problem? You love each other and you are going to get married anyway, right?"

"Are we rushing it? I just can't help wondering if it's too soon."

"It's only too soon if you think it is, because I don't reckon anyone else does," said Rob.

"I don't know, mate. It's not that simple."

"Sure it is. Why do you always make everything a massive drama? It's like you take some sort of masochistic pleasure in overcomplicating your life."

The truth of Rob's statement was impossible to deny, so Shane did not attempt to muster any argument against it. He always took the least direct path, preferred beating his way through unwelcoming and unyielding bush rather than motor along a well beaten and infinitely easier track. He guessed he was always trying to prove himself in some way.

"How'd you get on with Jam?"

"A subject change?" said Rob. "Okay. Let's do that. It was so great to see her that I cannot think of an adjective strong enough to define it."

"I can imagine."

"As you know I'd pretty much given up hope. I tried everything. You tried as well. Short of actually travelling to Thailand and conducting a ground search covering Bangkok and Had Yai, even though she may have no longer been in either of those places, I was dejectedly confident the hunt was over. Then she calls out of the blue, and throws my emotions off the cliff of stability and into the swirling anger of the waves. I was both excited and in appalling dread of what would happen. Every time a positive thought surfaced, a negative one jumped on its back and pummelled it into submission on the ground. I thought about getting loaded before meeting her but decided against it."

"A rare show of self-control?"

"Anyway, to cut a long story short, she told me she had become a Christian and had started a new life."

Shane almost laughed at the irony. The woman Rob had been running away from all his life, his mother, and Jam, the woman who he had been desperately searching for and pinning all his hopes for the future on, were now both Christians. Shane was also aware of Rob's encounters with Chris. It seemed he was marked man.

"Okay...so where do you fit into this new life? You are, or were a significant part of her old life?"

"She told me she tried to forget me, and even prayed God would take away her feelings for me. Does that even work? Is it possible? I don't know, but in her case it wasn't. In fact she said God told her it was okay to love me. Strangely that was not enough for her to jump on a plane. She said she needed to figure out what to do with her life. Career wise, you know?

Once she worked out what she wanted to do, she decided to leave Thailand and come to Australia to study. I told her that didn't make any sense if she was trying to move on, and she said sometimes we all do things that don't make sense."

"Shit yeah. When emotions take over locomotion duties, the train is bound to run off the rails."

"I suggested maybe she chose Australia because she knew she could not let me go, and she said eventually that was the only logical conclusion, and yet she feared contacting me because she was afraid of how I would react. She said she had not thought it out properly, but simply went on a gut feeling that things would work out somehow. I knew her when she was working in the bar, and I know what she did. I know the old Jam so how would I like the new Jam? That was her question; how would I like her now? How could I like her now? I told her that new or old I loved her, and if being with me was what she wanted and it made her happy, then I was ready to step up and be the man she needed me to be. If not, then I was prepared to let her go."

"That was magnanimous. Were you serious or just saying that in the hope she would say yes?"

"I don't know."

"And the result?" said Shane. "I thought you were abridging this story."

"We decided we would try. She said we should take it slowly, and she insisted sex was off the table, and we should therefore avoid situations where we might be tempted."

"And that was okay with you?"

"You know I like sex."

"Don't we all?"

"It wasn't even an issue. I didn't feel disappointed. I didn't even think at any time about being physical with her. I was so relieved to be looking at her face and hearing her voice that nothing else mattered. It's not that I didn't want to make love to her, but I didn't think about it. Not even when she said it was not going to happen. Suddenly it didn't seem important anymore."

"Sounds like you are in love, mate."

"As much as I understand it, yeah. I didn't know before, I mean, I didn't know what it was. It's hard when you have already become sexually involved, or when you start off a relationship with the intention of sex being the preeminent concern, to extricate yourself from the bonds of lust. There's the friendship thing, then there's the sex thing. Do you think a man and a woman can be just friends?"

"Depends on the man and on the woman," said Shane, as he watched a video highlights reel run in his mind, demonstrating all those times when he had failed to view a woman as a person and not just an object of sexual fantasy. It wasn't his default position but the highlights reel ran so long he had to switch it off. "It's tricky. If there is a physical attraction there on top of whatever else has drawn them together, then it's like you said. It's pretty hard to separate the friendship and the desire. Me? I could probably manage it, but you? Probably not."

"Thanks for the vote of confidence."

"No bullshit between you and me anymore, okay?" said Shane.

"On that theme then," ventured Rob, "Can I suggest you stop dicking around with the bureaucrats and either do something in the fair dinkum department to get those AHPRA rules changed, or drop it. And whatever else you do, marry Yan Ping. Don't let her go again. You wouldn't be that stupid, would you?"

"My capacity for stupidity is world famous, but listen," said Shane. "What about you? What about the murder, the cops? Did you two talk about that?"

"I asked her about it, and she said she had not seen or heard anything. She had not contacted anyone at Lipstick and did not want to. She thinks it is a dead issue, a cold case, but I told her that I still wasn't convinced I was off the hook. She really didn't seem at all concerned which made me feel a little better but...you can't just kill someone without consequence, can you?"

"We've had this conversation before, mate. You know what I think."

"Anyway, you have much more immediate problems than me and mine, namely, this AHPRA business. Just take my advice, okay? Sitting on your arse won't get you anywhere. Be bold, young soldier. Do something big, audacious, and risky, and make yourself be heard. Make it so they can't ignore you. "

Chapter Forty-five

The scene at the corner of George and Market Streets was nothing at all like what Rob had expected, even if he had known what to expect. The normalcy, the unremarkable buzz of the city in the middle of the day; shoppers, office workers, tourists bustling in and out of the cafes and shops on the ground floor, filling the air with the hum of human commotion. He pressed through the molasses to the elevator, where a policeman confronted him with a stony intransigence.

"I need to go to the seventh floor."

"You need to find something else to do. There's no access at this time due to a situation."

"I know, I know," Rob heard his voice rising in panic, and despite knowing it would not help his cause, he could not overcome the sense of urgent dread which coursed through his veins. "It's my brother. I need to see him. Let me talk to him." It was only then, as the officer shook his head and delivered a stern and unsympathetic apology, that Rob felt the heat of the crowd's excited curiosity and heard the buzz of whispered speculation. To call this a situation was akin to calling a five course meal, a snack.

A voice jumped from the sizzle of sublimated sound. "Sir, did you say that you are his brother?"

Rob turned to find the source of the voice. "Who are you?"

"Katrina Hang - Channel Seven news."

There were other cameras and reporters amongst the onlookers, which Rob had failed to notice as he marched through the ground floor mall of the Ernst and Young Centre. The closer he looked, the greater his surprise at all he had not seen. His head was spinning so fast, and he still had not recovered from the devastating knockout blow of the news that Shane had taken his advice about dealing with AHPRA to a dangerous extreme. When he heard something was going on at the AHPRA office, he had tried to call Shane. The lack of reply had placed all the ducks in a row, and Rob had quickly figured out his brother was in the centre of this maelstrom. Shane, version two, had become a monster of reckless unpredictability. Ignoring the reporter, Rob resumed his attempt to persuade the policeman to let him pass.

"Radio your boss and tell him I'm here. Let Shane know I'm here. I can help. Let me talk to him before he does anything dumb."

"I'd say he's already crossed that line, mate."

"Radio your boss," insisted Rob. "Please. Just ask the question, it won't kill you to ask, and it might help. You want to help, don't you?"

The officer raised his large hand and thrust a forbidding palm towards Rob. "Back up, please."

Without realizing what he was doing, Rob had pushed closer to the officer, and was clearly threatening rather than imploring. He retreated and collided with a body, presumably the Seven news reporter. The feminine grunt she emitted forced Rob to issue a perfunctory apology.

"Is there something you want to say to your brother?" said Katrina. "Speak to me. They've probably got a TV on up there. He'll get your message."

"Don't say anything to her," ordered the officer. "Wait."

He clutched his two way radio, pressed the speak button and identified himself. Rob held his breath as he listened to the gruff, scrambled voice at the other end. Then; "The guy's brother is here. He wants to come up and try to talk him down." The officer lowered his voice and turned away from the expectant faces of the crowd who had closed in tighter, filling the space with agitation.

Rob could not hear properly, but he noticed the officer nodding his head slightly and hoped it was a positive sign. Hope was a lighthouse; a faint beacon of light peeping through the maleficent darkness, distorted by the driving rain, dispersed by a demonic wind. It was all he had. He expected the worst, while simultaneously praying for the best. Yes, praying. Desperate times called for desperate measures, as the old adage said.

The officer turned suddenly and nodded, before pressing the call button for the elevator. Rob fidgeted as he watched the light trickle down through the numbers, finally reaching the ground floor indicator. A ding preceded the opening of the doors, presenting something that looked like an ominous chasm into which Rob would plunge and perish. The policeman ushered him inside with a firm hand and nodded again without smiling, as the doors closed.

His reflection in the polished stainless steel of the elevator walls glowed with the anxiety which ballooned within him. It was his advice, albeit taken exceedingly literally, which had compelled Shane to this act of lunacy. Rob had told his brother to stop whining and actually do something. Not something insignificant but attention grabbing, unmissable and impossible to ignore. He hadn't known at the time he'd said it what exactly he had in mind, or indeed if there was anything to be done. He was merely endeavouring to raise Shane's flagging spirits because he could see how the battle against AHPRA was dissolving his faith and sapping his energy. Now, it fell to Rob to right the wrong he had inspired. What would he say to Shane? What could he say? What frame of mind was he in? The steady predictable Shane that Rob had known all his life had recently undergone a dramatic overhaul. He appeared to be deliberately letting go, releasing control, denying even the need to be the master of his life and everything and everyone which interacted with it. The transformation was from a familiar solid to an unknown liquid, and although it was happening relatively slowly, it was happening, and it felt as though it must come to an inevitable and potentially tragic conclusion.

Bing! The elevator came to a sudden stop at the seventh floor and Rob held his breath as the doors opened. He was immediately faced with a wall which prevented him seeing anything other than the framed watercolour landscape which decorated it. Looking first right, then left, he noticed that either way would lead him into the AHPRA office, and for a moment he loathed the simple decision, to the point of inertia. He was still thinking of what to say to Shane, running through scenarios and possible conversations. Was he armed? He hadn't heard anything on the news about the man being armed, but if Shane didn't have a weapon, how precisely was he able to lay siege to the office, and what was it he wanted to achieve? Did he know? Had he thought it through, all the way through? Had the rational and calculating Shane Archer walked calmly into this office and taken charge, or was it a slightly deranged and desperate Shane with no capacity for peaceful protest?

A policewoman appeared in front of Rob's face, her sweet perfume filling his nostrils and contrasting dramatically with the severe expression on her face. Rob had only just stepped out of the elevator when the officer moved in.

"You're this man's brother?"

"Yes," said Rob, rattled by the intensity in the officer's voice and eyes. "Rob Archer. What's going on?"

"What's your brother's name?"

"Shane."

"He has a gun."

"Where did he get a gun from?"

"He has the staff in the manager's office and won't let them out. He says he wants the rules changed and he doesn't care if I, or that is we the police, know what he's talking about or not, because it has nothing to do with us. I pointed out that his waving a gun around and threatening people, has everything to do with us and I attempted to explain the ramifications of his actions which he has apparently not considered."

"It seems not. Let me talk to him."

"What are you planning to say?"

Rob stared at the officer as though he did not comprehend the question. The officer responded with a quizzical look which prompted Rob to say, "I have no idea. I was trying to think of something on the way up but...this is so unlike Shane. If you knew him, man, he's a model citizen, a stickler for the rules. I was the black sheep. He was the favoured one."

"Be that as it may," the officer replied, clearly uninterested in the Archer family history, "but he's put himself into a very unfortunate and dangerous situation. Whatever he's trying to achieve won't mean diddly squat if he hurts anyone, or if he gets hurt himself."

Alerted by the implied threat in the policewoman's words, Rob stepped towards her. Her blue grey eyes burned into his as though she was attempting to repel his advance, to warn him to keep his distance.

"What are you going to do?"

"Calm down," she replied. "The best possible outcome is for your brother to hand over the weapon and surrender himself to us. At the moment we are hoping to achieve that result peacefully, with words. Our words have thus far been ineffective. Perhaps you can talk some sense into him."

Not even remotely reassured, Rob said, "And if it *can't* be resolved peacefully? Are you going to take him down? Shoot him?"

The officer stepped back and showed Rob her palms. "Mr. Archer, please. You getting hysterical will hardly advance our cause here, will it? Just talk to him. Find out exactly what he wants and ask him to think about how far he wants to take this. I mean, seriously consider, do you understand? I'm not going to permit those people to come to any harm."

Rob nodded and followed the officer, who led him around to the left hand side of the partitioning wall and into the office where three other police officers stood with their guns trained on Shane. Shane had not seen him yet, which was just as well because the sight of weapons aimed at his brother, and the thought he may be literally nanoseconds away from injury or death, made Rob feel like vomiting. He glanced towards Shane who turned at that exact moment to face him. An unreadable expression, a mixture, Rob imagined, of surprise and perhaps relief.

"One more question," said the officer, grabbing Rob's arm and holding him back. "Do you think your brother is capable of killing anyone?"

"No."

The speed and certainty of Rob's response comforted him and inspired courage in him. He had not hesitated to answer in the negative. Of course, Shane was not capable of killing anyone. Neither was Rob himself, he mused, once upon a time. He banished that rebellious and unhelpful thought. That had been a completely different situation. Rob had acted in self-defence. Shane was simply attempting to make a point, to attract some attention, and he was succeeding mightily. Not that he knew that, because the police had prevented any reporters or cameras from coming up, but on the ground floor the swell was rising. With each passing moment, the suspense grew; insidious, mischievous and morbid. The drama sucked the interest and value out of everything else for those who were following the unfolding events on the seventh floor of the Ernst and Young building. That idea gave birth to another.

"G'day mate," said Rob to Shane.

"Did I make it on to the TV? Does everyone know what this is about?"

Rob continued his approach very casually as though it was an ordinary situation. "Yes, you're on TV, but no, I don't think people know what you're on it about."

The gun was being held captive within Shane's white knuckled fist, which he pressed against his chest with the barrel aiming past his shoulder to the ceiling. He showed no reaction at all to Rob's answer.

"I'm shocked to see you with that," Rob said, as he gestured at the gun. "Where'd you get it?"

"A former student."

"I didn't know you taught gangsters."

Shane responded with an almost imperceptible shrug.

"I always said we were running a risk by allowing those boat people to stay here." Rob scratched his head to initiate the inner search for something less banal to say. Even in the context of small talk, his flippant remarks were falling from the sky like shot ducks, and this was clearly not the time for small talk or political discussions. He turned away from Shane to address the policewoman in charge.

"Can we have the guns lowered? Are they necessary?"

"It's precautionary."

"It's inflammatory."

The officer frowned as though she was unused to doing so, before finally giving the order. "Lower your weapons but remain at the ready."

Rob thanked her, and turned back to Shane to find he was focused on his hostages. *Hostages?* Rob felt like a boat in the middle of a desert. "Let them go, mate," he said eventually. "This isn't going to work if you hurt anyone. You're already in a shit load of trouble."

"Come here," said Shane, beckoning with the gun.

When Rob had come close enough to hear his brother's raspy whisper, he could see the red lightning strikes in the whites of his eyes. His pupils were dilated, and his breathing laboured.

"Shit Shane. What's wrong with you?"

"I haven't slept for a while. I'm kind of tired."

"Kind of tired?" said Rob, putting his hand on Shane's shoulder and squeezing it. "You look like fucking death, mate. What're you doing here? You think they're going to change the rules because you've got a gun?"

"Fair fucking trade isn't it?" said Shane. He pulled away from Rob. "A simple stroke of a pen could save a few lives. Someone has the power to rewrite one line in these stupid fucking guidelines of theirs and that will be enough. That's all I want. The sevens don't need to be in the one sitting. Previous scores should count." Shane moved a little to the side of Rob and yelled at the police; "The sevens don't have to be achieved in a single sitting. Simple rule change!"

"Shane," said Rob, inserting his body between his brother and the police, inching closer. "You sound like a lunatic. They don't know what you're talking about. How long did you say you hadn't slept for? You're not on something are you? Fuck, mate. This is for real here, you know. What're you doing?"

The shove was completely unexpected, and resulted in Rob landing on his backside amidst a hailstorm of loud garbled words. He quickly looked up to see the police had raised their weapons again, and he turned to see Shane had done likewise and there they stood; a frozen montage of angry and incomprehensible insanity.

"No! Nobody fucking shoot!"

"Don't shoot. Lower you weapon!"

"Lower your fucking weapons. I'll shoot!"

"Don't shoot!"

"For God's sake, Shane, stop!" cried Rob as he scrambled to his feet and stumbled towards his brother. "Put your gun down Shane. Please. It's over mate. Please."

The brothers stood toe to toe, exhaling acrid fear into each other's faces. Rob could feel the police closing from behind and hear their breathing, their heartbeats. He sensed their dominance, the control and surety with which they now moved. He reached for Shane's gun and snatched it free of his grip, then tossed it on the floor. The police pounced, grabbing handfuls of Shane's clothing and throwing him to the ground, before one landed his knee on Shane's back and handcuffed him. Shane demonstrated a remarkable lack of resistance. The rage and frustration which had driven him to this conflagration had vanished in an explosive climax, a balloon pricked by a pin. As he lay still on his stomach, Shane resembled shredded rubbery remnants, but Rob was so overwhelmed by what had just happened, he felt no compassion or concern. He was too exhausted to even experience relief. All that subsequently transpired was a blurry, indistinct clash of sounds and sights. At some point, he wondered if Shane was okay, and later he would worry over the consequences of his crazy exploit, but mostly he was numb. He thought of Jam, and wished she was there, or that he was with her somewhere else. The misery which had shadowed him for so long was patently intent on his complete destruction.

The officer guided Rob towards the elevator and into it, once the doors had parted to extend the invitation. He felt so wretched, bereft of words, of emotion and of sensation; dead. The doors slid shut and he closed his eyes as he tried to reach out for the awareness of falling, for any conscious, tangible evidence of life. What now?

Epilogue

"He wasn't dead? Really?"

Rob smiled broadly, almost as though he was embarrassed by the good news and had not yet come to terms with it. "Unconscious. Not dead."

Shane said: "So the cops were never after you."

"The boss at Lipstick posted the picture. Pee Lek, the guy I thought I killed, is his nephew and after I bashed him up, I guess the protective Uncle thought he would try to find me and get some revenge. Nobody cared. The photo in the paper had a private number, and it seems as though most people, in true Thai tradition preferred to keep their noses out of other people's business."

Jam interjected. "We *do* get involved in the business of our family and friends. We're not heartless."

"Fair enough," said Rob. "How'd you find this out anyway?"

"I still have a few friends at the club," said Jam. "After things had settled down, I made contact and was told all about Pee Lek and how he was still running around the place complaining about annoying foreigners. I should have made that call earlier, but I was so confused about everything, and when I found out, I should have told you straight away, Rob. That was wrong."

"It doesn't matter now," said Rob, squeezing her hand lightly.

"Man, you were sure you had killed that guy," said Shane. "I remember pressing you, asking if you were sure, sure he wasn't just out cold?"

"I'm not a bloody doctor!"

"Yeah but you can tell if someone's breathing or not, can't you? Yan Ping?"

Yan Ping sat beside Shane with her hand on his thigh, absently stroking it. "Usually," she said, noncommittally. "Anyway, Rob, you were running for nothing then," she said.

Maureen and Alan sat opposite each other at either end of the covered picnic table which sat in the midst of a sparse forest of River She-Oaks. Sunshine danced on the surface of the Port Hacking River as boats plied the channel, towing water skiers through the brown water. Children played at the edges where the frothy wake kissed the grey sand, in and out of the water, alternately frightened and fascinated by the ubiquitous, large jellyfish which inhabited the river. A breeze caressed them and carried the sing-song chatter of the children towards them. Across the table from Shane and Yan Ping, sat Rob and Jam. Shane sat contemplatively, savouring the moment of togetherness, of genuine happiness. After such awful turbulence over the past year in particular, this felt like heaven. Shane could not imagine anything better.

"Actually," said Rob, "I think I was running from myself. Until recently, I think that has been my chief occupation."

"I don't understand," said Yan Ping, as she fixed her inquisitive glare on Rob.

"I never felt at peace. I always thought I had to push the envelope to experience new things in case I missed out. I was insatiable, always wanting more. Looking for a new buzz, a new high, and I hated being told, or even feeling like people were thinking I shouldn't be living a certain way. I just wanted to run and keep running until I found whatever the hell it was I was searching for. While I was chasing down that dream, I hurt people either deliberately or through careless neglect. I didn't like doing that because I felt like I was injuring myself at the same time, but I didn't stop. I rationalized my way through the pain, and simply swept all my feelings under the carpet. In the end, I think I forgot what I was looking for and became consumed with the damage I had done to myself and to others along the way. Then my running became about getting away from those feelings, attempting to escape myself, the person I had turned into. Does that make any sense?"

Yan Ping smiled. "Did you hear that excellent explanation Shane? I think your brother wants your job, to knock you off the pedestal as the most eloquent member of the family."

"He's always been full of hot air," said Shane, "As least as much if not more, than me."

Alan said, "You're both pretty long winded. I don't know where you got that from?"

Everyone laughed except Jam and Yan Ping, who instead exchanged the glance of the outsiders, with the knowing solidarity of those who have recently become part of a family unit much older than themselves, shared glimpses of the experiences of the Archer family available to them. In time they would carry the Archer name and they would come to know Alan and Maureen as mum and dad, and they would learn more. They would have their struggles against parental interference and influence, whilst trying to find their own way in new relationships. They would battle homesickness and inevitable personality clashes, many of which would be erroneously attributed to cultural differences. It would not all be smooth sailing. Shane was cognizant of the sacrifices both woman had made and would continue to make, but if he had learned one thing it was that true unconditional love demanded sacrifice. He took hold of Yan Ping's hand, and when she turned to him, he kissed her lightly.

"Go easy on the P.D.A's, mate," said Rob. "Be considerate, will you?"

Comfortable conversation flowed like the muddy river beside them, and Shane continued to reflect on his fortune. Following his arrest at the

AHPRA office, he had been charged with misuse of firearm, aggravated assault, unauthorised possession of firearm in aggravated circumstances and something to do with taking hostages, threatening to kill, to injure and more besides. While he had listened to the magistrate read the long list of charges against him, he thought they could have been summarized by a single charge of moronic behaviour. Luckily, he had not loaded the gun, so they weren't able to add anything to the charge sheet about intent. Jail time had been a definite possibility, but his lawyer had earned his money and Shane had escaped with a heavy fine and a probationary period. His previous clean record also assisted his case. The story of his ill-considered venture did make the national news, and even some international news services carried it as something of a curiosity and one to which many people could relate. Who hasn't been frustrated by bureaucracy at some time in their lives? The media exposure forced some public servants, including the health minsters, to answer some awkward questions about the processes surrounding the formation of the English language proficiency guidelines, and their enforcement. However, after successfully deflecting the heat of the debate for a few days, the issue fizzled and nothing more was said. It just wasn't sexy enough to maintain public interest. Behind the scenes, the Australian Health Workforce Ministerial Council was convened, and with nothing more than an update on the AHPRA website, the offending rule, the one which had sent Shane to the precipice of disaster, was amended. Yan Ping, together with thousands of other overseas born health professionals, was able to immediately submit her collective results and claim English language proficiency. Having done that, her registration was a formality which took a further three weeks. She found employment in the respiratory ward at Shellharbour Public Hospital before her registration had even been officially confirmed.

"How's the new job going, Yan Ping?" asked Maureen.

"I love it and sometimes hate it."

"Last job on earth I'd ever want to do," said Shane. “Speaking of jobs, Rob, what's doing on that front with you?"

"I'm tossing up two options; joining the police force or opening a bar. What do you think?"

"He's a cheeky bugger, your future husband," said Shane to Jam.

Jam took hold of Rob's arm with both of hers in an approximation of a hug. "I think he'd make a wonderful policeman."

Her straight faced delivery stunned everyone, and it wasn't until she allowed a furtive half smile that the joke was exposed. She laughed self-consciously, just as pleased with the reaction to her tongue in cheek comment, as with the joke itself. Shane nodded appreciatively. "You're certainly in the right family, Jam, aren't you?"

"So we're all good," said Alan. "This is wonderful. I'm so stoked to be here with you all. I really doubted such happiness would come to us. I mean you pray and you hope, and you hope and you pray, but sometimes you really wonder."

A reflective silence followed, during which a supernatural tranquillity landed softly on everyone, alighting on them like snowflakes. Shane looked at Maureen who was glowing in the glory of her reunited family, and remembered her frequent admonitions regarding God's grace.

"He doesn't give us what we deserve. That's grace. Sometimes our actions bring inevitable consequences and we must accept them, but sometimes we escape as though from a burning house with only the inconvenience of smoke inhalation and singed eyebrows. We might lose stuff in the fire, our possessions, even the house itself, but we survive. When we are tested by life's tribulations, we may be stripped and flayed but we survive."

"Or we die."

"In any case, grace remains constant." Maureen caught Shane staring at her, and smiled, raising her eyebrows to question him.

"But seriously, I think I get it now, mum."

"Get what?" she asked.

"Grace."

She smiled again. "I knew you would one day."

"Look what I have," Shane said, gesturing around the table. "Think of what I have done, and Rob? It could have ended so much worse, couldn't it?"

"But we made it."

"It won't stay like this though, will it?" said Shane.

"I don't know, love." Maureen stood and walked around behind him, leaning down to hug him tightly. "But does it matter if it doesn't last? Just enjoy it while it does. Life is not a puddle, or a stagnant pond. It's not even an ocean. It's a river."

About the Author

devolution_dacairns@hotmail.com

D. A. Cairns is married with two children and lives on the south coast of New South Wales in Australia where he works as an English language teacher and writes stories in his very limited spare time. He has had around forty short stories published (but who's counting, right?). He is the author of three novels: Devolution, Loathe Your Neighbour and Ashmore Grief.

www.ingramcontent.com/pod-product-compliance
Lightning Source LLC
Chambersburg PA
CBHW061927170626
46813CB00006B/2319